I0761618

# Crown of War and Shadow

# Crown *of* War *and* Shadow

J.R. Ward

TOR PUBLISHING GROUP
NEW YORK

This is a work of fiction. All of the characters, organizations, and events portrayed in this novel are either products of the author's imagination or are used fictitiously.

CROWN OF WAR AND SHADOW



Designed by Jen Edwards
Map by Virginia Allyn
Endpapers by Julie Dillon

A Bramble Book
Published by Tom Doherty Associates / Tor Publishing Group
120 Broadway
New York, NY 10271

www.torpublishinggroup.com

Bramble™ is a trademark of Macmillan Publishing Group, LLC.

*EU Representative:* Macmillan Publishers Ireland Ltd, 1st Floor, The Liffey Trust Centre, 117–126 Sheriff Street Upper, Dublin 1, D01 YC43

The Library of Congress Cataloging-in-Publication Data is available upon request.

ISBN 978-1-250-37362-5 (hardcover)
ISBN 978-1-250-37363-2 (ebook)



First Edition: 2026

Printed in the United States of America

10 9 8 7 6 5 4 3 2 1

*This book is dedicated to Jennifer L. Armentrout, who's been a leader for me and so many others. (Also, I just really like you.)*

*Always forward, never back.*

The Fulcrum

Altar of the Fulcrum

The

Kingdom of the South

City of Ruins

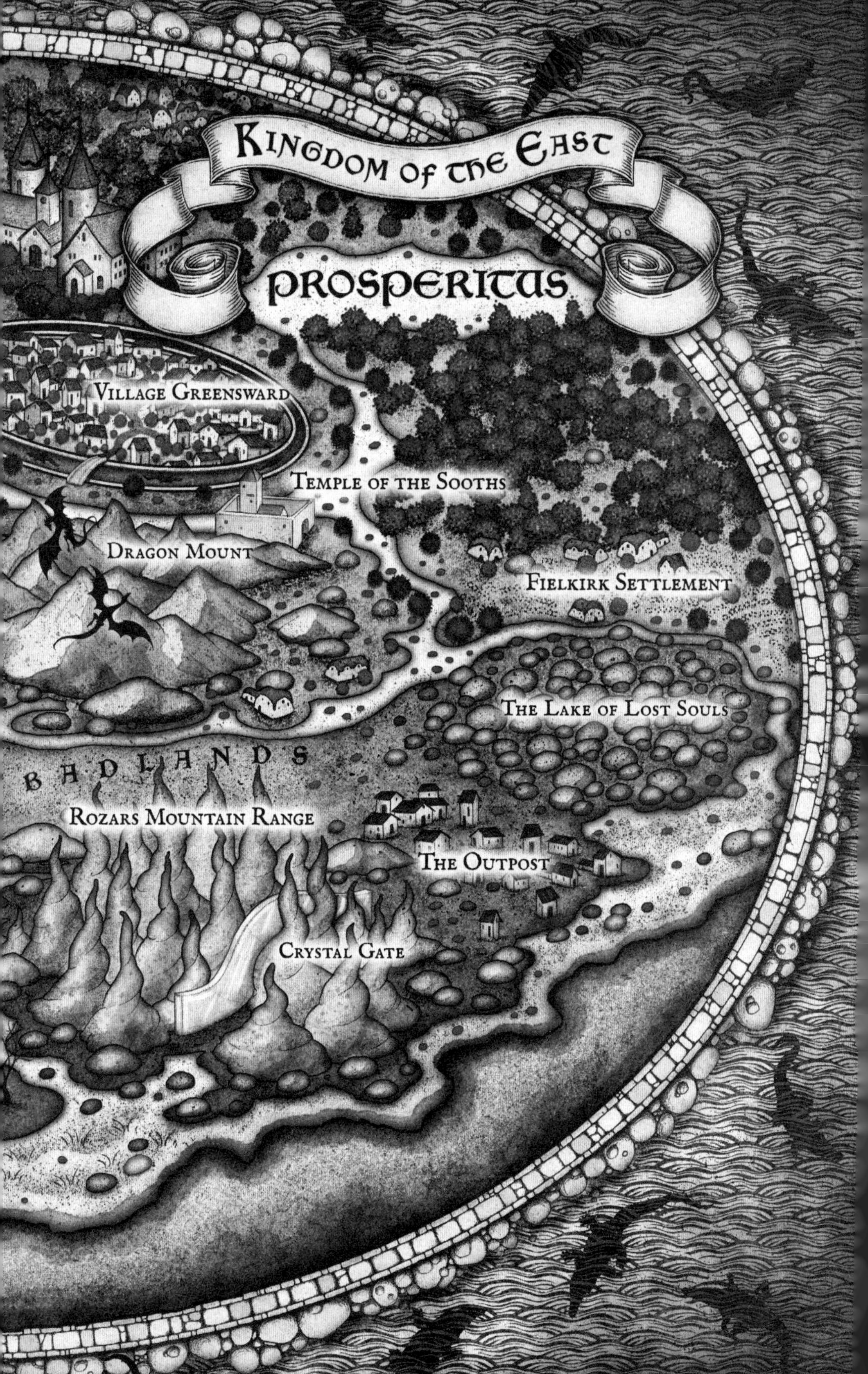

Kingdom of the East
Prosperitus
Village Greensward
Temple of the Sooths
Dragon Mount
Fielkirk Settlement
The Lake of Lost Souls
Badlands
Rozars Mountain Range
The Outpost
Crystal Gate

*Part One*

# Village Greensward

## The Start of All Things.

# *One*

# Demons and Departures.

"Where do you think you're going, Sorrel."

As Mr. Lewis heaps his rotund frame into my path, I shrink beneath my Pox cloak. The owner of the Gauntlet Public House is a mountain with a bald summit, and there is no going around, over, or through him, especially not for a barmaid like me. Keeping my eyes on his scuffed boots, I tuck the satchel of medicine I prepared under the folds of what covers me from aching head to tattered slipper shoe.

"I am to send word to the grain miller—"

A cresting of bawdy laughter and thumping fists cuts off the lie. In the glow of the lanterns, the pub's main door is just twenty lengths away, but the maze of rough-hewn tables is a congested landscape of sweaty, drunken clientele and faded-rose working women. With my employer blocking my escape, I can't even get to those obstacles.

"I have cleaned the hourly rooms," I offer by way of a toll to pass. "And I washed the pints for the tender, and the flour sacks have been brought in—"

"What about the stairs?" He pulls up the waistband of his sackcloth pants with the effort worthy of a stump removal. "And the sheets."

"I have brought the sheets in from the clotheslines and they are folded."

"The stairs, then." As another round of laughter explodes, Mr. Lewis points a pudgy finger over my shoulder. "You have to earn your room and board. I don't run a charity."

He reminds me of this at every turn, and if I am cast out from this place, I have no family, no money, and no prospects.

"You are very generous, Mr. Lewis—"

"I am *too* generous." He sniffs an inhale, as if he disapproves of himself.

"Get your broom then. You don't need to be out and about when things are busy here."

"But the miller needs to know the order for tomorrow's flour. It won't take long—"

"He always comes here after his wife serves him that bad food of hers. Without my ale, his gout would cripple him. You will tell him then."

"I can be right back—"

"Why are you still talking. And you'll sweep behind the bar, too."

I glance across at the tender, a perpetually cross man who is not going to want me back there.

Beneath the folds of my cloak, I fist the satchel in my hand. "Yes, Mr. Lewis."

Turning away, I reenter the back of house through the archway, and tell myself there's still time to get to Mare, if I make quick work of the duties. The elderly woman suffers without what I give her, especially in the cold and the damp of this interminable autumn, and I wasn't able to get free this morning. As I picture her in the nest of blankets I've made for her, fragile as a baby bird, I pray she's warm enough.

Bypassing where I sleep under the stairs, I go to the next closet. After I stuff the satchel into a pocket, I grab whatever handle comes to my palm, and mount the worn steps to start at the top—

A young man who's been lodging with us throws himself into a thundering descent as he pulls on his gray waistcoat. The tails of his untucked shirt bounce, and he's whistling under his breath, having clearly enjoyed his lusty pursuits.

"You missed a spot," he mocks as he pushes me aside.

He's been with us a week, having come down from Prosperitus, the royal seat of the East. His city ways have been the subject of provincial awe, and it's clear he enjoys the deference. The ladies have certainly enjoyed his coins.

I wonder when he's leaving so I don't have to do his sheets.

Arriving up top, I swear that Mr. Lewis lies in wait for me to have an unoccupied moment, and as I draw the broom from balustrade to bare wall, there's no loose dirt to sweep onto the next lower step. What there is plenty of is the muffled sounds of coupling. The grunts and theatrical moans ripple out from the closed doors of the ladies' rooms, and it's a relief to make progress so that I can't hear them anymore.

Sallae Mae, the women's unofficial madam, appears at the bottom with a charge. She's got blond hair that tumbles down her back, but with thirty years and four of hard living, there are lines on her face and a cynical twist to her smile and voice. The man leads the way, and as he ascends, I stop what I'm doing and try to make space for him to pass. Though I lower my eyes, I recognize his riding boots. They're very fine, with polished spur nubs that shine silver. It's one of the mayor's sons—

"Will you get out of the way," he mutters at me.

I try to become flatter against the wall as I remember attending his wife on the birthing bed last month. The son he's so proud to have is only alive because of me, and that means he and I have a dangerous, unlawful secret.

I tell myself that's why he hates me . . . that's why so many of the villagers hate me.

In his wake, Sallae Mae wafts past me in a cloud of perfume. Though I help her and the others on the sly with treatments for their various difficulties, none of them ever acknowledge me. But it's better than the active shunning.

Loneliness is about so much more than solitude.

As I resume my needless duty, the stiff straw head of the broom whisks over boards smoothed like river stones by countless footfalls. The Gauntlet has been a fixture of my village since before the Great Containment, or so they say, so it's got to be centuries old. I certainly feel as though I've been here forever, each night and day exactly the same, the grinding repetition a false sense of infinity.

With every step I descend, the time I'm being forced to waste is like someone screaming in my face. The medicine in the satchel is the last of the root I have prepared, and the pain reliever is more precious than any safety of my own. I tell myself that Mr. Lewis will soon get tied up with the other villagers, and that's when I can—

A resounding clap cuts through the pub's din, and I jerk my head up.

In the entry, standing in the pouring rain, the milkman, Mr. Cavenish, is holding up a cowbell that's covered in blood. In his other hand, a fistful of animal innards drips a gruesome stew down his pant leg and onto his knee-high boots.

"Demons!" he yells as he comes inside. "The Fulcrum is failing and they are coming for us!"

People duck as he swings the gore around and stumbles over to a table. In the yellow light of the oil lanterns, his face is a grotesque distortion—but worse is what he's saying, our collective, unspoken fears made manifest.

"Hunting in the gloaming, stalking us at night! She was snatched from the herd, her stomach clawed open—"

Villagers gasp and recoil as they're speckled in the face with blood, and he wheels on another group who have traded forced joviality for the very sincere horror that's been under all our awareness lately. "The demons are out of the Fulcrum and they're hunting us—the Dark King returns! It is his star that has appeared in the sky!"

I trip down the stairs, called by the confirmation of what we've all been worried about since the first of his herd was killed. But I make sure that I stay on the fringes as the alarmed hush that follows is broken with someone speaking up.

"There are wild animals in the forest. Many things will attack a—"

"The carcass was set at the south," Mr. Cavenish spits. "What animal slaughters cows at exactly the north, the east . . . and now the south! I warned you when this started two weeks ago! I told all of you! The wall that surrounds us will not hold—"

"Enough!" Mr. Lewis barks.

In the silence, clues tie together around a reality that surely will sink us—the slaughtered cows, the strange footprints . . . the pall of darkness that's all around our village. The others are thinking the same thing, I can tell by the hunched shoulders, the lowered heads.

This is probably the only accord I will have with them, not that they'd care I'm scared, too. Probably more than they are.

"Magic is in use," Mr. Cavenish lashes out. "The Fulcrum has weakened because of it, and the demons are harbingers of what is to come! The Dark King rises!"

Shrinking beneath my cloak, I step out of the lantern light. Not that anyone has noticed me.

Not that any one of them could point a finger at me without incriminating themselves.

"Get him out of here," Mr. Lewis says with exhaustion.

As he sweeps his hand toward the exit, a couple of men jump up from their frozen stupors, and Mr. Cavenish returns to his ranting as he's taken by the elbow and dragged back out into the cold rain.

"Magic has been used in violation of the law and all of Anathos will die because of it! You know this—"

Mr. Lewis himself closes the door and puts his boulder body against it. Though I'm careful to stay out of sight, it's clear he's looking around for something. I pray this is not the night I've always dreaded, the night when I'm banished, finally.

"We could go to the Sooths," someone suggests. "They'll know—"

"I already went," somebody else cuts in. "They will not speak of—"

"G'on now," Mr. Lewis interrupts. "Finish your ales. Next order's on the house."

This revives the mood a little, but he's got to make them stay or he'll lose the profit for the rest of the night—as opposed to them bolting home to their wives and children and securing their windows and doors. As Mr. Lewis waddles from table to table calming nervous chatter, I seize the opportunity. I scuttle off, shove the broom into the closet, and disappear through the empty kitchen and the rear exit.

Outside, the rain falls from the churning, restless sky, and the night feels like it's not just come early this evening, but is a season in and of itself. When I hear talk and a clanging, I whisper down the back of the Gauntlet and peer around the corner.

Mr. Cavenish is being walked along the main street, and the men with him are not being rough. The innards are no longer in his hand, but the bell remains. The soulful sound it makes is like a countdown, and I think of the deteriorating wall that surrounds my village. Even in its decline, the mortared stone bulwark is tall as the Gauntlet's thatched roof and thick as a mead barrel. Still, I find myself wondering if those creatures whose faces and teeth have yet to be seen can climb. Or fly like dragons.

Maybe the *balas* in the moat will give us some protection.

For my two decades of life, I have stayed cloistered inside Greensward's wall, only venturing out to gather the plants and roots I need. Otherwise, I don't even leave the pub unless I have to. I've never felt safe, even within our village, and as I think about what's stalking us? The news from the other territories on Anathos seem like forest fires of danger ready to consume me: There's been talk of animals, and even people, being attacked in the settlements that ring the various royal courts. I've heard so many fearful whispers at the end of the night, travelers sharing that which they refuse to acknowledge in the light of day.

The milkman is right. We are being hunted here, the wall that protects us both a defense and a target. But he's wrong that the Fulcrum has been weakened because of magic. I've been wielding a sliver of that sacred energy my whole life, and I refuse to believe there's been any bad repercussions—and everybody in this pub who ignores me feels the same way, too. Even Mr. Cavenish.

They hate that they've had to rely on me, but though I am a shunned orphan, I have learned one solid truth: There's nothing people will not do for their family.

No, the cause is something else.

And that's what we need to fear, even more than the demons, which are but the preamble to a much more deadly enemy.

*Two*

# A Mouse Among Rats.

I wait for the trio of men to get farther ahead of me, and then I ghost along in their wake, following the eerie clanging of the cowbell. My cloak soaks up the icy rain as if parched for cold water, and beneath my ratty leather soles, the cobblestone lane is slick as a mossy riverbed. The row houses that crowd up on both sides of our main thoroughfare have their shutters tightly shut and their doors bolted for reasons other than the bad weather, but their chimney flues are open, tendrils of smoke eaten by the wind.

When a distant creaking travels to my ears, I glance over my shoulder. The bridge that crosses our moat is being hauled up, and when the planks lock into place at the squat towers, the pair of sentries descend from their duty. That the men head to the Gauntlet is no surprise, and I wish they would stay where they were.

For all the good they could do with their pitchforks.

They are just civilians, like the rest of us. Our village is on the very fringes of the Prosperitus territory, and there are no royal guards here, for we are but a worthless trading post. That's why our wall is unrepaired and we have no protectors.

We must take care of ourselves.

Refocusing on my own journey, the lane before me is cast in a palette of grays, and wisps of fog curl and flatten in the downpour like restless phantom limbs. All I hear is water, dripping off roofs, splashing underfoot, tapping on my hood. Except I'm listening for other things. I'm looking for . . . other things. It's unlikely the sentries missed an entrance through the front. What if a demon came over the top? What if they possess dark magic, so that which is solid is nothing but air to them? And how did they get out . . .

Just as we have our wall, the continent of Anathos has the Fulcrum. The difference is that the latter was conceived to keep things inside and it was supposed to last for eternity. The Book of Time provides us with the story of the Great Containment, how after the Dark King gathered up and perverted the natural magic of the continent, and used it to subjugate the populations of all the compass points, the Savior came and rescued our ancestors from torture and tyranny. Working in secret, she extracted the tiny quantums of energy still left in the landscape, and then she seduced the evil overlord into a fissure in the ground and created the swirling force field that imprisoned him and his army of demons—

I stop and look over my shoulder.

Then I glance to the sky. With the cloud cover, I can't see that star that appeared months ago, so bright that it eclipses any others in its vicinity. I have to agree with the others. Its presence carries a portent of doom, somehow.

When I twist back around, Mr. Cavenish and his escorts turn a corner and disappear out of sight. For an instant, I feel like I'm the only one alive inside our wall, everybody else dead, the tedious, lonely life I trudge through gone and replaced by something so much worse. Anxiety seeds along my nerve endings, my hands and feet blooming with numbness, and I try to reach through the wave of panic and cold chills to connect to the world around me. I, too, have a turning, churning core, and I fall into its whirlpool of dread and terror at the slightest topple—

I shove my hand into my cloak's pocket and feel the bundle of herbs.

I can't afford to stop, and I certainly can't turn back.

Scurrying forth, my eyes bounce around at all the doors that are closed to me, all the windows covered. With each house, I pierce the veil of the clapboard walls and see inside. Never have I gone through the front entries or been welcomed as a guest at the meal table—I'm always snuck in the back, brought inside in secret, used for their purposes.

After which, I am worse than a stranger. I'm someone they know to their soul and wish they didn't—

My feet freeze once again. It's hard to figure out what's a genuine warning instinct and what's fear. But when a shadow in my wake shifts away into the fog, I know my eyes do not deceive.

Something in the street is tracking behind me.

I tremble under the cold weight of my cloak, and feel cracked nails prickle the skin of my nape, a warning that I've never felt before—

*Hide.*

That word, spoken in that assertive voice, takes the place of any other thought in my brain and all of the rushing anxiety in my blood. Throughout my life, the command has haunted me, as if it's the proper name given to me by whoever birthed and then abandoned me here.

Grabbing fistfuls of sodden wool, I set in to an escape, all kinds of horrendous creatures with fangs and claws populating my mind and leaping free of my imagination to pursue me. Except maybe the threat is more prosaic than a demon. I've overheard stories in the pub of traveling men who seek to inoculate themselves from the Pox by a rutting. Even though I wear the drape for a different reason, I can't escape what it means to everybody else.

All the lanes in my village channel into the market square, and if I can make it that far, there are places to hide in the empty vendor stalls, and also a watchman who makes rounds. He might help me because he has a daughter, and if I scream, perhaps I sound like her?

And I am not unarmed, I guess. I have my little knife tucked into my waistband, and through the jostling of my sloppy strides, I find the hilt with my hand and don't waste time looking behind me again.

As I sense the presence fall into the chase, I trust the instinct more than my eyes in the darkness. Closer to the square. Closer. *Closer—*

The figure that steps out in front of me is such a shock that as I wheel my arms and skid on the cobblestones, I do what must never be done.

I look directly into the eyes of the bulky, bearded man who blocks my way.

Following a split second of recognition, a blast of energy goes through me and I am blinded. Then I see the farrier not as he is this night, in the rain, in the lane, but at the moment of his death: His craggy, bearded face is burned on one side, the flesh blackened as meat cooked on a spit, the cheekbone a blaze of bright white in the midst of the wounding, the roots of his molars rivers of enamel that feather into his exposed jaws. Likewise, his eye is gone from its socket and his hair is melted onto his skull. He is gasping for air and then not—

The agony he's in floods my senses, my own face in indescribable agony, my lungs burning as if I'm breathing fire, the smell of smoke and cooked muscle coring into my nose. My body goes limp, my heart flickering before stopping as well, his death something transmitted into me, through me.

As he catches me in the midst of my collapse, his rough hands bite into my upper arms, and he keeps me from spilling onto the wet lane like something out of an upended basket. I feel myself get yanked into the shadows, and when he pulls me up to his chest, the unwounded side of his face comes into unbearable focus: The features are as he appears currently, no wasting from age, not even a change in the length, color, or thickness of his bushy beard.

His death is not far from him.

He does not know this, however. And this is not why he's captured me in the darkness.

"The bairn is dying . . ." he says in his gravelly voice. "You must come to my newly born son. *Now!*"

*Three*

# Wherein I Break the Law.

The farrier and his family of seven live behind his shop just off the market square, but he doesn't dare bring me in the front. Though time is precious, and the stink of his fear is a roar in my nose, he scuttles me down an alleyway strewn with dirty hay and manure to the back side of his combination workshop and house. His cracked and black-stained hand trembles as he grips the iron ring of his stout door, and I glance over my shoulder to see if we've been followed.

No one. Nothing.

I can't sense the stalking presence anymore, and I tell myself I was confused and it was just the farrier coming for me. The lie holds no logic as the danger was approaching from the rear, but sometimes I've got to construct a reality I can live with.

"This way," he says.

As I step through, he shields the entrance into his home with his hulking body, but it's not to protect me. I'm the last thing he wants in his house, and he's making sure nobody sees me, even though no one watches back here—

The smell is terrible. Fresh blood, old sweat, horse hooves, and melted metal. The kitchen is a mess, with chicken bones sucked clean of meat and gristle scattered across a planked table and the remnants of stew molded into the bases of tin bowls. Bladders of drink are lined up, but going by the acidic whiff of him, I'm betting they're full of mead, rather than milk or water for the children.

"He's down here."

The farrier's boots thunder over the floorboards, his weight like that of the steeds he shoes, and he makes no apology for the state of his home. Then again, that's women's work to him.

As he rips back a tattered curtain, the first thing I see are the young ones.

Four daughters are clustered together in ragged clothing, their pale faces dirty, their hair tangled and matted. All under five, born each year since the farrier took this wife. He killed his first one on the birthing bed, too, the fetus refusing to vacate the womb and souring inside of her.

There is also an older girl, one of teenage years, and I recall that she's a niece he took in at some point for labor. She has a gaunt appearance, and she puts a thin arm around the children. She shows no interest in me, her fearful eyes only worrying about where the farrier is, and I don't need to know how many beatings she's had under this roof. It's all in the way she hunches her shoulders and lowers her head.

I don't look any of the children in the eye. I already cannot bear what I'm seeing and don't want to know their futures.

I turn to the pallet in the corner. The young woman lying twisted as a rope on the bloody blankets is soaked with sweat and breathing in shallow pants. Her swollen lower body is fully exposed, her knees wide, the umbilical cord still tying her to the blue infant that lies waxen and motionless between her thighs.

The farrier speaks: "The laboring lasted most of the day and—"

I hold my hand up. "*Silence.*"

I want to slap him for forcing this breeding once again. I have memories of her before he claimed her as his birthing chattel, a girl of my own age, carefree and lovely, her dark hair streaming behind her as she danced with her sisters in the sunshine in the village square. Now she's here dying like a plow horse used too hard. And he will go on and get another to raise these unwanted daughters of his, and more importantly give him the son he wants, because he has the money to do so.

And if that one dies, he'll just return anew to the well of young girls.

Kneeling down at the pallet, I brace myself and look at the perfect little face of the infant. The eyes of the boy are open, and as I stare into them . . .

Nothing. No sensation, no images. I'm doing what others perform easily, meeting the pupils of someone else.

A familiar sorrow runs through me, filling my veins with a sour despair. I have to try to help the bairns, even if I hate the fathers—even if it means I am breaking the law and risk being flailed raw in the town square. When I was abandoned as an infant, a stranger cared enough to save my life. It's my calling to do the same, the only legacy I have to live up to.

Besides, even though their families will never acknowledge me, and they themselves will disdain me for being a *scur*, or the lowest of the lower class, my loneliness abates when I stare out of my hood at the children I've saved. As they go and live their lives, I know that they are alive because of me, and in this, they are the babies I will never have.

Though they shun me, I love them. And mourn them when I arrive too late.

"What of my son?" the farrier demands hoarsely.

I shake my head, and he begins to weep. He doesn't bother to inquire after his wife, and that brings me back to attention.

As I shift up to her, I want all the demons to come find him. "Elly?"

Her full name is Ellyne, and hearing her nickname seems to bring her around. Her lids lift and tears spill out and run down her temples. She hasn't the strength to speak, and as I take her hand, it's hot as a brand. I do not meet her eyes. Me feeling her death is not going to help either of us—

She murmurs something I cannot catch for the grunting grief of her drunken, rutting murderer.

"You must hang on." I gently stroke her stringy hair back. "I can get you medicine on the morrow."

And I can do something else for her. If she'll let me.

"Leave us," I command her husband. When he just stands there, sniveling, I glare out from under my hood. "And take your children with you. They have already seen too much."

The farrier wipes his nose on his dirty woolen sleeve. "So you can bring my son back?"

"No, but I will seek to ease your *wife*."

My tone is such that the young girls quake in their clutch, and though the farrier is above me in sex and station, he's too dumbfounded at my temerity to respond.

"*Go*," I snap.

With a dismissing hand to his progeny, he shoos off the gifts he finds worthless for they haven't a penis among them, and the lot scramble to their feet. The niece, who has red hair, puts a protective arm about the sisters, and as they squeeze past his girth, she looks back at me, her facial expression older than the sea.

What her eyes must be showing makes me feel ancient.

"Feed them something," I order him after they're gone. "And not that mead you buy with your coppers."

There's naught to sustain a fly in that filthy kitchen, and fates damn him, someone must charge him with his neglect.

The farrier skulks off, no doubt going for those bladders of fermented honey, and that he doesn't pull the heavy drape back into place for privacy enrages me.

I jump up and yank the folds across the doorway.

Back with Elly, I take her hand once more. "You must pass your afterbirth."

She's too weak so my words are naught but air, and I know what's coming next because I've seen it all before. Within a day, she'll be claimed by the infection that's already taken root in her womb, yet I'm going to forage for her anyway.

And that is as far as I will go. She has suffered enough in this life, and if I save her from the grave, it will be no kindness to her.

"I'll ease your pain," I choke out.

Going inside my cloak's cold, damp folds, I withdraw my little knife from its leather slide at my waist. I'm tempted to do horrible things with it.

If that brute had no testicles, many problems would be taken care of.

Instead of going after the farrier, I tremble as I saw through the gray, rubbery umbilical cord. Then I grab whatever stained blanket I come in contact with and pull a cover over Elly's privacy. She moans as the rough wool brushes her bloodied skin, and I murmur something soothing. Then I look once more at the bairn. Such perfect features, the little nose and wing of a mouth, cheeks that were full enough so that it should have survived. My vengeance is such that I'm glad the farrier's been denied what he craves, as if sons are the sole things of worth. Yet his quest for the only kind of offspring he cares about will continue to cost my sisters in our village their lives.

There's a tunic by the pallet, torn in half as if Elly ripped it in her laboring. I wrap the cooling bairn in the folds, and entertain a fantasy that I will bury the remains properly, in the Resting Place. But it's been a long, long while since any of us dared to go that far outside of the wall.

I don't know what will happen to this precious vessel, which has leached out its spark of life already. The same is true for Elly's body, and the distress I feel is deep enough that the pair of them might as well be of my own blood. In all my isolation, I find that my sentiments adhere to the villagers easily, though none have ever claimed me.

"My girls . . ." Elly whispers.

Putting my knife away, I focus upon her lax mouth. There's a broken front tooth that is new.

"I'll ensure their safety." I take her hand again, her blood and sweat fusing our palms as I make my vow. "They'll go to the Sooths."

The Temple of Sooths is known to take in abandoned females. The girls and the niece will be safe there with those prognosticators that I don't believe in. At least their wall is solid and strong.

"He will never . . . allow that."

My eyes move up to the tip of Elly's nose. "You are aware of what I can see, yes?"

"Yes," she says weakly. "And what . . . you can do. But death . . . is not always . . . a curse."

I shut my lids, aware that she and I are of agreement. I will not save her in the way I'm able. "Take ease then. The torment from him will not last long now, and when his time comes, I'll make sure your lovely daughters and his niece are taken in at the temple."

There is a flare of surprise from her, but it doesn't last. "Promise . . . ?"

"I promise upon my beating heart."

Going back inside the wet folds of my cloak, I take out the satchel I prepared earlier. Mare needs the herbs. Elly needs them more. They're supposed to be brewed as tea, but there's no hope of that. I wouldn't trust the farrier, and I can't stay here much longer. Someone could walk in, perhaps with news of what happened at the pub with Mr. Cavenish.

Now is not the time for me to be found next to the birthing pallet of yet another dying woman.

Lifting up the hem of my cloak, I go through the layers to reach my underskirt. With my knife, I cut a square of the thin cotton the size of my hand and make a table of my knee. After I open the satchel's neck, I empty all the dried flakes onto the center of the square. Then I bundle it up and use the little bag's tie to close the corners.

"I want you to put this in between your back teeth and chew." I lean in, and help her open her mouth. "This will soothe the pain."

I adjust the shape into a flat wedge, and push the medicine off to one side, so that it doesn't block the back of her throat. Closing her jaw, I hope that she holds the wad in place. With the herbs undiluted, they are going to be potent and I don't want her choking if she loses consciousness—

The relief that comes over her is quick and carries with it a brief aura of light. For a moment, I think she's leaving us, and with my word given, I will not stop the process. But no, the flare is a lie my mind creates because with her easing comes my own.

As she slips into the sleep that will hold her dear until her heart stops, I brush a tear from my eye, and realize I have marked my cheek with her blood. This feels right.

I gather up the bundle in the tunic, and rise to my feet.

I find the farrier at his planked table full of bones, the scatter of white sticks an allegory for all the consuming, the breaking, he has done in the calendar days and nights he has had upon Anathos's once-hallowed ground. He's got a bladder to his mouth, and has dribbled his beard with his haste to suck on the teat that muddles his mind.

The girls are nowhere to be seen, and I imagine they have a hiding place somewhere close by, a refuge outside of this domestic hell. That niece is going to watch after the sisters well, and I hope the farrier's fate with the hot fire in his forge happens very soon.

"You will come to me in two hours," I say as I place the dead bairn on the table, on the bones. "I will have herbs for her, and you will administer them."

It's too risky for me to enter here again, even in the darkness. I don't care about him, but those girls must be protected from my presence. Especially after what Mr. Cavenish brought to the Gauntlet tonight.

The farrier passes his meaty paw down his face with defeat. "She is still alive, then."

"Yes. And you *will* do right by her."

I bend down and stare across at him from out of my hood. As I meet his stare once again, like lightning splitting a tree, I am struck anew by his suffering, and I breathe in his hot pain with a nasty satisfaction.

The voice that comes out of my mouth, comes up from my soul, vibrates between us, deep and low. "*I will know if you do not.*"

The fear that sparks in his bloodshot eyes is the leverage I have over them all. In the daylight, in the safety of lanterns and numbers, the villagers shun me, but they've come to me. Each one, in their own way, has sought me out for unlawful things, and been witness to a strange and troubling miracle.

So even though the dance with death is my only distinction, they assume there are others I could wield against them.

I'm perfectly content to have this man worry about what I can do to him.

With my message received, I straighten. "Dispose of your boy properly as you did not the wife and daughter you first lost. And know that at the moment of your death, no matter where I am, or what I'm doing, I will know—and I will rejoice."

I don't tell him to mind being around that hearth of his. Don't warn him that there will be an accident, soon. Say nothing about the flames that will claim his flesh first and then his life.

I leave as I came in, sneaking back out into the freezing rain and the dangerous night. I'll have to see Mare tomorrow. With a full pub and the hour being late, there will be tables to wipe down, messes to clean up, tankards to wash. But none of that, and even my elderly patient being left without help through the night, is what's on my mind.

Another side of me, one that's mostly hidden and that I don't recognize as myself, has broken free, and like a horse bolted from a stall, there's no easy way to get the anger and vengeance back under control. It's just so hard to see the same thing played out, over and over again.

And to be used and discarded in my own fashion, just like these other young women.

As I retrace my route back to the lodging house, I almost hope I cross paths with whatever stepped in behind me. Though I ran from what stalked me earlier, my own truth cannot be ignored.

I am one of the things the villagers fear in the dark.

And with me in this mood, they're right to be afraid.

*Four*

# A Stranger Arrives.

The pub is especially loud. The village men are waving their tankards around, their heads flipping back as they project their laughter like cannonballs at what Mr. Cavenish's intrusion forced them to confront earlier. The air is thick with the stench of sour sweat and pungent ale, and as I skate over and pick up another empty tankard, I check the door. Since I returned, I've been able to sneak into my hovel under the stairs a couple of times and prepare more of the chews that will help Elly.

That husband of hers better show.

Grimly turning away, I weed back through the tables and chairs, which take up most of the floor. The bar runs down the far side, and I go to the end of its pitted, stained counter, adding my lot to the dozen or so I will have to clean before the end of the night—

There's a shout, and a crash of chairs falling over. Then an explosion of laughter, as three men who can't walk straight start to navigate toward the exit.

"Don't just stand there, get the mop," Mr. Lewis says.

He's emerging from the doorway in the corner, the one that opens into his private quarters. In all his grumpy disapproval, he is the opposite of the wife he lost a couple of years ago. I tried to save her, but didn't catch the timing right. I might believe he resents me for this, but the truth was, he didn't like me even before he became a widower.

"Yes, Mr. Lewis."

The mop and bucket are behind the bar, and the tender, who's yanking at the barrel pulls like he wants to tear his arm out of its socket, glares at me as I enter his territory. He is the one person I take no offense at when he shuns me. He doesn't like his job, doesn't like the pub, doesn't like Mr. Lewis. Doesn't like anybody or anything.

There's a water pump and a drain right by our employer's private door, and I steer the bucket with the mop into place under the spigot. The iron grip is warm as my hand as I throw my shoulder into the work of—

"Aye! Do it!"

"Do it—"

"—it!"

A chant starts up, and then the chatter calms a little. Sallae Mae casts a flirty glance at the sweaty, bearded man who's called out to her the loudest. She's wearing a sky-blue dress that's so low-cut, a deep breath would fully expose the top half of what she barters with, and that long blond hair of hers is a peekaboo shawl around her bare shoulders.

"A copper, then," she taunts as she goes over to him, lifts her skirting and plants an arched, stocking foot between his legs on his chair seat.

When the coin is in her hand, she holds it up and the customers hush into murmurs. With every eye in the place on her, she tucks the penny into her cleavage and sashays over to the bar. The tender looks as though he's about to quit, but he ducks under the counter and produces a thin glass on a slender stem.

"Thank you," she says with an exaggerated curtsy.

"Those aren't cheap," Mr. Lewis mutters.

Sallae Mae holds the flute high as she sits herself up on the bar. "Neither am I."

I've seen this parlor trick before—well, we all have, but the men like to watch her take a deep breath and I don't care about her respiration—so as she clears her throat, I take advantage of the crowd settling. Pushing my bucket over to where those drunken departures spilled several tankards, I flop my dirty mop on the floorboards. Over on the bar, Sallae Mae opens her mouth and projects a high note at the glass. The tone pierces like a knife into the ear, and she goes even higher and louder. Higher. Louder. Higher—

The glass shatters with a spray that shimmers in the lantern light.

The gasps and cheers are loud and prolonged, as if she'd lifted a plow horse up over her shoulder. Sallae Mae is delighted with the attention and stays right where she is, holding the slender stem while she fluffs her hair—

The front entrance opens.

What comes inside sucks all the sound and air out of the pub.

The man of war stands over six lengths high, at least. His heavily muscled upper body is clad in a drape of corroded mesh and a padded black leather surcoat, and his thick legs are wrapped in black leather as well. He has a dirk at his hip, a dagger upon his opposite thigh, and over his shoulder, the thick handle of a broadsword is within ready reach.

Nobody moves, not even Sallae Mae to slip off the bar.

He takes a single step forward and shuts the cold out with a clap. His hair is long and black, a braid on both sides keeping it out of his face. He's clean-shaven, his jaw square and pronounced, his nose straight as an arrow. I'm careful not to meet his eyes directly, but my peripheral vision tells me that one has been lost to battle, a scar slashing down through his brow and continuing to his temple, an opaque whiteness staring out into the world. The injury does nothing to diminish the power and authority of him, however—or the sexual charge that rolls off him like lightning.

He possesses . . . a brutal beauty.

And the working women clearly recognize the virility of him. All around at the tables, they plume in a way that has nothing to do with their profession. The men, on the other hand, don't seem to be breathing at all.

Mr. Lewis loops his suspenders, which have been hanging loose, up onto his shoulders. His voice is tense as he says, "Well, what d'ya want, then."

Like he's very much done with that door opening up to bad surprises tonight.

The warrior scans the pub slowly, and the drunks shift in their seats, making me think of a restless herd aware that a hungry predator has entered the grazing pasture.

As we all wait for the man to speak, I wager that most are thinking what I am: No royal insignia. So he's a mercenary looking for somebody, and when he finds them? There's going to be bloodshed.

"A room," he says in a low, resonant voice. "And some food."

*Five*

# The Dream of Horses.

"Take it to him. G'on then."

At the bar, the tender's command to me is impatient and he shoves a tin plate in my direction. There's a wedge of bread, a hunk of cheese, and a roasted turkey leg on it. All of the food is cold, having been prepared over day in the kitchen by the cook and myself. I'm surprised the tender isn't delivering. He hates dealing with combustibles, but Mr. Lewis doesn't want me near the eat or drink because of the Pox. I only deal with empties.

Glancing over at the mercenary, I don't want to go near the man, either. He's dampened the establishment like a fierce winter storm, dropping the temperature, causing us all to hunker down into ourselves. The pub has emptied out, most of the drunks stumbling off out of self-preservation, the women banished upstairs by Mr. Lewis.

Much to their disappointment.

Our employer is planted at a nearby table with two shepherds and a farmer, and he's listening in on me and the tender while his suspicious stare stays locked on the mercenary. When he nods impatiently in the man's direction, and then glares at me, I know I have no choice. Not that I've ever really had one.

"Yes, sir."

I dry my hands on my cloak. They shake as I take the plate, and the already hushed voices get quieter as I begin the trek through the tables. No doubt the men want to see what gets eaten. Me or the food.

The mercenary has finished his tankard. It sits at his elbow, empty. As I approach, I feel his stare on me and I become the mead, something he drinks in. I keep my eyes on his hands, noting the healed scratches, the calluses. He's missing the first sections of both pinkies, and I wonder how he lost them. I picture him captured, someone with a blade threatening him.

If that's how the mutilations happened, I also imagine whoever it was didn't survive to tell the tale.

"Thank you." His voice is surprisingly soft, and I pick up on an accent. "I am hungry."

Coming back to attention, I realize I've just been standing in front of him, and I place the plate on the table. When he doesn't move to take the food, I'm forced to lean over and push the meal toward him. Up closer, his chest is massive under the leather and steel of his fighting garb, and his arms seem thick as tree trunks.

Is he from Prosperitus? I doubt it. From what we've heard here, King Rehm the Just keeps strict control of his populace, and mercenaries aren't allowed inside the territory to disturb the order.

Well, most of the territory. A transgression here in our village wouldn't be so much excused as irrelevant to the King.

I clear my throat. "Would you care for more ale—"

"I would, yes."

He holds out the tankard instead of letting me pick it up. I'm careful not to make contact with him as I take the weight, but he moves his forefinger at the last moment. The stroke over my thumb is a shock, something sizzling between our flesh.

"I'll keep using this particular tankard," he says softly. "If you don't mind."

In a trance, I turn away, and I can feel his eye on me as I return to the bar. When I put the tankard in front of the tender, the man recoils as if it's contaminated, and I know what he's thinking. I've already been sacrificed to disease, and he doesn't like the idea of touching anything I have unless it's been washed first.

"He wants to use this one," I explain.

"Then you fill it."

Shuffling behind the bar, I take a cloth and cover my hand so as not to be accused of contaminating the drink. Then I draw the ale from the barrel's base, and too soon, I'm back over at the table. The mercenary nods as I place the serving by the plate, and as he shifts to the side, I jump out of range on instinct.

Although given the size of his shoulders, there is no out of range for him.

He stops in mid-motion. "You have nothing to fear from me."

The copper he takes out and slides forward makes a rasping noise over the rough wood planks. Everything about him seems very loud. Then again, he's sucked the sound out of the rest of the continent.

"For you," he tells me.

I shake my head and back away just as the pub door opens. Everyone except the mercenary looks to see what is arriving. What *else* is arriving—

The farrier steps through and locates me with ease through the subdued stragglers, his big belly turning toward me like it's homing in. I glance at the winding clock over the bar. At least he's on time.

"Friend of yours?" the mercenary asks me.

"Enjoy your meal."

I duck my head, even though it's covered by my hood, and hustle off for the back of house. No one stops me, not even Mr. Lewis.

Out by the stairwell, I bend down and spring the latch on my crawl space's panel. Squeezing through, I orient thanks to the light that filters through the gaps in the steps overhead. I have a sleeping pallet that I keep scrupulously clean, and an array of cloaks that hang from pegs I have driven into the underside of the staircase. Then there's my worktable, which is little more than a discarded board I have set on two stacks of bricks.

A collection of small earthenware pots contain various unguents, and my pestle is filled with dried leaves that I've not had time to continue working with. The collection of wads I have managed to prepare for Elly are bundled in one of my collection sacks, and I grab the medicine.

Reemerging, I confront the farrier, pressing the satchel into his meaty paw. "She must have a fresh one of these put into her mouth every four to five hours. Tell your niece to do it. I will bring more on the morrow."

He looks down at the little bag as if he's never seen one before. "And I shall bury my son at the Resting Place—"

"I care only about your *wife* who still lives. This will change her pupils so I'll know whether or not it's been given to her—"

We have an audience. Both Mr. Lewis and the scarred mercenary who brought the storm inside with him are standing in the archway. The plate I delivered is in the man of war's left hand and he holds the heavy pewter weight laden with food as if it's but a leaf.

"Take him to number eight," Mr. Lewis orders me.

The farrier drops his head and lumbers away like something that should be in a forest, not inside a pub or lodging house. Mr. Lewis makes room for him to pass. The mercenary does not. Him, the farrier squeezes against the dirty wall to get around.

"Yes, sir," I say.

Gathering my cloak, I start to walk up the stairs, and as the warrior falls in behind me, I imagine he's not led very often by another. My employer stays below, watching us, but not because he's protecting me. He's curious to find out, as the others are, what this killer in my wake will do to me as a way to judge what might come in their own direction.

The Gauntlet's second floor is a cave-like hallway of closed doors that's illuminated by oil lanterns that have stained the ceiling and walls with smoke residue. I go straight ahead, and given the sounds of moaning and creaking beds, I gather that business continues apace, in spite of our newest lodger. I blush ferociously as I take him down to the last room on the left, and I feel his presence looming behind me, the floorboards protesting under his weight, the soft jangle of his weapons and chain mail like the hiss of a coiled viper.

Though he brought the cold in with him, he makes me think of fire: At the moment, he is banked and contained, but the potential for destruction is never far, and I tell myself that it's because of this latent threat that my body is aware of every move he makes.

Yet I'm not afraid, for some reason. I feel . . . alive.

When we get to the door, I go to open it for him, but a long arm extends over my shoulder to push the panels wide. He smells like leather, metal, and cedar soap, and I breathe in deep as I stare into the darkness of the room he's been assigned. Only a slice of restless, golden light spills inside, and even still, he walks right in. The fact that he doesn't know what's awaiting his entrance seems not to worry him in the slightest. Then again, anything with a wink of self-preservation would get out of his way.

As he turns around, the illumination from the hall bathes him, and nothing else. He's not just of the shadows, he's tamed them.

"Are you not coming in?" he asks as he sets his plate and tankard down out of sight.

"Why would I . . ." I clear my throat. "I'm sorry, what?"

"Or has that villager already engaged your services?" I feel his eyes traveling down my cloak. "Never mind, I can wait while I eat my meal."

With a frown, I struggle to understand. "The farrier? I have no business with him—"

"Didn't look that way." He shrugs. "There's no need to be shy about our professions, is there? I do what I do best for pay, so I don't judge others for the same."

Someone orgasms across the hall, as if to back up his point, and all I can do is stare in disbelief at the mesh covering his chest. Incredulity aside, when I consider all the illegal things I've done, I guess it's far better to be thought of as a whore than risk anything even close to my truth.

"I'm glad you understand," I mumble.

"So you come back. When you've finished with him."

Lifting some of my cloak up, I lean in. "Do you not know what this is?"

"Of course I do. It's a Pox cloak."

Measuring the power of his body, and his long, flowing hair, I shake my head and think of the way Sallae Mae and the other women stared at him with hunger that hadn't been faked for effect.

"Whyever would someone such as yourself pay for something . . . like me."

His nostrils flare as he breathes deeply, and when he closes his eyes, his head falls back a little, as if he's savoring something. "Meadow flowers. Sunshine. And . . . a fresh, mineral spring in a basin of crystal stones."

He relevels his face, and his voice is something altogether different now. It caresses me: "You smell of a freedom I once had, a long time ago. How could you not be beautiful."

Before I can respond, he extends his hand. The copper piece he put on the table downstairs is in the center of it. "Take this. And come back."

In the pause that follows, the loneliness that's always defined me mixes with a need I've never felt before. I'm a virgin, utterly untouched, and up until now, my spinsterhood has always been the least of my concerns. Standing with this stranger? I suddenly find myself wondering what the sexual act is like.

And I decide that just once, I might want to share my body, especially with him—

"No," I say sharply. "I'm not coming back here."

"Why?"

I blurt, "I don't know you."

"You can call me Merc." He bows. "And you are . . . ?"

"As in mercenary?" And no, I don't want to know what he's called. He's already too close, no matter the physical distance between our bodies. "Your name is your job?"

"Precisely. So what does that make yours?"

"I am Sorrel." I lift my chin even though my face is hidden under my hooding. "That's my name."

His voice softens again, and I feel the syllables he speaks flowing over my skin. "Like the horses that run wild and free by the ocean."

My eyes flare wide. "What . . . ?"

"I have been to all the corners of Anathos. And some places no one should go. The most beautiful sight ever I saw was of the coastline where the wild horses hoof over the surf, and the ocean spray becomes their mane and tail."

My dream. The one I have told no one about.

Abruptly, my head aches, and for reasons I'll wonder of later, I stammer, "Sometimes I have visions in the night of horses that run on the beach . . . their hooves pound through the surf and their manes tickle my face while we race along the ocean's edge . . ."

He holds the aged penny between his thumb and forefinger, the stub of his pinkie cocked. "They have no black upon their coat, nor white. They are pure copper, and when the sun shines upon them, they gleam as this coin did when newly forged."

And then he speaks my name: "Sorrel."

When I refocus, he's right in front of me, having moved without sound. I want to meet his eyes so badly I shake, but I keep my stare locked on his throat.

"Take this." He presses the copper into my palm and curls my fingers into a fist. "For your services down below. We will see about what comes later."

As I unfurl what he's wrapped tightly around the coin, I'm confused. It was tarnished, but now the metal gleams as if freshly minted . . . exactly like the coats of those horses I visit in my dreams, and struggle to recall during my waking hours.

"What magic is this," I whisper.

"There is no magic."

My eyes lift to his lips, and everything disappears. The light behind me and the darkness around him, the Gauntlet and my village, the territory of Prosperitus.

Anathos itself.

"You lie." My words are mostly breath. Which is a curious feat, for there is no air in my lungs.

"Look at me," he commands. "You can't really see anybody without meeting their eyes."

Something in his tone awakens me out of the stupor, and I drop my stare to the copper. It abruptly appears as it was before, the surface dingy and dull.

"Never," I mumble. "I will never look at you."

"Is my injury so ugly . . . " His hand rises, as if he's brushing his scarred cheek. "That it disgusts you."

"No."

"Now you lie," he drawls. "Both my eyes work quite well, you know, in spite of what the one appears, so my ugliness is well familiar to me."

"I'm under a Pox cloak," I snap back. "Your physical appearance and any of its imperfections don't matter to me."

"So look at me properly and prove it."

By way of response, I hold the penny out. He does nothing. "Take this back."

"It's yours."

"No, it's not. And I'm not going to be indebted to you or anyone else."

"The services that earned its worth have already been tendered." He sweeps his hand off to the side. "My meal and ale have been delivered quite readily. And I have been delivered to this room."

I drop the coin, which bounces on the bare floor. It's still chiming as I leave him in the darkness by himself.

Yet I am the one who is alone as I flee everything that he wants, and all I must deny:

*Hide.*

*Six*

# My One and True Friend.

"Sorrel, your desire to cheat Death of its due is going to be the death of you."

It's the following morning, and I ignore that haughty proclamation for the pretense of stocking a small hearth with more hardwood. The kettle is almost ready, and I have the last of my dried *unslee* leaves in the base of a tin mug. As I measure the dwindling stash of oak logs, I know I need to gather more when I go harvesting outside the wall.

"Did you hear what I said," the former Lady Marehomen of Prosperitus demands.

"Stop deflecting." From under the hood of my cloak, I glare across my shoulder. "You're going to drink all of this, and you're not going to care if it's bitter."

"I will drink *some* of it and I will complain the entire time."

Over on the pallet, my elderly friend, Mare, lies swaddled in mismatched blankets that I've collected from the lodging house's stock and snuck out to this abandoned shoe shop. Lying there, so frail, so drawn, she's as an infant newly born into the world, incapable of caring for her most basic needs, relying on me to come when I can. Every time I show up here, I run the risk that we'll both be discovered, but she's a burden I can't put down. No one else in the village will care for her, and my conscience carries enough already.

I also happen to like her tart company.

"I am not here upon Anathos's soil for much longer," she says. "Why must you prolong my agony."

My friend's words slice through me. She was not my first stop on this glum and cold daybreak. I went to check on Elly and didn't get farther than the back alley behind the farrier's quarters. He was loading her body onto a cart, his daughters and niece hovering in the doorway as if they all wished they could follow her into her grave.

Assuming he even bothers to dig her one.

"You are quiet today," Mare observes.

"I am not, and you know this brew is just for pain relief." I glance back in her direction again. "Although I suspect your griping about the taste gives you a vital hobby. If you stop, you'll expire on the spot."

Her dismissive hand betrays the high station she once enjoyed, and I imagine jeweled rings on her fingers and her nails painted. "You will miss me when I am gone."

Leaning into the crackling flames, I wrap up my hand in my cloak's long woolen sleeve and still feel the heat as I take the brewing kettle off its iron arm. As I pour, the dried leaves swirl about in the tin mug and I imagine her ashes scattering in the wind.

I have to clear my throat.

"You're still drinking this," I repeat roughly, knowing that as I'm unable to treat my own pain, I soothe hers with a vengeance whether she likes it or not.

And she doesn't.

During the steeping, I pass a glance over the shabby interior. My only friend lives in what used to be the cobbler's shop before he moved closer to the village square. The shelves that once held the maker's inventory are the rib cage of the structure, lining all the walls. Here and there, pairs of shoes that were left behind are covered in dust, the fine layers buffering their contours just as the pilled blankets I pile on Mare bury her own aged body.

"So whatever have you overheard at that ratty establishment of yours?" she says.

"The Gauntlet is not mine." I stir with a dented spoon. "And there is no news."

"You lie, girl. Have there been any more slaughtered cows?"

Swallowing a curse, I shake my head and wonder why I told her anything. Then again, fear is like water. It will find any gap to penetrate for its expression.

Mare sniffs. "Well, that is a yes if ever I have heard one."

"I've said nothing—"

"So another demon has struck."

Between one blink and the next, I see Mr. Cavenish standing in the pub's doorway, bloody intestines in one hand, that mournful cowbell in the other. "We don't know that's what—"

"Is there something else out in the forest that is both brutal and intelligent—or do you think wolves of the wood are smart enough to know the compass? Which point did they hit this time."

I imagine her in the court of Prosperitus, dressed in silks and attended by servants, and I ponder the kinds of lives where a lack of memories is a gift. Her mind's still sharp, so she's spared nothing of her fall from such heights, this rickety, leaky palm that's caught and held her a shelter below the ranks and standards of even her groundskeepers.

Yet she's never complained. She's never talked about what happened, either. Maybe that's how she copes.

As the chatter from the fire grows loud between us, I lie. "We're safe here within the village wall."

"And you are the one who brings me wood for my fire and that foul medicine of yours, all of which is found outside of those crumbling rocks." In a softer tone, she adds, "I worry over you."

"I'm the last person you need to be concerned about."

Now that the leaf flakes have sunk to the bottom of the tin, I wrap the mug in a cloth and bring the brew over to her. When I hold out the cup, she takes it in her skeletal hands, even as she shakes her head.

"Tell me the news and I will choke this back. Otherwise, it is going to go cold."

As I meet her scowl with a glare of my own, I am careful to not look into her eyes. "Only you, Mare, could try and force a hand with your own well-being."

"Is it working?"

I sit at the foot of the pallet. Even though she can't see my face, I lower my head to hide a blush. "A man came into the pub last night."

I have immediate regret over the admission. This is precisely how I got into trouble with the demons, dead cows, and compass points. Then again, I have nobody else to talk to.

"There are a lot of men in that den of iniquity," she remarks dryly.

"Time to drink. Or that's all the news I'm sharing."

Mare grumbles, but takes a draw against the lip of the cup. "Oh, this is awful. You are no cook, for certain. Now tell me more of this man."

The details of the mercenary seep into my mind, his raven hair, his war togs, and his muscled body blinding me, even as my eyes remain open.

"After he showed up, it was the quietest night Mr. Lewis's pub ever had."

Mare snorts. "The only way to find anything resembling silence in that ale trap is to wrap one's head in a blanket."

"You've never been inside."

"One can hear it from the street." When I nod at the cup, she shakes her head. "You have not told me anything. We have an agreement. What of this man."

Blowing out my breath, I choose my words with care. "He was dressed for fighting . . . there were weapons all over him, but I didn't see any insignia. Are you aware of any kind of secret guard of the King? Maybe some soldiers who protect Him from positions in the shadows?"

Somehow I want that stranger to be moral. Or at the very least not an outlaw.

"How did you know he was from Prosperitus?" she asks.

"I . . . don't, I guess. I just assumed."

I can bring little to mind about the other three Kingdoms of Anathos, only spots of gossip I've overheard that don't make me want to ever visit any of them: Dangerous places with dangerous people. Why couldn't the demons target better victims than us?

Then again, if the Fulcrum is failing, maybe they are.

Mare takes a sip of her own volition, and as she scrunches her nose, it's as if she brought the warm mug to her lips out of habit and expected tea.

"Any soldier of the King's court must wear the royal coat and arms," she says briskly. "That has always been the regulation, whether on or off duty. So either your man is from another court with a different tradition or . . ."

"Or what?" Then I shake my head. "And he's not mine."

"Or he is a rogue for hire. In which case, he would be wise to leave even this lowly settlement on the fringes of Prosperitus. Our King does not care for the ugly business of mercenaries. The stranger will be hanged if caught."

"I haven't seen a royal guard or representative here, ever."

"That you are aware of."

Though I studiously avoid my friend's eyes, her mouth thins with resolve, and I wonder about all the things she hasn't told me about her past.

"But you have?" I prompt. "Mare, have you seen—"

"Now enough about armed men. What about the demons?" She looks at me sharply. "And do not insulate me, girl. I have a right to know anything you do."

Remembering my run through the darkness and the cold rain, I relive the shiver of warning that went through me.

"Tell me," Mare orders grimly.

"I fear something got inside last night. I was on my way here, and I sensed . . . something behind me." And because I'm not going to talk about the farrier, I tack on, "That's why I didn't come. I had to turn back."

"Demons." She makes the sign of the crescent moon over her chest, her forefinger and thumb a knobby C over her heart. "They are among us, for certain."

"But there was nothing out of order on my way here just now. No one hurt, no disturbances. Maybe my mind was playing tricks on me."

"You should *never* come at night." She exhales with exhaustion. "I have told you this before."

"I have to work in the kitchen preparing the breads and cheeses during the day—"

"And if you are killed by a demon while trying to help a dying old lady, how is that better than being slightly late for a shift you are not being paid for."

"Mr. Lewis provides me with shelter and food—"

"For which you work yourself to the bone. From now on, you will come only during the day—"

"Mare. It's better if no one sees me anywhere near here, you know this. In the eyes of the mayor, there's no difference between magic and medicinal herbs."

"He is an *aspinhaul*." As I gasp at the curse, she smiles as if she's enjoyed being sassy. "Besides, the villagers will not stand for anyone prosecuting you, not after all those bairns you've saved."

"They despise me."

"No, they *fear* you." Mare flicks her hand through the air in her fashion. "And they don't care about me. What happens herein is no matter to anyone."

"*I* care about you." I tap on the tin cup with my nail. *Tink. Tink. Tink.* "More."

Mare grimaces, and for once, does as she's told without argument. And in the crackle of the fire, I return to the moment I was alone with that mercenary in the darkened guest room. He was so unfazed by shadows that would consume a lesser man. He also thought I was like Sallae Mae, something to be bought for a short time. For his pleasure.

My face turns hot, but it's not from shame. I wonder what would have happened if I'd taken his copper and done what he'd ordered me to—and can't believe where my mind goes. I should be wary of him, and I am. There's something else for me, though.

Shifting my eyes to the little hearth, I stare into the flames, watching the undulation of the light, the way the flares of heat entwine and arch into each other—

Jumping back to attention, I look over at my dear old friend. She's lying back against her pillows, the empty cup lolling in her hand, her attention seemingly on something in the middle distance between us.

"Mare?" I take the cup from her and tap on her shoulder. "Mare. Look at me. *Mare*."

Just as I'm worried that I've given her too much, she turns her head in my direction like she's coming back from some place in her mind.

"I want you to do something for me, Sorrel."

Even though I try not to touch people, I take her palm in my own. "Of course. Anything."

When she goes silent again, I fuss with the blankets with my free hand, as if that will reanimate her—

"Go to those shelves." Her crooked finger points across the shallow room, steady as a knurled twig on a branch. "The third one from the top."

Her voice is not the imperious one she uses when she orders me about. I'm not sure what her tone is.

I set the cup down and go over to where she instructs. "Mare?"

"The panel, it is loose. Push where it meets the molding."

I find the fissure, and the wood yields under pressure to reveal a dark crevice. I look over my shoulder and await instruction.

"Go on," she says softly. "Take it out."

"What is 'it'?"

"Your future."

Extending my hand into the hole, I think of rats finding shelter from the cold and wet in the leaky walls of the shop. But instead of rabid little teeth, I feel something like velvet. When I go to pull whatever it is out, I'm astonished at how heavy—

The red velvet bag is tied at the top with a golden tassel that captures the firelight. "What's this?" I repeat.

"Open it."

With fumbling hands, I do as instructed—

Royal coins spill out into my palm and fall onto the floor, landing in a gleaming, tinkling chorus at my feet.

"Mare . . ." I breathe.

My elderly companion sits up in a way she hasn't been able to for a month. "When I was banished, I snuck them out in the skirt of my gown. As I was still legally the wife of a nobleman, they did not search me."

Turning a coin over in my palm, I am awed. "I've never seen even one of these before."

How beautiful they are. Each royal *dnaka* is marked with the proud profile of the bearded King on one side and the fierce head of a *grylon* on the other, and oh, the weight of them. They are dense with value.

"I want you to take it all and leave today."

When her arching order registers, I jerk my head around. "What? I'm not going anywhere—"

"We are not safe here for much longer. If you sensed something last night—"

"It was only my fear."

"I do not believe that." Mare eases back down with a groan. "My time is coming to an end, and I find that the only thing on my mind is you—"

When I go to interrupt, she shuts me up with that imperious raised hand. "My children were stripped of me when I was banished from the court, and none of them have bothered to try to find me or offer alms for my care and feeding. Therefore, you are the only daughter I have and you are due what worldly possessions I own."

I blink back tears, for no one has ever claimed me.

As if she senses my emotion, she says more gently, "When I die peacefully in this bed—and we have both agreed you will *not* intervene—you will have no more ties that bind here in this village. You must go, and go now, so that I do not spend my last days with all this worry."

I funnel what has stayed in my hand back into the velvet pouch. Then I crouch and pick up the other coins one by one. I inspect them all, turning them over, though they are exactly the same, the *grylon* and the King. The *grylon* and the King. The *grylon* and the—

No, there's one that's different. It's stamped with a younger version of our ruler, and the back side is marked with the image of a crown. No doubt it's an older one, from when King Rehm first ascended to his throne.

"Sorrel."

"You can't call me daughter and expect I'm going to leave you."

Also, the birthing women like Elly need me. And the bairns. But I don't speak that out loud even though Mare knows what I do.

And besides, I'm a coward. Though I have flares of strength, they never last, because it's not my true character. Even with all this gold, I would be useless out there, crippled by my anxiety and lost in the larger dangers of Anathos.

I cannot survive outside the wall of this village.

Mare wields that gnarled finger of hers again, pointing at me now. "There comes a time in everyone's life that they must choose themselves over others. You have to do this now. It is about survival. Take the coins, buy yourself a horse from Mr. Brownly, and leave."

"If I use one of these?" I hold the last gold *dnaka* up. "In this village or anywhere else? I'll be turned in for stealing. Only members of the court can use these—and anyway, I'm not leaving—"

"You *must* go." Mare's voice lowers even though it's just the two of us. "And someone who is capable of what you are is hardly defenseless."

"I don't know what you're talking about—"

*"Sorrel."*

My name is spoken with such urgency, I nearly meet her eyes. And in the silence that fills the space between us, I feel a crushing fear that thunders my heart.

"I can't . . . survive out there alone," I protest. "I'm not strong enough."

"So find yourself someone to protect you." Mare nods at the coins. "And those will help you—the gold can be melted down. Its value is not in the imprint of the King, but the metal itself."

"But what about you? Who will bring you food and water—"

"My sleep these days is so deep, I have to claw my way back to consciousness, and I have no thirst or hunger. Soon enough, I will drift unto the horizon and rest eternal with my father who loved me and my mother for whom I was a shining joy. I have had my fill of Anathos, and am ready for this. My only worry . . . is you."

I slip the final coin back into the pouch, and as the sweet chiming is muffled by the red velvet, I picture the mercenary in the pub, the grip of his broadsword extending up over his heavy shoulder.

"This place leaks." I look pointedly at the puddle in the corner by the boarded-up front window. "We should use some of these to move you to better accommodations."

"*No.* You will take it all and secure your future with what I have left in this material world."

I put the small fortune back into the hidden nook and re-cover the space with the board. "I'll return with food and more medicine at nightfall—"

"Sorrel, I have never asked you for a thing, not even when this started between us."

I return to when I first saw her in the market square a calendar ago. She was struggling to hold a loaf of bread and a gather of walterberries as she limped along in rags. Even though it was noontime, I stepped in and helped her, and was surprised to find her living in what all of us assumed was a vacant storefront. I have been coming back ever since.

"You are more important than this village," she tells me gravely. "What you can do must be preserved—"

"I do nothing."

Unable to stay still, I get busy with useless effort, unfolding and refolding blankets at the end of the pallet, rearranging the pitiful stack of wood by the fire.

"Come here, child."

My body answers Mare's call before my mind can decide whether I want to approach her or not: The next thing I know, I am sitting by her.

"Will you not ever show me your face?" When I make no move to remove my hood, she sighs. "I do not care if you are scarred."

Mare is the one taking my hand now. Hers is so different from my own, stripped down to its component structures, the bones and ligaments stark under thin skin mottled with age spots. With her silence, she pleads more loudly than if she'd spoken further, but there are so many reasons I cannot do as she wishes, as she commands.

Chief among them is that I feel as though if I take the coins, I'm hastening her death.

And I don't know what I'll do in this village, in this world, without my one true friend.

*Seven*

# A Trip Outside the Wall.

It's very late in the afternoon when I go out the Gauntlet's back door, and head for the guard towers and the bridge over our moat. I keep my eyes on the cobblestones, but sense the flow of villagers around me, their chatter, their sloshing buckets of water, their bundles of creaking wood balanced on their shoulders, the kinds of things that calm me even though they shouldn't. I see the evidence of normal life as proof we're not in danger, and that's faulty reasoning—

"—'nother one, aye."

"In truth? At what compass point?"

"The carcass was to the south. 'Tis time we count all the cattle—"

I duck my head even more in hopes my hood will prevent me from hearing the talk—and when that doesn't work, I realize only men are around me. In the regular course of things, women would be coming and going, too, bringing in the herds of small *untas* that are allowed inside the wall when it's dark out, shooing children toward home to prepare the evening meal, carting in the wash from the river. I wonder if this is an edict from the mayor that I haven't heard about yet or if all the husbands, fathers, uncles, and brothers are collectively putting their feet down.

And Mare thinks I can survive on my own, even with all that gold?

A stone arch links the two guard towers, and there's a brief echo chamber as I enter the tunnel. Glancing up, I try to focus on the sections of stones that are sound, not the ones where the mortar is crumbling, and as I reemerge into the waning sunlight, I search the meadows that undulate out toward the distant forest edge. The pasture fences are as they've always been, solidly constructed and without breaks, but there are no horses in them. Likewise, no sheeplings or cows munch in the grasses beyond the barns. Clearly, the livestock have been locked down under cover in the barns. Not unlike the women in the houses.

Yet no one stops me as I cross onto the bridge.

The planks I travel over are slick with mud, and nailed together, they're wide as our village's main lane. I refuse to look down at the muddy water. We're up at least ten or fifteen lengths to make sure we're well out of reach of the *balas*, the red-eyed, horn-backed, many-teethed thrashers that churn the moat, but I don't want any reminders of how hungry they are.

I wonder how a demon would match up against our reptilian guards, and fear my conclusion.

Reaching the end of the bridge, I step off onto the dirt road that snakes around to both the left and the right. Various footpaths, well-trodden, but swampy from all the rain, are tributaries from these bigger sources, and I hook up with one that takes me on a decline through the meadow to the tree line. Nobody else goes this way, so I'm on my own through the green-and-yellow blades. Overhead, the sky is a ringing blue, and the sun is also vibrant, although with its low seat at the horizon, the temperature is cool and I'm grateful for my cloak.

But none of that is what I dwell on.

Even with the daylight, the troubling star that suddenly appeared in our sky is bright enough to be visible. I swear it's getting closer, and the sight of its fierce glow makes me long for cloud cover.

So instead, I focus on the snow-covered cap of Dragon Mount. At the moment, none of the great scaled creatures are patrolling their lair, but many times, I've seen them flying in great circles around the craggy apex. They're fearsome terrors for sure, except they're like wasps protecting a nest. As long as you leave them alone, they're content to stay in their fire-breathing introversion, and besides, they far more prefer *grylons* to we stringy humans for their meals.

Now what about a demon against one of them? The dragons would probably win.

That there might be a doubt makes me walk quicker.

As I arrive at the tree line and penetrate the weave of branches, my path disappears, but I know where I'm going. Good thing, as there isn't much of the waning sunlight filtering through the leaves, which have turned such a dark purple they're nearly black. This final stage of color change means they're about to fall, and by spring there'll be a fresh layer of soil for the plants I need to grow in.

Underfoot, the ground is spongy, and the smell is thick and earthy in my nose. Usually this reassures me, and these gathering trips are a time for me to relax. Not anymore. I pull out my little knife, and my heart skips in my chest as I keep my strides even and quiet.

I don't want to be out here so late in the day, but I've decided Mare needs something more than the *unslee* I've been giving her. Night-blooming *alsaag* is what I am after now, for it has healing properties for the heart and for the breathing. If I can give her body greater strength, perhaps she'll stay with me a little longer.

I glance at the sun's position, now even lower on the horizon than when I left the Gauntlet's kitchen. The gloaming is required for my harvesting, as the flowering buds must be picked just as they bloom or the components are worthless—

I smell something foul and stop.

The scent of corporeal rot is in the air.

My first thought is to race back to the village, but fates, what if it's Elly. What if that horrible husband of hers has just dumped her out here?

As I track the horrible stench, leaves and branches hinder me like hands trying to hold me back, and as I fight through, veering farther and farther off track, my mind spins—

"Oh . . . fates," I whisper.

The dead cow is on its back, the poor animal's heart-shaped hooves lax on the ends of its splayed, spindly legs. The belly is torn open in a ragged maw, the innards cast aside as if whatever had taken it down had been choosy in what it had eaten. I stumble back, and cover my mouth and nose so I don't throw up. The remains have been here awhile, given the laziness of the flies, which have already gotten their fill, and the day's warmth has rekindled the stench.

Looking into its milky, blank stare, I see nothing, I feel nothing. Then again, its death was at least a week ago.

I lift my eyes, all the while knowing exactly what I'll see—

The setting sun is directly in a line with the remains.

To the west. The final compass point.

A pleading sound escapes my lips and I stumble back until I slam into a trunk. "Fates . . . we are doomed."

Everything inside me screams that I've got to return to the village, and tell the others—and I know they'll believe me because the carcass is here. The remains speak for themselves.

But then I think of Mare. I need those special leaves to help her stay alive, especially now that she's claimed me the way a mother does.

Even though the gathering could cost me my life out here with what ate that cow.

I'll just be quick about it.

Tripping and falling and flailing, I beat back branches and search the ground as daylight continues to drain at an alarming rate, that evil star growing ever more prominent as if it's coming after me. My collecting pouch slaps against my hip, and my cloak snags on brambles and branches, my hood tugging back until it almost falls free of my head.

*Alsaag* is a shy plant that hides under the plate-sized leaves of the forest undergrowth, and I know I've got to slow down or I'll miss its eerie glow. Yet as my blood rushes in fear, I go still faster and farther, faster and farther—

Abruptly, I realize I've gone very deep into the woods.

I stop and look around. So many shadows, closing in on me, stalking me, just as it was the night before as I ran down the village lane.

Maybe I've missed the plant's telltale luminescence, but if I double back and find nothing, it will be too late to venture this far out again. I keep going, trying to scan the underbrush, while all my eyes really do is seek demons. I picture them as twice the size of a full-grown man, with the teeth of a predator, the claws of a *grylon*, and the—

Something tickles my nose and I brush my face under the hood. When it happens again, I notice there's something in the air. Black wisps are swirling around like snowflakes, and there's a buildup on the branches, on the dark leaves, on my sleeves. Before I can wonder too much about it, I catch the first glow.

Finally.

There's a patch of *alsaag* throwing gentle shadows under some broad-leafed *wallsa*. Scrambling over, I throw myself down, and pinch the heart-shaped blooms from their nests of foliage. The stench of a dead body blooms in the cooling air and takes me back to the cow, not that I need the reminder. How something that can so powerfully sustain life smells like a corpse left in the heat has always struck me as one of nature's worst jokes, and I choke back nausea.

More is growing nearby, but my harvesting is slowed by the many times I look over my shoulder and bat at the tufts that are falling from the sky even though there are no clouds above—and this is no snow that I've ever seen.

I move farther into the brush, and the sense that time is running out trembles my hands. Images of Mare struggling to sit up spur me on, and I'm even more determined than ever to keep her alive—

Abruptly, the rushing sound in my ears tells me I have gone *way* too far.

It's as though there's a river near me, except I know there's no water here. I'm also aware of what the subtle roar truly is.

Later, I will wonder why I went forward, but one thing is true.

My whole life changes as I break out of the forest and step into the pale, loose sand that's encroaching on the trunks and killing the root systems of the arboreal perimeter. Standing among the skeletal *cangjas* and *tallsi* trees, I crane my neck and look up, up . . . up.

The Fulcrum is a towering churn before me, a horizontal band of storming energy that stretches as far as the eye can see in both directions. Tall as the sky itself, it circulates to the right, and the dull roar burrows into the mind. The marvel is not actually made of the bleached particles that have been trapped in its twist. Rather, the ground has been dehydrated and sucked up into its circular force, thrown free at the top and drawn back in at the bottom in an endless cycle that's been going on for centuries.

I have seen this marvel only a handful of times before, and a shiver goes through me, my body reacting to the electric charge. The Fulcrum is pure magic, all of the elemental energy that remained after the Dark King rose to power and took control gathered by the Savior and concentrated here during the Great Containment.

To hold the evil and its army of the undead in.

Except something is terribly wrong.

In the midst of the swirl, a black contamination has weeded through the pale waves. Bands of the rot have threaded into the entirety of what protects us, and it's from these that the black snow spins off.

The milkman is right. The Fulcrum is failing.

And inside of it, the Dark King and his demon soldiers are poised to—

At first, the cacophony to my left doesn't register over the hum of the Fulcrum and the horror of what I'm seeing. But then my ear locks in.

Shouting.

Someone is in trouble.

# *Eight*
# An Evil Comes for Me and Thee.

As I scramble forward, my soft shoes struggle for purchase in the sand and my cloak slows me down even after I grab its folds and yank them out of the way. The high-pitched sounds of yelling get louder as I track them along the face of the Fulcrum, and I worry about the women, whoever they are. Who would be out this late and this far from the village? At least here in the open, there is a little more light left—

From the corner of my eye, I see a shadow coming at my head, and I duck so that the bird of prey doesn't get me. Except it's not a bird. Stumbling off balance, I pitch face-first into the loose ground and roll over just as a black arm-like extension from one of the Fulcrum's bands swipes at me and then retracts into the swirl.

Whatever it is comes at me again, and I shove myself back farther, kicking up sand, not knowing how far the reach is.

Fates, the contamination is alive and prescient, a predator made of black magic, and it throws off more of the black snow, flurries of evil falling all around.

"Forsake thee!" I shout as I make the sign of the crescent moon over my heart.

I glance at the ragged tree line, but then the screams pierce my consciousness again. Bursting into more paddling movement, I refuse to give in to my own fear as I go round the curvature of the Fulcrum—

The tableau that's revealed makes no sense, and the components become apparent in a series of focal points—the first of which is that it's not women or girls. It's a trio of young boys, aged about ten and two. And they're not in danger.

They are the tormentors.

A dragon is down in the sand, its iridescent scales dulled to a sickly white, one wing twisted at a bad angle, its long snout open and gray tongue lolling as it struggles to breathe.

"Again!" one of the boys shouts. "Throw another!"

The blond-haired of the three goes over to a dead *cangjas*, tears off a branch, and advances in a kind of dance, bouncing on the balls of his leather boots. His friends cackle as the dragon jerks back and its muzzle twitches.

"Do it! Do it—"

The boy moves fast, rushing for the great beast's head. With a savage blow, he hits at its eye. There is a wince of pain, a groan, and the dragon paws weakly at the sand—

"Stop it!" I yell. "Right now!"

The boys wheel toward me, and instantly the guilty shock on their faces is replaced with the disdain they've been taught to have for me.

"She's no bother," the blond one says. "She's just poxed!"

The other two fall into a singsong taunt I've heard before. "Poxed, you are, poxed, you are, ugly and poxed, you are, you are—"

I march toward them, rage making me forget who I am in the hierarchy. "If you hit that dragon again—"

"You'll do what?" the blond boy taunts. "Give me the Pox? My father will put you in the stocks!"

Flushed with excitement, he dances around the dragon, hitting the creature again and again with the stick, until it no longer flinches or twitches. It just lies where it's fallen from the sky, dying slowly, circled by a fly that degrades its last moments.

"Stop it, right this moment—"

"You can't make us!" one of the others says as he goes for a branch and joins his friend.

The two run laughing around the dragon, the magnificent beast closing its eyes with resigned exhaustion—

Riding a piercing fury, I put my right palm out. "You will leave him alone or I will curse you!"

All of the boys freeze, even the blond instigator who's by the dragon's wounded wing. And as they stare at me in total shock, I lower the tone of my voice, some other part of me breaking free and attacking.

"You know who I am," I growl. "You know what I do. *Leave the dragon alone.*"

The branch falls from the blond boy's hand—

From out of the Fulcrum, one of the contaminated bands whips free. Before I can warn the child, before the other boys see it, the blond tormentor is wrapped in a fist of black sand and plucked from the ground like a weed.

With a high-pitched scream, he flails against the hold, his arms and legs spinning in the air, the sound he's making akin to what had called me to him and his friends, except now it's what I'd thought it was:

He's in mortal danger.

And he continues to beg for help as he's drawn higher and higher, not as the miniature man he was trying to be, mimicking the worst expression of male aggression, but as a bairn of his rightful age—

"You're a demon!" the boy who's stayed at the tree line yells at me. "I'm going to tell them all! This is your doing!"

As he runs off, the other friend tries to help and gets too close. He's caught just as the blond boy is swallowed into the black sand like a meal, those rippling screams fading into the roar as the next victim's start.

Bolting forward, I skate by the dragon, and jump up to grab the remaining boy's foot. Locking on with both hands, I hold on for everything I'm worth, and am slung around like a fish on a line, my cloak blooming out as it catches air.

"Heeeeeeeelp!" The boy's tortured pleading is the stuff of nightmare. "Help me! Help—"

"I've got you, Fergus!"

We have history, he and I, even if I'm the only one who knows this. After he was born, he struggled for his breath, and I'm the only reason he's lived long enough to die here at the Fulcrum.

And die he's going to.

I lose my strength and his shoe comes with me. In the instant we part, my eyes go straight to his, and the electrical bolt that sluices through my body precedes a pain I've never known before. Searing, tearing, penetrating— I writhe as I plummet to the ground and he's pulled into the black band.

My landing is hard, the breath knocked out of my lungs, my head kicking back such that there's a ringing impact at the base of my skull. There's no time for recovery or to try to race off. The evil comes for me next. A black spool of sand licks out at me, and I kick at it as I crab-walk backward for the tree line, my hood sloping forward so I can't see. If I can get among the dead *cangjas*, I'll have those trunks to hold onto—

My leg is snagged and I'm dragged toward the Fulcrum. I paddle for any kind of grip on anything, but sand slips through my grasping fingers and then I'm off the ground again.

That's when I see the horned face in the black band.

Something horrible stares at me like it knows me.

*Sorrelllllllllll . . .*

As my name wafts out, I scream and know there will be no getting free of this.

The evil is claiming me as if it's been waiting for the chance.

*Nine*

# The Dragon and the Knight.

A flash of the sun saves me.

Just as I'm being consumed, my cloak twisting around my body and locking me up tight, my feet sucked into the Fulcrum with the rest of me certain to follow, a gleam of gold flies by my face. Then there's an unholy screech that's so loud, it registers as pain in my ears instead of sound.

The Fulcrum's grip on me slips for an instant.

And then there's another golden flare. Another blaring screech.

Now I'm falling again.

I slam into the sandy ground once more, this time landing face down with my hood flopping over my head. As I pull in a breath, I get a mouthful of sand, and through the coughing and wheezing, I try to understand why the sun itself has taken human form—and is defending the likes of me.

Then I turn my head and see . . . what surely must be a myth. A dark-skinned knight in golden armor on a blinding white stallion is battling the black band with his golden sword, the blade glinting like fire as he defends me. He is both grace and strength, subduing his warhorse while he wields his weapon, parrying and jabbing—

All at once, the contamination retracts into the Fulcrum, the discoloration disappearing, the strange snow stopping, the squealing dimming until it can't be heard over the normal roar of the magical barrier.

My savior reins his stallion toward me and dismounts at the same time, his golden chest piece amplifying the sunset, his striking face set off by the halo created by all the precious metal that's on his body.

I almost meet his eyes, but catch the mistake just in time. His mouth is moving, but I can't hear anything except my own thundering heartbeat—

He kneels down and I can feel his stare on my cloak's hood. "Maiden?"

With a shaking hand, I yank what covers my head farther down—and get sand in my eyes. I'm blinking and rubbing at the grit as I stammer, "You . . . saved me."

"Not for long. I know not what that was. Are you from the village Greensward, *dreah*?"

Little one, he calls me.

All I can do is nod. I feel like I've swallowed half the Fulcrum, but that's only part of what's paralyzed me. That face I saw in the black band, my name called out to me, those boys now dead, this knight appearing at just the right time . . .

"We must return you to your family." He indicates the nearly dark sky with the tip of his golden sword. "You are not safe here."

Without waiting for a response, he takes a firm grip of my arm and pulls me to my feet. As I wobble, I look at his broad chest. The insignia of the Prosperitus Court is no surprise, and neither is the reflection of my sandy, sloppy cloak.

"My lord," I croak as I attempt a curtsy.

"Worry not of all that nonsense."

He half carries me to his magnificently saddled steed, and the horse looks over its shoulder at our approach with disinterest like it's seen so much, a draped woman who smells of sand is nothing worth reacting to.

As I'm being lifted up and settled behind the saddle, I hear a groan and glance toward the sound.

The dragon remains on the verge of death, suffering and hopeless on the ground. Its great rib cage lifts up as it inhales raggedly, and on the exhale, the beast closes its eyes in defeat—

"Wait!"

Just as the knight puts his boot into the stirrup to mount up, I scramble off the steed and race toward the beast. I hear the knight shouting and ignore him, and I stop just out of reach of the dragon.

It seems even bigger up close, and how beautiful the scales are, each perfectly fitted to the next all over its body, the iridescence still visible even as the green and the purple have leached out. All of the rows undulate as it respirates unevenly, and in response to me, the winged animal laboriously moves its huge back legs and little arms. When its wing lifts briefly, I imagine him in flight, high above the snowcapped apex of his home, where he seeks only solitude and peace.

I whisper hoarsely, "I'm so sorry—"

"What are you doing! Get away from that thing!"

The dragon's muzzle curls and he attempts to lift his enormous head as the golden knight skids up to me.

When the court's warrior takes my arm, I pull myself free. "No! I have to help him—"

"Are you mad? The thing's not dead yet—"

"That's the point! I can help him because it's not too late."

The golden knight is momentarily shocked by my tone, and before he can recover from the insult to his station, I go right up to the dragon's head, by his jaws full of razor-sharp teeth and his fire-breathing nostrils.

The creature does what he can to keep track of me, but he's obviously at the very end of his strength. Kneeling down, I take a deep breath . . . and stare directly into its eyes—

I suck in a gasp and only have a split second to note the oblong pupils before I'm swept into his suffering. The pain in my side and left arm is intolerable and my breathing becomes labored, but there are further injuries. And then I see and feel the death, and it is awful. The dragon suffers all night long and is toyed with by nuisance predators before his heart finally stops as dawn's light pours over his broken body.

A ragged grunt is released from the snout, as if my commiseration brings some relief—

My body jerks back, and for a second, I think it's a spasm from what I'm feeling. But then the knight tries to take both of my arms—

"Unhand me!"

As I yank out of his hold, my savior jumps back and focuses downward. To my shock, I see my little knife in my grip—an absurd show of self-defense against his armor and his greater power, but I'm desperate and that gives me an edge.

"Go," I order him over the din of the Fulcrum. "I am nothing to you—*leave*!"

"You are bleeding!"

Ignoring the man, I kneel once again by the dragon. "I'm going to take care of you. Trust me."

The beast blinks, the dual sets of lids crisscrossing vertically.

The pulsing vein that runs up the side of the throat is hard to find because the heart rate is so slow and I'm not sure of his anatomy. But I locate it, and keep our stares locked as I lean forward.

I put the tip of my knife to the pattern of scales that are so much softer on the underside of the massive chin.

"I'm coming in after you," I vow. "I'm not going to let you go and I'm not going to lose you."

Even though I've never actually tried to resurrect an animal before.

Taking my own deep breath, I lock my jaw—

With a hard jab, I drive my knife into its throat, right at the vein. The dragon barely flinches, and as its purple blood floods my hand, warm and slick, I lower myself until we are eye to eye, nearly nose to nose. The head is almost the size of my entire body.

As I stare into its soul, what I foresee changes. The light of dawn around the body at the moment of death gets sucked down into the horizon, and replaced by a night sky full of stars. They pinwheel in a fat circle, that strange, new, brightest one the only celestial light that stays put. And then there is the gloaming, the very last of the sunset's bloom of peach and pink and orange flaring at the west—

We are here, in this moment.

Right now—

I take another deep breath, and my skin tightens as if my skeleton and muscles are expanding, an anticipation growing inside of me like I'm about to leap.

It has to be just right. A second before, a second after, and this illicit energy I somehow command will not work—

There's a great burst of illumination and the dragon is suddenly bathed in a mirroring effect that erupts from his body, coating the limbs, the wings, the barbed back and tail. It's the life force within him, finding physical expression before death ushers in its departure.

They say there is no magic left in Anathos. That's a lie. Life is magic—

*Now.*

Catching my breath, I make the sign of the crescent moon and then I dive into the pool of energy headfirst. The shock is always new, no matter how many times I do this, both icy cold and burning hot. For reasons I've never understood, I'm a magnet for the life force; it attaches to me as I swim through the shimmer, heading for the source of the wellspring.

In the center of the dragon's chest, where his heart is, a breaching has occurred, and as I penetrate the leak with my body, everything that has escaped comes with me.

Now I am in the *kwale*, or the sacred interior space where the soul resides. I'm standing on a slick, yet solid grounding, and I look around as the iridescent level at my feet begins to rise, everything that has followed me back in returning to where it's been held—

There's the tear. Up at the top of the *kwale*, a breaching that reflects the mortal injury that has occurred, and I extend my hand up. I cannot comprehend how I do what I do, where the gift comes from, or why I've always known my role, but as I present my palm to the ragged hole, it seals up so that there's only enough of an aperture for the soul to continue to come home.

The level of the silvery effect ascends my body, coming to my knees, then my hips, my waist, and higher still . . . reaching my chest, my throat, my chin. I always feel a panic as my mouth and nose are covered, though I'm not breathing in this other realm. I'm my own energy and nothing more here. My extraction occurs when the vessel is full, pressure building until I'm expelled as the interloper I am, my exit sealing the hole in my wake—

The reentry into my own body is painful, and I hear a gasp as I draw in air, but it's from a distance. As I slump off to the side, I'm aware I fall into the sand, but again, it's a distilled sensation as I hit the ground.

What is clear is that the great dragon explodes into action. Leaping up onto its powerful rear legs, the wings unfurl to their full span and the beast lets out a stream of fire that I cannot feel even as the flames flicker around me. His scales are now back to an emerald green and a range of purples that vary from deep amethyst to pale lavender—and on that right wing, the injury that brought it out of flight has an uneven, but fully healed, repair.

The beast doesn't spare me glance nor growl as he takes to the air, the great buffered gusts as his wings draw down blowing my cloak around my numb body. Up, up, and away he spirits from the pit in the sand that was his premature grave, and as the dragon soars higher and higher, he crosses in front of that brilliant, troubling star. The celestial illumination on its scales is a light show worthy of a rainbow, and how I envy his freedom as the creature flies for the snowy cap of home.

Staring out from under my hood, my eyes water from sadness, for I know I will never travel so far—

The golden knight leans over me, and though I'm careful not to meet his gaze, I can tell his noble, dark face is drawn in lines of awe.

"'Tis you," he says with reverence. "You . . . are the one I seek."

*Ten*

# A Bloodthirsty Crowd.

"Julion Wyse of Prosperitus, at your service."

The golden knight removes his helmet and bows with a gallantry that surely makes women fall in love with him on the spot. Then he looks to the dark western horizon and extends a hand to me.

"Now, we must go, yes?"

He's worried about the night and the Fulcrum. I'm worried about why he thinks he knows and needs me. Hard to decide which is the bigger danger, and that's saying something.

I accept his aid in getting to my feet because I feel so wobbly, but we need to part ways, he and I. "No, thank you. I'll get back on my own—"

He picks me up as if I weigh nothing and carries me over to his steed once again. The previously laconic stallion, who wasn't even bothered by a dragon getting resurrected and flying off, suddenly begins to mince in place and snort.

Its shrewd eyes are focused somewhere past the sandblasted outer ring of the forest, on the shadows lurking in and among all the dense branches of the healthy trees.

Where I found the dead cow.

"I think I will accept a ride," I mutter.

"Your honor is safe with me, I assure you."

The knight gathers the reins, plants a boot in the stirrup, and somehow manages to get us both up onto the saddle in one smooth movement. As I'm settled behind him like a sack of grain, the horse rears up, hooving at the air.

"Hold on tight!"

The steed bolts before the knight finishes speaking, and I grab on to whatever I can. Ducking my head behind the smooth gold plate across his back, I look over my own shoulder. The Fulcrum looms like an evil entity in and of itself, rather than a containment for one, and I search for black bands in the last wink of daylight—

The horned face appears again, this time in gigantic proportion, the features pressing out of the swirling sand. The mouth is open and the eyes are hungry, and it's rushing out toward me with a booming war cry—

I scream, and the knight twists around.

"Fates!" he hollers over thundering hooves.

"He's coming for us!" I yell.

That's a lie. Whatever it is comes for me, and me alone.

The steed responds with a surge of speed, except clearly the horse already senses what's happening. And though there's a proper trail some distance away, the knight veers us right into the scrub brush and dead wood. It feels like an eternity, but then we hit the tree line proper and are lashed by branches. By the tinging of metal, I know the knight is taking the brunt of the impacts, and I'm glad the armor is on him for his sake.

There is no slowing down.

Still going at breakneck speed, we link up with a narrow, winding animal path, and go deeper into the dark forest. The steed jogs left and right, jerks his head, shifts his weight. We do the same, the knight and I, while I hold on to the male body before me for dear life, and I keep glancing in our wake, expecting to be pursued by what is trapped in the Fulcrum.

And trying to get out.

Fear chokes me and I hunker in under my cloak, squeezing my eyes shut and recognizing that there's nothing I can do to help in this madcap retreat except not fall off. I can go no faster than the horse and I have no skills to fight like the knight, so I'm at the mercy of whatever destiny will befall us in these trees.

Thank fates the armor is made of a sturdy gold, or surely I'd crush it like paper.

The escape seems to last years, and my whole body, especially my teeth, hum from being clapped by the horse's surging efforts, nothing but trees, trees and more trees until I'm certain the knight is lost and we're going in circles—

We break out of the arboreal congestion like something expelled.

The brace of fresh, cold air rejuvenates me, and the horse obviously feels the same. Our speed increases even further as the stallion stretches out his neck and becomes a bird over the ground, the herky-jerky jostle gone, now only a lightning-fast, smooth flight over the meadow's long grasses toward my village's wall.

I've never gone this fast in my life, but the knight has. He's one with the horse, as steady and true in the saddle as a statue, my anchor in the windstorm.

When we pull up short in the lee of a barn, the horse lets out an angry war cry and rears up again as if he's frustrated his gallop is being taken away from him. I nearly roll off his butt, just managing to catch myself on the knight's arm.

As we land with a bump, I forget all the aches in my bones and stinging in my molars. In the icy moonlight, the bridge over Greensward's moat is raised, and the murky circle of water churns with *balas* thrashing in excitement as if they've already had some sort of a meal.

But that's nothing compared to the unrest inside my village.

An orange glow rises up from inside the wall, billows of smoke punching at the night sky and charging at the timid stars emerging from their daylight retreat. A great chorus of shouting echoes upward from the market square, and it's so loud, we can hear the anger even here. On the outside.

It's as if all that fury is the cause of the bonfire.

"They think I killed the boys," I say as I right my hood on the crown of my head.

There's a clanking as the knight glances back at me. "You fought for their lives—"

"No one will believe me."

With hauteur, he says, "My word is bond. *I* shall tell them what happened."

It must be nice to have that kind of authority, but I fear he underestimates the problem.

*Hide. You must hide—*

My head pounds as I shake it, and I cast myself from the saddle. When I land, my legs are weak, and the knight catches me with a quick hand.

I stumble back from his aid. "I am not the one you seek, and I'm not going any farther with you—"

"Do you mean to go in there and face that alone?" He nods at the wall. "I heard what the boy yelled at you as he ran off. Come away with me now. I know where a royal hunting cabin is not far. We can stay there until dawn—"

"No!"

The knight removes his golden helmet and places it over his breastplate. "My honor will not permit me to just leave you here."

"And your integrity is the least of my problems."

He drops down out of the saddle and takes my hand. For a moment, I stare at the link between us, his rich brown skin against my freckled own. We are from two different worlds, and his is so far above mine, we might as well be separate species.

"You *must* allow me to be of aid to you."

From under my hood, my eyes shift back to the fearsome glow and furious, billowing smoke. The wall that I previously measured and found wanting now seems more solid than a mountain, and fates, what awaits me there.

I have no choice. I have to leave.

Panic flows through me, running off all the blood in my veins, and as I drop his hand, I force myself to think logically. First, I want to stock Mare with some provisions, and I should have some for myself. Except as the din of the riot inside that wall gets even louder, I don't know how I'm going to navigate the mob. And then I look to the forest, try to imagine what's waiting for me out there, and think only of the desecrated cow—

I can smell the blood and hear the lazy flies as if the carcass is right in front of me.

There's no way I can survive on my own.

Squeezing my eyes shut, it's a number of heartbeats later that I say with defeat, "I am still not the one you seek. No matter what you saw back with that dragon."

"Then I shall aid you anyway. A gentleman never leaves a lady undefended and he expects nothing in return for his service to her virtue."

This . . . said to a barmaid in a Pox cloak.

Blinking away tears, I choke out, "I have someone I need to provide for first, but there's no way we can get inside with the drawbridge up. And fates, that riot is over me—"

"It is no problem at all."

The calm response makes me worried he's insane, but with no options and Mare on my mind, I find myself once again up on the warhorse and holding on to the knight's armor.

"Duck down behind me as if you are a saddlebag," he orders as we trot off.

"With pleasure," I mutter.

After a short distance, the whistle he makes is loud as a pig squeal. Peeking up from around his elbow, I see two men peer out at us from the guard tower on the right. It's the pair of farmers who took Mr. Cavenish back home the night before.

"Oy," one of them shouts down. "What are you on about—"

"Lower your planks," the knight commands.

The two glance at each other as if wondering whether they heard that right. "We'll do no such thing," comes the reply. "Move on."

"You will open your gate and lower the planks right now—"

"Move on!" the other guard shouts as he points a musket out of the arch. "Your body may be covered, but your head is not and I never miss—"

"If you do not lower the bridge this very moment, I shall return with an army and tear your village's irrelevant collection of sticks and stones to the ground. And may I further point out that I am a member of the court of Prosperitus, so I do not recommend you pulling any trigger in my presence—unless you want to be in the gallows before dawn."

Roaring from the crowd rumbles through the night, and I swear I can feel the heat of that fire, too.

"I. Am. Waiting," the knight snaps.

A moment later, the farmers disappear and the great bridge begins to come down with the sounds of heavy chains clanking through gears. The planks are still falling in that controlled way when the knight spurs his steed on, the warhorse leaping up and riding the end of the descent into the short tunnel between the towers.

As we emerge on the main thoroughfare and the knight hauls back on the reins, the guards are already raising the bridge up again, and for once, the Gauntlet is not the source of rowdy noise. Lantern light bleeds out of its foggy windows, but there are no shadows passing in front of the bubbly glass on either of the floors. The place is empty because people are gathering pitchforks to go after me—

*Hide.*

"Keep going," I say over the clapping of the horse's impatient stomps. "Down this lane to the square. I need to see the crowd for myself."

Before I upend everything and make Mare die alone, hungry and in pain, I should verify it's truly me my fellow villagers are protesting. Maybe they're mounting a defense over demons? This is probably false optimism talking, but when the knight surges on, I take it he agrees with me.

Cleaved to his armored body, I shrink down to be as small as I can make myself. The row houses flash by, and the sharp rapping of the warhorse's iron shoes echo like the warning something dire is afoot. As we come to the fringes of the crowd, the knight pulls back on the reins once again and the stallion minces in a jog.

No one pays us any mind. Attention is focused on the platform in the center of the square. The boy who ran off is up on it with his father, his uncle, and his grandfather, the frantic light from the bonfire agitating their already animated bodies and faces. Tears stream down the child's face, but he has a slight smile under the theatrical sobbing, as if he's delighted by the drama and unable to comprehend the loss of his friends and the rage of the adults he's inciting.

"—working unlawful magic. She must be killed!" The father, a heavily built laborer, picks up the boy. "You heard him!"

He shakes the lad, like a music box that must be primed to function, and then the son's higher voice quiets the crowd.

"The Pox girl said she cursed us, all of us!" The boy speaks what he's obviously already spoken faster and faster, the words running together, the excitement of youth mixing with a first taste of power. "She killed Thaddeous and Fergus! She was going to kill me with her magic, but the Fulcrum's black band attacked her!"

"The Fulcrum is weakened because of her!" The father takes over. "We were wrong to use the dark magic she plied us with—*she* is the reason the demons are free and why we are endangered! Who here will stand with my blood so that we may spill hers and save us all!"

The crowd yells and stomps so loudly the ground shakes and the stallion rears up and hooves at the smoky air.

Having gleaned what I required, it's time to cut loose from the knight. I take advantage of the jostling and slip off the back of the saddle. As I disappear into the shadows, the knight wrenches around, and searches for me while trying to control his mount.

I used him only to get inside the wall.

The truth is, he's better off without me, even with his threats of bringing an army here. He doesn't have anyone else with him right now and if that crowd gets ahold of him? But moreover, I cannot be the solution to whatever problem brought him here in search of me, especially not after tonight. Mare was right. Representatives from court must have come here at some point, and overheard whispers of what I'm able to do.

And sooner or later, he will insist. Anyone as used to giving orders as he is will have to address his own needs.

Hauling up my cloak, I mist down the alley that runs behind all the empty row houses. I'm dizzy and breathing so hard that my lungs pump as fast as my legs, and all along, there's a single driving voice in my head.

*Hide. Hide. Hide—*

The drumbeat is relentless. As soon as I check on Mare, I'll steal some provisions from these vacant houses, give her most of it, and find a place to hide out the night. After dawn? Maybe I can catch a hidden ride in a hay cart or something—

There's a sudden commotion out on the main lane. Shouting. Racing footfalls. And it's approaching me, rather than heading in the direction of the mob.

When I come up a passageway between two blocks of houses, I duck in and try not to make too much noise as I catch my breath and look out to the thoroughfare. Four men are pounding down the lane, and the knives in their hands flash like heat lightning as they pass by the hanging lanterns. I know where they're going. They're racing for the Gauntlet to try to find me and bring me to the crowd—and those blades of theirs are already bloody, so they must have sworn a mortal oath for their violent duty.

No doubt up on that platform, to the cheering of the crowd.

I flatten back against whatever house I'm next to and clap my hand over my mouth to keep my terror from coming out in a scream.

After they go by, I lean around once more.

And that's when I see him.

The mercenary is sauntering down the center of the lane, heading for the market square and all the commotion. When a couple of stragglers come out of their houses, they give him a wide berth, and he pays them no mind—

He stops. Lifts his nose.

And then turns to my hiding place in the passageway.

Another man hurries by him, and when the lane is empty, the mercenary walks down toward me. His massive body and all of his weapons represent a threat I'm not going to get away from unless I start running now—and oh, the coin he could make from kidnapping me and charging the village for the delivery of their source of torment.

Yet I'm frozen. My legs are jelly, my heart is flickering instead of beating, and there's not enough air in the whole of Anathos to cut the suffocation in my lungs. I am the deer stalked and unable to bolt.

And now he's standing right in front of me.

I'm careful to look only at his jaw, his chiseled, strong jaw, with its frame of black braids and waves. Unlike the golden knight's, this warrior's armor and weapons are of the darkness, and seem more deadly because of it.

"You aren't going to see what the fuss is all about then," he drawls.

Not a question. And now I'm narrowing my eyes on his chin. "You already know. You heard it in the pub."

"So it's true." The mercenary's tone is bored. "You cursed those boys, and killed two of them."

"Absolutely not. But there's no defense to the accusations of a murderous crowd."

Footsteps approach out on the lane, and suddenly he's blocking any possible view of me with his body, pushing me back against the clapboard wall. As I go face-to-face with the blade of his enormous broadsword, he takes a wrap of *wensel* from his fighting vest with a steady and sure hand. As he lights it, the smoke is fragrant in the cold air, but it's the scent of him that really registers.

Unprincipled though he may be, he still smells so good. Clean male and leather. And that cedar.

I remember what he said about my own scent.

"You've got to leave this place," he says softly on the next exhale.

Before I know what I'm doing, I blurt, "How much."

He glances over his shoulder, and I trace the tail end of the braid that falls my way. There are black beads on the leather thong that ties it, stacked one atop the other. I wonder who put them there, for they seem too frivolous for him to have wasted the time on the decoration.

"You cannot afford me."

"I can't go alone." My eyes flood with tears as my reality falls onto my head like boulders from our crumbling wall. "And I can't stay here."

And the golden knight wants to use the very magic that got me into this mess.

"I have . . . to hire you."

*Eleven*

# A Terrible Discovery.

"Exactly where are you going?" When I don't reply, he exhales a stream of blue smoke and pivots to face me. "My price depends on the engagement. Where are you going?"

"The Badlands," I mumble. "I want to go to the Outpost in the Badlands."

When he chuckles, I glare at the lobe of his left ear, and note in my peripheral vision how the brow over his pale eye arches.

"Why not Prosperitus? Closer. Safer."

No, my reputation not only precedes me there, but is going to get me in more trouble. "Badlands. Outpost."

"There are only outlaws there."

"What do you think I'll be if I make it out of here alive." As he stares at me, I shift my weight back and forth. "Name your price."

He draws on the *wensel*, and releases another cloud that glows blue even in the darkness. "One thousand *emras*."

My breath leaves me in a rush. "Th-that's a fortune."

"Do you have any idea what is between this village and the Badlands?" The smile is cold. "Forests full of wild beasts, the Lake of Lost Souls, *grylon* territory. And there's been talk of demons. This is not a leisurely stroll through the long grass."

"In my lifetime, I will not see even a hundred *emras*."

"Hm. Pity." There's a stretch of silence while he smokes. Then he drawls, "But it appears as if this is your lucky day."

"That is *not* what I would call my present circumstance."

"I happen to be headed to the Badlands myself." My brief flare of relief is quickly dashed. "However, I don't work for free under any circumstances. I have a code, you know."

"One that's clearly not of honor."

"Honor doesn't mean anything on Anathos. You're in the process of learning that right now."

Oh, I already knew that the first time I was shunned by someone I'd helped. "So what do you want, apart from an absurd amount of money."

"What else do you have to offer." His attention goes down to the hem of my cloak. And then returns to my hood, slowly, as if he's envisioning me naked. "What else do you have that I might want, I wonder."

My body warms in a rush, to the point where I swear the ground beneath my feet has given way to a hot spring—

Off in the distance, the crowd begins to chant.

"Your time is running out." The mercenary tilts his head toward the lane. "What are you going to do. Leave with my help or stay here and get burned in that big fire down there."

Tears come to my eyes and I tremble, but not because I am frightened of him or the situation I'm in. Although both warrant fear. No, the response is because I'm a virgin, and I've made peace with dying one because I've had to. I just never thought there'd be a chance to feel a man's touch, a man's lips . . . a man's body . . . against my own because he wanted me, and I wanted him.

The sacred mystery not overheard, but experienced.

"I'll be gentle with you," he says in a low, resonant voice. "What I do for a living won't be what I bring to the bed, not with you."

"Why," I whisper.

"I only fight what fights against me." His scarred dagger hand reaches out, and runs along the hooding as if it is my hair. "And you can't hurt me."

The crowd roars anew, and I'm reminded of what's going on outside of this charged privacy we've created in the passageway. Except the bartering we're doing over my body seems far, far more dangerous.

"I'll get you the money," I croak as I must turn away, not so much from him, but from myself. "Follow me—"

As I try to continue down the alley, he snags my hand and pulls me back. His palm is warm and callused, and it's as if he touches me over my entire body, all at once.

My lips part and I stare at his mouth. "What."

"I have to have you," he says with urgency.

"You must be mad."

"I am very sane."

I gather up some of my cloak. "Are you *certain* you know what this is?"

"I can assure you, I do not wish to bed your woolen folds."

He steps in to me, his body emanating a sexual energy that cannot be denied, ignored, or diminished. It's what is under his surface, all the time, what every woman reacted to the second he walked into the pub.

"It's quite another fold I am interested in," he murmurs as he drops his head so his lips are by my ear, separated only by the hooding of my cloak. "A place that is warm and slick and welcoming to a male. Where I can leave something of myself behind, inside of you."

I think of all the pleasure he's surely given to so many females and take my arm out of his hold. Yet I can't look away from his lips.

I sense his stare narrowing. "Why will you sell to others so easily what you will not give to me in return for a job I am very well good at? Especially when your life is in this kind of peril. I'm starting to take this personally."

There are other ways of hurting a woman, I think to myself. And what is for him a transaction will be, for me, a piece of myself.

But do I really want to die untouched?

As I take a deep breath, I'm aware that there are two totally different negotiations taking place, and he's only aware of the surface one. He thinks the terms are about sex, whereas I'm bartering with a bit of my soul.

"All right," I tell him roughly. "If you take me to the Badlands, I'll . . . give you what you want. But only when I say."

His satisfied chuckle is deep in his chest, and very masculine. "Of course. I'm a mercenary, not a savage, you know."

"Is there a difference?"

"I'll prove it right now if you want. But there's something to be said for discretion, don't you think?"

My heart pounds, and I know I have to refocus. "We'll see about that—"

As I go to take off once again, he recaptures my hand. "We have to seal the deal. It's not official yet."

Instead of shaking on it, however, he turns my palm over, and bends down farther, ignoring the danger we're in. I stand transfixed as he massages the inside of my wrist with his thumb—and then presses his lips to my lifeline.

I have to close my eyes as he straightens. For the first time in my life, I can't meet a man's stare for a reason other than I don't want to know his death: If I looked into this mercenary's eyes right now, I'd burst into flames.

"Come on," I say roughly. "I lead the way."

I start running, following the alley farther down. The mercenary stays right behind me, his movements so silent I don't hear him in my wake, even with all his weapons. When we get to the intersection of another alley, I pull up short and check for stragglers.

"To the right," I say softly. "We go to the right—"

"I thought we were leaving the village." He points over my shoulder. "The gate is back there, and now is a good time for me to overpower those two guards. They're going to be distracted by the noise."

I frown over my shoulder, focusing on that hard jaw. "You can't kill them. They're just farmers."

"Oh, I assure you I very much can—"

"No!" I grab his arm and then retract my hand. "You *won't* hurt them. I hired you and I'm in charge."

Against the backdrop of the distant yelling, the mercenary scrums down so our heads are on the same level, and I have to look at his boots to make sure he doesn't see inside my hood.

"They'll kill you. Each and every one of them, including the two that are between you and what's outside that village wall. You can be in charge all you like, but some decisions are mine and mine alone."

Abruptly, I'm furious at him, and not just because he's making a kind of sense that my conscience can't live with. I'm angry because I can't be mad at the Fulcrum. Or those cruel, dead boys. Or those families who are suffering and scared, but also prepared to condemn me to a brutal, public slaughter, even though I saved their bairns, and eased their pains—and had nothing to do with what happened in all that sand.

And fates, I have just become this mercenary's whore.

I lift my chin. "We go to the right."

That chuckle comes back, and he inclines his head like he's humoring me. "Lead on. For the moment."

I am more than happy to get running again. It's a better outlet than so many others.

The cobbler's former storefront is around the next corner, and before we make that turn, I have to force myself to stop to make sure no one is ahead. In our pause, I'm breathing hard. The mercenary looks like he's been out for a stroll.

I feel like kicking him in the shins.

"Stay here," I tell him.

"Why."

"Because I said so." Stepping out into the lane, I glare at him from under my hood. "I'll be right back."

Tears gather in my eyes as I tenderfoot it to Mare's door. I don't know how I'll say goodbye to her—

The entry is ajar.

I glance around. Push the rickety panel open a little farther. "Mare?"

There's a smell that registers, but my brain refuses to label it.

"Mare."

Ordinarily, I never wait for a response from her when I come here with my herbs. I wait now, even though I am hunted. On the threshold, my heart thunders—and I know what's happened, even before I see it—

The mercenary elbows me aside and goes in first.

His black boots leave footprints in the blood as he enters.

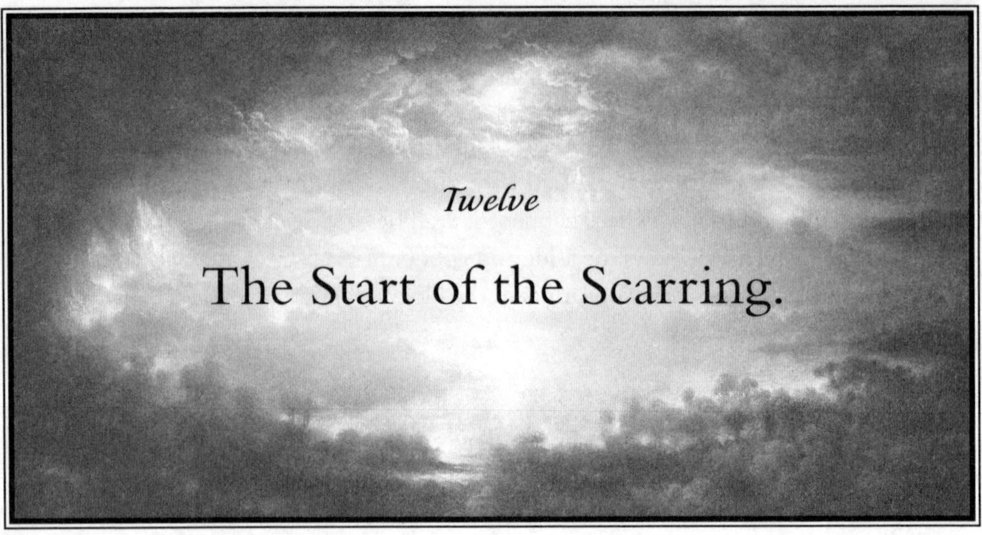

*Twelve*

# The Start of the Scarring.

A scream rips from my throat and I claw him out of the way. A bloody trail marks the way to the bed, and my dear friend's withered body is lying on her pallet, on top of the blankets I brought to her. Her chest is cut open and the cavity inside her ribs is empty, and I fixate on the smell of burning meat that crowds into my nose.

They took her heart and lungs out and threw them in the little hearth that is aflame with the wood I gathered for her.

And that is not the worst of it.

Two daggers protrude from her eye sockets, one from her mouth, and a fourth has been stabbed into her lower abdomen. The hilts are cockeyed because the ritual murder was committed in a hurry.

Her hand is still gripping the edge of the pallet.

She was alive when they started, when they took her eyes first.

I fall to my knees and sob. "*Mare . . .*"

Over the pallet, on the only flat wall in the abandoned shop, a crude crescent moon has been drawn in her blood, the depiction sloppy and still dripping, it's so fresh.

Those four men I saw, with their bloody knives out. That was no mortal oath of the hunt, sealed with the streak of a blade across their palms. They were the ones who came here, thinking she was hiding me.

My dear friend is dead because of me, and it's unbearable that her hand is still warm as I take it in my own. "I'm so sorry . . ."

The tin cup with the herbs I served to her this morning is crushed on the floor, some heavy boot nailing the thin metal flat on the floorboards. They think I've been working black magic on her. They slaughtered her to ward off evil, and also because they just want to kill and couldn't find me. Yet.

"It was not supposed to . . . end like this."

She was so frail, she wasn't a threat to anybody. She was going to die peacefully, fading away from old age. Not in this manner, brutally sacrificed like an animal to the superstition of villagers who know nothing of true magic.

And if I'd left this morning when she told me to, none of this would have happened.

A surprisingly gentle hand rests on my shoulder. "You are not safe here."

I wipe my face under the hood and know that the cleansing ritual is only halfway done. To finish the job, they have to cut her arms and legs off, lay her torso face down with the limbs running to the cardinal compass points, and light the rest of her on fire.

They will be back when they can't find me at the Gauntlet.

"But I can't leave her here like this—"

"You have no choice."

Outside, villagers run by, their torches flaring in the cloudy windows.

"She is dead," the mercenary says more forcefully. "There's nothing you can do for her now. But you can save yourself."

"I'm to blame—"

"Are those your daggers?" He jabs a finger at the body. "No? Then you are not to blame. Come *on*."

He pulls me to my feet and all but drags me over to the door. I'm almost at the threshold when I slip out of his hold and race back for the shelves. I find the seam by feel alone, release the latch, and push my hand inside the hidden compartment. Taking out the velvet bag, I tuck the weight of the royal coins into the pocket of my cloak, and take one last glance back at the bed.

"I can't leave her."

I say this as I'm returning to him, and I only know we're outside again when the cold hits my slippered feet and bare hands. He leads me back into the alley, and as we get into the shadows, he's talking to me as we go. I can't hear him and have to stop.

Wrenching over, I gag as my stomach attempts to evacuate itself, but there's no food in me to throw up. The next thing I know, I'm arguing with him, even though I don't know what we're going on about.

"—at the Gauntlet. I *must*," I hear myself saying.

"You're determined to make this difficult, aren't you."

And yet he takes me forward in the direction of the pub, leading with his body. We go quite a distance, using crisscrossing side lanes to stay out of sight, before I realize he's got a dagger in each hand. As I catch a glance at another couple of men thumping down the main thoroughfare with torches held high, their meaty faces red and twisted with rage, I don't want to be in this mercenary's world—

I stop again, and he doesn't notice. He keeps going.

Backing up against the side of a row house, I hang my head and struggle for breath, thinking of all the bairns I saved, all those little gray bodies I brought back to life by something I've never understood. Then I think of what they did to Mare.

What if they decide to kill everybody I've helped?

The mercenary's in front of me once again, his heavy boots like a pair of boulders on the cobblestones. "What're you doing—"

"I have to go turn myself in." I shudder, waves of fear swamping me. "If they don't kill me and cleanse the village, they'll go after the bairns I've attended to on the birthing bed—"

"Are you mad?" he snaps.

I picture all the children I've brought back, at the ages they are now, and see them just like Mare, their eyes, mouths, and guts pierced by knives, their hearts and lungs taken out and burned, their bodies laid out in the market square for another bonfire. The smoke that will rise from their mangled corpses is supposed to be a sign that the cleansing has worked, the black magic is gone.

"You don't understand what I've done," I say. "All those families . . . they're going to kill the children unless—"

"You really think this is about you?" His voice is strident. "All that mob wants is a target for their fear. I don't know what you've done with their offspring, but they're not going to hurt their own. They're after you because you don't matter, and the same is true with your friend back there. Both of you are nothing, so you're an easy sacrifice."

I exhale like he's punched me.

As he grabs my arm and drags me forward, I yank against him. "Let go of me, I have to go to the square—"

"You're going to live through this whether you want to or not—"

"Why do you care!"

The mercenary wheels around and nearly shoves his face under my hood. "I did the noble thing once, and it proved to be a curse I set on myself. It ruined my life. You obviously don't know how things work so I'm not allowing you to make the same mistake. *Never* sacrifice yourself for another. Survival is all that matters, and you'll thank me for this in the morning. When you're still *alive*."

Catching a sob in my throat, I squeeze my eyes shut as if I can make it all go away. "I don't want to live in this world."

"Neither do I."

As he drags me along with him, I'm too scattered and numb to keep arguing. But when we get to the Gauntlet's front corner and pull up short, I force myself to focus.

"You stay here," he says. "What do you need and where is it."

Pivoting, I rise up onto my tiptoes and look in one of the opaque windows. I can't see much, but there's nothing moving and there's not a voice or a sound inside. All I can think of is those four men with the knives striding down the main lane. Did they kill everyone? Sallae Mae, and the other women? Mr. Lewis?

The mercenary stamps a boot. "We can't waste any more time. We need to find a hiding place before the crowd scatters—"

Without thinking, I bolt away from him, running down the front of the lodging house and skidding to a halt at the door. Which is partially open.

"Dearest moon in the heavens," I whisper as the mercenary curses at my elbow.

The pub is ransacked, the trestle tables knocked over, the chairs scattered, tankards all over the floor with puddles of ale everywhere. Over in his regular spot, Mr. Lewis is seated at the only upright anything in sight, as if he watched them do the vandalizing from his perch.

A lantern flickers before him, the light playing over his downcast, pudgy face.

As Mr. Lewis looks over at us, he shows no surprise.

"Sit down," he says gruffly. "So I can finally tell you about your mother."

*Thirteen*

# Revelations.

I drift over to Mr. Lewis as if I'm in a dream and lower myself onto the bench across from him. There's a dust-covered satchel and a sizable box next to the lantern as well as an untouched tankard of ale. My employer's flushed, sweat-run face becomes pensive, and he stares off somewhere over my shoulder, seeming not to notice me or the mercenary.

"What about my mother," I breathe when he doesn't speak.

"I didn't believe him." Mr. Lewis shakes his bald head and swipes his face with his meaty palm. "When I was told . . . I didn't believe any of it. But here we are, and it's exactly what my father said. A night when the villagers take to the square and bring their flames, on the hunt, for the one who saves."

He abruptly looks at the mercenary, who's stayed by the door. "You're even in the prophecy. I should have connected it all when you walked in last night, but who is ever ready for destiny to unfold."

"What of my mother—"

Ignoring me, Mr. Lewis shoos off the mercenary. "You must leave us now for a moment—no argument, wait outside. She and I will be done here directly, and I'll call you back in. And no, they won't return here. They've already looked for her twice. *Leave us.*"

There's a pause, and I brace for a set-to. Instead, my escort just turns and walks out.

The man only argues with me, I think bitterly.

When Mr. Lewis and I are alone, my employer shakes his head.

"Now I know why you wear the Pox cloak," he says in a soft voice. "But like so much else, I did not believe . . ."

"Mr. Lewis, I don't understand any of this—"

"Every firstborn son in my line has been called to the deathbed of his father and given these." He places his palms on the satchel and the box. "We are told of the promised one who lives under this roof, the one we must shelter beneath the stairs . . . the daughter of the Savior, creator of the Fulcrum, subduer of the Dark King."

As I gasp, he pushes the objects toward me. "These are yours. One is a compass that will guide you on your quest, the other is the point of it all. You must leave tonight with the knight of swords, and seek out the warrior queen who sees no one to give her her due. Only then will she unite the Kingdoms of the North, South, East, and West, and defend Anathos such that the Dark King shall never rise again."

His words are spoken from what feels like a vast distance away, and they make no sense. I am but a barmaid, who dabbles in herbs and is frightened of her own shadow—

"I have no mother," I hear myself say. "I was orphaned on the birthing bed, and left in the village square—"

"You were entrusted to the care of my bloodline by your mother, the Savior. After she consolidated the last quantum of magic that remained, before she lured the Dark King into the fissure and created the Fulcrum, she gave you over to us." He does not look at me, and seems to be reciting a practiced speech. "This is your duty unto Anathos. You must finish what your mother began."

"No." I shove the bag and the box back at him and jump to my feet. "I am not anyone. I was orphaned on the birthing bed and left in the village square where . . ."

"Go on," he says in a tired tone as my voice drifts. "What then. Tell me."

"I was orphaned," I parrot weakly as I sit down once again. ". . . on the birthing bed. And left in the village square . . ."

When I can go no further, he motions impatiently with his hand. "What next."

Except there's nothing after that combination of lines that I've repeated to those few who have asked about my origins. My mind is . . . utterly blank.

"I was but an infant. How would I know what's next?"

"The question is why you know anything at all." He puts a hand to his chest. "I certainly never told you your story. Who did you hear it from then?"

I open my mouth to reply. And find there's nothing to say.

"The Savior lived . . . hundreds of years ago," I protest. "I can't be her daughter—"

"Fourteen generations to be precise." Mr. Lewis laughs in a harsh rush. "Do you know that I was relieved when my wife couldn't give me children? I didn't want any sons to carry on this burden—and here you are, ending it anyway."

"I am not hundreds of years old—"

"I don't care what you do from here on out." Mr. Lewis talks over me as he shoves the satchel and the box in my direction. "But my family's due to you is done this night. I've upheld our responsibility all my life, and I've finished this finally. Now you're going to take those things and leave before my livelihood is what that mob burns down."

Mr. Lewis whistles toward the front door, and as the mercenary steps back in, he gets to his feet with a grunt. "Follow me. I'll take you both to the tunnel."

"Tunnel?" I say as I get to my feet.

As Mr. Lewis walks over to his private quarters and the mercenary follows, I pick up the satchel. It's heavier than it looks—and so too is the box.

Glancing to the pub's door, I want to run, but what's out there is deadly—and the mercenary is right. Those villagers who've used me and then ignored me in public won't sacrifice their own children. Self-interest will keep their eyes closed to their own transgressions and complicity while they seek to sacrifice me—which will do nothing to stop the Fulcrum from degrading, and the demons from coming, and the Dark King from . . .

My mother is the Savior?

Surely Mr. Lewis is mistaken. Hundreds of years have passed—

*Hide.*

In the chaos of my mind, that old, familiar voice gets me going even though every logical instinct tells me to stay where I am and wait for reality to make more sense. I scramble after the men, tripping on something—a chair?—and having to catch my balance on one of the overturned trestle tables.

As I join my employer and the mercenary inside the owner's quarters, I'm not surprised that a framed drawing of Mr. Lewis's wife has pride of place over his messy bed's headboard. After he shuts us all in, he goes across to a drape-covered arch and groans as he bends down and pulls an ancient trunk out of his closet. A cloud of dust wafts up as he lifts the lid, and the pack inside has cobwebs all over it.

"This is what I'm supposed to give you." He tosses the bag to my feet and it lands with a rustle. "Along with some provisions."

Over at his galley, he takes two loaves of fresh bread, and a bladder of what could be water, milk, or mead, and stuffs it all into a woven sack. Back with us, he pushes the comestibles at me and I struggle to keep ahold of them and what he's already insisted I take.

"This way," Mr. Lewis tells us.

The blank wall he goes over to makes no sense—until he lowers his shoulder, and pushes a narrow, hidden aperture open. As lantern light pours inside, I see . . . absolutely nothing. It's a black hole, as if what's been revealed is a tear in the fabric of time and Anathos itself.

"There's a torch on the left." Mr. Lewis pulls his sagging pants up over his belly, but as he has no waist, they slip right back into place under his girth. "You can light it with this."

He presses some matches into the mercenary's hand, then looks back and forth between us. "Well, go on then. Get out of here—"

"Where does the tunnel end up," the mercenary demands.

"Not here. That's all that matters—"

The man of war steps in to him, and I notice the dagger is back in his grip. Mr. Lewis sees the weapon as well—just as outside the private quarters, voices announce that a contingent has entered the pub proper.

The mercenary deepens his tone to an order. "*Where.*"

"It goes under the village wall and then the moat." Mr. Lewis puts both his hands up, as if the knife is pointed at his chest even though the weapon remains at the mercenary's side. "I don't know because I've never been down it. But my father told me that it is the way out for her. When you're inside and I close the panel, you throw the switch by the lantern and it's done. No one can get in there. Ever."

The voices get louder and there's some thumping, like fists are beating on the bar counter.

Turning away from the men, I square off at the black void. Then before I can think too much, I extend my foot—

A powerful arm bars my way. "I go first."

There's the threatening sound of metal on metal as the mercenary draws his broadsword from its sheath. Leaning into the darkness, he reaches to the left, and his opposite hand comes out with the torch. Instead of using the matches, he goes to the hearth, and lights it from the embers that are glowing there.

The flames crackle in their seat as he reapproaches the darkness and steps inside without hesitation.

I envy his confidence.

Pausing on the threshold, I look back at Mr. Lewis, though not into his eyes. "That's why you never wanted me to go out, especially if it was night. You were protecting me."

"Don't get sentimental." His stare shifts to the portrait of his wife. "I was just doing a job. Now will you leave. Finally."

Pain as familiar as that voice in my head lances through my chest. Did I honestly expect anything else from him, though? From anybody here?

As I enter the tunnel and Mr. Lewis closes the panel on my hooded face, I know deep in my soul that I will never, ever see him again.

And I'm the only one who cares.

*Part Two*

# The Quest Begins

## A Gathering of Skills.

*Fourteen*

# The Tunnel.

As our only source of light licks and spits in the darkness, the agitated illumination brings the mercenary's hard features and long black hair out of the void. In my fear, I nearly meet him in the eyes, and only the habit of a lifetime stops my gaze at his nose.

To the left of the torch's empty bracket, there's not only an ancient lever set into the sloppily mortared stone walling, but several lengths' worth of dirt-encrusted pine boards that are taller than I am. As the din out in the pub rises so much that we can hear the cacophony even in here, I imagine the angry villagers bursting into those private quarters and somehow sensing our presence. Dropping the load I'm balancing at my feet, my hands reach forward without any command from my mind, and I grip the cold, corroded metal. Murmuring some kind of prayer, even though I don't know whether to the crescent moon or fate itself, I pull—

I get nowhere with the switch, and vacillate between feeling trapped and wanting to run out of this dank, oppressive chute and being utterly panicked that I can't protect myself by locking us in. As I try again, the mercenary's free arm extends past my head. His palm locks on to the handle below mine, and the way he pulls the thing down so easily galls me to my core.

A rumbling starts, like underground thunder that's off in the distance. And as some kind of momentum is gathered, vibration comes up through the uneven dirt floor and dust wafts out from those pine boards beside us—

The broadsword enters my vision as the mercenary's arm makes a bar across my chest. He yanks me back just as the wooden planks explode into splinters and an enormous stone disk rolls into place over the hidden entry with a roar and then a bone-shattering thud.

In the aftermath, my harsh breathing harmonizes with the hissing of the torch and the subtle rainfall of pine slivers and grit. Mr. Lewis is right. The spring-loaded boulder is a barrier so total it's a horizon. There's no getting over or around it, and certainly not through. There will also be no moving the thing, not with the size and the way it's set into a groove in the far wall. We are both protected . . . and trapped.

There's no going back, not that retreat was an option anyway—

Abruptly, everything warm and firm and very male at my back registers. I jump forward with a squeak—and that's when the muffled yelling grows even louder. Did they hear all that? Have they found the seam in the wall?

Putting my palm on the flat, cold stone, I glance back. "Will they hurt Mr. Lewis?"

"What do you care. He's one of them."

"He was . . . kind to me."

"Oh, really? Looked like he was cutting loose a burden and glad about it as he locked you in here." The mercenary shrugs. "Let's get on with it, then. No reason to stand around."

As he extends the torch out in front of him, the silhouette of his shoulders and head—and that broadsword in his hand—is as if the darkness before me has coalesced into a living form. But I remind myself he's a weapon under my control, and even though I don't know what we will face, I'm certain of one thing:

I am not going to die in this tunnel. Maybe somewhere else, but not here, and not tonight.

With that resolve, I open the pack and find that everything, including the box, fits inside. As I sling the weight onto my back, the mercenary turns away to face whatever's ahead of us.

"Wait."

He turns his head to the side, his profile harsh as any predator's. "What."

"What's your real name?" I feel an urgent need to know what it is, and when he remains silent, I press, "We need to be on cordial terms for the duration of this . . . journey."

"Why's that?" He slashes the broadsword with impatience. "Never mind. And I told you what you can call me."

"Please. What's your actual name."

"I don't have one."

"Everyone has a name—"

"Not me."

He steps forward like he can handle anything we'll encounter, and I have no choice but to draft in his wake or be left behind.

"I'll call you Merc," I announce as a downward slope starts under my slipper shoes and the air becomes dense with the smell of earth and mold. "'Mercenary' is too . . ."

Well, too close to the truth for me to constantly be reminded of it.

"Fill your boots." Then he gives me his profile again, a half smile on his lips. "Sorrel."

His strides are long and I have to hustle to keep up, especially as we bottom out and proceed at a much lower level. Overhead, cracks in the arched ceiling leach cold water that dampens us and fills the puddles at our feet. I feel as though I'm drawing soil itself into my nose and it's turning to mud in the back of my throat—

A squeak and scurry introduce the rats that presently become our traveling companions, and I try not to notice their plump gray bodies and fleshy pink tails as they rush by us and evaporate into all I cannot see. When there's another angle of decline, I put my palm out to the wall to steady myself—and take it back. The slimy feel is more than I can bear, and makes me think of the cow innards that Mr. Cavenish brought with him into the pub.

As I rub my palm on my cloak, a tingling starts at my sternum, and my stomach flip-flops in the cradle of my pelvis. Then my throat closes as if it's been taken in a grip.

Suffocating, my lips part and my breath goes in and out as if I'm running, the high whistle through my front teeth like a bird warning of a barn cat hiding in the hay. My balance suffers as my feet abruptly go numb, and I collapse against the oozing wall. Bracing my hands on my knees, I become a table with three legs as I try to keep from passing out—

Merc has to backtrack to put the torch to my hidden face. "What's wrong with you."

"Can't . . . breathe—"

"Well, get that stupid hood off your head. It's hot in here."

"I-i-it is—no!" I jerk away as I feel him tugging. "No, no, *no*—"

I lock my hands over my head. "I can't do this—I can't breathe, I can't—*I can't do this*. I've got to go back, I can't do—"

A grip locks on my biceps, and he gives me a shake. "Yes, you can—"

"N-n-no, I can't! We need to go back—I'm going to die here!"

So much for the resolution that had seemed so hearty mere lengths ago.

Merc's face thrusts into my own, and I squeeze my eyes shut to avoid his own. "We are going forward—"

"I can't—"

"You *can* and you *will* because you have no choice." His sharp voice echoes up and down the tunnel. "Stop this right now, and get walking. Only forward, never back!"

Merc pulls me forward and I'm so shocked that I forget the rioting sensations in my body. As he drags me along, I paddle at the puddles with my leather slippers, the cloak tangling around my legs.

"Let go of me—"

"Make me."

"That's unfair." I yank at his hold. "You're bigger than I am. Stronger. Harder—"

*"Make me."*

"What are you—"

"You want me to let go?" He jerks me around and shoves the torch at my hand. "Lead on, and I will. But either you're walking ahead of me or I'm dragging you behind. One of two is happening here, and that *is* your choice. But going back isn't, and stopping here isn't. What's it going to be."

Between one blink and the next, I see Mare defiled in the nest of the blankets I stole for her.

"This isn't fair," I choke out.

"What makes you think life is." His words are edged with a savagery that draws my stare to the scar on his face. "Don't be weak *and* stupid. Nothing is fair, no one is going to save you except yourself, and going back isn't an option. So am I dragging you or are you stopping this right now."

How has this all happened? I wonder. What am I doing here—

"I was orphaned," I find myself repeating in a numb mumble. ". . . on the birthing bed. And left in the village square . . ."

"What way are we doing this. That is the *only* response required."

I'm trembling so hard, my cloak is like the torch's flame. The whole of Anathos feels against me, from my village to this man who is yelling at me to the fate that has stripped me of everything, down even to those precious herbs and the cheap mementos I'd collected in my hovel under the stairs. And then there is this supposed past of mine, of which I have no conscious knowledge—and don't believe, no matter Mr. Lewis's apparent conviction.

"I was orphaned, on the birthing bed," I whisper as something prowls around my subconscious, something more threatening even than this tunnel or the hard, frustrated mercenary before me. "And left in the village square . . ."

"And you think that makes you special? We're all abandoned the instant we're born."

"Why is fate so cruel."

There's a long pause, nothing but the sound of dripping water and the hiss and spit of the torch between us. Then his grim response: "You don't know what cruelty is."

I think of all the times I've been shunned, by all the villagers whose bairns

I saved. Lifting my chin, I say with force, "You have *no* idea what I've endured. And that crowd wanted to kill me over a lie—"

"But they *didn't.* So are you going to do the job for them after you got away?" Merc points over my shoulder with a jab. "You stop now and you might as well have marched into that square and let them set you afire back there."

I open my mouth to respond, but all I have is a roar in between my ears and a pounding in my chest.

He drops his arm. "I was wrong."

"A-about our arrangement?"

"No, there's a third option." He steps back. "I leave you here. I am not wasting my life on your weakness, no matter how much I want to fuck you."

With that, he pivots away and starts walking again, taking his presence—and all the light we have—with him.

The darkness crashes into me as he rounds a bend and goes out of view.

I am alone in the tunnel.

## *Fifteen*

# An Impasse.

The smell of copper brings my attention to my hand, and I become aware that my palm is stinging. I'm bleeding there, but I can't assess the depth of the wound in the darkness. It was probably from the wall, and my unhelpful brain kicks out a suggestion that I wash it and rub *talrow* root on the abrasion to keep it from getting infected.

As I lower my arm, I'm back at Mare's bedside again. If she'd had my youth and health, she would have run. She would have . . . heard the crowd banging on her door and gotten out through the trapdoor under her bed.

Or maybe she wouldn't have, but I would have, had I been the two of us combined.

And as much as it galls me, Merc is right. There's only one thing I need to do now.

With my uninjured hand out to the side for navigation, I know I have to get moving not because of what he said to me, but because I imagine my old dear friend in that bed, so helpless as the men set upon her. I imagine their murderous faces, their knives, the rank stink of their sweat. The echo of the horror she must have felt surges through my suffocation and panic, and I take a step forward. And another.

And another.

Her gold is on my body, in a pouch in my pocket. I mark my progress by the way its weight slaps against my thigh.

After I make the turn, another decline dips beneath the soft soles of my slippers, and I can feel it, the sensation in my feet returning. Right after that, as if in reward for my bravery, the glow of the torch flares in the void up ahead. As it gets brighter and brighter, I realize that Merc's waited for me.

I exhale in relief. He's giving me time to catch up to him, and if I didn't, he clearly would have come back for me.

Evidently, there was a fourth option—

Oh. He hasn't waited for me. Voluntarily, that is.

Merc's crouched down at the edge of a pond's worth of water, moving the torch around as if assessing the depth of the pool as well as where the far edge of it intersects the slope of the tunnel ceiling. The firelight sparkles over the black water, making it look like oil, and all I want to do is tell him to get back before something leaps out at him.

"You better know how to swim," he says grimly.

Rising to his feet, he shoves the torch at me, and I take the grip that's been warmed by his hold and squeeze my hands around it. After he sheathes his broadsword at his hip, rather than his back, he starts to unbuckle the heavy weapons belt at his waist.

My eyes lock on his scarred hands yanking at the leather strapping, right over the laces of his britches. Right over . . . the seat of his sex.

A flush roars to my face and I drop my eyes.

"What are you doing?" Even though it's obvious—and how far is he going to go?

"I'm going to see if there's a way through. I suspect the tunnel's collapsed somewhere up ahead and this is moat water."

"Wait! There are *balas* in the—"

"I know. But there's no going back, remember."

Dropping his pack, he shucks all of the holsters on his torso, then removes his leather overcoating and the chained breastplate, revealing a long-sleeved black sheath that stretches over his muscled chest, shoulders, and arms. Dimly, I wonder where all of his other clothes are—they must be in that pack—and then he bends over and starts to undo the buckles on his heavy boots.

I have to turn away as it looks like he's indeed about to drop his pants.

Crescent moon, he probably is going to take his leather pants off. And fates protect me . . . I want to see. All of it.

All of him.

Closing my eyes, the sounds of the shifting of clothes, of his breath, of the creak of what covers his lower body, are too intimate to bear, and for a moment, I am back at the Gauntlet on the second floor, listening to Sallae Mae and her ilk do their business.

When I hear a splash, I whip back around. Merc's already wading into the fetid flood—

Okay, he's kept on the black sheath, and it's long enough so that it covers down to his mid-thigh. I can't decide whether I'm relieved or disappointed. What's clear is that given our circumstances, his nakedness or the lack thereof should be the very *last* thing on my mind.

"Where's your weapon?" I blurt out.

Merc glances over his shoulder, and I jerk to the side just in time to miss his eyes. "I'm coming back for them. And you."

With a messy fumble, I get out my little knife and offer it to him, even though the stumpy blade is pathetic compared to what he normally carries. "Take this. If that is moat water, the *balas* will scent you through the currents, and at least you can swim with this easily in your hand."

When he just stares at what I'm holding out, I turn the blade around so the hilt is facing him. "It's better than nothing."

In the firelight, his half smile is a beacon all its own. "You have that with you always?"

"Even a mouse needs to bite if threatened."

Merc steps out of the water and takes the blade. Then he gently unfurls my fingers and lays it back in my grip properly.

"You keep this."

"What if you don't come back?" I blurt as he turns away again.

"Then you'll either try the water yourself or you'll starve to death here." He glances back at me. "Don't worry, though, I won't be gone but a bit. I have to live long enough for you to show me what's under that hood of yours, yes?"

For a split second, he stares at me with his head tilted to one side, and I wonder if he's trying various hair and eye colors on me. Then he chuckles and turns to the oily black water.

Bending down, he wades in as far as he can, which is not all that much because of his bulk and the way the tunnel's ceiling angles sharply into the pool. Then he starts huffing and puffing, blowing air in and out of his lungs. Finally, he draws in a long, slow inhale that seems to go on forever—

He goes into the murky depths like he's been sucked down.

The disturbance on the surface doesn't last long.

And I know what's coming, if I'm lucky: He's going to reappear and tell me I have to follow him through that water.

Panic immediately returns.

I cannot swim.

I've tried before, in lazy streams and still-watered lakes. In ponds, too. I sink like a stone, and have all the coordination of a seizure.

Glancing around, I find a fissure in the wall that's big enough to shove the handle of the torch into. It takes a couple of tries to get the stalk to stay put, but finally, it holds. Then I sluice the pack off my shoulder, and bring my hands up to my hood.

I have to breathe deeply once or twice, just to convince my brain I'm not already drowning. Right before I drop the folds back, I glance at the pool. Then I wrench the hood off my head—

Oh, the air is good. Even as musty as it is here, just the ability to draw in freely as well as the temperature drop on my face calms me a little.

Releasing the cloak from my body helps, too. The weight off my torso and arms makes me feel like I'm floating and a chill tickles away the oppressive warmth that's had me locked in a vise. Underneath, I have two layers, an outer linen tunic that falls from my collarbones to my ankles, and beneath that, there are my intimates, such as they are. As opposed to the corsets and thigh-high silken leggings of the working women, I just have shirting and a pair of loose men's bloomers.

Quick as my shaky hands will let me, I take off my sheath, tie a knot in the top to close the neck hole, and pull it back over myself, seating the length on the crown of my head. As the folds of thin material settle around me, they are a veil that doesn't compromise my vision, but still hides my face.

Then I go back to the cloak. Fishing around the folds, I take out Mare's heavy bag of gold and wonder where I can stash it. There's a button pocket on the backside of the bloomers and I shove what my friend wanted me to have in there and refasten things. To cure the drag on the waistband, I tighten the leather slip I have to wear to keep them on my hips in the first place.

After which, I just stand there and stare at the pool.

The surface is so still, it's a mirror of the rough stone walling and the arching ceiling above.

Time spools out into eternity, and my heart beats faster as I imagine the burning in Merc's lungs as he holds his breath and uses those broad, callused palms to propel himself through a cold darkness that surely must feel infinite to him, too.

My thoughts begin to cannibalize my consciousness. I picture him turned around in the weightless void, unable to find his way back.

I glance at the torch. Hopefully the light will be his guide? Assuming the glow even carries through the soup.

I wait.

And wait some more.

As I sense myself spiraling again, my mind escapes to folktales I've overheard in the pub for as long as I have memories. If Anathos still had its magic? If that invisible power, the sacred energy given to everyone and everything when our continent was created, remained in the air and the soil and the water? I maybe could have marshaled it and provided him a sufficient homing signal. Or perhaps I could have gone with him, suspended in a protective bubble that I could drive like a ship—

We could have both been in my magical underwater vessel.

Yes, a bubble under the surface. With a lighting glow and confines that were great enough to withstand even the teeth of the biggest *balas* in the moat—

My racing thoughts slam into the barn side of reality: In the ancient times, there wouldn't have been the Fulcrum to claim those boys. So we would not be here at all.

And in that scenario, Merc could have summoned the *granthe* himself and visualized the safest escape.

"Merc . . ." I cup my hands to my mouth. "Merc! Come back!"

Trying not to panic, my eyes shift to the pack, and I blame all of this on the stupid story Mr. Lewis laid out—even though the real problem was the angry crowd.

*Hide*, that old familiar voice commands me.

And then it follows up with something new:

*Seek out the warrior queen who sees no one and return what is hers. Your salvation is there.*

Staring at the still water, I shake my head bitterly. "I'm just going to get out of Greensward and survive somewhere. That will be *quite* hard enough, thank you very much."

*Sixteen*

# The First Monster.

Merc's got to be dead by now.

Hot with alarm, I'm pacing at the pool's edge, as if any movement of mine can help him. It's been too long, far, far too long. Even though I've always nervously avoided water, I know that breath is limited, and that's before you add in the effort of arms and legs—

A bubbling sound gets my attention, and I pivot to the water. Air is escaping from somewhere and rising to agitate the surface, and I think of that day a man horrifically fell off the moat bridge. He was immediately captured by a *balas* in a thrash, rolled under the water, and then . . . nothing but bubbles.

I crouch down with my little knife, and tell myself to dive in.

The waves come next, the pool coming alive with—

A two-headed monster explodes up in a tidal rush, coming right at me.

With a scream, I leap out of range, and it's as I slam into the slimy wall that I decipher the churning, twisting mass before me. Not a two-headed beast, no. Merc and a *balas* are in mortal combat, their bodies locked against each other, the snapping jaws of the animal looking for purchase, the man's arms bulging with muscle as he attempts to control the fight. They land in a tangle at my feet and the *balas* begins to roll, the thick, spiked tail thrashing and slapping as it attempts to get Merc on the bottom.

Later, I'll wonder what threw me into action, but in the moment, I swear to the crescent moon that there are no conscious thoughts. I jump around them, stash my useless knife, and go for Merc's broadsword. With the knobby, tough hide of the *balas*, the only hope we have is something as heavy, as sharp, as that weapon.

The sickening sounds of solid mass slamming into the tunnel floor spur me on, but I'm unprepared for the sword's ungainly weight. The thing is heavy as a mountain, and all I'm trying to do is get it out of the holster. Sinking down into my thighs, I throw my back into the effort. The hilt's textured grip bites into my palms, and nothing shifts. At first. The instant the blade starts to give way, I stamp a foot on the strapping and yank, yank, *yank*—

The broadsword bursts out of its leather cage like a beast released, but I can't straighten, the weapon tethering the upper half of me to the ground—and the folly of my impulse becomes clear as the *balas* pins Merc once again. The animal's black and mucky green scales eat the torchlight, and when I heave at the weapon, I end up tossing myself right into the thrashing tail. My legs are swept out from under me and I land on my shoulder—

The *balas*'s craggy head turns on me and its jaws snap with a terrible sound, the fence of enormous yellowed teeth locking shut—

"Give . . . me . . . the . . . sword . . ."

Merc's own teeth are like his attacker's, gritted in the midst of his fierce battle to kill another living thing before he himself is done in. Jumping to my feet, I do my best to drag the broadsword closer, but I'm dodging rear claws and that vicious spiked tail.

The *balas*'s fangs flash back and forth between us, and every time the jaws open, I focus on the pink meat of its mouth. If Merc lets go to grab the hilt, assuming I can even get over to him, he's going to be a meal—

The beast bangs him into the wall, then throws him at me. As Merc lands at my feet in a crumple, his body goes lax—and without thinking, I look him square in the face.

I don't meet his eyes, for they roll back into his head.

The *balas* lets out a hiss of triumph and focuses on me, opening that maw.

Between one blink and the next, I see what to do. My hands release the broadsword's handle, and move carefully to the sharp blade itself. Taking it flat between my palms, I wedge the hilt against a catch on the floor, tilt the sharp tip upward, and get the angle right.

That beast is going to lunge at me with its mouth open.

And I'm going to feed it one hell of a dinner.

"Come on, you bastard! Bite me!"

The ripple up its spine announces the moment of attack, and as I scream at a high pitch, I find a flow of energy, and do my best to hold steady. My control isn't going to last long, and if I get the angle wrong—

Our eyes lock, and my lungs jerk an inhale as those oblong pupils suck me in. The moment of the *balas*'s death imprints on my mind—

Not how it dies. Not with me and the broadsword.

As the vision overtakes me, the weapon slips free of its catch on the tunnel floor and clatters off to the side. The *balas* has an expert predator's sense of space and timing, and comes right at my head—but as I've been pulling back on the weapon, when it goes out, so do I, my momentum to the rear carrying me off my feet.

Those jaws snap closed on thin air—

My hard landing stuns me and my vision dims. When it returns, Merc's somehow back in the fight. He's got hands under the *balas*'s lower jaw, his arms vibrating as he holds off all those teeth again while trying to get the beast away from me—

My little knife finds my hand, and I jump to my feet, the vision I just witnessed laying clear my strategy: Two running leaps. Then like a *varthig*, I am airborne and full of vengeance. Now I know exactly what I'm doing.

The little blade knows, too.

The moat's beast and I are suddenly face-to-face, and just as my premonition showed me, the tip of my knife pierces the *balas*'s left eye. My trajectory along with my propulsion does most of the work to drive the blade deep into the socket, but somehow, I manage to flip my body around and straddle its nape. Pulling back with both hands, the hilt of the knife becomes the pommel on a saddle as the *balas* lets out a roar of pain and rears up. Ducking, so I'm not knocked out by the ceiling, I ride the monster's knobby body, while beneath us, Merc's arm stretches out.

The broadsword finds home in his palm as if called.

With what must be the last of his strength, he hefts the impossible weight, and his expression is one of pure vengeance as he stabs the *balas* through the throat.

Instinctively, I release my hands and leap free. I don't know if the broadsword can come out the back of the skull, but I don't want to find out—

*Crack!*

The sound is as loud as an axe splitting dried hardwood, and for a heartbeat, I have no idea what could have made such a noise.

Then the pain in my head registers and all I can do is lie where I land in a heap, an odd numbness replacing the feeling in my limbs, my stomach flip-flopping, my eyes shifting over to the *balas* while they struggle to focus.

Merc is still under the gruesome blanket of the beast, and he turns his head slowly to me. His black hair is a tangled halo around his face, which is flushed from effort and stained with green and red blood, what is leaking out of the *balas* mixing with what's in his own veins.

As I barely remember to avoid his eyes in time, I have a thought that I'll recall this scene always. Assuming we get out of here alive—

It dawns on me that his lips are moving like he's speaking to me, and I try to respond. I don't have any idea what's coming out of my mouth. Then my lids grow too heavy to hold up, and everything starts to dim, what I see, how

I breathe, what pain I feel, as if the numbness is an infection taking over my flesh.

The last thing that registers as I lose consciousness is the two blades: my smaller one in the beast's eye, the tip of Merc's far larger weapon extending out the back of the head.

It's exactly what I saw as I stared into those oblong pupils for that moment, and I know that Merc would have died without my effort.

It's satisfying to think even a mercenary could be helped by someone as insignificant as myself.

We're a good team, all things considered.

*Seventeen*

# A Shared Meal.

The smell of cooking meat is so strong, my hunger is like a sword in my gut.

I'm at the Gauntlet, and for reasons that I cannot explain, I'm relieved that everything is as it has always been: the familiar customers at the tables, Sallae Mae and the working girls, the tender of the bar who hates his job . . . Mr. Lewis who dislikes me. The voices are loud, and the air thick with the sweet smell of ale and the sour stink of bodies that are washed but once weekly.

It is precisely how I have spent every evening of my life. Yet something is . . . off.

All of the things I don't like about the place are soothing to me, as if I miss them, and this makes no sense.

Also, there's a fire pit in the center of the pub.

Why has Mr. Lewis allowed a ring of stones to be set right in the middle of the floor and filled with flames—

Somebody is cooking strips of meat on the flat blade of a massive broadsword.

And I'm wrong. It's not a proper fire, as in one set with logs, and there's no flat hearth to contain it. A torch is being held upright between a pair of leather-clad knees, and the sword is being held over it.

Confused, my eyes trace the corded thigh muscles that run down, right-angled, into the profile view of a hip. Rising up from that anchor, the torso of a man is clad in a long-sleeved black tunic, and tilted against a rough-cut wall, waves of long black hair drying in corkscrews—

I wake up in a rush, my lids flipping all the way open, the sound of the Gauntlet crowd dimming in a flash, the familiar glow of the pine tables and floors extinguished as if all the lanterns in the place are turned off at once.

Just a dream.

And where am I? I seem to be lying on my side with my cheek on a damp stone floor, and an essential exhaustion keeps me in that position as I try to figure out—

*Merc.*

Through the linen veil that covers my face, my eyes take in all the details of him, and my brain connects his grim presence with our grim present. A ringing disappointment blooms in my chest: I am in the tunnel. With him . . . and the *balas* that followed him out of the moat.

Which he's turned into dinner.

The predator we bested is on its back by the murky pool, and a wide block of flesh has been taken from its ribs, the anatomy far too obvious and bloody for my tender eyes.

So my gaze returns to the man with a greed I don't want to acknowledge. In the torchlight, Merc's legs and clothes are clean of both colors of blood, so I guess he gave himself a thorough bathing. And as he monitors what he's cooking, the planes of his lean, aggressive face are remote, his stare fixed on what he's doing, even though I suspect his mind is far away.

I trace the scarring across his eye. Where have his thoughts gone in a private moment like this? To his family, whoever they are? A woman he once knew and loved? Children he's had and misses dearly?

A wife he provides for by doing brutal things for money?

As misplaced jealousy digs into my hollow gut, I lift my aching head—

"So you're awake then."

His voice is low and deep, full of gravel. And then he turns his head and looks at me. As I am careful to focus on his throat, I sense that his eyes are hooded, and watch as his mouth flattens into a tense line.

In any other circumstance, I would ask him what's wrong. As it goes, that would be a long list and all of it is very obvious.

"We need to eat as much as we can of that beast." He returns to staring at the meat. "As much as you can stand. And we won't be able to take the bread with us through the water, so we might as well consume it, too."

I sit up, and the tunnel swings around like the bow of a ship. Throwing out a palm, I brace myself to keep from falling back over. The thought of swallowing anything but air makes my throat tighten to a gag.

"We wait until dawn." He brings the broadsword around to inspect his cooking. "I could not find a way through the collapse in the dark. The daylight will show the way. If there is one."

Not yet satisfied by the meat's appearance, he returns the blade to the torch, and the sizzling resumes.

"You did well," he mutters gruffly. "With your blade."

It's as close as he can get to thanking me for saving his life. And I'll take it. "You're . . . welcome."

"I've cleaned and sharpened it for you." He nods toward my feet. "That little thing was made well, by someone who knew what they were doing."

Right within my reach, the knife is gleaming like a gem, and my hand trembles as I pick the familiar object up. Somehow, he's brought it back from the dull and grungy state it's always been in, and now every part of it shines as if new.

Clearing my throat, I say hoarsely, "I found it in the village square. After the traveling merchants' day a couple of years ago."

"Somebody is still missing the thing, I'll tell you that. Made of fine steel and the handle's honed *alaight*."

"I don't even know what kind of wood that is."

"It grows in the northern territory." His face seems to soften. Or maybe I'm about to pass out again? "Those trees are the only thing that live on the mountain slopes. They're small, and their trunks are twisted, yet the branches are only ever straight. You have to hike to reach them, and when you get in range, the *raagles* will come after you because they nest in them."

"What's a *raagle*?"

"Scavenger birds." He shakes his head. "With a wingspan as wide as my arm. While you fight them off, the barbed branch you want will fight with you, too. Those ugly trees grow in tight knots of a dozen or more, and they hold on to their arms and legs jealously—and with good reason. Their wood is nearly as strong as what this sword is made out of."

As I measure my find, which I had always assumed had been discarded due to age, Merc concludes, "But if you prevail in your gathering, the reward is the handle on a little knife that will never rot, and retains a certain purchase, even when wet."

"You have spent time in the north, then?"

There is a long silence. "I was born there. A very long time ago."

It's hard to imagine him as a young man, still growing into his full height and stature, harder still to picture him as a boy. And it's utterly impossible to see him as a bairn, wrapped in swaddling cloth, all wide, innocent eyes and button nose.

"Is that where your family as yet resides?" I ask.

His head shakes a brisk "no" as he refocuses on the meat, but that pensive look stays on his profile.

"It seems like a place you miss," I murmur.

His expression closes up again, his mouth flattening, his eyes narrowing on our meal. "Mourning anything is wasted effort. People, locations, objects.

There are enough prisons around that you don't volunteer for. Sentiment shouldn't be added to that list."

I think of my hovel beneath the stairs, and wish I could smell the subtle spice from my herbing, and set my head upon my bundled cloaks, and fall asleep under the sound of footfalls going up and down those creaky wooden steps. The yearning I feel is so strong, it's painful, and I have an inkling that he may be right. After the events of tonight, dwelling on what I've been forced to flee from seems like an agonizing waste.

And I can't bear what was done to Mare.

Picturing my last view of Mr. Lewis, my mind revisits his astonishing revelations in no particular order, as if my thoughts circle something left for dead, and then my eyes shift to my cloak and the pack. They are where I left them—

"Here."

The flat plane of the broadsword swings in my direction, and I jerk back.

"You really think I'm going to hurt you?" Merc mutters.

It seems pointless to reply that I was just surprised. He seems spoiling for an argument.

"Use your knife," he orders. "It's too hot to touch."

Doing as he says, there's something intimate in my blade meeting his as I spear what he offers. But then I have a problem. Over the course of my life, I've only eaten four things: greens that Mr. Lewis cultivates in his garden beyond the wall, milk that was delivered daily by Mr. Cavenish, bread that was the staple of the Gauntlet's working girls, and *psears* from the trees that grow on the south shore of the moat.

Part of the dietary restriction was economic. I was at the bottom of the social hierarchy and very poor. Any delicacies like meat, candies, or exotic fare the travelers brought to market went into mouths that could afford such things, and I certainly was never invited to those tables. The other part was practical. If my knowledge of herbs taught me anything, experimentation with growing things can be perilous. Just because a fruit or vegetable sprouts and matures for the sun doesn't mean it's safe, and if I guessed wrong? No one would have helped me if I succumbed to a bad mushroom or root.

"Is there a problem," he says.

"I've never had meat before."

"You lie—"

"It's true. Who's wasting that on me?"

Sniffing at the still-steaming piece, I'm surprised that my mouth waters and my stomach growls at the scent. With a piercing anticipation, I bring it to my mouth—

The linen sheath is in the way.

"You might as well show me." His voice is remote. "Considering our agreement. Or do I need to remind you of what I'm getting in return for my efforts on your behalf."

Shifting around, I bring the sheath up until I can lift the veiling enough to get my knife under the cover. I've never been so glad to have my face hidden. Then again, I'm blushing so furiously, maybe I'm casting a red glow.

"No kissing," I blurt.

"That was not part of our—"

"Working girls do not kiss the patrons."

He chuckles deep in his throat. "That, my dear, is not true."

The idea he's paid for women before shocks me. Then again, would it be better for him to have found a true love and never strayed out of loyalty? And why in fates do I care about his bedding partners.

"Sallae Mae never kissed the patrons," I retort. "None of the working girls at the Gauntlet do."

"Is that the woman who brought you into the trade?"

Ignoring him, I nibble off a bit with my front teeth, cautious in case my nose has misidentified things, and it is something tough and tasteless—

My mouth blooms with the most delicious taste, and I can't help but moan while I eye the carcass. How anything so tough on the exterior can provide this singular delicacy, I have no idea, but my stomach doesn't care about the particulars—or the bloody mess we took the meat from.

It just wants *more.*

"Oh, crescent moon . . ." I chew slowly to savor the experience. "This is—"

"Lewis was an arse who did not take care of you well enough. Here, have more." Then Merc tacks on dryly, "Brace yourself, my sword's coming at you again."

As I glance his way, there's a sexual charge to the comment and my cheeks get even hotter. "What about you?"

"We feed you first. Then I'll see about me."

I'm so touched, I nearly forget everything and meet his eyes. But that warmth fades as he announces practically, "If you're going to make it through the journey that awaits us after our swim, we need you properly fed."

The disappointment that hits me is as misplaced as my speculations about his lovers. And really, after all I've seen, why should I ever assume tenderness from any man?

"And one more thing."

I finish chewing and take another piece. "What is that."

"I am going to kiss you." His voice lowers into a silky drawl. "Before we leave here."

*Eighteen*

# An Abrupt End.

Merc feeds me as if I'm a pig to the slaughter. All of the bread, all of the meat he's cut from the ribs of the *balas*, and he makes me drink everything that's in the bladder Mr. Lewis pushed into my hands. I'm now chewing on a root of mint wood, cleaning my teeth thanks to a supply he keeps within the folds of his surcoat. Following his announcement about our mouths meeting, he's remained silent, but in my head, we're arguing back and forth—

No, wait. I do believe I'm fighting with myself.

I *want* him to kiss me, and know that's a stupidity from which I'll not easily recover. The problem is, even with the full belly he's given me, I'm not likely to survive what we must do next—whether that's somehow getting through that pool or whatever's past that. Do I really want to go to a watery grave without knowing what it feels like to have a man's lips on my own?

Merc's lips.

Going on this theory, we might as well have the sex now—

"*What*—" Merc sputters. Then he puts his broadsword aside and shoves the butt of the torch into a fissure in the wall. "I mean, *yes*. Now—"

"Wait, what—"

Merc rises up on his knees, and he's magnificent in the torchlight, his hair one with the black of his tunic, his harsh face carved with a mating need I've seen before on other men—but never had directed at me. His blunted fingers yank the knot out of the laces that close the front of his britches, and behind the leather, the bulge of his sex thickens and extends out to the side in its confinement.

I'm so shocked, I can't respond. I must have spoken my thoughts aloud—

"Only a kiss," I blurt.

And then wish I could take that back, too.

He freezes, his corded forearms in mid-flex, his hands run with veins. I have a thought that his palms must be callused from fighting, and I shock myself by wondering what they would feel like on the inside of my thighs as he spreads me—

Merc redoes the knot. "All right, a kiss then."

And still the length and thickness of his sex grows. And grows.

"My veil stays on."

That's the last thing I say. I suddenly can't breathe, but in contrast to my earlier panic, this suffocation is sweet. Behind my sternum, my heart skips beats, then thunders.

"Just a kiss." Now his deep voice is a purr. "With your veil . . . still on. Yes, that'll be fine."

He falls forward, and just when I think he might land on his face, his hands flatten and his palms catch his weight on the tunnel's stone floor. Then he prowls toward me in a crouch, his long, black hair hanging down, those braids swinging freely, his massive shoulders larger than ever before.

"Are you going to eat me," I whisper.

"Yes. I am."

Good. I want to be consumed. There's lightning in my veins, a heady combination of fear and desire—except I'm not ready for all of him, not yet. Still, he's so big, and we're alone down here. I don't think he'll take what I'm not offering, but I don't know that for sure. I'll find out, though.

Right now.

We are face-to-face, separated only by the shift of linen. I can smell the leather and that spice of cedar coming off of him, and the scent kills the mold and mud in the air. My stare stays on his mouth, but I can feel the heat in his scarred gaze, the raw sexual need.

He tilts his head, and as he does, the beads at the end of the braids that frame his face make a chiming sound.

"Give me your mouth," he growls.

With a surge, he comes at me, and his lips find my own without any searching, homing in even though surely the veil conceals most of my features—

Everything fades away. The tunnel, the dead *balas*, our situation. As something warm and soft brushes back and forth over my mouth, the world is reduced to him. To us. To what this leads to, surely as a landslide rakes down a mountain, taking all with it. I tremble with a sudden, clawing need, the core of me opening as if he'd finished the job with his britches, and was lifting my skirts to get at my sex with his own.

When Merc eases back, I'm not sure whether time has stood still or a thousand years have passed.

I want more. Yet he just stays where he is.

Until he backs off to his previous spot.

He's brooding as he stares at the torch.

Oh, no. He didn't like it.

With a curse, he eases to one side, and shoves a hand at his hips as if he's rearranging something that's been caught in a crease. When he resettles, he clears his throat.

"What's wrong?" I ask roughly, my breath tight.

"I'll still do the job." His words are gruff. "As I told you, I'm heading to the Badlands anyway."

I touch my mouth through the damp veil and can still feel his lips.

Before I can ask him what's wrong, he leans back against the tunnel wall, extends his legs, and crosses his arms and his ankles. I know that he's closed his eyes by the stillness of his body, and risk a glance at his face.

With his lids down, I can finally take my time studying him. His forehead is broad and his brows have no arch to them at all, just two straight lines from the frown that breaks across the bridge of his straight nose. His cheeks are well-defined, the hollows under them valleys before the cut of his heavy jaw. There is no shadow of a beard, and I dip down to the neckline of his shirt. It's too high to see if there is dark hair on his muscled chest.

I refocus on his mouth, the lower lip so much fuller, the upper marred by a tiny scar at the bow on the top. It's a scratch that healed into a barely noticeable line, something so much less than what injured his eye, and I wonder how many other wounds of varying severity have left their markings on his skin—

"Sleep if you can," he orders me. "When the torch is almost out, dawn will be close by, and I'll try again."

I feel deserted in his silence, only the fiery chatter of our tethered flame and the drumbeat of the incessant dripping from the ceiling entering my ears.

But that isn't all I hear. In my mind, his voice is on repeat: *I'll still do the job . . . I'm heading to the Badlands anyway.*

One kiss and he's released me from our arrangement.

Mirroring his pose, I shut my own eyes and resolve to rest with the same level of commitment and exertion that I would approach a cliff climb—

My eyes pop back open again. Without any kind of permission from me, they drop down to his sturdy boots and travel slowly up his leather-clad calves to his knees, and then his thighs. With his legs outstretched, I can see the front of his britches. He remains erect, and the finely worked hide is a second skin that once again obscures nothing of his anatomy.

The outline of the head and the thick straddle of his shaft are so clear, he might as well be naked.

His potency is no surprise. As if his arousal would be any less imposing than the rest of him—

"You keep staring at me like that," he says with a hint of amusement, "I'm going to think I guessed wrong, and maybe you do want me, after all."

Flushing bright as that torch, I look away. Then frown as meaning catches up with his words. "Is that why you stopped?" I clear my throat. "I mean—"

"I told you, I'm not a savage. Your lips never moved against my own and I'm not going to take what you aren't willing to give me. Now do us both a favor and go to sleep."

I lift my fingers back to my mouth. I want to tell him that I don't know how to kiss, that he is the first and—given what we are about to face—the only for me.

And that I would like very much for him to teach me how to please his lips.

Instead, I close my lids and order sleep to take over.

Some things are best kept to myself.

## *Nineteen*

# On Matters of Fish.

"It's time."

I must have fallen asleep at some point because I wake up to find Merc standing over me. He's wet again, so I guess he's done a little more exploration, and in the dwindling torchlight, the sheath that cleaves to his torso like a second skin gives me quite a show—especially as he picks up his mesh armor and straps it on.

With every movement, his muscles contract and release, the power in him as transfixing as flame. And I grow warm.

At least until he continues talking.

"We have to do it now." He nods toward the pool as he begins strapping on his weapons. "We need to get you away from the village before it's broad daylight, and there's just enough sunrise for me to navigate the collapse—"

"I can't swim."

That shuts him up sure as if I've slapped him. "What do you mean you can't—"

"I tried a couple of times when I was younger." I'm flushing again, but this time, it's with embarrassment. "I can't do it."

"Of course you can't," he mutters as he pulls on his leather coat and his pack. "How is this possible?"

"I sink—"

Merc slashes an impatient hand and then goes digging into his pack. "It's as if I knew—and that's why I brought this. Stand up."

He holds out a rope, and when I just stare at the thing as if I've never seen one before, he pulls me to my feet. Stepping in close, he reaches around my waist with the twist of fibers—

The scent of him washes over me and I breathe in deep. How can he always smell so good? This is the only thing I'm thinking of as the band tightens across the small of my back, and I nearly take a step forward just to keep us together.

"I'll do the swimming." My body tugs back and forth as he ties things in a tight knot. "You just need to hold your breath and not fight me."

His strong, sure hands test the tie at my belly button one last time. "You have your knife?"

"There. By the pack."

"Tuck it into your waistband. You're going to need your hands free."

On reflex, I bend down for my cloak.

"You're not wearing that. It will drown you."

"But I have to bring my—"

"That thing is going to absorb enough water weight to equal two of you. I'm not dragging it through the currents as well."

As I stare down at the folds of ugly brown wool, I wonder how many more parts of myself I'll have to jettison during this journey. The idea of leaving the thing behind makes me sad in the same way I feel when I think of my nook beneath the stairs.

"You're not actually going to argue with me, are you."

I shake my head. "I'm just thinking about how habit will turn even a hovel into a home, and a rough cloak like that into comfort."

"You're going to do *so* much better in this world, as soon as you drop the sentimentality."

"I'll keep my emotions, thank you very much."

Looking at the pack, I decide to leave it behind. After thinking things over before I fell asleep, I've decided nothing that Mr. Lewis told me made any sense, and I'm not heading off on any quest just because he tossed a bunch of lore around. I'm going to try to hide and survive in a town of outlaws under the theory that there's a kind of safety in numbers, especially with people who have good survival instincts. Surely that's a better option than being alone in a landscape where demons are escaping the Fulcrum. Or some half-cocked story spit out at me by a man trying to save his business—by making sure I leave his establishment and do him the kindness of either getting myself killed, or at the very least, never, ever darkening his door again.

This was why I didn't bother to look in the satchel or the box. I don't care what's inside either of them—

"Hold on." I glance up to Merc's chest level. "Do you have a compass?"

"No. Why?"

"How—ah, how sure are you that you know the way to the Badlands?" Although it isn't as though we have a map—

"I know the way."

And what if we get separated? I think. Or something happens where I have to go on my own? I've heard it's to the south and west. How will I know which directions they're in if I get turned around, or it's at night?

Glancing down, I decide I could use a compass. And even if I don't need the thing for navigating, I could maybe use it to barter.

Grabbing the pack, I slip the straps on my shoulders, and before he can argue, I flash my palms at him. "Hands free."

I just hope the water doesn't destroy the mechanism of the instrument.

Merc is muttering as he ropes his own waist, straps his broadsword onto his back, and slaps at various places on his body, all of which have some kind of weapon secured by some kind of belt or holster. Then he nods as if he's both his own master and protégé, and this is part of his training.

"Well, come on. Let's get this over with."

As he turns away, I grab his forearm. His head snaps toward me, and I open my mouth. Except what is there to say?

"I don't know," he drawls with a shrug. "Maybe we make it, maybe we don't. But I'd rather die trying, wouldn't you."

"I'd rather not have to do this at all."

"Talk to the crescent moon, then. Destiny and its exigencies are far, far above anything that has to do with me."

Merc wades into the pool, bending his prodigious height until he can proceed no farther without going under the surface. As I measure the taut rope that connects us, my lungs start to pump and then I shift my eyes to the black water. I look back at the torch. It's almost out of reed to consume. Soon, there'll be nothing but darkness, rats, and the moon knows what else in here.

"I'm not waiting for you much longer," he says impatiently.

One foot in and I feel as if I'm being consumed already, the cold wetness chewing through my soft-soled slippers and going right for my flesh. Something about the way the fetid, viscous tide rises up my calves without my going a step farther makes me want to scream.

"I can't do this—"

"No choice, remember." Merc holds out his hand. "And I'll be with you all the way. I'm not going to leave you in there."

As if to prove the point, he tugs on the rope that links us. "No more wasting time, though. This is not getting any easier, the longer we stay here. You're just going to get more and more afraid."

"I don't think that's possible," I mumble.

When I still don't move, he pulls me forward, and the tunnel floor takes a sharp decline that makes me wobble and splash. No doubt it's dropping under the moat.

When the water is up to my thighs, I'm by his side. I don't have to bend as he does, and I'm grabbing at the air in jerks of my rib cage, like a fish in the bottom of a boat.

"We're going to take three deep breaths together."

His voice is so calm, I feel like the only one who's stuck in a tunnel and having to swim through *balas* to safety is me—

"One."

My nose burns as I inhale. And when he exhales, I do the same, focusing on that wide chest of his as it deflates.

"Two."

I repeat the draw again, until my lungs sting from the stretching, and my sternum feels as if it'll break open. I glance back at the carcass and remember the fight.

Countless more of them are waiting for us.

"Three—"

At the height of the final inhale, things happen fast. Merc sinks beneath the water level on a lithe dive, and before I can even approximate what he's done, I'm yanked under by the waist. The shock of the cold water swallowing me whole causes all the air in my lungs to explode out of my nose and lips.

I lose every bit of it. And then I gasp—

The moat enters my mouth in an icy fist. Flailing around, I try to cough out the water while I fight the rope, my brain telling me we have to go back and try again after a resurface. Merc is going incredibly fast, though, and I grab on to the tether that binds us and attempt to pull on it, in hopes of signaling that drowning is already happening.

He just keeps swimming, his powerful strokes dragging me along.

My eyes bulge in the watery darkness, and I close my mouth so at least I don't get more down my throat. As my arms and legs become useless, my mind tangles and spins, my thoughts like the rushing in my ears, all noise, no meaning. I bump along the sharply descending angle of the tunnel's ceiling, well aware I'm going to lose consciousness yet again, the wholly unfamiliar buoyancy terrifying me—

Suddenly, my head stings with that familiar, sharp pain, and a vision bursts through the cold, midnight void:

The ocean.

The beautiful ocean at sunrise.

And I'm spearing into the salty, warm waves. Under I go, but there is no fear. There's only joy and surety, my arms cleaving out and pulling back, my legs frogging at the heels and kicking in propulsion, my coordination as natural and comfortable as drawing a breath. Again and again, I stroke through the sea's sweet, surging body, my heart singing.

I swim without needing air, for I am one with Anathos's best natural barrier, that which has protected us from sieges and helped us to thrive for millennia, not isolated, but safe, from whatever is past the horizon.

I swim as a fish does.

Perfectly.

*Twenty*

# The Last Meal Retaliates.

A dull glow guides me. The illumination hovers in the murky water like a lantern on the far side of a dense curtain, and as a moth, I zero in, stroking faster and faster. To reach the beacon, I must begin to rise, and rise I do, until I'm hindered by some kind of drag upon my torso. Unable to progress farther, I claw at the water, pulling on my slippery submersion—but then I'm abruptly free. Just as my lungs begin to burn with the kind of urgency that cannot be denied, I'm liberated and approaching the surface, and this gives me the extra energy I need. As shockingly comfortable as I am propelling myself with strokes, a timer is ticking in my marrow. I know I must take a full breath, soon.

Closer and closer. Bigger and brighter, now the light—

Bursting to the surface, I tear the linen from my head and crest with my mouth wide open. My inhale is not panicked. It's steady, as sure and deep as my entire body, as if every muscle and all my bones have their own sets of lungs and the whole of me is filling with air at once. This happens with a confidence I've never known before—

Settling into a bouncing float, reality returns in a rush. This is not the beachside. This is the fetid moat, and through the muck that coats my face in a thick layer, I look around frantically for *balas* in the midst of the browning lily pads. I don't see any of their knobby, bobbing sets of eyes—

But neither do I see Merc.

Spinning in a circle, the village wall rises above me, a towering mountain made by the hands of men. This is the back side, almost directly behind the bridge and the gate. I can tell by the dappling sunlight that dances on the weathered stone and crumbling mortar. It needs to pass through leaves to get that effect.

"Merc," I hiss so that I don't attract any guard that might be up walking our defense's parapet. "*Merc.*"

Abruptly, I remember the rope. My hands snatch at the knot he tied at my waist, and I pull, pull, pull on the lax—

The end arrives without preamble, and I bring it up out of the water. The twist has been sliced cleanly.

"Merc!"

Grabbing a breath, I plunge under, but can see nothing as I wave my arms around and pull myself deeper. When I have to replenish my lungs, I resurface—

As I'm breathing in to resume my search, bubbles appear three lengths over from me: My agitating movements have called one of the beastly guards to me. Fates! I'm going to get eaten—

Even though I should maybe stay still, I start stroking for the moat's stone banking. The fact that it rises a full body's length above me makes me realize I'm in a bowl set for the aquatic predators, and just as a serving of stew has no hope of besting the rim that contains it, I can't imagine being able to get up and over to the grass above.

The *balas* I ate and am still digesting is about to be avenged by its brethren. Even if they don't know they're settling the score—

A great breaching explodes behind me, and as the beast lands on the surface with a slap, a tidal wave pushes me along, giving me an advantage that will be closed instantly. I paddle faster, slapping at the water with panic—

"Wait for me, why dontcha," comes an impatient voice.

I roll over in surprise, and keep gliding from my momentum. "M-Merc?"

Against all odds, he's surfaced, and he seems equally flabbergasted to see me.

"What happened?" I exclaim.

"You can't swim, huh," he mutters as he shoves his braids back and pulls a hand down his face. "You have fucking fins—"

"Behind you!"

The first of the *balas* appears, its red eyes glowing out from beneath its knobby glower. Merc doesn't bother to assess what I've reported. He starts for me with powerful strokes, and I know the only way I can help us is by leading the charge to the impossible moat edge.

When I get to the stones, I try to set my blunt fingers into the seams between the algae'd, smooth-faced rocks, but there's no purchase, the slime preventing me from securing any kind of hold. I keep attempting to find some sort of grip, even as I glance back once again. Merc is coming at me so fast, he has a wake behind him, but the disturbances have called even more to us. Four or five other *balas* have zeroed in from way across the water, their tails swirling back and forth with the lazy movement of cats on the hunt.

Right before the mouse is toyed with.

Merc arrives at me and throws himself at the walling. He fails as I do, but doesn't keep up with trying. In a single move, he comes about and unsheathes the broadsword, the tip breaching the surface and gleaming wet in the sunlight.

There's no way he can defend us, and they're all closing in, the monsters bickering back and forth, their jaws snapping in a fanged argument over who gets first bite. And behind the lineup, there are countless others ready to strike.

I go back to throwing myself at the slick stones, and a scream gets trapped in my throat when I notice that there are a similar series of pawings, long stripes of something—or someone—desperately trying to extricate themselves in a losing battle, the kind of epitaph that terrifies me—

Out of the corner of my eye, I see one of the *balas* rushing in on me from the side. It's decided not to take the common frontal approach, and it's going to get me and Merc as a reward for its thinking.

To hell with the guards on the parapet. I start to scream—

That's when the snake lands on my head.

## *Twenty-One*

# The Snake and the Grave.

Furious at the unfairness of a reptilian counterstrike, I bat at the snake, but it's tenacious, wrapping around my head and falling down my shoulders. I look to Merc for help, but he's got his own problems—and they're all about protecting me. He's put himself between me and what's now a ring of *balas*, his arms spread wide, that broadsword at the ready as he treads water to stay afloat. The countdown to the attack has started, and the predators are focused now, no longer biting at each other.

As the one coming at me from the right opens its jaws into an evil smile, full of filthy yellow teeth, I grab at the snake and yank it off me—

What's in my hand makes no sense.

While the rope comes into focus, a male voice from above says, "I shall pull you out! Hold on!"

In the back of my mind, I know I've heard the man before, but I'm too confused to make the connection. All that matters is that maybe this is a way out.

"Merc! A rope!"

I grab a length of his hair and yank back. He doesn't shift his position, but he as glares over his shoulder, I shove the rope in his face.

"Start pulling!" I holler at our savior.

Taking the loose length, I wrap it around myself, well aware that I haven't the strength required to hold on. Instantly, I'm rising out of the water, and the scum, green and brown and viscous as old treacle, clings to my hair and body as if the moat is possessive—or at the very least on the side of the *balas*.

"Take the rope!" I yell at Merc as he turns back to our attackers. "Merc!"

Higher and higher up I go, but now I'm fighting the rescue, trying to backpedal against the slippery stones.

"Merc!"

Just as I reach the lip of the walling, the first of the *balas* goes for him.

Hard hands grab me and yank me up onto the embankment, and the instant I flop onto the dry ground, I crawl back, throwing myself over the lip.

Just as the biggest of the *balas* lunges forward with a foul splash, jaws wide open and trained on my mercenary's head.

"Merc!" I fight against whoever's holding me in place. "*Merc—*"

"You must stop," someone says crossly. "This is no good. At least you are safe—"

The *balas* strikes with deadly accuracy, the teeth clapping together on the arm he raises to cover his face with—and then the feral beast goes under the surface and takes its prey with him.

Merc is gone.

The horror of it silences me, and in desperation, I search the churning water for anything, well aware that what I will see could certainly break me: A leg. A hand. Fates preserve us . . . a head, where I can finally meet those mismatched eyes because death has already taken the most extraordinary man I've ever met—

I fall into the moat, my body tumbling forward.

Instantly, I'm yanked back up again and shaken as a rag doll. "*Stop it! He's not worth your life!*"

The golden aura imprints on me first, and then the handsome, virtuous face and the royal insignia come into focus. "Julion? What are you doing here?"

"You are all right," he says in a gentle way.

I have a thought that I'd love to hear that tone from Merc. And this snaps me back to attention.

"Not without him, I'm not." Freeing myself from the rope I wrapped around my body, I throw the length back over the lip and lean out once more. "Merc, the rope! Take . . . the rope . . ."

My voice trails off. So far below me—an impossible distance down from where I lie, coated with scum, soddened and saddened—the moat water is restless, but the water bubbles are ceasing. No matter how desperately I look for those black braids and that harsh face, the broadsword and broader shoulders, all I get is an occasional *balas* tail that slices up and curls back into the murky depths.

And then everything begins to still.

A kind hand lands on my shoulder and I jump. "Fear not. I shall protect you."

Except I don't want the knight in shining armor. I want the mercenary.

"Merc . . ."

Putting my head in my hands, I fall backward and weep as though I've known him all my life. We were so close to getting away. If only he had—

"Fates!" Julion barks.

As I drop my slimed hands, I . . . can't believe what I'm seeing. For reasons I cannot fathom, Merc appears to be riding on the back of a cresting *balas*, the broadsword like a bit between those jaws, his powerful body straddling the back of the neck as he steers the forward motion by jerking on the hilt or the tip by turns. Meanwhile, the *balas* is in an absolute fury at its passenger, and this anger is the propeller that sends them both on this hellfire ride—

He's coming right for me. Right . . . at the wall.

Like he's going to drive that beast—and himself—directly into the stones.

"What are you doing!" I scramble to my feet. "Merc—"

With an athletic surge, Merc jumps up and plants his boots on the knobby spine, balancing as if he surfs upon a board. And then at just the right moment, he yanks the broadsword free of that mouth full of teeth, whips it around—and stabs the *balas* in the rear. As the ugly, red-eyed head arcs up and the body of the monster breaks out of the water, its master leaps forward, one step, two steps, three steps—

He jumps off the nose of the *balas*, throwing himself at the lip of the moat's walling.

Fates, he's not going to make it. As the other *balas* retrench their positions, and form another circle, he's going to smash into the stonework, knock himself out, and fall back into that horrible water and all those yellow teeth.

"Merc!"

At the last moment, when surely he's going to make a full-body impact, he trains the tip of the broadsword at a mortared fissure. The penetration is spot-on, and he double-grips the hilt, lithely swinging his legs up and around—

Just as one of the *balas* launches out of the water after him.

As those jaws snap at nothing but air, Merc is flying free, a perfectly executed tumble planting him upon the grass with both boots under him, and that sword still in the grip of his very sturdy palms.

He's breathing heavily. But he's utterly alive, and smiling like a god.

"Well," Julion remarks, "I did not know one could ride those wretched creatures."

I don't even think. And that, of course, is a fault of mine when it comes to the mercenary.

With a cry of joy, I launch myself at him, and Merc catches me with one arm easily, his laugh so deep and masculine, the satisfaction in it is warmer than the sunlight itself—and he keeps laughing as he swings me around and around, my legs spinning out as I find myself sharing in the happy release.

And then comes the moment of pause, our silly spinning stilling, our faces almost too close together, our bodies totally too close together.

The way Julion clears his throat, we might as well be naked.

As I push myself out of Merc's arms, I flush and then panic about having shown myself. Except there's no worry on that. Punching out my arms, I see nothing of my skin, just muck from the moat. From my face to my feet, I'm covered with congealing slime.

Cloaked in it, one might say.

"So I gather you two are of acquaintance," Julion says with disapproval.

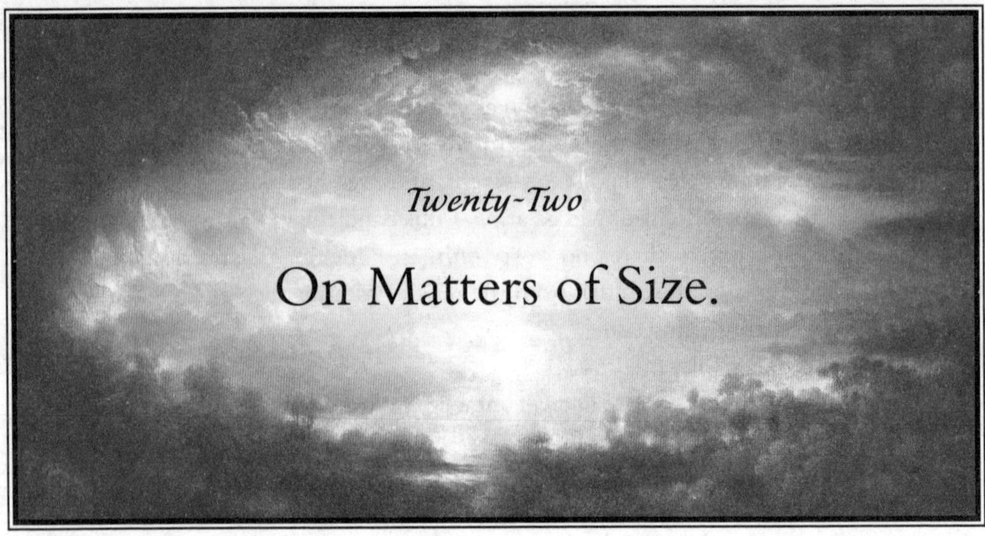

*Twenty-Two*

# On Matters of Size.

Deep in the autumnal woods, behind the thick trunk of a *thimbe* whose leaves have gone red and orange, I'm peeling off my absolutely disgusting underclothes. The chill in the air makes me goose-pimple all over, until I feel for sure my bones have turned to icicles. Julion has given me an entire bladder of fresh water to clean with—for all the good it can do against what coats me—and I grit my teeth, brace myself, and empty the rush over my head—

A beautiful scent blooms around me, of roses and other flowers I have never smelled before.

It's not water.

As a tingling enlivens the root of every strand of my hair, I bring my fingertips to my nose. Then I rub them together. It's an oily substance, astringent in nature, and it's doubling and redoubling. Glancing down my body, the fizzing trail it leaves on the way to my feet generates heat.

I pour the rest of the bladder over my head, closing my eyes and luxuriating in the unexpected gift. Soon enough, I am as covered in the cleanser as I am with the muck, and just as I'm wondering how to rinse off, the solution starts to evaporate. Steaming off my hair and scalp first, the moat's stench and slime leave with it, and I watch my forearm as my freckled skin emerges. When I reach up to my head, I'm surprised to find the locks of white hair dry and fluffy—and as I bring some forward to my nose, the flowered scent lingers.

What would Merc think of it?

As he comes to mind, it seems right that the warmth that's flowed into my body and kindled my internal organs flares up even more. I enjoy the sensation for the moments it lasts, and miss the soothing comfort when it's gone. Ultimately, I'm left cold and aware that I'm bruised and cut in many places.

Time to get dressed, and fortunately, this bathing bounty is not all Julion's provided me. Draped on a branch, there's a pale blue men's undershirt, of such finely spun wool, it's like air. There's also a heavier navy jacket and pair of riding pants, both of which have a pattern on the hems that appears to be sterling silver. Finally, I've been given a turban that is made up of coils of that blue fabric, and accented by more silver stitching.

Shivering, I throw the clothing on. The undershirt is absurdly baggy, and I roll the sleeves up. I have a little better luck with the jodhpurs, as they're meant to fit tightly; they just pool around my ankles and calves. A fine leather strap from Julion's saddlebags slips through the loops to keep the waistband from sliding off my hips, and then I glance at the sodden slop heap of what I had been wearing.

I'll have to somehow fashion a face covering out of something. But I hate the idea of any of it on me now that I'm clean and in fine, dry clothes.

On that note, I turn to the pack. Amazingly, there's a puddle of scum around it, the fabric seeming to reject that which everything I'd had on had absorbed like a sponge. When I bend down to open the throat, I'm also shocked to find the interior is totally dry—

*Hide.*

That old familiar voice cracks like a whip, and as a horse that's drifted off its trot into a walk, I snap back into action and inspect the turban-like hat. Yanking all my hair together, I wind it up high and force the dressing onto my head. Given that it's made up of bands of fabric, I tear free the end of the top layer and the length falls down over my face, buffering the world in a haze of blue. To keep the veil in place, I tuck it into the shirting and finish things with the heavier outer coat.

The last thing I do is take Mare's velvet satchel of coins out of my bloomers. The bag is nothing of its former pristine self, but the coins inside gleam like sunshine. Pouring them all out, I twist, twist, twist the fine material, wringing out the murky sludge. Then I use the very last of what's in Julion's bladder.

Like with me, it's a resurrection.

I refill a dried, clean sack, and tuck it into the inside of the navy coat.

When I step out from behind the tree with the pack over one shoulder, both of the men who are waiting redirect their glowering expressions to me.

"You look like a boy," Merc says dryly.

"She is perfectly dressed for discreet travel—"

"Assuming you want her to get mugged for all that silver."

Julion's jaw works in a circle, as if he's chewing on insults he'd prefer to spit out. Next to him, Merc's staring like he wishes the knight would open his mouth and let it all fly.

To ease the tension, I bow toward Julion. "You're most generous. Thank you."

Julion places his hand over his gleaming gold breastplate and inclines his torso in return. "You are most welcome."

I hand him back the empty bladder. "What, may I ask, is that wash?"

"Oh, is it not lovely? My staff makes it from the garden at the—"

"Not to ruin this chatty conversation," Merc cuts in, "but *may* I remind you that there's a village that still wants you dead. And they live on the far side of that."

His heavy forearm swings around like the boom on a frigate ship, and my eyes follow where he's pointing out of the tree line at the wall.

"Allow me to be of aid." Julion steps in to me and takes my hand. "I have a steed, and a home that is very safe. No one will find you there, and if we leave now, we can be there by sundown—"

Merc closes the distance, too. But instead of gallantly assuming my free palm on the other side, he looms in all his black leather and hard-worn steel. "She and I already have an arrangement. I will see her where she needs to go."

"It's up to her—"

"She's already decided—"

"And she can reconsider—"

"Enough!" As they both eyebrow at me, I shake my head. "Merc is right. He and I have made . . . an arrangement. He is going to ensure my passage to . . . safety."

Not that I expect much of that. Along the way or wherever I end up.

"He's going to get you killed." Julion glares at the other man. "Because he's going to desert you when it's convenient for him or he gets a better offer. That's what men like him do."

"You don't know me, *jyrth*."

I nearly gasp. Not because I'm particularly lady-like—but because even after all my years at the Gauntlet, I've only ever heard that word used once before.

Julion does gasp, and rears up on his spine, like a prized stallion coming to attention. Maybe because one of its shod hooves touches excrement.

"I *beg* your pardon."

"You can beg for whatever you want," Merc drawls. "And something tells me you're probably the kind whose preferences run in that vein. But pardon isn't something you're getting from 'a man like me,' now or ever, and especially when you're in my way."

With a slow, steady draw, Merc unsheathes his broadsword and then begins to idly flip the massive weapon in the air, like it weighs no more than a stick.

Each time he catches the hilt, it smacks against his hand, and I'd be willing to bet my virtue, he's picturing himself paddling Julion's butt each time the sound rings out through the trees. Or worse.

Oh, wait, I've already bartered with my virginity.

"Do you honestly expect me to be impressed by this show?" Julion says with hauteur.

"Well, mine's bigger than yours, so yes, I do—"

"Can you each please stop," I say with exhaustion. Then I turn to Julion. "Thank you, for rescuing us—"

"I rescued myself," Merc cuts in.

My eyes narrow in his vicinity. "And I'm about to toss you back into that moat if you don't cut out the instigating."

His smile is devilish, and he lowers his voice into a stage whisper. "I'd like to see you try. At the very least, I'd enjoy the effort—and I'd make sure you did, too."

I'm muttering under my breath as I refocus on Julion. "Thank you for your concern, and your timely rope."

"Where are you going?" Julion asks.

Merc cuts in front of my voice: "That's none of your concern—"

As I shoot another glare at him, he gets precious, making a little zip-the-mouth, throw-away-the-key motion over his lips. Then he shoots a shimmy in Julion's direction.

For a moment, I picture Merc getting eaten by *balas* after all, while I ride off into the horizon with a golden nobleman who's been so kind.

Julion clears his throat. "So be it, then. But before we part, I will have a word with you." Though I do not meet his eyes, I can sense the nasty look he sends Merc. "*Alone.*"

*Twenty-Three*

# An Invitation Politely Declined.

"He is very protective of you, I shall give him that."

As Merc walks off, his massive shoulders part the orange and red foliage, which appears brown and purple due to the makeshift blue veil I look out of. Even after I can't see him anymore through the trees, I can still sense his presence. Then again, convincing him to leave was harder than getting us out of the moat.

In the silence that follows, my fingertips trace the silver detailing on one of the outer jacket's sleeves. They're so long, the hems hang over my hands, but I'm glad for the warmth.

"He is." Then, even though I know what this is about, I ask the knight, "What is it you wish to speak to me about."

"I need your help."

When Julion doesn't immediately continue, my eyes shift over to his gold breastplate. My distorted reflection stares back at me, the blue turban and the veil, and the silver stitching on the togs, presenting a picture that looks nothing like who I was back inside the wall of my village. This is good camouflage, I tell myself, but not so good that I can remain anywhere near my home.

And then it dawns on me. Julion is alone. I have a thought that he must be good with the—yes, it *is* smaller—sword that's holstered in a bejeweled sheath at his hip. The trip down from Prosperitus is fraught with thieves and bandits, and for certain, he must be confident of his ability to defend himself.

And successful at doing so.

"Tell me," I prompt in a low voice.

"I saw what you did to the dragon." There's a pause, as if Julion wants me to confirm what he witnessed. When I stay silent, he continues, "I have heard of you, a young woman on the fringes of the Prosperitus territory, who can bring people out of the cave of death—"

"That is not me," I lie. "I cannot do anything for you—"

"There's a threat that we face in this Kingdom, one that comes in the darkness, from out of the failing Fulcrum. Surely you have heard the talk. Or perhaps you have seen the carcasses in these very woods."

"You know of our dead cows all the way up in Prosperitus?" I find that hard to believe—

"No, we have our own around the city."

"Demons stalk the court?" I breathe in fear.

"And I did not know you had them, too."

Uttering a curse, Julion begins to pace around, and the gathering sunlight that filters through the colored leaves glints and flashes on his golden armor. His mood becomes grim, his profile drawing into an aggression that shouldn't be a surprise given that he is a fighter.

"The uneasy peace," he says, "that has reigned over Anathos since the Dark King was banished during the Great Containment is hard enough to sustain in times of bounty. The four Kingdoms of the North, South, East, and West are not, and have never been, aligned, for we compete for resources to survive and there is no trust among us. If what I believe is happening is fact rather than myth, there are . . . decisions that must be made for the good of our people, for the good of Prosperitus."

He stops and stares through the branches at the far-off wall of my little village. It's then I notice the dull wafts of smoke that as yet rise up from inside of the barrier's crumbling confines, a reminder that I must go, and the sooner the better in all this daylight.

"There is a very certain courage that I require at this time." The knight looks over his shoulder at me. "One I find I have lost somewhere along the way and cannot access."

"That sort of resurrection is up to you, not anybody else."

"You're wrong. I can find it as long as my love is by my side." Though I am not meeting his dark eyes, I can feel his stare narrow on me. "And that's why I need you. My betrothed is dying. She has . . . days left, if I am lucky. I need you to keep her alive, so that I can serve in the capacity I must for the citizens of Prosperitus—of which you, yourself, are among."

Shaking my head, all I can see is Mare. This nobleman is physically stronger than her, and certainly has more station and resources, but you cannot trust a mob—or predict what they will destroy in their madcap rushes.

"You do not want what is coming after me," I say roughly.

That he gets all regal is not a surprise. "I am afraid of no mortal thing upon Anathos."

"Superstitions make men with weapons and flames very dangerous, particularly in a group."

"And I have an army."

Julion begins to pace again, and I catalogue the weapons on him, thinking also of what that warhorse of his might be carrying. Maybe he's right to be so secure—in the usual course of things. But I fear that version of Anathos went by the wayside some time ago; it's just taken us a while to catch up with the disintegration.

"I saw what you did with the dragon." His voice grows strident, his footfalls turning into stomps that crush the ground cover. "You killed it first. Then you brought it back."

"I did no such thing." Again, the falsity leaves my lips easily. "And I fear your desperation is making you mad—"

"I shall pay you." He stops again and looks across the lengths that separate us. "I am not without means."

"I don't need money, and even if I did, I have nothing but my sincerest sympathy to give you. At any price."

Julion curses and approaches me. "Why are you withholding your gift? You could alter the course of my life and so many others—"

I open my mouth and quote from the Book of Time, or at least as I've overheard it: "'In the right and proper order of things, there is nothing that shall escape the call of death.'"

"Spare me pabulum from the past." He leans in to me, and the energy rolling off him shifts. No more a hero, he becomes an aggressor. "Besides, if you really believed that, you would not have brought the dragon back—"

"That beast spontaneously revived. It happens—"

"After you drove your knife into its throat, and then disappeared from sight right before my eyes. Or did you think I could not see what happened? I witnessed it all, and I need you to save my beloved so that I may do what I must to protect this Kingdom and its citizenry."

Turning my head, I stare through the changed leaves, searching for Merc's black-leathered figure. We should have had a signal for when it was time for him to return. A whistle or something like a birdcall.

"Fates, I do not understand you." Julion wheels his arm about as if he's trying to loosen a knotting in his shoulder. "You are an outcast, with no resources and no one to help you but an unscrupulous man who is out for himself. And I stand before you, prepared to provide you shelter, protection, and money, and you will not give me what you imparted to some dumb monster for free."

I picture the dragon, lying there in the sand, the color gone out of its scales, those boys taunting its pain and beating at its head with sticks.

"People don't tell you 'no' very often, do they," I hear myself say.

This seems to pull him up short. "Indeed, they do not. But then I am not in the habit of asking things of senseless women very often."

"So if I do not acquiesce to your request, I am to be relegated to stupidity?"

"I am offering you *so* much more than you have!" Now he walks around in a tight little circle, as if he's on a lead that's staked to the ground. "In return for a work of . . . compassion and grace in the midst of a cruel and unfair fate. Yet you fight against me—"

"Do you remember the crowd last night?" Anger sharpens my voice. "That mob is what I have been waiting for—and fearing—every moment since I can remember. If I actually possessed the power you say—and I deny having any such thing—and I were to use it to bring anyone in your court back from the grave that awaits them—however unfair that grave is—that violent crowd would absolutely come after you, too. They'd just be wearing your army's uniforms, instead of the tattered clothes of villagers, and their weapons would be so much more than torches and rakes."

He stops dead. "No, they would not."

"You're so sure of yourself."

"You do not know who I am."

"Your ilk is more common than you think." As he tosses his head back and looks at the sky with annoyance, I study his profile in a way I've not been able to do—and recognize him in all his grandeur. The wealthy and beautiful, be they men or women, are a tribe, far apart from the likes of me. "You're a well-bred man of means, who gallivants through his mortal time on Anathos, doing what he wishes, going where he pleases, and bidding others to his whims because he was born to nobility and the court. And he's so certain of his position that what was merely the luck of his birth he ascribes to his own intelligence and doing."

"And you're a commoner with no prospects who's being offered the kind of security a woman of your station cannot even hope to marry."

"Wrong," I snap back at him. "But you're close. I'm a commoner with no prospects who's turning your arrogant offer down—and you should thank me for it. You can't handle what comes with my aid."

After what happened to Mare? I am never, ever drawing on that power again. *Ever.*

"I thought you said you have no special gift," he drawls. Then he says in a very low tone, "I can force you, if I have to."

That uncharacteristic fury within me kindles and I nearly look him in the eye as I start to unbutton his coat: "Try it and see how that goes. Wouldn't beating a woman sit badly upon your spotless conscience."

Abruptly, he covers his eyes and turns away. "What are you doing?"

My fingers attack the fasteners. "I'm giving you your clothes back—"

The high-pitched whinny of a horse cuts through the forest, and we both jerk toward the sound.

"Fates," Julion says bitterly, "your helpful friend better not be stealing my stallion and leaving us both in the lurch."

We take off running. He's in front, cutting through the branches without holding any to the side for the person drafting in his wake. I don't care. I'm shorter than him, and easily duck to keep from getting smacked in the face with the orange and red leaves.

In a clearing not far from where we were, his fine white stallion is tethered to a tree, and Merc is indeed standing before the magnificent warhorse. As he eyes the steed while it throws its head and whips its tail, he does look as if he's sizing up a leap into the saddle, and I wonder if Julion's opinion of the man I've so blindly put my faith in may be closer to the truth than I can bear to admit.

"Off hand thee!" Julion shouts as he breaks out into the knoll.

Merc's head twists in the aristocrat's direction. Then he raises his palms. "I'm not touching anything." After which he assumes a smirk as he measures me. "More than I can say for you, evidently."

I pull the coat back together and hastily redo the buttons. Meanwhile, the stallion keeps mincing in place, those finely shod hooves prancing divots into the ground like it's warming up for a full-out bolt. Julion strides over to the horse and soothes it with a calm stroke on the snorting muzzle and soft words quietly spoken—

With eerie clarity, I see a beautiful young woman with deep brown skin and long, flowing black hair, reclining against silken sheets, fading away.

"I'm very sorry," I say in a hoarse voice.

Julion takes a deep breath and glances over his shoulder, looking through Merc to me. "Please. Help me. There are things . . . I must do that I am unable without her."

All I can do is shake my head and drop my eyes to his finely made riding boots.

"Keep the clothes," he tells me with defeat. "If you change your mind, come to court and ask after me. I shall receive you at once."

As he releases the reins from the branch he wound them around, he says, "Fates be with you."

"May the crescent moon watch over your trail as well," I whisper.

The golden knight mounts with an elegant economy of movement, and the stallion hips backward, clearly not willing to associate with lower-class women and men of questionable scruples for even a heartbeat longer. With a swoop of the reins, Julion turns the warhorse about and gives it free head, those hooves thundering off through the forest for the main road that leads north and east away from my village.

Not that it's mine anymore.

I glance back at Merc, focusing on the beads that are tied on the ends of his braids. Before I can speak, he demands, "How much did he pay you for your service."

"Nothing. Nothing happened—"

"Why are you *so* determined to deny your job."

On the contrary, I'm not going to argue about how those buttons got unfastened. "We must leave now. Before the herders take the sheeplings and cows out to the pastures—"

Merc comes over to me, and even through the muck that covers him, I can smell the cedar fragrance I've become so addicted to.

His scarred hand reaches out and touches the veil over my face. "Did he kiss you? I might have to kill him, you know."

"He has an army," I hear myself say.

"That hasn't stopped me yet." I sense Merc's eyes narrowing. "Is that all he wanted of you? Sex."

I lift my chin and stare off over his shoulder, noting how the blue veil changes the colors of the landscape. "Yes."

"You're lying to me."

After a long, tense moment, Merc backs off with a curse. My deflation is immediate, as if both my heels have been punctured and all of my strength funnels out into the *coney* needles underfoot. I hate the lie, but the truth is so much more complicated—and so much worse.

"The Badlands are a full day on horseback if we don't sleep," he says brusquely. "On foot? We're looking at two without any breaks. So we need to find some of what your noble charge just left on."

When I don't respond, he shoots me a glare. "Don't tell me you can't ride."

I take a deep breath, and say with resignation, "Okay. I won't."

## *Twenty-Four*

# Something to Ride.

"What in the gods' damned fate have you been doing with yourself? You can't swim, you can't ride, what the hell can you do—"

Merc stops himself and puts his palm out. "Never mind. I can guess."

I'm too weary to correct him. The reality, though, is that when you have no one to teach you the ways of the saddle, and nowhere to go, and no money, traveling is not a priority, and swimming is not something you do unless you've fallen in the moat and are trying to save your own life.

As for that vision of the ocean I had? Like so much else, I can't explain it, and don't really care right now. Real problems await, once again.

"I'm willing to try," I offer lamely. "Riding a horse, that is."

With another curse, Merc puts his hands on his hips and stares at the messy ground the knight's stallion chewed up before its departure. Then he looks out toward the road Julion disappeared down. I can just imagine what he's thinking.

"No one's keeping you here," I tell him. "You're free to go."

"You won't survive even the daylight hours without me."

"Maybe that's true, but you're volunteering to do this." I almost want him to leave—just so I don't have to worry about *when* he's going to desert me. "And anyway, aren't you the one talking about letting go of emotion? Stop feeling sorry for me and proceed forth on your own destiny."

As he swivels his head in my direction, I drop my gaze to the ground just before our eyes meet. "Pity is *not* what I feel for you."

His voice is that low, velvety one, and instantly, I remember what he looked like going for the tie on his britches, his sex hardened for me.

Or . . . hardening for any woman. He doesn't even know what I look like.

"I don't understand it," I say under my breath.

"How you've managed to stay alive this long? Neither can I—"

"Sex must be easy to find for a man like you." I almost keep the bitterness out of my tone. "Why barter this mess with me in return for what you could so readily have in any number of beds?"

When there's only silence, it's clear he thinks that's a rhetorical—

"You're different."

My breath stops in my lungs. "Why."

Merc turns away, and I measure the breadth of those shoulders, the tightness of his waist, his spectacular . . .

Well, arse. Not to put too fine a point on it.

He ignores me and looks to the path the knight cut through the brush. "I need a horse. We need a—"

"I know where to go. For one."

I expect him to pivot back around. He doesn't. He stays where he is, still staring off into the trail of the other man, the one that leads to the road that will take anybody far, far away from where we stand now.

"I mean it," I say. "You can go at any time."

After what seems like forever, he shakes his head, the beads on the ends of his braids chiming softly as he turns his back on Julion's way and whatever destiny would await him if he gave in to what he so clearly is contemplating.

"Lead on. Show me to the horses."

As I take off through the branches, I don't bother to see if he's following me. He will or he won't, and even though I'm terrified about being alone, I'll do what I have to because he's wrong. It's not a wonder that I've survived this long. I've survived this long because I've kept a low profile, and if it's left me stunted?

*Hide.*

Better off than dead.

I head away from the sun, penetrating the forest more deeply so that we have a buffer from the village's pastures, and the going is slow, not just because of the dense branches, but because I stop often to listen. The day is already coming into its own and all kinds of people will be moving around soon. We can't risk being seen, and as quietly as we shuffle through the leaves and the undergrowth, I swear we might as well be bringing a trumpeter with us.

I'm also uneasy about taking something that isn't mine. I tell myself that I'll find a way to return what we must borrow—and besides, their owners were going to kill me last night. Surely that creates a certain moral leeway here?

It feels like we go forever, and I even catch a glimpse of the Sooths' Temple, the craggy, gray fortification protecting those sacred women like a mountain rising up in the middle of the forest. But then the meadows to the southwest appear on the far side of the forest rim. The acreage is flat and intersected by clean streams and paths worn into the grass by hooves and feet, the plots of land separated by split-rail fences and generations of ownership.

"We're just in time," I say, pointing out of the branches that shield our presence. "There they are."

Merc steps in beside me. "You've got to be kidding."

I chew my lower lip. "Well, I know they're not horses. But surely they'll do—"

"Those are *donkeys*."

Merc walks out of the trees as if he owns all the land, everywhere. Then again, he isn't hunted, he's a hunter. Following him out of necessity, I draft in the wake of his larger body and remind myself that I'm wearing entirely different clothes, richly adorned clothes with silver threads that would cause poor villagers to duck their eyes in deference.

"We have to be quick," I whisper. "The other herders will be back with—"

"I don't think the entire lot of them could carry me. So this is a waste of time—"

"Not at all." When he glances over his shoulder, I can sense the annoyance in his expression and resent it. "We'll just string four of them abreast, and lay your delicate self across their backs like a fallen tree. I'll walk alongside and make sure they don't get away with you."

There's a pause, and then Merc barks a laugh. The sound carries, and the fawn-colored clutch of donkeys restlessly shift in their pen, their big ears pricking nervously. Courtesy of the sound, we also gather the attention of the guard dogs, who we've been downwind of.

The two enormous brindle canines, which are the size of wolves, rush out from their posts to position themselves between us and their herd.

Their growling is backed up by a great baring of fangs, and smartly, they're solely focused on Merc as the threat.

Cursing, he pulls at his leather surcoat. "I reek of *balas*. That's what they're picking up on." He takes my arm and draws me back into the trees. "If I go at those dogs, I'm going to win, but the fight's going to be loud, and the commotion will attract attention. Also, while I appreciate your efforts on our behalf, I have a better way to get us under the saddle. Stay here."

Naturally, I follow tight on his heels. When he turns around to argue, I put my palm up, right in his face.

Before I can open my mouth, he shakes his head. "Well, what do you know."

"I'm sorry?"

"I don't care enough to fight with you on this," he mutters as he pivots back around. "It's your life. You might even be doing us both a favor if you get yourself killed."

He strides off once more, angling away from the village, and as I bob and weave against branches coming at me, my strength returns, probably because I have something to fight against. If he's going to block my way, he's going to have to use sturdier stuff than this forest I've already cut a path through.

Some ten lengths on, the wide, bouldered river that feeds all the smaller grazing streams cuts in close to us, and Merc takes us to the very edge of the tree line so that I can feel the warmth of the sunlight. As he looks around at the bend in the flow, I measure the forest on the far shore, but no one comes here, so there's no need, really. Water is more easily accessed elsewhere, we are a distance from the travel road, and with the dead cows?

"You better get back in the woods," he says casually.

I step in closer to him for protection. "What have you seen?"

"Unless you want to watch." Merc takes off his pack and then his hand goes to the dirk holstered at his hip. "In which case, you're more than welcome to stay here."

As he takes the weapons belt off, I frown. "What are you doing?"

"I reek of *balas* and need to get the stench off me and my clothes as best I can." He removes his leather surcoat and tosses it to a rock at the shore. "Or most of the domesticated animals, and all of the wild ones, will alert to our presence."

With that, he strips the mesh breast cover away, and goes for those ties on his britches. Flushing, I can feel his eyes on me, as if he's daring me to stay where I am—

I shoot back for the forest so fast, my face smacks into the very leaves I've been defending myself from. Sputtering and shoving branches away, I dive deep into the cooler shadows, and make sure I keep my eyes focused in the opposite direction. I have to give him credit. Given the density of the forest and the way it crowds up to the river edge, this is as safe a bathing place as any—and he's got a point about the animals.

Also, going by all the splashing behind me, I'd say he's making quick work of his very big body . . .

My mind becomes inappropriately sharp as I ascribe all kinds of nudity to him—as well as what those callused hands must look like cupping the water and carrying it to his bare skin. I swear, what my imagination conjures is so vivid, it's as if I'm watching him. I see the droplets falling off the ends of his hair, and rivulets sluicing down the pads of his chest and the hard clench of his abdominals to his—

"Stop it," I hiss.

But . . . I don't.

I can't.

*Twenty-Five*

# Trust Issues.

As I listen to Merc bathing, my sense of direction evaporates even though my inner orientation has always been pretty good: I become totally lost in the familiar woods I've been through my whole life, and that doesn't bode well for the journey that's awaiting me.

And then something occurs to me.

Relieved to have another focus—*any* other—rather than mercenary nudity, I shift the pack off my shoulders and kneel down. My hands shake as I loosen the flap that kept things so tightly sealed, but it's just the cold, I tell myself. Yes, in spite of the sun, the air temperature is quite chilly, especially here in the woods—

"So why won't you tell me what he really wanted?" Merc calls out from his bath.

Shoving my hand inside, I stall. "Who?"

There's a pause in the water noise. "That dandy with the golden halo and air of superiority."

My movements get jerkier as I fish around because all I can feel is the box. Where is the compass in its satchel? And I hate that my first thought is whether Merc has taken it.

"I don't know what you're talking about—"

The washing starts up again, and Merc's voice takes on that tone of dry amusement I'm coming to know very well. "Why did you apologize to him as we left?"

Glancing in his direction, I nearly fall on my face.

He's all the way in the center of the river, the water level at his waist, his bare chest and sculpted abdominals glistening, wet and strong, in the sunlight. Unlike so many of the Gauntlet's clients, he is utterly hairless, nothing obscuring his musculature.

Thus the scars that mark him are obvious.

There are . . . too many of them. And yet the fact he's survived that much makes him seem like a god demoted to be among those of mortal make.

"I just want to know why you said you were sorry," he prompts sardonically as he paddles a palm of water at his pecs.

I shake myself back to attention and continue shoving my hand around inside the pack. "It's nothing that concerns you."

Did he go through *this* while I was passed out in the tunnel? And take the compass? There's no way, with the pack as sturdy as it is and its ties being so tight, that the instrument could have fallen out.

Over in the river, there's a big splash, followed by a slapping sound, as if he's dived under and reemerged with a toss of all that black hair. Even though I try not to, I imagine his long locks coming out of the water in a fan, flipping over his head with a spray of clean droplets . . . and landing on his bare back.

Are there scars there as well?

"Everything about you concerns me," he says brusquely. "Especially if you've made yourself an enemy of the court."

"Julion left us on good accord."

"For now." A scenting now, spicy and pleasing. Soap that he keeps with him? "Is he one of your regulars? That why he was so determined to save you?"

"What would a man of his station want with me—what is that smell?"

"Arrow lily. There's some growing right beside these rocks. It, and all this water, will take care of animals thinking I'm some kind of predator."

Oh . . . great. Now all I can picture is him peeling the first layer of the stalk back with his sharp white teeth, and rubbing the red interior meat all over his—

"You must be very good at your job," he says dryly.

"I'm sorry?"

"For that nobleman to be so concerned with your safety. And I really doubt you have anything to apologize to him for."

When I don't respond, silence flares between us, and I think of the lighted torch we had down below ground, a contained flame that could be destructive under different circumstances. Lack of trust is the same, a warning instinct that can consume.

There's another round of splashing, much quieter, and I have to look again. Merc is cleansing his black shirting now and he's using the contours of his abdominals as a washboard for the thing, rubbing the arrow lily in until frothing bubbles drop into the river. The way the suds flow down and swirl in front of him makes me think about what's right below the surface at the front of his hips.

I have to turn away, but I continue to listen to him as he works on his leather britches and then his weapons.

That he isn't bothered by the cold is a sign of his discipline. That I can't keep my eyes off him is evidence of my lack of self-control.

Finally, he walks out of the river, and there's a series of rustling and clanking, as he gets re-dressed and re-armed.

"You can turn around once again," Merc announces as he hangs his pack off one shoulder. "I have all my naughty bits re-covered."

On the pivot, I mutter through the leaves, "I don't know what you're talking about."

"Courting tackle?" He comes toward me, entering the trees with his dripping leather surcoat hanging off his hand. "Sword and pouches? Hammer and stones—should I continue?"

Reclosing my pack, I sling the weight back onto my shoulders and I cover my ears. "That's more than a sufficiency of terms, thank you."

He's laughing easily now, and even through the cup of my palms, I like the way it sounds. So I drop my hands.

When he's right in front of me, he says, "I need you to stay here—"

"No—"

"—so I can get us a proper horse from the traveling road."

"I'm coming with you—"

"No, you're not."

Crossing my arms over my chest, I think of Julion's warning about him. "Why not."

"Because you're not going to approve of how I do this, and I'm not interested in your opinion. Not unless we can throw a saddle on your censure and ride it out of here." He drops his pack and his surcoat and points at them. "You stay here with these—they're too wet for me to move well with them on. The daylight is properly arrived, and if we don't get you out of here, you'll be where we were last night."

I know he's right. We've already wasted a lot of time, and even though most of the villagers will probably stay within the wall, there'll be those who must venture out—and they'll have weapons on them, I'll bet. Or at the very least, voices to call for people who are armed.

"Don't hurt anyone."

"Of course not," he mutters as he starts to walk off. "Why*ever* would I do that."

I stand there with his soggy things, watching him disappear anew into the trees, and then I'm left alone with my suspicions and my fear. After I look around for a moment, I drop down to my knees by what he's left behind. Flattening out his leather surcoat, I double-check he's still gone . . . then shove my hand in one of the big front pockets—

There's a subtle chiming, and something that crackles? The weapons are . . . too many to count. A length of brass chain. Folding knives (two)—

"Ow," I hiss as I'm stung by something.

Snatching back my hand, a row of pinpricks on my fingertips bloom blood, and I brush them off on my hip before proceeding with greater caution. What spools out is another length of chain, except this one has barbs. Like everything else—and my own knife now—it's clean and very well tended, and it's not hard to picture what it could do around someone's throat.

I glance up again. Look behind myself.

Then I carefully put the thorned steel back, and go through the rest of the surcoat. Every square *nic*. All I find are folds of damp leather that smell like him, arrow lily, and more weapons that can do dreadful things to people.

Absolutely no compass.

Then again, would he have left the instrument here with me if he stole it? Perhaps it's stashed on him somewhere—

A rustling of undergrowth rips my head up, and I flap the surcoat around, trying to remember what it looked like when he dropped the heavy weight. Then I wait, with just my pounding heart to keep me company.

Nothing comes of it, and I eye his pack. Even though he probably did the same to my things, the idea of going through all his possessions makes me distinctly uncomfortable. I go to my own strapped bag again, and this time, instead of just rummaging through it, I pour the contents out—

The satchel is the last thing to fall free, and it hits the ground with a dull thud.

"Thank the crescent moon," I exhale.

Falling back into a sit, I go to work on the plain brown satchel's tie. As my sloppy fingers make messy work, I find myself murmuring, "I was orphaned on the birthing bed and left in the village square where . . ."

As my words dry up, I wonder why I've never noticed that that's as far as I ever get, but then the compass pours out into my hand and everything stops for me.

The weight of the palm-sized instrument registers first, and after that, all I can think about is how ancient it appears to be—yet it's so very well preserved. With covers on both sides, and a release mechanism on the top, the yellow metal of the casing is untarnished, and I wonder if it's made of gold . . . or perhaps just a brass that was polished to perfection before it was stored with care away from the air. What appears to be the front cover is etched with a fine attention to detail, the directions of *North*, *South*, *East*, and *West* spelled out in beautiful cursive. In the center, there is a knobby outline that I know in my gut is Anathos itself.

Squinting, I focus on the area where my little village is located, on the lowest edge of the Kingdom of Prosperitus's territory. Merc said it was a day's ride to the Badlands, and I extrapolate how much farther south I'll have to travel if I'm to make it to the Outpost, which I've heard is the last settlement in that area.

I can't help but notice that the Kingdom of the South is, comparatively, not that far away.

And according to what I've overheard in the pub, there is a warrior queen on that throne who has an appetite for war and will see no one.

Travelers regularly came through our little village and tarried at the Gauntlet for their rest and refreshment, and they've always brought with them news and history from all around Anathos. That queen's reputation proceeds her, to the point where few ever wanted to go all the way south, for she defends what is hers with a fierce army of a thousand mounted soldiers.

I've even heard she feeds her victims to her men.

My thumb hovers over the release button on the compass's top, and as I hesitate, I tell myself if I can survive the tunnel and the moat, surely the effort required to flick the tiny latch is nothing. But I cannot do it. For some reason, I'm frightened of what's inside—

I shove the compass back into the satchel, and go for the box. It's made of wood, and at first I think the grain is stained with an onyx bark solution, but that's not it. Great age has darkened the container, and the little latch that holds the top and bottom together is corroded. I score my fingernail as I try to get the hook free, and just as I'm about to give up, it slips out of its dock.

I have to claw into the seam that runs around the sides of the container, and when I finally pry the box open, the hinges creak—

"What am I looking at . . ." I whisper with awe.

*Twenty-Six*

# Unexpected Travel.

The sunlight that slants in through above hits a collection of black spikes, and as the illumination is refracted up and into my eyes, it's like a rainbow at midnight, all the colors that exist flowing through ribbons of dense darkness.

I've never seen anything like it.

Drawn by the iridescent display, I go to touch what turn out to be crystals—and the pad of my finger is sliced sure as if I've been bitten. As I jerk back my hand, my blood, red and vital, falls in drops that slip down in between the various levels and seem to be absorbed. Even though that can't be right.

"This is not for me," I hear myself say.

The box very nearly shuts on its own, and it's a relief to flip that latch back into place. For good measure, I return the lot of it into the pack and resolve that I will never, ever touch the thing again.

And then I wait some more.

The compass ends up back in my hand. And then my thumb shifts over to the release at the top. Bracing myself for a revelation that is equally mysterious and beautiful, I trigger the mechanism and the top pops open to reveal—

A bog-standard white face with a black arrow and black directional demarcations around the outer edge of the circular face. Nothing special at all. It's not even pointing in the right fashion, for the sun rises in the east and the tidy little pointed head indicates north as I pivot my palm toward the rays that pierce through the treetops.

At least it doesn't try to draw blood.

It's as I'm shutting the cover with disappointment that something stops me. I lean down, staring at the face more closely.

The compass is looking back at me.

That's the only way I can describe the eerie feeling as my gaze becomes captivated by what is actually nothing much, visually speaking. I find myself searching the tidy black N, S, E and W, and the combined letters NE, SE, SW, NW—

Both the hand and the directional markers begin to spin, slowly at first, then faster and faster, and warmth comes with the movement—

The black of the tempered steel changes to red, as if it's gotten hot as a horseshoe newly from the forge.

"Magic . . ." I whisper as I trail my fingertips over the glass.

Folktales have described the force that used to weave through everything on Anathos, and hushed voices have speculated over what the Dark King harvested and corrupted for his evil ways. And indeed, books have recorded both the history and the embellishment of what actually happened. But I've never actually seen any magic outside of the Fulcrum—my strange dances with death notwithstanding.

Maybe not all of the sacred force is in that swirling barrier, after all?

Abruptly, an image of the black bands of contamination and the floating black snow comes to mind, and I think of the root of all evil and his army of demons—

A subtle pull registers on my right side, as if my arm is being tugged. I even jerk my head up, expecting to see Merc hauling me to my feet. I'm alone. And as soon as I look back down at the compass's face, the spinning intensifies until—

*POP!*

The vortex claims me and the world disappears. My only anchor becomes the compass face, and it's no longer standard at all. The simple letters on the outer rim are multiplying, and then they swirl off the instrument, lifting up such that the optical illusion becomes not alphabetical, but . . . linear? Lines, lots of lines, now, that twist in and stretch out, to form a jagged pattern that closes in on itself.

Anathos. It's the pattern that is etched on the front cover.

And beneath the mirage, the now-red directional arm stops.

Tilting forward, I look down through the map until a dot in its center lines up with the anchor for the directional arm . . . and a shiver goes through me. Just as I could pick out my village on the etching, I find my position.

And it's where the arrow is pointing to.

Except it doesn't stay there. As a vibration shimmers into my palm, the red arm slowly swings in a southerly direction.

Until it stops.

On the face of the compass, the original black letters reappear. Dead south. The arm is pointing . . . directly downward.

At the Kingdom of the South.

The journey Mr. Lewis presented me with—

The swirling returns, the flow churning in the opposite direction. Instantly, the magical map disintegrates, the lines are sucked back into the face, and the heat as well disseminates. Another *pop!* sounds somewhere in my head, and I gasp as scents of the forest fill my senses once again—

Something has changed, and alarm rings in my chest.

I'm still in the glen of trees, except I'm no longer sitting on the ground. I'm up on my feet, and a moment of pure panic has me whirling around—

The pack is on my back.

Ripping it off my shoulders, I shove my hand through the bag's throat—

The box is in there, and so is the compass in its satchel.

When did I put the latter back?

That's when I notice the sunlight. Through the canopy's interlaced pattern of leaves, I can tell that the angle is all wrong. No longer low to the horizon, the bright, piercing beams are directly above me.

It's noontime.

"Merc?" I turn about. ". . . Merc?"

As I go to pick up his pack, I grunt as I get it off the ground and settle its weight on my shoulder, and his leather surcoat is just as heavy with all its chains. Neither are as wet anymore, and I worry I've lost not hours, but days.

Paddling through branches with the heavy load, I fumble and trip my way along the forest's maze of trunks, blindly running. I have no idea how far I go or in what direction, but when I hear horses off in the distance I freeze and duck down. Through the branches, the travel road that winds its way around to the entrance of the village is barely visible, but I see enough to assess the men who appear in the distance.

It's our mayor. His plump figure is jiggling in the saddle, with both his threadbare suiting and the faded red banner that proclaims his pitiful status straining to confine his girth. He's flanked by two of his three sons, who function as his personal guards, such as they are. Given how much they share their sire's affection for ale and bread, it's hard to see them offering much defense if the lot of them are set upon, and they also share his current dissatisfaction. None of them seem pleased about whatever outing they've been on, their ruddy faces set in thin-lipped frowns.

I'm guessing this has something to do with me, although I can't imagine they went all the way to Prosperitus to report what happened to the King's court. Besides, they couldn't return this quickly—

Unless I have lost days.

Triangulating their position, I decide no, they've probably just been to the

Temple of the Sooths for advice, and going by their expressions, the foretelling was a grim one—

I sense a presence looming at my rear.

Before I can stop myself, my lips part in a startled scream.

Only the hard palm that slaps over my mouth keeps me silent.

*Twenty-Seven*

# Lies on All Sides.

"Shh—it's me."

Merc's voice is a hiss in my ear, and his chest is a solid wall behind me as he holds me against his body. When his hand drops away from my face, the warmth of his palm lingers on my mouth, and I feel as though the hottest month of summer has calendared in my gut.

He takes what I've been carrying for him as if it weighs nothing. Speaking softly, he demands, "Where the *hell* have you been—"

"Right where you left me—"

"You've been nowhere *near* this forest." He draws his leather surcoat on over the broadsword sheathed on his back. "And what made you decide to come back?"

"I'm telling you," I shoot back at a whisper, "I never left."

"Then why have I been looking for you in these woods for hours?"

"I guess we've just been going in circles."

After that, neither of us moves except to breathe, as the mayor and his sons close in at a slow trot. With every inflation of Merc's lungs, his pecs push the buckles of his holsters and the padded contours of his muscles into me, except I can't let the feel of him consume my thoughts. As much as I've never particularly cared for the mayor—or his sons, who were regulars at the pub and frequently made fun of me—I don't want them to cross paths with us. I can't explain the time loss, but if Merc's still looking for a horse, those men are in his crosshairs. And then what if they see us first? They could alert the entire village—

Out of the corner of my eye, the hilt of Merc's broadsword hovers over his shoulder like a snake head that has risen and is ready to strike.

"Let them go," I say softly as the trio are almost upon us. "There will be other horses."

"These are the first in four hours."

"*Four* hours—"

"Shh."

The horse of the son closest to us snorts, and then the animal stamps to a halt and wrenches about to face us. Its eyes pry wide and lock on our position, and the alert is a contagion that spreads quickly to the other steeds. Forelegs get braced, rumps are raised high, and nervous whinnies percolate like the whimpers of small children on the verge of wailing.

"Oy!" one of the sons shouts as he lurches off-balance. "Stupid horse!"

He digs his spurs into the poor thing's hide, but in so many ways, the animal is smarter than the owner. It refuses to pass and rears up—

The result is a boulder rolling down the side of a mountain, the rider's tumble sluggish and ungainly, the landing a thump that reminds me of a bag of grain hitting the ground. As mud splashes, the horse bolts in the direction they approached from, and the other two members of the little herd take its advice.

Except they are less successful at shifting their loads.

The mayor grabs on to the mane and hunkers down as he tries to keep astride, his combed hair frothing out of its plaster of oils and spiking up like he's been hit by lightning. The other son, who's bearded, is the better rider and manages to keep his seat, but he can't get his mount to go forward.

Both are so consumed with avoiding the mud bath of their blooded relation that they don't notice us.

"Keep my pack," Merc says softly.

As I fumble with the load, he jumps out into the road. This spooks the mayor's horse all over again, and as that fleshy fisted grip is lost, my mercenary snags the reins and takes over. Even as the chestnut bay leaps into the air with all four hooves, he somehow retains control of the steed as the father follows the first son and lands in the mud.

The fact that the sound is the same, and so is the splash, makes me marvel at the way traits are passed down through generations.

The bearded son, who's stayed in the saddle, takes one look at Merc—and then lets his steed have its head. Off he goes, from whence they all came—

"Roy!" the mayor yells after him. "*Roy* . . . !"

So much for the loyalty of progeny. And the father doesn't waste time bemoaning what he's raised: "I carry no coins."

"I'm not here to rob you." Merc keeps a hold on the reins of the panting, panicked horse as he offers the man a hand up and then does the same to the muddy son. "I'm taking—well, borrowing, one of your mounts. You see? Over there?"

The elder and his son look in the direction that he points.

And then it happens so fast, none of us can track the actions.

Between one blink and the next, the two shorter, pudgier men are tied up together with the smooth chain I inspected earlier. I don't know how Merc did it so fast, but the father and son are now back-to-back, their sets of hands wrapped like the hooves of a steer, the chain around their waists.

When Merc's evidently satisfied with his work, he shoves them off-balance, and when they start to topple, he eases them down to the mud once again.

"Do you know who I am?" the mayor asks weakly. As if he's addressing himself in search of courage.

"You said you weren't here to rob us," the son protests.

"I lied." Merc leans down and in a pleasant tone remarks, "Just one of your horses I'll be taking, and I thank you for the good tack—"

"You can't do this!" The son's ruddy complexion goes bright red. "You heathen! I know what you are—"

Instantly, everything about Merc changes, even as his body position doesn't shift—except for the hand that rises up over his shoulder. To the hilt of his broadsword.

"If I were you, I'd be more silent than spoken. And I'll help you with that right now, if you want."

In the midst of my camouflage of leaves, I take a step forward to stop what's about to happen. I'm not going to let these men get slaughtered—

Merc's face whips in my direction just before he unsheathes his weapon. As I shake my head furiously, his fingers flare at the grip. After a tense pause, he drops his arm, the broadsword staying where it is.

Meanwhile, the mayor's son keeps his mouth shut, as if he knows exactly what he was just spared from.

"Someone will come along soon enough." Merc snatches the red sash off the mayor's ballooned torso. "Maybe even before the demons roam after night-fall."

The chestnut horse has settled some, so Merc is able to tuck the ends of the reins into his hip pocket as he bends over the men and wraps their heads together so they're unable to see. I notice he makes a rather nice bow, like they're a present to be unwrapped. And though they would sooner deliver me to flames in the village square, I don't want demons to be what finds them.

Merc motions for me to come forward, and puts his forefinger up to his lips for quiet.

I'm not feeling talkative.

As I slip out from my hiding place with his pack, the chestnut gets mincy again. His flaring nostrils pull at the air—and I can tell when he catches my scent. He eases some, sensing I'm no threat in spite of my odd costume. Or perhaps he's smelled me before from the village and remembers me.

Merc takes his pack, ties it on one side, and mounts with a fluid movement. His control over the animal between his legs is immediate and he extends a hand down to me. I can feel his eyes on me, intense and commanding. Like I'm little different from the horse.

I don't like any of this.

I don't want to ride this stolen animal.

I really don't want Merc's help up.

But there's no way with the mud and no stirrup offered and this being the first time I've ever gone astride that I can get my body where it needs to be on the horse. With an odd disassociation, I watch my own hand extend to his. The instant contact is made, I flush under my blue veil.

And then I'm flying.

Merc hoists me onto the chestnut's rump with what seems like no effort, and I nearly forget to split my legs. The saddle is large and comparted for travel, so there's a place for me behind the contours of the seat, the leather shelf big enough for a bedroll to be tied on. I brace myself to feel unsteady—

The instant I'm in place, I feel as if I've come home.

As unnatural as this should have been, especially as the horse shies from the extra weight it's been asked to carry too far down its spine, I settle and relax. Oddly, the palm of my right hand tingles as if something should be in it.

The reins. I should be holding . . . reins . . .

And that's when it happens.

An image takes over, erasing everything around me.

I'm plunging into the ocean again, that memory of something that never happened returning to me. Except this time, the sequence of the dive runs in reverse. I am sucking out of the entry into the cresting salt water—and landing on the bare back of a sorrel horse that's hooving through the surf and kicking up waves of white spray.

I'm laughing, and the sun is on my face, and my hair is streaming behind me like a flag unfurled. There are no reins in my hands, but rather I hold on to the base of the mane, and in spite of the speed, I am as secure in my seat as if in a solid chair.

I am not hiding. I am free—

"It's not so bad, then." The dry voice brings me back. "And all you have to do is hang on."

The hilt of Merc's broadsword is right in my face, but that doesn't last. As he sets us off at a trot, his battle-hardened hand reaches back and unholsters the weapon from under his surcoat, the metal-on-metal shift ringing close to my ears. I expect him to sit it at his hip.

He keeps it in his palm and down at his side, a reminder of what we are going to face along the way.

We're heading in the same direction the mayor and his sons were traveling, and I glance back over my shoulder. The bound twosome are sitting immobile where we left them, not even trying to get free, and I picture tethered goats, which seems mean.

"Do you really think someone will come along?" I say. "Before nightfall?"

"Doesn't matter to me, one way or another." He glances back toward me, his scarred profile cutting through the backdrop of red-and-orange trees. "Now where the *hell* did you go."

The rhythmic beat of the hooves beneath us seems loud, as does the soft squeaking of the saddle, and I have known all this before: the sensation of the shifting gait of the horse, the swishing of the tail, the way the landscape moves by at a quick rate. As I probe the wheres and whens of the image, a headache blocks me from going any further from the cantering down a coastline I've never seen before and the lithe dive that submerges me in the ocean's warm, salty embrace.

That I have never swum in before—

"*Where* did you go?"

The repeated demand refocuses me.

As I struggle to answer him, the headache fades like a guard dog no longer triggered by a trespasser.

"I had to hide." I look around his heavy upper arm at the well-trodden thoroughfare ahead. "We must have left a trail of sludge out of the moat because a village patrol came searching the forest."

Lying comes at a physical cost. At least for me. Did Merc's throat feel tight back there when he was first reassuring the mayor? Did his lungs burn as he told them they were not going to be robbed?

I doubt it.

"We need to get on to one of the less traveled trails." I try to orient myself properly. "I think there's one up here on the left—"

"Don't do that again."

"Do what."

"You're *not* that stupid."

I almost respond with the truth: That I didn't "do" anything, and if

Merc expects me to promise the strange lapse in time won't repeat, it's impossible for me to take that vow as I don't know what happened in the first place.

Then again, I'm never looking at that compass again. So problem solved.

"Up there," I order him. "Turn off *there*."

## *Twenty-Eight*

# A Chilling Husk Presents Itself.

"Get under my surcoat."

The sharp words rouse me from a doze I'm unaware of having fallen into. As I jerk to attention, I look around. Long gone are any trails or even landscape I might have been familiar with. Now we are on a broad swath of road that cuts through a dense forest, and the shoulders of the packed route have been cleared, as if to prevent kidnapping and the thievery of carriages. There are no more *thimbe* trees with their autumnal foliage, but rather prickly *statchz* set in a craggy and sparse undergrowth. The sun is low in the horizon, on the verge of setting—

*Hide.*

For a moment, I'm confused. The voice in my head doesn't sound right—

Merc twists in the saddle and hisses, "Duck under, will you. You've got to *hide*."

The gathering cold flushes out of me, and in what has become a practiced maneuver, I pull up the back of his leather coat and dive beneath the heavy weight. The next breath I take is heaven. All I can smell is him, and as I turn my face to the side and rest my cheek against the valley of his spine, I slip my arms up the rippled flanks of his torso.

The first time I did this, we were approached by a brisk pair of riders dressed in royal garb. When Merc gave the order to go under the surcoat, I didn't know what to do with my hands. As I fumbled, he solved my problem with an under-the-breath order to just disappear them, he didn't care where. So I ran my arms up the sides of him, and was shocked by how the thin material of the long shirt he wears hid nothing. And it hides nothing now. I'm just used to fitting myself to him, and feeling his torso.

He's so warm. And hard all over.

Closing my eyes, I pray to the crescent moon for our safe passage, and realize that's such a stupid entreaty given we're going to a place that I've heard is more dangerous than the treacherous roads and territory we've got to cross to get to it: The Outpost in the Badlands is a savage place. But at least Merc's authority and control have never wavered yet. Though I bow to the aches and stiffness all over me, though I have flagged and fallen into exhaustion in spite of our precarious situation, he's remained alert and prepared to fight.

Pride's the only reason I haven't asked him how much farther—

Three horses pass us—or at least it sounds like more than a pair. Merc says something to whoever it is, the rumble in his chest transmitting into me, and my panic returns. Word will have spread throughout Prosperitus about what happened at the Fulcrum with those boys—

"All right," Merc clips.

With reluctance, I release my hold on him and leave the cocoon. When the cold air hits me, I tremble from the temperature change and a curse floats back from him.

"We've got to stop before it gets too dark."

"Here?" I offer. Even though I have no idea where we are.

"Somewhere."

The blooming of peaches and pinks in the western sky announces the day's grand finale of illumination, and soon enough, a moody gloaming takes over. With every blink, more light drains, and even though my eyes adjust, there are way too many shadows in those spiky, evil trees on our periphery.

And then the true darkness arrives.

My instincts prickle and my stare scans the borders of the road, seeking sets of glowing red eyes while my ears drown out the sounds of hooves and leather tack, in favor of a growl or a snort.

What do demons sound like—

"Trust the horse," Merc says. "He's going to alert before we do."

I must have spoken that out loud.

We press on because we must, the road seeming to go on forever, the landscape offering us no true shelter or coverage. Time condenses into a focal point of the persistent present, no future ahead of us, no past behind. Only the single heartbeat of each moment repeating to the beat of the horse's plodding gait.

At least the tension that coils in my gut chases away the chill that's settled into my bones.

Overhead, the three-quarter moon rises, but offers little illumination to go on, as if it's determined to remain neutral with regard to our travel and destiny. A strange desperation grips me, unlike anything I've felt before: I know the safety I yearn for will not magically appear whenever we find a place to shelter ourselves for the night. We will still be out on our own, and in the best course of things, we'll only be attacked by robbers or a landowner defending his—

All at once, we round a curve and the forest gives way to a meadowed valley that seems big as Anathos itself. The terrain change is so abrupt, I wonder if I'm dreaming as I look out over the fields that unfurl like carpet to the base of a mountain range far to the southwest. In the moonlight, the long grasses are cast in shades of palest blue, and I know it's not just because of my veil. In the autumnal daytime, the thread-thin stalks are yellow instead of green, the seasonal change having come upon them. The lunar light, however, is an artist who paints with platinum and steel rays, and along with those delicate blades, the road ahead, and even ourselves, glow in the cool palette of the night sky.

"There."

Merc points with his broadsword to a settlement cluster halfway between where we are and the first of the snowcapped summits. The farmhouses are too small in number to count as a village, too many to be a single homesteader, and I'm hoping the inhabitants have it in their hearts to welcome strangers.

Given the tenor of things, I doubt it—so I don't bother to ask if it's safe to approach. The answer is no.

It's a better shot than risking demons in the forest, however.

Merc stays at the ready as he urges our tired horse on. He doesn't ask for a trotting, just as he's stopped twice at streams to make sure that the chestnut is offered a drink. We all need a rest and some food.

"I don't want to steal anything else," I warn.

"We'll see."

The farther along we go, the more exposed I feel out in the open. And yet when we were surrounded by trees, I was surely stalked.

Spoiled for choice.

Merc scans the fields, and here in the open, the moon does give the eye something to work with. After I measure that bright star that nearly throws its own shadows, I vacillate between jerking my head over my shoulder to make sure there's nothing coming up behind us, and fixating on the outcropping of buildings as it grows larger and larger.

And then I only look at what's coming.

There's something wrong with the settlement, and as I narrow my eyes to tease out what it is, a chill of warning tickles the back of my neck. And then a strange scent blows our way, the acrid sting in the air making me sneeze.

It's not until we are halfway across the meadows that I realize it is a proper town. But most of the structures . . . they've been—

"Quite a fire," Merc remarks.

"Oh . . . dearest *fates* . . ."

So many of the homes and stables have been burned to the ground, only a couple of surviving structures remaining at the far edge of what turns out to be quite a large community. And then it dawns on me.

"Is this Fielkirk?" I whisper. "How can this be?"

"You know the town?"

"I do—I mean, I've never been here. But they would come to us on market days with grains and hay on offer. Crafts and clothing, too. What happened?"

I try to recall what the men and women looked like, but of course, I didn't spend much time on their faces. I do remember thinking that their clothes were just like our own, and so were their accents, and now I wish they'd had a wall to protect them, even if its mortar was breaking down in places.

And a moat. And *balas*.

Soon enough, our horse's hooves cross over onto scorched earth, the flames having spread out from the core to the grazing fields on the perimeter. Yet the stink of ash and smoke is not too overpowering. This happened a week ago at least, and there has been plenty of cold rain since. Fates, though, the fire must have been an inferno. The burned carcasses of cattle and sheeplings break my heart, their charred ribs still retaining shape, the ghostly spaces where internal organs had once been like the rafters and chimneys that are the remains of the homes in the distance.

"Who did this?"

Merc offers no answer, but as if he'd have any? He pulls up on the reins, and the chestnut docilely halts. Then, for the first time since we started out, he twists in the saddle, and I'm forced to turn with him or risk getting pushed off by the breadth of his shoulders. In a slow swivel, he pivots all the way back around, like an owl.

"We have to stop, but I don't like this."

"Has any part of this journey been enjoyable," I mutter.

"Oh, I can think of one."

As I flush under my blue veil, he sets us off once more, and soon we are passing by the first of the burned-out homes. The stony foundation remains in place, charred, but otherwise solid, and the same is true for the hearth and its spine of bricks. Some boards and rafters have survived, although they are burned into ragged points. Personal belongings, however, are almost exclusively reduced to ash, although a cluster of overturned kettles and pots around the fireplace undulate beneath the blanket of soot, the table they were on no match for the inferno they were able to withstand.

We pass a couple of variations of this, but then less and less of the structures remain, until we arrive at what must have been the center of the fire. Here, not even the mortar could beat the heat, the foundations naught but rubble, all the wood and textiles consumed, even the chimneys crumbled—

The snort of our horse makes me jump, and the chestnut shakes his head as if the pungent stink is irritating his nose, too. As the reins jangle loudly, I look to the snow-covered peaks far to our west and wonder if the sounds will awaken the dragons in their moonlit lairs.

At last, we come out to the far side, reaching the houses that are still standing. It's obvious the blaze was carried by a northwesterly wind, for here, the damage is nothing but blackened stucco and closed, toasted shutters.

Merc pulls us to a halt in front of a two-story home that, given the flashes of paint up under the eaves of the tile roof, was painted with an elaborate pattern of lozenges. Everything else on the exterior has been stained with soot.

"Stay on the horse," he orders as he throws a leg forward over our steed's mane and drops to the ground. "We can't lose him, not that he's got any run left."

The reins are pushed into my hands, and I gather them on reflex.

He frowns. "You hold them right for someone who's never been in the saddle before."

"I . . ."

My voice drifts into a tense silence as Merc squares off at the front door, his broadsword up.

Just as he makes his approach, the smoke-stained panels open.

## *Twenty-Nine*

# Water for the Parched.

Merc stops in his tracks and sinks down into his thighs, his body collected and ready to pounce. Through the crack at the jamb, the interior is darker than the moonlit night around us, so nothing is revealed. When no attack comes, Merc presses forward. I figure he'll open the door the rest of the way with the tip of the broadsword. He doesn't. He double-fists the hilt of the weapon and punches out his boot, kicking the thing wide.

There is a sharp *clap!* and he catches the panels on the rebound.

"Be careful," I whisper as he enters.

In his absence, our horse comes alive, its ears twitching front and back, its tail swishing. There's no stamping of hooves, but I know that's from exhaustion. He'd be rearing up if he had the energy, and all because he wants to stick with our protector—

I jerk around. Scan what's behind us.

The lane that we've come through on is marked with our lone hoofprints, the scuffing marks in the soot making me think of the black snow drifting from the Fulcrum. I know that the containment is quite far from here, but if the demons are already around my village?

They have to be here, too.

Merc reemerges with his sword still at attention, but his stance out of that crouch. "Nothing."

But he's not at ease as he comes over and offers me his hand. I shake my head and slip down to the ground on my own. My legs immediately protest the weight they're expected to support, and I think of the animal who's so faithfully carried us.

Merc and I go for the saddle girth at the same time.

"No," I tell him. "You need to worry about what's around us. Let me take care of him."

I glance at that open door as I free his pack, and let it fall to the ground. Then I go to work on the buckles under the flaps of leather. Peeling the saddle and woolen pad off reveals a block of sweat in the horse's short hair, and the groan of relief and the full-body shake that comes next make me feel both better and worse on his behalf.

We're just going to have to do more tomorrow.

"Take him inside." Merc is over at the far corner of the house, looking around it. "I'll bring the saddle in, but first I'm going to try to find an uncontaminated water source."

As I glance at the horse, I'm careful to focus only on its muzzle. The last thing I need is to learn that it's slaughtered by a demon while that sweat stain is still drying. I've got enough to be terrified about in this burned husk of a settlement already.

"Come on," I say, and tug on the reins.

The horse follows me, even though it has to duck its head and the narrow jambs brush its flanks. Then again, it's probably been brought indoors during very frigid nights on occasion, and after the ordeal of these hours, it's come to trust us out of necessity.

Or maybe it's more like attrition.

After I close us in, my eyes adjust, but only to the extent that I'm able to make out the contours of things. It's similar to the way the ash cover coated what survived the blaze, no distinct edges on anything, just shapes: a table and a couple of chairs in front of a hearth, a collection of cooking supplies, and then an orderly lineup of heavy coats hanging on hooks. In the far corner, a set of steep stairs leads to the second level.

I stare at the ceiling, my ears straining. As the horse drops its head to the floorboards and nuzzles around as if hoping to find some hay somewhere, I try to drown out the soft sounds.

We wait. And wait some more.

My anxiety returns with a tingling that starts at the nape of my neck and flows down into my arms. The go-nowhere warning redoubles until my chest feels as if it's going to explode. I'm so far from home, such as it was, and I miss my hovel under the stairs as if it's a family member off to war.

Except I'm the one out here in the cold night, aren't I.

Pacing around, I cross my arms and blow out my breath. I make a circle around the interior. And another. And another—

Merc's going to need a bucket.

The conviction comes out of nowhere, and is the kind of rescuer I didn't see coming. I've had attacks of panic my entire life, and nothing has ever derailed them. Ever.

In this moment, though, the urge to help Merc gives me . . . a job. And as I start to look around for something that we can fill with water, my flare of terror begins to subside: My brain's focus shifts to something of greater import than the impotent fear that's been my constant shackle for as long as I can remember.

This is a private triumph that may well have legs. If I can derail the fear now? Maybe I can do it in other situations when I am crippled.

All I evidently have to do is focus on keeping us alive. And fate knows I'll have plenty of opportunities to practice this between here and the Outpost.

Shaky, but resolved, I go to the hearth area and start patting around a series of wall shelves with my hands. In the darkness, searching by touch reminds me of my home under the steps, where things were always dim. I easily recognize cups and plates, rough forks, the sharp blade of a kitchen knife. A pot. A—

The door opens with a creak and I spin around.

Merc is in the doorway and he has two buckets with him. "Found water."

He goes over to the horse, and puts one of the loads down. As the chestnut drops his head and drinks with abandon, I fumble to find some cups.

"Don't bother, come here."

As he holds up the bucket, I go over and lower my lips to the wooden rim. Breathing in, I smell nothing at all, and a test sip reveals a sweet clean taste that makes me whimper. I ape the horse, but force myself to stop before I am satiated so there's plenty left for—

"Keep going," Merc says softly. "I had my fill out there to make sure it was safe."

He always puts me first, I think as I continue to drink.

Before my emotions get too far ahead, I remember what Julion said. As it was a lifetime ago, the golden knight's concerns seem like they were about two completely different people than my mercenary and me.

Giving my thirst free rein, Merc keeps tilting things forward as I swallow. When I finally straighten, I glance up and stop my gaze at the tail end of one of his braids.

"Thank you."

He nods and puts the bucket down. Going over to the horse, he strips off the bridle and there's another good shake, after which the chestnut clops over to a corner and lowers its head. A moment later, one of its back hooves turns up.

"We need to find food for all of us." Merc starts going through cupboards. "There has to be some around here."

An offended squeak reminds me that rats are everywhere, and the scurry of small rodent feet depresses me, even though there are bigger and better things to be discouraged about. Still, even after you lose your leg, a shard of glass in your remaining foot hurts, and sometimes the brain can only process bites of tragedy, as opposed to the whole rancid meal.

I hurry to join him, working the lower level of things.

All we find are rats and food too spoiled or nibbled at to eat—

When I stumble, I don't even try to right my balance and fall to the floor. With my hip ringing in pain, I just lie where I land, my head happening to fall on my angled arm. Oh, how nice.

Comfort, like beauty, is relative.

"Are you dead or just overjoyed at being off your feet."

Focusing on the tips of his boots, I marvel at how he keeps going. "A bit of both."

"Fair enough." Merc goes over to the door. "I'm going to have a wash-up."

"What's in your hand?"

"What I believe to be a bar of soap. Either that or it's a fragrant rock."

He departs, leaving me and the horse to ourselves. The idea that Merc is out somewhere behind the house, getting naked and pumping the handle of a well in the moonlight, gives me a burst of energy and I sit back up.

My ears listen for falling water, and so keen are they, the silence around me crackles. Getting to my feet, I shuffle around, and I swear I catch a whiff of something cedarish. The horse doesn't seem to notice me or any scent. Is it possible to pass out while standing up? As time spools out, I yawn and wonder if I won't try that theory myself—

The door opens again and I breathe in deep. "Oh, that soap . . . smells good."

"Do you want a go?" Merc shuts things, and puts our saddle down. "It's cold out there, but I could carry some buckets in so you're away of the wind."

I bring my sleeve up to my nose. Whatever that oil of Julion's was, its scent still lingers. "I think not."

"I wasn't going to recommend it. There's a chill even in here."

"You're cold?" I shift around. "Maybe I can start a fire—"

"Let's try for some sleep."

"But we could warm ourselves by the hearth? There's wood set."

"We can't risk any smoke coming out of the chimney. I'll be fine."

Merc doesn't lower himself down in front of the door. He throws himself onto the floor as a dog would, all sharp impacts that don't seem to bother him as he settles himself with his back against the panels and his legs outstretched and his broadsword in his hand.

As he stares across at me, his face seems to glow as if it's in moonlight, though there's no illumination inside because all the windows are shuttered.

What's he thinking of?

"Tomorrow's another long day." He crosses his ankles, the heavy blade of his weapon bisecting his thighs. "And we don't know what the rest of this night brings."

After he falls silent, I pick a spot by the cold hearth and lower myself down with a groan. All of my muscles are freezing up, and when they stop cramping, I steal a glance in his direction. Even though it's very dim, and I refuse to get anywhere near his eyes, I can tell he's exhausted. There are lines carved in those harsh, handsome features that haven't been there before, evidence of the exhaustion he's hiding from me.

Maybe hiding from himself.

He's utterly spent.

My eyes travel to the bucket—the one he held for me to drink from.

"Thank you," I say softly.

A quiet snore weaves through the still air between us, and I return to staring at him. His body is powerful, even at rest, and I have no doubt that if anything or anybody tried to come at us, he would spring up and fight to the death to keep us alive. I also know that he'd hate to think anybody watched him in his repose, and the stolen intimacy warms me in spite of the temperature.

Or maybe that's the desire I feel for him. Even though I'm also tired beyond measure, I'm acutely aware that we are alone in this house, and I have a thirst for more of what we shared in the tunnel.

On that note, I close my eyes, and breathe deep. But it's not to relax and try to find repose.

I love the smell of him.

*Thirty*

# The Veil Is Dropped.

Something wakes me.

The thudding sound comes again as I lift my head, and my sluggish brain can't place the disruption, even as it provides an instant awareness of where I am. As I look to the door through my blue veil, the darkness is so dense, it's a tangible solid.

"Merc?"

Except I know he's not here. I can sense his absence, even as I plumb the void for the shadows of his broad chest and his long legs.

I'm alone. In the wasteland of the burned village.

Fear hits me like a physical blow, and I paddle at the floor with my feet and hands to stand up. "*Merc.*"

My body is stiff and unbalanced, and when I'm finally vertical, the shivering that rattles my teeth and my limbs is a reminder of just how far the temperature continued to drop. I rub my upper arms to generate warmth as my eyes trace the doorjambs. Wan gray moonlight seeps in through cracks in the planks. Dawn isn't even close—

He's out with demons.

Merc heard something outside and was ambushed when he went to check on the sound.

An internal roaring knocks out my sense of hearing, and as I begin to choke on panic, that thin covering over my face thickens into a sodden woolen blanket. Batting at the fold that falls from the turban, I open my mouth to get more air in, and when that doesn't help, I have a sudden paranoia that the water was contaminated and I've been poisoned.

With shaking hands, I tear the veil off my head, and yank in some deep, unrestricted breaths. My head begins to spin, and as I throw out a hand, I catch my balance on the ash-dusted wall. The air is instantly filled with fine particles, and it turns out that makeshift face cover offered my nose and throat a kind of protection. Coughing, I feel like I have to run. Run fast and far. Where am I going, though?

And what awaits me if I leave this abandoned house—

Abruptly, I frown.

Wait . . . am I dreaming? *Is this real?* I glance around again, noting the horse in the corner—and brace for the chestnut to turn toward me with its eyes glowing red from an evil possession. Even though the steed does no such thing, I think of the old wives in the village, who always warned that however frightening the dark of night can be, it's nothing compared to the dangers of the dream world. There, the demons are not alive so they can't be killed when they come out of the shadows—

"Merc, where are you," I beg the silence.

Unable to stay where I am, terrified of what I'll find outside, I start for the door, the toes of my slipper shoes hitting objects that rattle as I kick them out of my way. I don't care about the noise. I want something to come at me, so at least I can stop worrying about when it will—

The door swings open, and lunar light streams in, blinding me.

I gasp. Or wait . . . someone else does.

"Merc?"

By the width of those shoulders and the scent of cedar soap, I know it's him. Except he just stands there in the jambs, his one hand on the door's handle, his other raised with that broadsword in his grip.

"Where have you been?" I say hoarsely, my breath coming out in clouds that pass through the moonbeams.

The tip of the broadsword slowly lowers. Then he continues to stay where he is, staring at me, even though he should shut the door.

Not that that flimsy wood can protect us from much.

"Are you all right?" I take another step forward, kicking something else that clangs. "Are you injured? What happen—"

He wrenches around, ducking his head and putting his free hand out to stop me. "Your veil."

"What?"

"Veil! *Your veil.*"

I stop in confusion, and that's when I hear the thud for a third time. It turns out to just be the horse, stamping a hoof as he repositions himself in the corner. That's what woke me up.

And in a similar way, the sound brings me fully to my senses.

With a squeak, I reach up to my head. The length of fabric that I draped over my face is back on the floorboards where I ripped the thing off.

"Did you put it back," Merc demands in a rough voice. "Can I turn around."

My eyes return to the heft of him. His torso is twisted about on his hips, the leather surcoat stretched tight across his shoulders, his thighs thick with leashed power. In the moonlight, his black hair gleams in shades of navy blue and brilliant silver.

*Hide.*

Suddenly, I feel as though I'm back in the water of the moat, my body flailing and weightless, my lungs burning with suffocation: For all my life, I've listened to the voice in my head, I've heeded the warning. I have . . . behaved.

But now I'm here, in the night. In this burned-out village.

In danger from whence I came, facing only danger to which I go.

I'm done with the hiding.

"Sorrel, is your veil back in place?"

"Yes," I whisper, as, for reasons that make no sense, I suddenly feel more calm than at any other time in my life.

Merc exhales a long, deep breath, and the tension in him eases as he uncoils and turns back around—

He freezes once more.

I can tell nothing of his expression, for the illumination that streams in from behind him turns him into a shadow, and blinds me where I stand.

"You lie," he says in a voice so deep, it's nearly inaudible.

There's a long moment, and I have the distinct impression he's giving me time to reconsider and re-cover. Keeping my eyes on his boots, I lift my chin, by way of answering.

Merc continues to stare at me as he reaches behind himself and shuts the door. The moonlight is cut off by inches, as if it's a living thing and being slowly killed, and when the darkness consumes us both, I find myself shivering again.

But it's not from the cold.

I'm ashamed.

I know how odd I look. I kept a shard of mirror in my nook beneath the stairs, and from time to time, I'd take a glance at myself, expecting something to change: Colorless, wavy hair, that I have never cut, not once, and keep pinned up in a knot at my nape. Skin that is freckled. Features that are unremarkable. Eyes that are such a pale gray, only the rim of them defines the iris.

Never have I seen anyone who resembles me. Clearly, that's the same for Merc, and as things remain silent between us, I regret revealing myself. Did I honestly think that my attraction to him meant he'd feel the same as soon as he saw me? As if there aren't enough undercurrents in our awkwardly constructed partnership—

"Why."

The word he speaks lingers between us like smoke in a cave.

"I don't know," I mumble.

"Yes, you do."

His voice has a different tone than I've heard, and not just because it's a full octave lower than usual. No, this is something else.

"At least now I know why you hide yourself." There's a long pause. "You are . . ."

When he stops there and clears his throat, I touch my face as if it's someone else's. The idea he thinks I'm ugly has me backing up, bending down . . . picking up the thin blue cloth from where it drifted into the soot.

"There's no reason to put that back on." His tone is brisk now, and I hear the weapons he wears on his body shifting in their metal holsters as he resettles on the floor against the door. "Besides, it's dark as the inside of a hat in here. I see nothing."

Before I can sit back down in my own spot, I go over to where the coats are hanging on pegs. I know that the night will only grow colder as it goes on, so I take one of them off its wall secure. The folds of wool smell like smoke, and there's something that seems all wrong about putting on a stranger's clothing. But I have to get some sleep, and it certainly seems like winter as I lower myself back down and tuck my knees up to my chest.

Silence. So much . . . silence.

The weight on my shoulders reminds me of my cloaks, and I look at the length of cloth I've used to cover my face. It's thin as a wisp in my hand, and I marvel at how such a delicate thing can be so powerful. Shame makes me want to drape myself in bolts of heavy fabric, but something deep within me rebels at that.

I've always felt as though I had to hide, and not just because of that voice in my head or all the things I've done in my village in secret. There was another level to it, I've just never bothered to look into why—and I don't have the answer for that now. But I am clear that I'm done. I'm tired of suffocating under fabric, especially as we head off into a territory where no one knows me or what I can do.

And if Merc thinks I'm that hard to look at, then his eyes can go elsewhere.

Winding my arms around my steep-angled legs, I let the piece of turban fall back to the floor.

"Where did you go?" I ask.

"I do rounds to ensure our safety." Now, his tone goes dry: "Such as it is.

Go to sleep. We have about three more hours before the sun's up, and we'd be wise to head off as soon as we can see properly. I'd like to enter the Badlands in broad daylight and we're still hours away."

There's a determined exhale, and I don't know whether it's about continuing the journey before us, or him trying to follow his own order to sleep.

"Stop thinking," he says.

"You cannot read my mind," I snap. "And I'm not thinking of anything."

A grunt comes back at me. "Sleep . . ."

There's another word after that one, spoken so softly, it barely travels. Yet my ears in all their straining hear it well enough.

*Woman*, he calls me.

*Thirty-One*

# A Harvest of Sorrow.

When I wake up again, the morning has finally arrived. All of the windows and doors leak threads of the dawn's light, the closed shutters not nearly as tightly fit as I thought. Merc and the horse are gone, but his pack and his leather surcoat are by the door next to the saddle, so I know he hasn't left me.

Or at least . . . I can't imagine he'd leave without so much of his gear.

Rubbing my eyes, I get to my feet and stretch, my bones realigning themselves in a series of pops and snaps. As I look around, my face registers the subtle currents of the drafts in the room, and it feels good for my nose to be unfettered, my eyes to be unobstructed, my skin to feel the air, even with all the ash. When I bring up my hand to brush some wisps of hair back, another part of the turban unwinds, and on reflex, I start to pull the length over my forehead and nose.

I stop myself. And tuck the soft fabric back into the twist from which it came.

Then I go for the door, following the path of footfalls in the soot made by Merc going in and out during the night.

With the early daylight coming in so many kinds of gaps, it's impossible not to properly notice the overturned chairs, the dishes that are broken, the things that have been scattered around. Whoever owns—or owned—this house left in a hurry, which is what one would do when a fire has broken out in your neighbors' places and you want to save as much as you can of your things. Even though I don't know the people, I picture the merchants who traveled to my village, and pray they're okay.

A gust of wind blows against the house, whistling through the seams, and making the shutters vibrate against their—

One of them rips open, and light pours in.

The massive blood splatter is to the left of the doorway, under the window.

Most of it's on the floor, but there's a splash up the wall that speckles the glass panes . . . as if someone with many injuries was thrown there on a surge of great violence. Most of the stain is brown, indicating that a number of days have passed since the incident, but what marks the window remains a brilliant, bracing red.

Fates, that was a tremendous amount of blood. And with a feeling of piercing dread, I pivot around—

My hand rises to my mouth and locks on. There's another stain over by the hearth, big as a puddle in a lane after it's rained for nearly a week.

Right where I've been sitting all night long.

With a feeling of foreboding, I walk over to the stairs to the second floor. I fear what I'll see up there, yet I can't stop my feet as they mount the creaking, soot-dusted steps. Rounding the rough-hewn bannister, I look across an open, raftered space that's streaming with sunshine. Another set of shutters has blown open . . . so the rust-stained quilts on the tiny bed and even smaller crib are cruelly visible.

The parents were killed downstairs. The children up here.

Did they hear their mother and father fighting off the intruders? The breaking of furniture and the scattering of things down below?

Squeezing my eyes shut, I moan in the back of my throat, and my descent back down the stairs is a trip and fall that nearly lands me on my head. With a shuddering shamble, I bolt out the door—

The ruination from the fire overwhelms me.

In the shadows of the night, when I was worried about being ambushed, it was bad enough. But now the devastation is unlike anything I've ever seen before, and all I can do is imagine the heat and the flames, the people and animals panicked and fleeing and burning alive . . .

Except that's not the way it happened, was it.

And when I put it all together, I'm even more horrified.

Across the narrow lane, a beam of sunlight at a low angle rounds the corner of another house that's managed to survive . . . and the brown marking on the stucco beside the door is highlighted as if something unseen is demanding I pay attention to the symbol.

The sloppy swirl was made in a counterclockwise direction, given where the brush ran out of blood. The drips that flow down from the design suggest it was done in a hurry, and I know, even before I pivot around, that the same marking is going to be beside the door I've just come out of.

It is.

As I turn to the lane we rode in on, and look at all the burned-out shells, I don't need to inspect any of the other surviving structures to know that they've been marked with the symbol as well. It's an *S* and a *P*, intertwined.

Salvation and Protection.

I've only ever heard about the dark-magic warning before. Supposedly, it's made with the blood of a goat or other cloven-hooved animal that's slaughtered in a prescribed way. What it means is that someone came through here, killed the farmers and their families, along with all the livestock, and then marked the little community as contaminated with evil.

And everything was burned to the ground because when they stacked the bodies and doused them with the same oil used in the lamps in Mr. Lewis's pub . . . the fire was so hot, so intense, so big, that it spread throughout the buildings.

The goal was to incinerate the people's remains, not the houses.

"Merc . . . ?" As I call out, it feels as though I am forever saying his name in that pleading tone of voice. "Where are you?"

I have to find him. I cannot be alone in all of this revelation, though surely he knows what's transpired here, too.

Assuming he hasn't left me.

As I set to walking, ash squeaks under the soles of my slipper shoes, and the smell of faded smoke and dead bodies becomes all that I know, the noxious combination staining the insides of my nose and dripping down the back of my throat. Falling into a run in spite of how stiff I am, I try to outpace the stench.

And then I don't think any more about it . . . or anything else.

I pass by the final two houses and a long view to northwest unfurls before me. But instead of the fenced-in grazing pasture and then the outer rolling farm fields, it is the lone figure standing in the midst of the grass that draws all my attention.

Merc has his back to me. His black hair is waving in the wind that blows into him, and he's bathed in the golden light of the dawning sun, the broadsword in his hand glinting silver. Beside him, our horse is cropping great yanks of green blades, tethered by a lead line looped around his chestnut neck.

I'm tempted to call Merc's name, but something chokes the syllable in my throat.

I've never seen the man so still, and I worry he's spotted something dangerous off in the distance. I scan the horizon, all the way to the slopes of the snowcapped mountains to our west. The sheer breadth of the vista is unlike anything I've ever seen before, and a sense of vertigo threatens to upend my balance.

There is nothing moving in the landscape. Nothing coming at him . . . or me.

Meanwhile, he just continues to stay planted there like a statue, his focus unwavering, that eerie lack of motion making me wonder if he's noted the symbols by the doors, knows what they mean—and is disturbed by where we've had to rest the night. Yet that makes little sense. He's a mercenary who's traveled anywhere and everywhere to maim or kill on behalf of whoever can pay him most. He has seen such violence before, in one form or another.

May have even committed it from time to time.

As moments pass and dread curdles my gut, I figure I should leave him be. But I should know better than to think I can be sensible when it comes to the man. Unable to stop myself, I step through a fence's open gate and proceed into a pasture that's intersected by a sluggish stream.

He doesn't turn toward me. Not even as I surmount the rounded back of a rickety bridge, my steps causing creaks as I cross the crystal-clear water. The horse hears my approach, however, and cranes his neck around for a brief, disinterested glance—before he resumes his vigorous munching with a nicker.

And still Merc doesn't seem to notice I'm here.

Pausing to look around again, all I see between us and the mountains are fields planted with crops that were not harvested before the first frost that hit this territory mere nights before, the gourds and melons bruised and browned out, the leaves shriveled up—

Merc drops the lead and starts walking away, as if in a trance. When he gets to the two-rail fence that contains the farming plot, he sheathes his broadsword, ducks through, and continues over to the first of the planted rows. Crouching down, he pushes his hand into the dark soil. As clumps fall through his fingers, his head rises again to the distance.

Wherever he's gone in his mind, it's not for the company of others to witness. And because of this, I cannot turn away. I circle to the right, until I catch sight of his profile—

The anguish on his face carves new features into the planes and angles I've become so familiar with. He seems twice his age now, and exhausted to the point of illness. Instead of bending down by choice, he appears crushed by burdens so heavy, even he can no longer bear their weight.

A single tear trembles at the corner of his scarred eye, tangling in his long black lashes.

And I'm wrong. His gaze isn't on the horizon.

It's on the crops. He's staring at the cultivated rows of plants, and if I didn't know better, I'd say he was regretting the loss as if he were the farmer who had nurtured it all—

The tear makes its escape and travels the slope of his cheek into the hollow underneath his hard jaw. He doesn't brush it away, even as it slips down the side of his throat. He doesn't seem to notice he's crying any more than he does me or the horse.

The image of him staring out with such yearning over that which had been carefully tilled and tended should have been touching. Except he's not a farmer. He's dressed for war. And those plants have borne food that is now inedible because the people who should have harvested and consumed the vegetables are all dead.

So it's a scene of sorrow and loss, a cautionary visual of what happens when violence enters a community.

"What ails you," I say softly.

Merc wheels around, and for once, his hands don't go for his weapons and he makes no aggressive response. He puts his arms up defensively, bracing for blows, and in the process, falls backward into one of the rows, crushing the shriveled leaves and rotten vegetables.

As he shrinks away from me, I almost meet his eyes—and for once, it's not what I don't want to know about a person that saves me. I want to afford him some privacy.

But it's too late for that, isn't it.

"I'm sorry." I fan out my hands, and try to look unthreatening. Not much of a stretch, really. "I'm . . . I was just worried about you."

All he does is stare over at me, like his mind is fighting the reality that's just intruded on wherever he was.

Later, much, much later, I will reflect that this is where I started to fall in love with him. At the moment, I'm too concerned to think much about what I'm feeling. All I know with surety is I have suddenly seen that he and I have something in common: Underneath my cloak and his strength, we are not as dissimilar as I thought.

He, too, suffers in his own way.

"What are you doing here." Merc's voice cracks and now he scrubs at his face like he's trying to get feeling back in it. "Why are you—"

"I saw that the horse was gone."

"And you thought Julion is right about me and I took off."

His head turns toward the field once more. When he doesn't say anything, and makes no moves to get to his feet, I take a few steps in his direction.

"Talk to me, Merc." As a strand of white hair waves into my face, I pull it away with impatience. "How can I help you."

It's a while before he answers: "I was a farmer, once." He digs his hand into the soil again and clenches another fist full of the rich, dark crumble. "Before . . . I became something else."

"You don't have to live and die by the purchased sword." There's no response to that, so I press, "Can you not return to the north? Surely there is vacant land in the place I know you love. I heard the longing in your voice when you spoke of the mountains and the trees there."

His reply, when it eventually comes, is low and carries a kind of defeat that I do not associate with his strength: "You know nothing of me."

"You're wrong." When he shakes his head, I counter, "I've only been able to survive as I have by judging the people around me, especially the men. And you can decide where you go and what you do, more so than most people."

"There is no going back for me."

I think about what he said to me in the tunnel. "Then make a different forward."

"I can't."

"Why."

"Because of you." He casts the soil aside, surges to his feet, and impatiently brushes his palm off on the seat of his britches. "I'll meet you back at the house. We leave soonest, but the horse needs to eat more."

Maybe that's true. That's not why he wants to stay out here alone, though. "All right."

While I turn away, his vacant expression as he looks toward the horizon haunts me, the kind of thing I know I will never forget.

Both of our veils have dropped.

But only one of us is prepared to acknowledge this.

*Thirty-Two*

# One Final Parting Gift.

I'm sitting on the stoop of the house next to the saddle, our packs, and his surcoat when Merc finally returns. I don't look up at the man or the horse, because I'm afraid of what's showing on my face. With me no longer hiding behind a hood or a veil, I'm going to have to work on composing myself when I'm anything but composed.

And I'm not talking about what I found upstairs. No doubt he saw the bloodstains on the first floor, too, and as if more would be a surprise?

Merc clears his throat. "You look ready to go."

Getting to my feet, I brush off the seat of my makeshift pants and glance back at the door. "I collected any food that seemed remotely edible in a sack, and I found two water bladders and filled them. But I'm not sure whether we shouldn't leave it all behind—"

"Don't worry about the symbols." The horse shakes his head as if in disagreement. "They don't mean anything."

Is he serious? "Only enough to ensure the violent deaths of every living thing here."

"I'm referring to whether we should be concerned with contamination. All three of us drank the water last night. Dark magic goes there first. If this place was actually cursed, we'd feel it by now."

"Or be dead," I say with horror.

"And we didn't eat any of the crops that were poisoned."

"I thought . . . that was frost."

"No. All the grass is still alive."

Fates. But at least he sounds like he's back in control, as if whatever happened at that field was left behind with the ruined vegetables and wilted leaves.

"We're in this together, Sorrel," he says brusquely as he saddles up the chestnut.

"At least until the Badlands."

There's a pause. "Yes, that's right."

I nod, as if we've reshaken on our agreement.

"I'll just be getting my things, then—"

"They're right here." I'm surprised he hasn't noticed. "So. Shall we saddle up?"

He says something that I don't catch, and then he's over at the pile I made of his things. With sure hands, he takes off the shoulder holster that mounts the broadsword on his back, pulls his surcoat on over the steel mesh on his chest, and then restraps the weapon's heavy weight. While he's tying his pack on the side where it was yesterday, I go to put on my own, and stop as the wool coat I've been wearing since last night registers.

My eyes shift again to the *S* and *P* marking by the entry.

Before I can think too much, I take the coat off and go back into the house. As I return it to its place on the peg, I take a last look around. My eyes linger on the bloodstains. I don't want to wear the clothing of a dead man, as if a violent mortal event is something you can catch, like a cold.

Back outside, I feel Merc watching me as I pick up my pack and put it on. I don't wait for him to help me onto the chestnut. With a move that feels practiced, even though I have no conscious recollection of doing it before, I jump, find the stirrup with my left foot, and swing my right leg over the horse's rump. My weight finds the back ledge I was on before as if I were made for the saddle or the latter was made for me.

"Well, you've come a long way."

The comment is a throwaway from him, made as he puts his boot where my slipper shoe just was and mounts by swinging his leg forward, over the mane.

As he unsheathes his broadsword and sets us off, the words linger.

I start to think about all the things I've done that I couldn't possibly have imagined as recently as a day ago: I've swum to freedom, I've ridden a horse—I helped kill a *balas*, for fate's sake. I've eaten meat, traveled a great distance, run when I had to, hidden when I needed to, survived the forest, the night, the daybreak . . .

My own panic.

My no longer hiding my face.

And I've been kissed.

I've also lost the only friend I've ever had, the only home I've ever known, and the relative safety of the village wall. And my own past, as well. Or at least . . . what I thought it to be—

No, I still have that. Because I refuse to believe anything Mr. Lewis told me or charged me to do.

As we link up with the road we will take to the Badlands, I remember the night I was out in the rain, all alone, trying to get to Mare's and being sidetracked by the farrier. I had no idea the wild changes that were in store for me. And now I'm pressing forward into a territory that even the village blowhards spoke of with fear in their voices.

With a man who's a dangerous stranger. Well, not really a stranger anymore.

While I consider my current reality, the strangest conversion takes place. Before all this, the sole strength I had was rooted in the gift I've never understood. It's only ever been in my dance with the deaths of others that I've felt powerful. Outside of that, I was indeed a mouse among rats, weak, scared, scampering for cover in hopes of being left alone, yet painfully lonely in my exile.

But I had it all wrong. My gift doesn't give me strength: I felt that way when I used it because it was the only time I claimed my own power.

This horrible journey is forcing me to find resilience.

So I have been strong.

Which means . . .

I *am* strong.

And as I look out ahead of Merc's shoulder, at the road that continues past the burned settlement toward the mountains, I know that where we're headed next, things are just going to get ever more dangerous and deadly.

*Bring it on,* I vow as a curling aggression settles in my gut.

Bring. It. On.

*Part Three*

# The Badlands

A Gathering of Allies.

*Thirty-Three*

# Humor in a Hard Landscape.

The lush green valley continues for what seems like an eternity, running parallel to the mountains that I expected us to have to find our way up and over. Instead, the road we are on proceeds along the base of the great, craggy elevations, and under other circumstances, the ride might have been rather enjoyable what with all the fair, lovely weather, and the amiable amble of our steed.

That all changes.

Abruptly, the grasses disappear and the ground level declines into an inhospitable territory of gray rocks. No more trees or vegetation, no humidity, no streams or rivers. All we have are clusters of boulders, some big enough that the trail must wind around them, others of varying sizes from ones you could build a wall with all the way down to pebbles and sand.

The temperature changes, too, as the sun becomes unrelenting rather than pleasant. It's risen ever higher and higher in the piercing blue sky, but the heat that gathers around us like the cinch on a sack is about more than just the strength of the rays. The baking dryness is a different climate entirely, a summer's day at high noon that never fades and is never relieved by a rain shower.

Merc keeps our pace slow and steady, and he stops to offer our horse one of our two bladders of water. The poor thing drinks all of it. Merc then holds off for himself and tells me to sip from the other. I decline. I'm sure I'll regret this later, but if he's not drinking, I'm not drinking.

As we resume our progress, we don't talk much—which isn't to say there hasn't been conversation of sorts. My brain fills the silence with all kinds of exchanges between the pair of us, and I dub in his side of things as I wish he would respond. I have to wonder how close the fake past I create for him tracks the actual one he's led—

"How're you back there?"

His deep voice cuts through the plodding of the horse's hooves and the creak of all the tack. And even though he's asked this with some regularity, I jerk to attention like he's never addressed me before.

"Ah, yes, fine. You?"

Babble, babble, babble, I think to myself.

"We've made good time." His head cranes up to the persistent blue sky. "We should be arriving at the Outpost by late afternoon."

Though he seems quite satisfied with our progress, I'm crushed by the idea that I'm going to be on the back of this saddle for what surely will be another four hours at least. I've got chafing where a woman would prefer to have absolutely none, I'm hungry and nauseous at the same time, and my tailbone is numb. You'd think that last one would be a benefit, but it isn't. It's the precursor to a stunning pain that's surely going to come when circulation resumes.

Meanwhile, I'm not certain Merc's fatigued at all. His roaming gaze never stills, his broadsword never dips down, his grip on the reins never relaxes. In this, he's as hard as this unforgiving landscape we're trudging through. I'm grateful.

It's also hard not to resent the strength a little.

As he falls silent once more, I twist around and look over the chestnut's ample rump. The way behind us is the way ahead is the way off to the east and the west.

Rocks. Rocks. And more . . . rocks. As far as the eye can see.

I didn't know there were so many shades of gray, and gone is my previous captivation with the breadth of the vista. Still, the summits of the peaks to the west do gleam like diamonds in all the sunlight, and I tell myself that I can see the dragons circling round their nests. I'm not sure whether that's an illusion created by the waves of heat, however.

"Anybody riding up on us?" Merc demands some time later.

I search the sharp black shadows thrown by the sunlight hitting the cluster of boulders we just passed. There isn't enough space to hide in the fissures and crevices—at least, not if you're bigger than a sheepling. Our only real risk, it seems to me, is an ambush set in the lee of one of these larger groupings, but with our ability to see so far and wide, whatever threat would have to have been in place well before we arrived.

"No one." I turn back around to look ahead, down the trail of gray sand. "And I can understand why this isn't a well-traveled route."

Given what I'm escaping, not crossing paths with a single soul is arguably a good thing, be it beast or man. The isolation is intimidating, though.

As my mind nibbles on whether to worry about how far we are from water and shelter, a familiar tension grips my ribs, and I begin to feel as though I can't breathe—and maybe it's a symptom of my weariness, but I'm annoyed at the anxiety. How a wide-open landscape can make me feel so claustrophobic is a new one—

"This used to be a vast lake."

As I home in on Merc's voice, I'm beyond grateful he's talking. "Really?"

"Yes." Merc points off to the left with the broadsword, then sweeps the horizon up and over the horse's bobbing head and lolling ears. "This is the Lake of Lost Souls. You can see the old shoreline all around us. And check out the marking toward the tops of these tall rocks we pass by. That's the old level of the water."

Even though I've been looking around for hours, this is a revelation that now seems too obvious to have been missed. We've indeed descended into a massive basin of sorts, the distant edges of which nudge up in every direction. Instantly, my mind recasts the landscape, and I imagine an ocean's worth of water filling the depression, with boats under sail navigating around the rocky protrusions, far, far above from this stone-filled bottom.

"I didn't notice," I murmur.

"A landscape never lies." His head swivels back and forth as he scans. "The signs of what has come before are written in the topography, the soil, the stones themselves. These clues are a physical manifestation of the passage of centuries."

I recall him spearing into the soil with his hand, and try once again to picture his life before he learned how to wield that broadsword. Farmers are not fighters, not unless they're defending their land, I suppose. I don't think he'll ever tell me much more about himself, and I crave his secrets like they're a meal I can consume.

Then again . . . I also wonder some about my own.

"What will you do after we get to the Outpost?" I ask.

"Whatever comes next." His laugh has an edge. "There's always work for a man like me in a place like that."

From what I understand, the Badlands is a catch-all name for this stretch of territory that runs between the southernmost edge of the Kingdom of Prosperitus and the outskirts of the Kingdom of the South.

"You've been before?" I ask.

"Its reputation is well-known."

He's right about that. Back at the pub, I overheard travelers talk about the town and its debauchery, and I can remember thinking that I was glad I would never have to go there. Ah, fate.

"I have two rules for you at the Outpost," Merc announces. "And we might as well get them straight before we're anywhere near that place."

Maybe it's the heat. Maybe it's my hunger. But I become churlish at his attitude. "I do believe I am in charge—"

"Rule one. We're going to stay together while I'm there."

I frown. "I'm sorry . . . what?"

His head turns to the left, his profile briefly carving an outline through the vista. "You and I will be in the same room."

Stiffening in my seat, I mostly keep the bitterness out of my voice. "Still interested in collecting on our deal?"

"It's about safety, not sex."

So I'm right. He's changed his mind and doesn't want me. "You still think anybody else would lust after me? I'm flattered."

"What's that supposed to mean."

"I'd guess that my natural attributes are deterrent enough. Now that I've decided to be done with facial coverings."

Merc reorients forward again. "I don't know what you're about."

"How am I going to pay you?" I wonder aloud. "If sex is off the table?"

Merc pulls the horse to a halt, and swings his leg over the chestnut's mane to drop to the ground. As he lands, he does that thing with his hands, clapping his torso under his surcoat, at his hips, then his right thigh, left thigh. He's absently checking for his weapons.

"Yes?" I prompt when he just looks around.

After what feels like too long, he turns back to me and our horse. "Rule number two—"

"I haven't agreed to the first one—"

"You will cover your head again as soon as we get in range."

This takes my breath away. And I want to keep the raw emotion to myself, I really do. But as I lower my head, my voice comes out small and soft.

"You are . . . that ashamed, then."

But come on. A man not finding me attractive isn't nearly as hard as nearly drowning in a submerged tunnel or almost dying in a moat. Or falling off a horse. Or being eaten by demons, cursed by black magic, lost on the way to the Badlands—

"Well, too bad," I answer for myself. "I like the air on these features of mine, such as they are, so you're just going to have to deal with it. If you have a difficulty being seen with me, we can part ways anywhere you wish."

In the periphery of my vision, I absorb the details of him, and am struck by an absolutely penetrating conviction that he's about to leave me and the horse—and I swear to the crescent moon that he'll do it by disappearing into thin air, as if he's an alter I've conjured in my mind, rather than a living, breathing person—

The chuckling that rumbles out of his broad chest is the very last response I expect from him.

And then he laughs at me properly.

*Thirty-Four*

# Whereupon We Are Both Fishermen and Bait.

"What are you laughing at."

When Merc ignores me, I dismount and lower down next to him. "I said, what are you—"

"I heard. You weren't exactly shouting from a rooftop up there."

Finally, he looks at me. As I have to lower my eyes, I'm not completely sure what he focuses on, and that's probably a good thing.

"I didn't fancy you one who liked to fish." His voice is smooth, too smooth. "But I don't mind being caught, if it's on my terms."

The next thing I know he's stepping up to me and sheathing his broadsword on his back. Then he reaches his long arm out toward my face.

"What are you doing?" I say hoarsely.

By way of answer, his hand circles round to the back of my head, and I feel a tugging at my nape. My hair uncoils as if it has been waiting all these years just for this liberation, and he pulls part of the heavy twist over my shoulder. In the sunlight, there's the slightest golden cast to the deepest waves, but most of it is cloud white.

As Merc's fingers fan out and comb through my hair, it's as if he's moving in slow motion, and I notice every scar on them and also that his nails are blunted and clean. And though I imagined him leaving me just moments before this, now I can never see us parting. It's as if we were always supposed to be here, in this barren wasteland, standing beside this tired, stolen horse, with him touching my—

"Give me your hand."

His voice is a low command in my ear, and before I can think why I shouldn't, I give him what he wants. The contact is gentle, and the calluses from his sword grip rasp against my skin as he guides my palm downward. I don't understand what he's doing—

My hand is turned around and pressed in between his legs . . . onto the very large, very hard ridge that fills out the front of his leather britches.

Instantly, he releases his hold of me, his arms raising up as though I'm trying to rob him with a musket.

As my palm stays right where it is, he growls, "There are many things you can question about me. Morals, scruples, the very air in my lungs. But never doubt that I want you."

"How?" I whisper. "Why . . ."

His fingers return to the ends of my pale hair, and I marvel at how his hands of war can be so careful with me. Then his touch travels upward. He brushes my cheek with his knuckles and concludes with a pass of his thumb over my lower lip.

"How can I not?" He smiles, just a little. "I've never seen anybody like you before—and I knew that before I ever saw your face."

On some level, I can't believe I'm standing here with him like this, and I sternly order my hand to remove itself and go elsewhere. Anywhere. Unfortunately, my palm does not find this order commanding in the slightest. Instead, I press into him, exploring the contours of his arousal, the length and thickness of his shaft, the blunt head of him, the—

The hiss is such a surprise, I nearly meet Merc's eyes, but as my gaze stops at his mouth, I see what I'm doing to him. His teeth are gritted, the front ones so white and straight, his canines prominent with their points. The grimace on his face suggests that I'm hurting him.

The throb of his arousal tells me I'm not.

After all, I may be a virgin, but some things are self-explanatory, even for the uninitiated—

Merc steps back sharply. Turns away. Cocks one leg out to the side and sinks down, while both his arms disappear in front of his hips. There are a couple of grunts as he rearranges things, and all I want, all I care about—Badlands, and the Lake of Lost Souls be damned—is to race around and watch him.

Is that callused hand inside the britches? Or is he attempting to relieve a very critical constriction from an external approach—

Merc curses under his breath and starts to walk off, that broadsword returning to the palm that put my mine where it . . . went.

"You're not leaving me then?" I say.

He glances over his shoulder, and I swear he's rolling his eyes at me. "What do you think."

With casual, brutal grace, he begins to flip the broadsword in the air, the honed blade spinning in the sunlight before the hilt is caught. I'm momentarily distracted by the show of coordination and strength—as well as the very real possibility that if he misjudges the re-grip, he's going to hack off his forearm.

"Well, you could be running off," I remark.

"Oh, yes. That'll happen, sure." He tosses the broadsword behind his back and over his shoulder, catching it with both hands this time. Then he weaves the blade through the hot air in front of him, as if he's parrying and jousting with an invisible foe. "At least you don't have to worry about me taking that horse. If I try and get up into the saddle now, I'll be a gelding."

I wince as he throws the blade behind and over his shoulder again. "Isn't that more an issue with the testicles?"

"Oh, I've got one there, too. Trust me."

"You sure are walking funny."

Another glare comes lancing in my direction, and to back it up, he points the broadsword's tip at me. "You try to sit astride with a log shoved in your pants. Then you can talk to me about—"

We both see the attack at the same time. An enormous black bird of prey, the size of one of the trestle tables from the pub, has come out of nowhere, and is shooting down toward us from the brilliant blue sky like a tear in the fabric of space and time itself. Its wingspan is easily twice as long as I am tall, and with a black beak sharp as a—

"Get in the saddle," Merc barks. "Now!"

I don't think twice. I leap up onto the horse and gather the reins, pulling the gelding around.

"Go! You go!"

"What? No, come with—"

"I'm too heavy!" Merc cuts me off with a slash of that sword. "He needs to run like your lives depend on it! I stay, you go—"

A horrible, high-pitched scream pierces through the entire landscape, as if the ear-numbing sound emanates from everywhere, all at once.

*"Go!"*

Merc smacks the chestnut's rump with the flat plane of his broadsword, but our steed doesn't need the encouragement. As if it's heard what Merc's said and taken the order to heart, the chestnut bolts off at a dead run—

I'm nearly thrown out of the saddle from the sudden burst of speed, and my attempt to stay aboard overcorrects the problem and makes things worse. As I lurch to the far side, my left slipper shoe, which has no heel or firm sole, shoves out the front of the stirrup such that my ankle becomes trapped. This sends me even further off-balance until I nearly pitch off the racing steed—

Beneath the blur of hooves, loose gray stones flash by, and I can already feel my skull raking over them until I black out from blood loss—

Through the galloping rear legs, I look back and catch sight of Merc standing braced with his broadsword angled toward the sky, as if he's declared war on a thunderbolt send to smite him. In his black leather clothes, and with his black hair blown back from his harsh face by the hot, dry wind, it seems as if he's the only possible match for what is coming: Directly above him, the massive bird of prey is crying out in its meteoric descent, and Merc is yelling back, man and winged beast squaring off and prepared to battle to the death.

With their collision course locked in, and the distance collapsing to nothing at all, the avian predator abruptly changes its position. Throwing out its massive wings, it treats the air as a solid—

And brings its full set of deadly sharp talons forward.

As if Merc is a fish about to be plucked from a pond.

## *Thirty-Five*

# The Air Assault.

In spite of the galloping speed and my utter lack of purchase, I've got to regain my seat if I'm going to help Merc. Throwing my hand out, I manage to lock a grip on the pommel, and then I don't know how, but I drag myself back up and into balance on the saddle. There's no time to catch my breath, no time to capture the other stirrup.

As if it's second nature, I haul the horse around and stay fused with my seat. The chestnut bucks and rears as it gets an idea of what I'm going to ask it to do, still I wind a grip into its mane, squeeze my thighs, and dig my heels into its flanks.

The great black bird attacking Merc is a horrible sight, as if all of the shadows in the dry lakebed have coalesced into one menace, but he's an equal force as he wields the broadsword in a great heave at just the right time. Sparks flash and scatter as talons meet forged steel, and the bird angles off—only to promptly return. Merc is ready for it. He twirls around, black leather surcoat flaring out, his raven hair like the great vulture's feathers.

Another strike, another parry. More sparks.

And I'm still so far away.

The horse fights me, and keeping us on track to intersect the fight is a battle of my own—especially as there's another round of metal lightning, those viciously sharp talons streaking along the broadsword's blade. Heart in my throat, I pray for Merc's strength as his arms bulge from the effort to hold off the attack. I have no thought of my own safety as I thunder to him, and also no plan—

The bird swoops down once again, and Merc manages to nick its belly just before he must duck and roll to avoid having his head severed from his spine by a slash of those knifed feet. A great cry of frustration rings out from the bird, and there's no pause for Merc to get back up and reset his position.

I can see what's going to happen. As he rolls over to defend himself, the bird's going to go for his belly.

And rip him open like what happened to those cows.

I yank back on the reins, and as the horse lets out a whinny of terror, I don't understand why the black-winged attacker doesn't seem to notice us.

It only has eyes for Merc—

And that's when I see the air beast's feral stare in my peripheral vision. Though I cannot—and will not—get a full picture of its eyes, they seem to be just planes of white in slits of black.

That are locked on the flashing of the broadsword.

The bird is all but blind, and every time the sunlight catches Merc's blade, it knows where he is. That's what brought the scourge to us, the frustrated show of toss-and-catch with the honed steel weapon.

I form no conscious thought, and yet I move with purpose: I shove my hand into the pocket of the navy outer coat and take out my little knife.

The one that Merc cleaned and polished for me with such care.

The instant my blade catches the sun's rays there's an amplification of light that I've never seen before. For reasons I can't explain, the composition of polished metal not just reflects them, it refracts the illumination into an explosion of rainbowed colors so brilliant, I have to look away or be blinded—

Though my eyes squeeze shut, I know by the horrible call of the winged predator that its attention has been secured.

That and the way my horse shies away with a violent shove of his hindquarters.

Even without the use of either stirrup, I manage to stay astride, my body absorbing the jolting whirl on a wave that channels the energy from my hips, up my spine, and out of my barely tethered skull. Then I go low over the horse's neck and give him his head, letting the gelding thunder away from the bird.

While I hold that little knife over my shoulder.

"No, Sorrel, no!" Merc screams hoarsely as I leave him behind.

Great buffers of wind push at me from the downstrokes of the bird's wings, my hair whipping back from the galloping speed, shoving forward as my attacker swoops in above me with a great flap of its wings, whipping back again. At this point, the folly of my impulse becomes clear. In the next heartbeat, the air beast will be upon me, and I have nothing to defend myself with—

The downward attack occurs, and out of the corner of my eye, I see one of the black talons up close. The claw is nearly as thick as my wrist, and as pointed as an iron spike—

My hair is caught and yanked, my head ripped to the side, my torso forced to go with it. Though I need every hold I've got, my hand slips free of the mane and I feel myself getting lifted from the bolting horse—

The knife.

Re-angling my arm, I shove the blade into the tangle of hair that's been caught, and brace myself for a ragged gnawing to cut through—

Merc has sharpened the knife to such a degree that it slices through the thick rope of locks with no effort from me at all. The instant the tie is cut, the release pitches me backward in the saddle so that my head bounces on the surging rump of the horse.

I also get an upshot view of the bird as it circles and zeroes in on me once more.

Even as I bounce and jostle from the gelding's violent, panicked strides, I become frozen at the sight above me.

My stomach is what's going to be ripped open. And as soon as I hit the ground, I'm going to be snatched and carried back to a nest or a feeding spot, my muscles and fat and very bones nutrition for—

Gritting my teeth, I clench all the muscles in my body and drag myself upright against the rush of air. We're not going to outrun this. Sooner, not later, the horse will either stumble or it'll slow such that a perfect alignment can be made between those talons and my shoulders—

Even through the roar in my ears, the shattering, careening call is right over me once again, those beating wings creating their own gale-force winds.

Up ahead, there's a rock formation created by a tumble of boulders bigger than my valiant horse and the nightmare bird combined.

Angling the reins into the side of the chestnut's neck, I force a reroute toward what once was an island. As our course is altered, I bring the knife across to my left. It's nearly impossible to control any part of my body outside of maintaining my position in the saddle—nearly. With a similar focus to what saved me from being dragged to death, I bend my knee up and expose the stirrup strap.

As my little blade slices through the hardy leather quick as a gasp, I free what's trapped my foot from its tether and resolve to never, ever allow the thing to become dull again.

Putting the reflective knife back up over my shoulder—

My arm is gored.

I cry out in agony, but I don't lose my little weapon. I also don't lose my attacker, and that's the plan. The bird, showing no signs of fatigue, abruptly switches tactics, angling around and coming at us from the front. I have another full view of its outstretched black wings, their span such that the whole of the horizon is blocked out, and also of its slashing talons, and its straining black beak—

Waves. The ocean.

All at once, the vision that made no sense first in the moat, and then when I initially sat astride the gelding, returns to me. It's so vivid, so clear, I can taste the salt spray in my mouth, feel the sorrel horse running free under me—

Reality snaps back into focus and I release my hold of the reins.

With a punch down into the stirrup that remains, I leap free of the saddle, going airborne with a coordination I shouldn't possess. And as I dive through the air toward the stony ground, I have the thought that this is even more stupid than me going to help Merc in the first place.

That bird wasn't going to be able to pick up and carry me and a horse.

Just me? Well, that's lunch, is it not.

Somehow, I roll myself in midair and land in a run, as if I've practiced this maneuver—which I most certainly have not. I keep going with as much speed as I can, the knife with the light show over my head, my legs churning strongly even though I've been in the saddle for two straight days. The stirrup I cut clanks on my ankle, the strap flaps against my lower leg, and I can feel my own blood from where I'm injured at the arm, but these are very minor details as the bird tracks me, not the horse.

I'm easier to catch, but more than that, I have the lure.

I've never run so fast. Especially not with one arm over my head—

My feet lose traction all at once and slip out from under me. Just as I go down, I flip around. The bird is making what surely will be its final pass, coming at me like something that is avenging a wrong I once committed.

Reaching down deep into my marrow, I gather the very last of my strength and throw the knife as hard as I can at the boulders that are but three lengths away.

And are the same gray as everything else.

End over end the knife travels, each alternating cycle of handle and blade a mini-variation of what Merc had been doing, the rhythmic flaring what I hope, what I pray, will be enough. It isn't. Once again, the black wingspan eclipses all my vision, and the black-feathered scourge comes upon me. There's no time to roll in a ball and protect my inner organs. I'm laid out, about to be flayed out—

At the last possible moment, the bird veers away.

And follows the brilliant rippling light.

I roll on my side, just in time to see the knife skittle into a fissure between two boulders. The bird doesn't lead with its talons this time. The head extends forward and its neck thins out as the wings duck in against the body and its speed redoubles.

So it's nearly at the velocity of a free fall—

As the winged predator slams into the rocks.

The cracking impact is as loud as its call, the snapping of its spine so violent, the bird's death knocks the formation out of alignment, and rocks bounce down and travel. Landing in a heap, the beast's half-hearted flap of one wing is followed by a series of twitches.

And then . . . the kind of stillness that only a life lost brings.

Panting, dizzy, and in pain everywhere, I think of the *balas* meat, and know that we'll have a meal, if we choose—yet I'm saddened at the death, even though it was him or me.

Her or me?

"Sorrel!"

The sound of Merc's baritone voice is so sweet, I shudder with relief. And I intend on getting up—or at the very least, sitting up—to greet him. I don't have the energy. I flop over onto my back once more and continue to pant as I look toward him.

He's running faster than I did, nearly as fast as the gelding, the broadsword sheathed on his back, his arms pumping like he's punching the air. With his black hair streaming out in his wake, and his leather-clad body propelling him forward, Merc is the very study of a powerful man in his prime—and not unlike the predator who nearly killed us both. And it's good that weapon of his is put away, I think numbly, in case there are more of those birds around. We need to keep all flashes of light to an absolute minimum.

I try once again to sit up, and fail. So I lie where I am, in this field of gray rocks, that could well have been my grave. Overhead, the sun is so intense it hurts my eyes, yet I can still see that odd and worrisome star—

Merc skids to a halt beside me, gray pebbles kicking up and skipping across my dead-weight legs. As he falls to his knees and takes my hand, I start to smile.

"You didn't leave me," I say hoarsely while I search his body for injuries.

"And you *should* have left me." Leaning over, he brushes the hair out of my face. "Are you all right, woman?"

As my lungs get tight with emotion, I open my mouth to answer him. Except then, caught up in the moment, I do the one thing I must never, ever do.

I meet his eyes with my own.

*Thirty-Six*

# A Man to Die For.

My gasp seems as loud as the bird of prey's call, and I grab on to the front of Merc's surcoat, prepared for an assault that, though it will not kill my body, I know without a doubt will kill my soul. Bracing myself, moaning, kicking my feet into the pebbles, I prepare my weak body for what he'll feel as he dies—

His one uninjured eye is dark. So dark that, with the sunlight streaming in behind him, I can't tell where his pupil ends and his iris takes over. The other side is the opposite, so white that there is only the faintest hint of a ring around the faded center.

The slashing scar is nasty and jagged, and surely what would have killed a lesser man.

"Sorrel." He says my name roughly. "I need to get you out of the sun—"

As I reach for his face, he falls silent and I know now is the time. It's coming, the flash and the agony, the knowledge I don't want, shouldn't have, can't change. My curse, showing up here to spoil—

The world recedes as I become lost in his gaze, that midnight darkness enveloping me as the white expanse pushes me away . . . but instead of driving cold, or creeping terror, or crushing suffocation, I feel cocooned. Safe. At home with this stranger who knows only violence and solitude.

After he was a humble farmer who loved the land.

It's as all this occurs to me that I realize: Time is passing. And still I hold his eyes with my own. I see nothing, other than the two universes that stare back at me. I feel nothing, outside of warmth and reassurance. I know nothing, apart from him leaning over me while I lie on the hard pebbled ground, the blue sky stretching over us, a cloudless blanket of daylight that will usher in danger when it fades into the very color of half his gaze.

A sense of utter disbelief causes me to recede from him, and that means the death vision is finally coming. Any moment. Yes, right . . . now . . .

The death vision, the moment of his demise—and all the physical and emotional sensations that go along with it—is going to take me over, and make me writhe, and cause me to know that which I can never, ever share—

*Hide.*

"Sorrel." Now he's sharp with me. "Can you hear aught?"

As I reach up, he captures my hand and gives it a squeeze. "You're bleeding—"

"Shh."

When he falls silent, I go for his face again. My fingers make contact with his temple and then the scar that intersects his pale eye. His skin is warm, and where he might have a beard it remains smooth, though I don't think he shaved this morning. More than this, I notice his eyelashes. They're thick and long on the top, thick and short on the bottom, and the frame they make serves to emphasize his deep-set, intense stare.

And that is all.

For the first time in my life, I have the details that every other person registers in the normal course of things: Eye color, placement, lashes. And where the individual's stare is directed.

Merc's is not leaving mine.

"I'm getting you to shade," he says brusquely.

When he goes to pick me up, I stop his hand with a light touch. "Your blade. Let me see it."

"What—"

"Please, I need to . . . see myself."

He's impatient with the request, but he unsheathes the heavy weapon, and though we shouldn't garner more attention from things that come out of the sky, I have to know.

Directing the blade, I angle it to my face.

And meet my own eyes.

All I see—all I've ever seen—is their strange pale irises and the pupils in the center. I've never gotten a hint of my own death, and it's been something I've always been grateful for.

Like the host must not know of its own demise.

"Let me check the back of your head." Keeping the sword steady, Merc lifts my torso up gently and cranes around behind me. "No blood."

The relief in his voice warms me, but I can't dwell on it. My brain is scrambling as it tries to frame within my previous experience the lack of—

The broadsword is sheathed, and I feel his hands go behind my shoulders and under my knees. I'm lifted with care from the rocks, and Merc's long strides take us over toward the dead bird. He goes around the now-tumbled boulder pile, and finds a wedge of shadow to put me in.

"Look at me, Sorrel."

I take a deep breath. Maybe I got nothing because I hit my head? Or the chase has exhausted me? And I could always resume my normal course and avoid his gaze, except then I'd never know whether the anomaly is this situation or him.

My focus swings back to him and I tighten my grip on his surcoat again . . .

Though I'm in the cooler shade, the brilliant sun slants into his face. I see now that there is a faint delineation between the dark iris and pupil, and I recognize this because of the way his uninjured eye adjusts to the ray's intensity.

"I'm going to check your stare," he informs me.

I almost laugh as he carefully pulls my lids apart on the right side, then the left. As he exhales, his mouth lifts into a brief smile of approval.

"What do you see?" I ask hoarsely.

"If you hit your head, you're all right." He sits back and brings up my wounded arm for inspection. "I've had many a man knocked in the skull, and if their eyes aren't the same, they die shortly thereafter. Now let's see about this bleeding."

The rocks against my back are no more comfortable than the ground was, and yet I recline into their bumpy profile as Merc curses and then goes to work on the fastenings down the outer coat. Meanwhile, I just stare into his face.

Maybe the curse is over.

The instant this idea strikes, I doubt it. Over the course of my years, I've had slip-and-falls, head bumps, stressful things. I think of the Fulcrum, those boys, and what I was still able to see of the dragon's plight. So fear and anger don't affect . . . whatever it is I have.

"Let's sit you up a little bit more." He cups my shoulder and does all the work of the repositioning. "And now we get this off."

I assume he's talking about my jacket. Instead, he takes off my pack, which I have wholly forgotten about, and then he resettles me.

"There, you should be more comfortable."

Well, in fact I am. What I assumed were rocks was in fact the contours of the compass and the box. But who really cares about all that. I want to understand why I can look into his—

As he strips my arm out of the baggy sleeve with its fine silver embroidery, a familiar clip-clop suggests an approach, and sure enough, our sweated steed rounds the boulders, his head down low, his ears lax as a dog's, his feet trudging through the loose gray stones as he still catches his breath from our sprinting.

Turning my head, I hold out my hand. The chestnut glances at Merc, but it comes to me. Meanwhile, Merc is talking to me, and pushing at my arm. I ignore both whatever he's saying and the brief flares of pain that mark his exploration. Instead, I focus on the horse as I palm the loose reins.

Taking a deep breath, I slowly lift my stare from those frothy, still-flared nostrils, up the graceful bridge of his head . . . to his doe-ish brown eyes—

Like a crack of lightning, my body is racked with electricity, and my arms and legs stiffen. The barren lakebed disappears, and so does Merc, as I am consumed by the connection with the horse—

For once, there is no pain. There's just peacefulness. I see no violence, no fire, no blood or gore . . . only a redolent green meadow, a peaceful pasture, a broad realm tree overhead. The horse is lying down on its side, its hooves and spindly legs curled in, its head slowly sinking to the fragrant green grass. I can feel its heart as my own, and the beats become slower, slower . . . ever slower. There's a brief flare of breathlessness, but that passes soon enough.

And then all is still.

Death is kind to this animal, and I can't help but tear up in gratitude for its destiny—

"Sorry," Merc says as he pours water on the ragged wound in my skin, "I know this hurts, but we must clean it."

His words return me to my own timeline, and I release my hold on the reins. "Stop. Water for him. More important."

Merc looks at me. "You come first—"

"No, he does."

As our eyes meet again, I'm filled with wonder, but also a confusion that derails me.

"Give him all the water," I say. "He needs it more than I, and he deserves it for his efforts."

Merc's brows drop down in a glower. But then he shakes his head. "You have a thing for salvation, don't you."

Shifting away, he makes a basin out of the side of his surcoat and pours the water into the leather bowl. The horse goes in immediately and starts drawing, the two turning into a painting, the man at a kneel, the animal bending down.

Salvation.

I look at the hilt of the broadsword protruding out of the top of its holster, but what I see is the flat of the blade . . . and my own eyes staring back at me.

I've always thought I don't see my own death because I'm so close to it—and because my survival instinct is so strong that my free will is too disruptive to any final fate, at least at the age I am now. And I think the latter is the key right now. Given the journey ahead of Merc and me, and for however long our destinies are linked, I know I'm prepared to fight for him as I'd fight for myself: Of the many deaths I've seen, not once, ever, was I willing to give my own life up for any of the people—or animals—I set my eyes to. Why is Merc different? He's my protector.

And also maybe it has something to do with what I saw in him as he stared over that field this morning.

By virtue of our circumstance, I'm too close to him, too.

Perhaps, at the moment we separate, if I were to look into his eyes, I'd see what awaits him for his last breath. Until then? His mortal destiny is so inextricably intertwined with my own that the time and circumstance of his grave is not something I'm going to know.

It's such a relief.

"All right, then," Merc says. "That's your fill whether you like it or not."

He flaps his surcoat, water drops flicking around, while the horse lets out a satisfied groan and shakes its head with a rattle of tack.

"I've got a cloth to wrap up your arm."

I'm so deeply in my own thoughts, I can't figure out what he's saying. But then he takes a clean stretch of red fabric from out of an inside pocket and begins to wind it around my forearm. When he's finished, he tucks the end into the top and sits on his heels.

"We have to get moving. Do you think you can get back in the saddle?"

I meet his eyes yet again, and cease my flinching.

Instead of answering him, I hold out both my arms. With a nod, he brings his chest down to my own to pick me up—

That's not what I'm after.

Winding a hold around his massive shoulders, I close my lids and burrow into his neck, smelling the leather and clean sweat and the cedar spice that is him and him alone.

"Let's get you—oh, we're not . . . all right. This is what we're doing."

He's so awkward in retuning the embrace, it's actually charming. Or would have been, if I hadn't started to well up with emotion.

"It's okay," he says softly as he wraps his arms around me. "That was a big one. Let yourself go for a moment."

With a shudder, I give in to a good weeping, and I feel myself getting repositioned in his lap. As he holds me to his steady, beating heart, his sword hand makes a slow circle on my back, soothing me.

"We made it," he says in a deep rumble. "You're foolhardy and far too brave for your own good. But we're both okay, and it's all down to you—and don't *ever* do something as stupid as that again. Are we clear."

He thinks my emotions are about what we both survived. They're not, but I can't tell him my truth.

Never before in my life have I met someone I'm willing to die for, and who knew there would be such a liberation in that potential sacrifice—or such a relief from the loneliness that has defined my pitiful existence.

Also . . .

Well, he happens to have the most beautiful eyes.

*Thirty-Seven*

# The Quenching of Thirst.

Merc insists on walking to give our horse a break from his weight.

The chestnut seems to prefer him up ahead, rather than at our sides, so he's out in front, the reins a graceful curve running between his left hand and the bit in our steed's mouth. Astride, I am drowsy from the mosey, the back-and-forth rocking like the rhythm of my own breath, something that happens to me, rather than anything I control. And like the regular contraction and expansion of my lungs, the ho-hum hooving over the gray ground is nothing I notice anymore.

In the back of my mind, I recognize that I'm in pain in many places, but either from exhaustion or new habit, I don't notice the signals anymore.

"How we doing back there, Sorrel?"

Three . . . two . . . one—

As Merc looks over his shoulder, our eyes meet. I've learned not to answer his inquiries quickly so he's forced to visually check in. I can't get enough of his face, and though those black and white eyes will always be my true north, I also enjoy the sight of his mouth, his cheeks, and those almost-always-furrowed brows. The vista of his visage has yet to grow old on me, and I feel like this is permanent.

"Fine, yes. Thank you—"

He does this thing where his left brow arches while the other stays down, and I find it endearing. "Your color's bad."

"Is it?"

"Too pale with cheeks too red." He reorients back around. "But it's not much farther."

I'm not sure I trust the "not much farther."

Things have changed around us. The mountain range off to the west has come closer and closer, and we've mounted a gradual rise that I think might be, finally, the far end of the lakebed. I have no idea how far the Outpost is from us, though, and I'm not asking.

At least the sun is lower and there are clouds coming in. I tell myself the temperature is dropping. It's a lie. The rocks have been warmed all day long, so they're taking the balance of the heat's graft over from the declining strength of the rays overhead, a hearth still warm even after the fire has dwindled. I have some faint hope, as we crest the incline, that whatever's on the other side—

"Oh . . . fates," I whisper through my aching, dry throat. "It's beautiful."

Merc halts our progress, and everyone looks around: Him, me . . . the horse. There's green, everywhere.

"Water . . ." I croak as I point a shaky hand.

We all see it at the same time, and each have the same thought. Merc and the horse put feet forward, and even I, up in the saddle, lean in the direction of the rushing stream, as if I'm a water diviner. The rope of churning, crystal current, in its carpet of luscious, healthy grass, is such a welcome sight, I get teary and I don't even bother to wait until we stop. I dismount halfway there, imagining the cool flow down the back of my throat, the sweat gone from my face and eyes, the—

My legs crumple beneath me.

Before I fall on my face, Merc whips a hand back and captures a hold of my uninjured arm. With a jerk, I'm up against him, and I throw a clutch around his waist.

When he releases the reins, the horse continues on without us. "I can carry you?"

"I'll walk." He's worked harder than I have on this stretch. "Crescent moon, I've never wanted a drink more than—"

As I stumble, it's clear I'm not walking anywhere. My feet are dead at the end of my numb legs.

Merc sweeps me up into his arms as the horse chugs right into the rush, dropping its head, the reins washing away in the brisk flow. The stream is five lengths wide, and appears to go to infinity in both directions. The bottom is all rocks, and even with the speed at which the water runs, you can see right down to them.

There's nothing cloudy, no weeds or even fish, and I can already taste it.

Merc wades in with me, and I wince as he shifts me down and places my feet in the little river. The water comes to his knees. For me, it's halfway up my thighs—and the incandescent delight of the cold rinse hitting my aching, hot feet and stinging, throbbing calves makes me moan.

"I've got this," I say as I nudge free of him.

Cupping my palms, I bend down—

My legs give out on me again and I splash into the stream. Merc reaches out again with a curse, but I brush him off with an ugly squeak that, were I not so dehydrated, would have been a proper laugh.

I totally submerge myself by lying flat and holding myself under with a grip on the smooth, clean stones at the bottom. There's a shock to it all, my hot skin, hot clothes, hot hair, exploding at the tingling chill, and then there's my injury, which positively screams. But I don't care. As invisible fingers scrub down to my scalp, and every chafed, gritty, sweated place is rinsed off, I am renewed even before I start to slake my thirst.

Opening my mouth, I take in gallons of water as if it's air and I've been suffocating for days. The taste is exactly as I thought, so sweet, it's like an apple—

Abruptly, Merc pulls me out, and on a sputter, I mistakenly blow spray into his face. "Oh! I'm so sorry—"

"I thought you were drowning." He laughs in a burst. "And worry not, woman. Everything that matters is wet on me, too."

Indeed, he's put his whole head in the stream, or poured as much as I've drunk over himself. Clear water is dripping off the beaded ends of his braids, and his long, black hair has twisted into damp corkscrews. Droplets even cling to his long, thick lashes, and I stare, mesmerized, at the way the diamonds glimmer around his obsidian eye.

"I'm going to ask you something," he says in that deep voice that goes into me as if my marrow is a tuning fork for his song.

"What," I whisper as our horse wades out and starts to crop at the grass.

"Why're you looking at me now?" He reaches to my face and touches my wet cheek. "You never did, before."

*Hide.*

I don't like to lie to him. But how could I possibly explain the truth?

"After everything we've been through?" I smile a little. "Let's just say, our sustained discomfort has led to a certain . . . comfort."

"Ah." He cocks a brow. "Quite a price for eye contact, then."

Worth it. So very worth it.

I brush my wet hair back. "I would much have preferred sharing a pint and a nice meal, it's true."

Merc throws his head back and laughs properly, and the way the muscles on the sides of his neck flex remind me why he's good at a job that requires strength. And as he relevels himself, I have the traitorous thought that I want to be unforgettable to him. After we part, I want him to remember me as I'll remember him—

Before I think better of it, I rise up on my tiptoes and bring his face down to my own. Our lips meet with such ease, it's as if we have been kissing each other for years, and when his tongue seeks to enter me, I want the penetration.

I want him inside me in another place, too.

After all of the travel and the heat, I feel like I'm soaring on the first pleasurable moment I've had . . .

Ever.

I want more of him. I want *all* of him, his naked skin, his sex in my own, his weight bearing down on me.

When we finally ease back, I stare into those eyes of his and remember the way he stopped before. Flushing, I stammer, "Sorry."

"Don't apologize for the likes of *that*."

A precious moment follows—one I know I'll recall when I try to sleep tonight, wherever that may be—where we cling to each other's gaze and both go so much further in our minds. Clearly, I've misinterpreted his earlier reversal. Or maybe I was right then . . . and now is somehow different.

Mortal near-misses make people restless, perhaps?

Although for certain, his "further" is very much more accurate than my own fantasies. Something tells me he'll teach me, though.

Except then he looks out to the south, and I know, even before he frowns and steps away, that the moment is gone.

Nor should it continue.

A rider approaches.

*Thirty-Eight*

# The Outpost Arrives.

Merc puts himself in front of me, but leaves the broadsword holstered on his back. His hand finds instead the dirk at his hip, and he unsheathes it discreetly, keeping the weapon down by his thigh.

Peering around the meat of his biceps, I narrow my eyes against the low sunlight. A man in a black top hat approaches from the west. He's dressed in a formal gray and black suit, and astride a very fine black trotter. All the silver flashes on the tack suggest—fine clothes aside—that whoever it is has some wealth. Yet he's traveling alone.

So, like Julion, he's either stupid, arrogant . . . or sufficiently dangerous that he doesn't need a defender.

But unlike the golden nobleman, this is not someone to trust.

"Don't say anything." Merc shakes his head as if I'm already arguing. "At all."

My impulse is to give him some lip—and not the kissing kind. But the rider is on us, pulling up and halting beside our horse. Under the lee of the top hat's brim, he has dark sideburns, and the kind of smile that strikes me as a warning, as opposed to a greeting. That I can't see his eyes is a good thing.

A man like him will come to a violent end. It's the way of things.

His chuckle is deep and velvety. "A pair of lovebirds in a poisoned stream."

"What!" I croak as I scramble free of the water, jumping out on the opposite side from him. "Oh, crescent moon—"

"Relax," he says. "All is quite well. Just a joke."

As his foreign accent registers, I pat at my wet clothing the way Merc checks his weapons, for all the good that will do. If the water is indeed contaminated, it's in me, on me. Still, I grab my hollow stomach and take special note of its equilibrium.

"Not much of a joke." Merc also gets out of the stream, but unlike me, he chooses the side the rider's on. "I think you need to be moving on, mate."

If the other man's dark grin is a warning, Merc's stance is a fight already in progress. He's no longer bothering to hide the dirk, either.

"Quite inhospitable you are," the rider in the top hat drawls. "Then again, I gather you all have somehow managed to cross the Lake of Lost Souls. On that . . . old nag. A feat that requires a bit of grit."

Merc says nothing, and I can imagine what his glare must look like.

The rider points to the south and west over his shoulder. "You're going to the Outpost, then? For a rest and a recovery. You'll find it not far off in that direction." That chuckle returns. "Something tells me you'll be just fine amongst the colorful characters therein."

The man's attention returns to me. "I'd keep her well in hand, however. There are many who will seek to sample what you have already enjoyed."

Touching the brim of his hat, he inclines his head—and yet somehow remains unbowed. Then with a *chk-chk* between his molars, the black stallion lopes off in a canter that suggests those hooves have plenty more speed at their disposal.

Merc continues to stay where he is, until the rider has hooked up with a well-grooved road many lengths away, and continues forth toward the dark clouds that are gathering to the northeast. When my mercenary finally turns back to the stream, his eyes burn with aggression that's not directed at me.

Wordlessly, I cross through the water, hop out, and gather the reins of our horse—who is *not* a nag. Lifting up one of the saddlebags, I shove my other hand in and fish around, and when I feel what I was hoping to find, I pull out an empty cloth sack. I imagine that the mayor or one of his sons probably kept a sizable load of provisions in it. Orange fruit, going by the scent that lingers, no doubt an offering for the Sooths they went to see.

I really hope that muddy, bound pair made it back to the village safely.

With a jerk, I rip apart the bag, the flimsy seams releasing without much force. When it's all unfurled, I take off the blue turban, wrap my lower face and hair up with the sackcloth so that only my eyes show, and then replace what was on my head to hold the draping where it is. As I tuck the tail end into the navy blue coat, I look at Merc.

"We should move along," I say. "I don't like the look of that weather."

His face softens, though it's nearly imperceptible: If I didn't know him so well, I would think there is naught behind his hard, cruel exterior save more of the same.

Nodding at him, I gather the reins and mount up on the saddle's leather ledge, landing in a soggy astride that feels unpleasant.

Compared to the heat, I'll take it.

Merc remains where he is for a stretch of time, and I don't rush him. He's scanning around, and then rechecking the road off in the distance, as if to make sure the rider in the top hat stays on his own journey—and keeps it separate from our own. Only after that black stallion has disappeared somewhere around the base of the closest mountain in the range does Merc walk over.

As he swings up into the saddle, I release my hold on the reins and lean back to give him room. He settles with a solid thump, and our horse grunts beneath us. No doubt it wishes for a return to the lighter load of just me.

Merc directs our not-nag to the road the hatted man approached on, and the twin lines of packed earth suggest that stagecoaches travel the route with frequency. I twist around and look back. The storm is continuing to gather strength, the bad weather ushering in great black and purple swells that will soon eclipse all the blue sky. At least there's still no hat man—and the breadth of the lakebed we've crossed astounds me. I can't see the far-off shore where we started the descent I didn't take much note of, and all those gray boulders, gray rocks, gray stones, and gray pebbles are as inhospitable an environment as I could ever imagine.

The Lake of Lost Souls. How apt, and I'm glad I didn't think too much about the name as we headed down into that basin.

As I turn back around, every instinct I have tells me we're heading into another kind of inhospitable.

"What are the clouds doing?" Merc demands.

"Coming fast."

As anxiety travels up my spine and fuels unhelpful thoughts, I tell myself that I've seen many a storm before—except all I can think of are the black bands in the Fulcrum. I pray to the crescent moon the things in the sky really are just clouds, however gloomy and dark they appear—and not evil energy come to hunt us.

But the top-hat man proves to be right. Soon enough, a sizable town kindles on the horizon, and when we reach the farming fields on its periphery, the low stone plot fences and orderly lines of mature plantings are a surprise that shouldn't be one. No matter the debauchery, people need to eat. At the moment, nobody is working the rows of bright green bushes, but they are well looked after, without weeds or leaves damaged by pests. And as Merc lingers his attention on the crops, I wonder if he isn't making an expert's assessment of the beans and grains.

My heart aches for him.

Grazing pastures with over a dozen horses working at the grass come next.

These meadow lots are separated by rail fences, and after them come the first of the structures. The stables are flat-roofed and closed up, the weathered boards the gray of the lakebed, and in their midst, trees have been allowed to grow up, perhaps to offer a buffering from the sun. These arboreal specimens are like none I've ever seen, tall, bushy, and triangular, the branches spindled with dark green spikes, their trunks craggy from what appears to be a perpetual molt.

Though voices thread over on the breeze, I don't see anyone. Merc hears the chatter, too, his head turning the moment the conversations register in my ear.

He still has that dirk out by his thigh.

"We're being watched," he says softly.

My eyes shift all around, but I can see nothing in or between any of the stable buildings. "Where—"

"Up."

That's when I see the camouflaged blind, set about halfway to the top of the nearest tree. I don't know how he saw it, but there's another. And . . . another, up ahead.

"I guess they take their horses very seriously," I say in a lowered voice as thunder sounds out behind us.

"It's about the gambling. You have to be careful with sore losers and big winners alike."

"Oh."

And now we arrive.

The town is nothing that I imagined. "Outpost" suggests a couple of grungy buildings huddled together while men and women do dirty deeds in not-so-secret ways. This is very nearly a city. There are too many houses, shops, and trading posts to count, and the road breaks off into different routes that run into the thicket of commerce and residences. There's no charm to any of it. Unlike my village, where the lanes are cobblestone, and lanterns hang by rounded doors, and the stuccoed facades come in colors, everything here is weathered wood and utilitarian. There's also a battened-down look to it all, no open windows or doors, anywhere.

Something tells me it's not because of the heat or the approaching weather.

Faded signs announce that there's a grain merchant, a mercantile and clothier, and finally, something that piques my interest: Herbist. And interspersed among these going concerns are unmarked porches that I assume are attached to homes—

Another roll of thunder reaches my ears, and I glance over my shoulder again. A flicker of orange lightning teases the undersides of the dark clouds that continue to close in fast, and dread makes me shiver. I've never seen it that color before.

"Everything here is made to hunker down," Merc remarks. "And going by the condition of the wood siding, I'm thinking it's bad weather—in addition to bad manners."

"Do you know where we're going to stay?"

"No, but something will turn—"

Up ahead, a pair of men crash out of a set of double doors, and Merc has to pull up our steed. The two drunkards are in mid-slug, their sloppy fists and slippery boots the kind of thing I'm well used to from the pub, except this is the late afternoon, not midnight.

There are two other sets of doors under the short overhang, and those exits break open, shaggy-haired people dressed in well-worn clothing spilling out into the lane. The audience is little different from the combatants, and up on the second floor, seams open all along the facade, faces peering out of shuttered windows. There are a lot of beards, and the women seem as tough as the men.

"Ye bastard! She's mine—"

A leveled, sailing fist makes contact by luck, rather than skill, and the accusation is cut off by a crack that makes me think teeth have been compromised. Assuming there were any in that mouth to begin with.

The knockout flop is like a bag of oats tossed off a cart, and the concussed lands with the same finality—though he's face down in the dirt, he doesn't lift his head for air. The victor lifts both arms over his head and starts to dance around, at least until he trips over the boot of his foe, loses his own balance, and lands across the knocked-out guy.

Same flop sound. And he also doesn't get up.

At this point, there's a long pause, the audience falling silent. Then the arguing starts, all kind of fingers pointing to the men who've passed out in the street. The volume of the voices rises until there's a sharp whistle from a fat, mustached man who looks annoyed.

"He fell first, that's what it be!" he says.

Fates, it's like Mr. Lewis, just with hair.

The announcement brings all kinds of grumbling, but coins start changing hands as people turn away and reenter the building. Upstairs, the curious faces retract, and the second-story shutters close up, tight as ticks.

That's when I notice the faded sign mounted just above the overhang: WIDOW'S PEAK INN & TAVERN.

"We stay here," Merc announces.

*Thirty-Nine*

# A Reminder of Things Unchanged.

The check-in process is smooth. We're assigned a room, our horse is likewise taken into boarding, and going by the way everybody steps carefully around Merc, it's clear that trouble will not be immediately looking for us. Further, he tells everyone I'm his wife, and he pays with a silver coin, not a copper one.

"It's the best room in the place." The brusque woman leading us up the creaky stairs speaks between grunts. "Just cleaned, too. Meant to be."

I can't tell what age she is. Her hair is gray, and she's a bit stooped, but she's solid and no-nonsense. In this way, she's like all the buildings of the Outpost, battened down and hearty. As with a lot of the women in the pub, her skirt is made of heavy, felt material in a deep red that flares out in a straight circle to the floor. I was wondering how she sat down—and how she was going to make it up the stairs—but the front of it bends as if hinged. On her top, she has a short vest of the same fabric and a loose gray blouse that billows out around her arms.

I'm not sure what's so significant about the felt. Some of the men have pants and outer coatings also made of it, though their clothes are brown, and the uniformity of the dress helps me pick out who's part of the community and who's passing through. But it can't be comfortable—

At the top of the stairs, I find myself in a hall that stretches out a building length in both directions. Somehow, the second floor is twice the size of the lower, suggesting the space has been retrofitted over the other stores and enterprises of commerce on the first level.

"This way," the woman announces, as if she's a herd dog and we're sheeplings.

I glance at Merc, who's planted his boots. His eyes are narrowed, but it's not at the innkeeper who's scuffing her way off to the right. He's assessing all the doors, particularly the ones that are going to be behind us if we follow our felted leader. It's like he can see through them, even though I know he can't.

I wait for him.

What a dreary place this is. Though there are regularly spaced lanterns throwing yellow light, it's a dingy gloaming up here. Then again, even the interiors are done in that weathered gray boarding, leading me to believe the town either got a deal or felled an entire forest of whatever tree it is.

When Merc gives me a brisk nod, I start walking to the right. The number of rooms is nearly unfathomable to me, and I can hear people on the other sides of the doors, the men and women emitting . . . certain noises . . . that are familiar to me.

It's clear that mead, iffy food, and shelter are not the only things on offer.

Fortunately, the "certain" sounds diminish the farther down we go, suggesting that the hourly rooms are the ones at the top of the stairs, and the lodgings are at the ends. This makes sense, given the traffic.

"Here ya go," the woman says as she throws open the very last door.

As luck would have it, there's a flash of orange lightning just as I step into the darkness, and the peachy illumination flickers in through the closed shutters.

"The lamp's here on the table." As she turns the glowing wick up, thunder offers a threatening commentary. "You get one measure of oil with the price of the room. Extra costs. If you'll be wanting soap, it's extra. But the blankets are included and so is the en suite. You said one night, but you're going to be here longer, Mr. and Mrs., so I'll be needing more payment tomorrow morn before the bar opens at ten."

Merc's still out in the corridor, and I have the sudden thought that he's going to stay there and guard the door as I sleep.

"We're here for tonight only," he announces.

The innkeeper laughs as another streak of lightning licks into the room, like something that's locked out and testing weak points for entry.

"The rain's comin'." She points to another doorway. "The en suite. It's the only one in the building. You're lucky. Only one meal included downstairs."

"You'll bring the food up here to us."

Merc presses a coin in the woman's hand as she opens her mouth—and she checks to see what it is before smiling.

"Whatever you be wantin'—"

"Tell anyone you care about not to open that door without an invitation." He points to what she unlatched for us. "Otherwise, they'll be dead before they hit the floor. And the same goes for any of our possessions. If they're moved even a hair, I will know and I will do something about it. Are we clear."

The temperature seems to drop, not just in the room, but along the corridor and throughout the building, and the woman's expression of bored tolerance shifts into a something entirely serious.

She nods once as she eyes the scar on his face. "What time do you want your food, sir."

"Now. My wife is tired and hungry."

"As you wish."

She closes the door silently, and I look at the gray panels as the sound of her shuffling footfalls disappears.

Suddenly, the reality that we are here, in the Badlands, at the Outpost, settles on me like a cloak of nettles.

Our arrangement has been fulfilled. At least on his side.

And I wonder how long he will stay with me. Only the night, apparently.

For all the distance we've traveled, and all the time I've had with my inner thoughts, I never considered what I would do when I was finally here: The trip was so dangerous, the destination seemed irrelevant.

I'm not ready to be on my own yet—

"You need to sleep," Merc informs me. Like he's diagnosing an injury.

My eyes go to the bed.

It's very large, and I'm entirely unsurprised that the blankets are made of red and brown felt. There are two thin pillows set side by side, and the headboard is of course made up of that gray wood that reminds me too much of the rocks in the lake basin. As I slip off my pack and put it at the base of the mattress, I glance around. The rest of the room is just as simple. There's that table with the lamp, and a dresser that looks as exhausted as I feel. Across the way, a bowed-out section, marked with the set of shutters, offers a window seat, but there are no cushions. Just more of that wood—

*Clunk.*

Merc throws the heavy bolt that runs from the door panels through the jamb and into a seat screwed into the wall. Then he yanks at the handle. With a comment under his breath, I'm unsure whether or not he approves.

"I want you to engage this anytime I leave." He taps the latch. "*Every* time."

He goes over to the en suite. As he disappears inside, I lay my hand on the footboard of the bed and wonder what the sleeping arrangements will be. After that kiss at the stream, I find myself hoping for things I very much doubt I'm made for—

My ears perk up and I glance at the door.

Singing. I hear . . . a woman singing.

It's muffled, but the sweet, high notes are a surprise—

"I'm going downstairs." Merc comes back out, shrugs off his pack and puts it on the window seat. "I don't know what they'll bring up for food, and if it's not appetizing, I'll find something that is."

"I can go with—"

"You're asleep on your feet. Have a wash-up and a lie-down." He frees the bolt and looks back at me. "I am waiting on the far side until I hear this latch—and don't touch it until my voice returns on the other side."

"How will I get the food."

"I'm bringing it up to you."

All of his weapons are on him as he opens things, and even he seems surprised as he notices the singing. Past the heft of him, I see a diminutive, brown-haired maid with a bucket and scrub brush backing out of the room across the hall. The second she notices Merc, she shuts up and makes no eye contact, and with the way she hunches over as if bracing for blows, I worry that she's been beaten in the past.

"Was that you singing?" Merc asks.

"Forgive me, sir," she says, and cowers against the wall.

Before I have a cogent thought, my body's moving, and I duck out under Merc's arm. "You did nothing wrong. You have a beautiful voice—"

Without thinking, I look into her lovely brown eyes, and gasp.

*Forty*

# A Dangerous Resolve.

The murder of the young girl spills into me on a series of body blows that I feel as if my own head and shoulders are absorbing them. I fall back and put my arms over my face, but the sequence has been initiated and there's nothing I can do to stop it, block it, swerve away. Crumpling to the floorboards, I land in the position she will and hunker down, trying to protect myself against the attack.

That's when the iron skillet comes at our head.

I look up through the crisscross of my forearms.

Clear as if it's happening in the present, I see the man who stands over her, his paunchy face twisted in rage, his loose mouth open as he yells at her, the veins in his sweaty neck popping as he starts the downward motion that will lead to her death—

"Sorrel!"

The sound of my own name pulls me out of the vision, and then I feel Merc's hands bring my arms to my sides. His face is right above mine, and I duck my eyes and flinch away, only partly myself, still mostly the maid—and I cannot bear the pain of the girl with the sweet voice's demise.

"Look at me, are you ill?" Merc strokes my cheek. "*Sorrel.*"

"Perhaps she needs food?" The maid is so tentative as she comes a little closer. "I could go get her some bread and water?"

Merc shoves his hand into his pocket and holds a coin out to her. "Come back fast."

She bows to him. "Yes, sir."

The maid doesn't take the coin and hurries off, her red felt skirt like the base of a bell. In my stupor, I imagine a tiny pair of feet in brown leather slips going at a fast whisper over the gray floorboards of the corridor. Were the shoes brown in my vision? I don't know why I think they're brown—

The world spins and shifts as more thunder roars, and the building shakes. For a moment, I fear we've been struck by that orange lightning and the roof is collapsing, but no. It's Merc. He's picked me up off the floor in the hall and is carrying me into our room and over to the bed. The way he lays me down, as if I'm something that could break, brings tears to my eyes.

Especially because I have the sense that maid with the lovely singing voice has never been treated so kindly.

Merc sits next to me on the edge of the bed, his hip tilting the mattress so that my body rolls into him. He has all those weapons on his body, but with the way he looks at me, I feel as though he's disarmed.

"We traveled a long way today." His callused hand goes to my chin and he untucks the sackcloth I've used as a face cover. "You did very, very well."

"Especially with the bird?"

He smiles. "Especially with that."

As he pulls the fabric free of me, the cool air is nice.

"I am tired," I say roughly.

"I know. You rest here. We're getting you what you need."

*You're here*, I think to myself. *That's what I need.*

He brushes my hair back, and I close my eyes instead of look into his. I can't take any more of anything right now, especially as the aches in my body blur to the point where I cannot distinguish my own pain . . . from what that young girl is going to go through: Between one blink and the next, the vision of the attack's perspective swings around and I see her cowering, her face already bruised and cut, her eyes wide with terror.

"I'm not leaving," he says as he shifts off the bed.

*Yet*, I tack on.

Merc goes to the door and faces out, filling the jambs with his body, his broad shoulders and planted boots more solid than the panels and that latch. He's waiting, for the food and drink, and he's protecting me.

For as long as he's with me.

How will I do this without him? Where will I stay long-term and what life will I live here?

As I move my hand over to my hip, I feel the satchel full of Mare's gold coins. If only I knew how to use them safely—or does the court imprint not matter here? Fate knows we're a long way from Prosperitus territory—

The young girl arrives with a tray, and Merc allows her to pass before shutting the three of us in together. She comes right over to me, and puts what she's brought down on the floor by the bed. With both hands, she offers me an earthenware cup.

"This will refresh you after all your travails."

Her voice is soft, and in the syllables, I hear hints of that songbird voice. My heart tightens as she holds the cup to my lips, and I smell lemon. When I hesitate, she nods and takes the rim to her own lips. Her swallow is not small and very obvious, her slender throat undulating as she completes the sip.

"'Tis safe, I promise."

But that's not why I hesitated. "Thank you."

Sitting up, I hold out my palms, and as she places the beverage in them, the bruises on her wrists show as her sleeves ride up.

She must catch my gaze going to them, because she moves back fast and pulls things back into place.

"This looks good," I murmur, making a show of taking a drink.

The taste is lemony, and there's a tingle in my body as I empty it in one tilt. When I right my head, she trades me for a plateful of fresh bread that has been torn into bite-size pieces, no doubt by her gentle hands. I only take one and it's just because she's brought them to me, but the delicate flavor awakens my stomach. Hunger is indeed the best spice, and I decide, as I take another ball and it melts away in my mouth, this is quite possibly the best meal I've ever had—

Another gust of wind rattles the shutters, and orange lightning flashes a circuit around our room, starting with what I believe faces the lane, and continuing past the corner.

And then the rain starts. The pitter-patter sound makes me think of the rats in the tunnel, their feet traveling fast and lightly.

The girl exhales with an exhaustion that has nothing to do with lack of sleep, and between one blink and the next, I again see her right before she is killed, cowering away, begging for the beating to stop, that skillet raised above her head. Her face is black and blue at the temple, and there's a band of bruising around her throat.

She's not any older than she is now. And her hair, which is cut short as a boy's, is no longer—

More lightning strikes with a crackling, and she's almost able to hide her gasp.

"Storms pass," I say hoarsely as I put more bread to my lips.

"Not here, they don't. Here, they linger, for days." She forces a smile. "But you are lucky, you have shelter. And . . . safety."

Her stare darts in Merc's direction, and I wonder if she's aware of how she shrinks into herself.

"Days?" I say, just to keep her with us.

She nods. "And then there's the flooding. I know not where you are headed, but the way south will be closed for quite some time."

"Why?" Merc demands as he sits down on the bed again.

She almost catches her flinch, but it's too quick for her self-control, the burst of fear escaping through her muscles, her fragile body jerking from head to toe under all her red felt.

In a gentler tone, Merc says, "Tell me more about the southern route? Please."

The maid sits down on the floor, her skirt folding up in a regular series of creases, like a fan. As she links her fingers and sets her hands in her lap, she's like a living doll, her porcelain skin contrasting with the fringe of dark hair that frames her heart-shaped face.

"There is only one way to pass through the peaks of the Rozars," she replies. "And if you had come yesterday, you could have made it. With this rain, the flooding will force you to wait."

"Mountains can be traveled, even in a downpour."

Her head shakes. "The dragons protect their breeding grounds so one must stay close to the ground, but the flooding of the way through will make that impossible, especially as the Old Trail is blocked."

"So there's two ways, not one?"

"I'm sorry." The maid shakes her head again, her hands twisting as if she's afraid of upsetting either of us. "I shouldn't have said—I mean, the Old Trail is quite impossible, no matter the season or the weather."

"Why?"

"The Crystal Gate shall not allow anyone to pass—"

I put my hand up to stop the interrogation. "Thank you for the bread and drink. I feel much better."

"Oh, mistress. Of this I'm glad." The maid gets up to her feet, the red skirting uncreasing in a stair-like progression. "You have a proper meal due to you, which I would be pleased to bring—"

There's a shout off in the distance and the girl wheels toward the exit. Like a bloom wilting, she deflates into her fear.

"If you will excuse me." She bows to Merc and then to me. "I shall return with your meal as soon as it is ready."

She doesn't so much leave as dematerialize, a living ghost chased by a death that I would bet, if I were to ask her and she were to be honest, she well knows is coming for her—and soon.

"If I could get my hands on the man who's beating her," Merc mutters.

I refocus on the plate, which still has bites of bread on it. "You'd do what."

"Kill him."

"But that would be murder."

He laughs in a short, cold way, and leaves that as his reply.

Putting another piece into my mouth, I can feel something unfamiliar building within me, and I try to push it aside because the emotion is so dark. But I'm tired of the cruelty in the world, and sometimes, though it's just a fantasy, it feels good to imagine evening the scales.

"I'm going to go downstairs and get the lay of the land," he says as he gets to his feet. "If you're okay now."

"Looking for your next job, already?"

In the silence that follows, I meet his eyes—and mean to. I also know that black and white gaze will haunt me after we part.

For what will feel like forever.

"Are you going to the south tomorrow?" I ask him.

"I'll wait for you to pull the latch into place." He opens the door. "Before I leave."

For a moment, he glances over his shoulder. The yellow light from the lantern on the table finds every shadow in his features, from what's beneath his frowning brows to the hollows under his cheeks and the cut of his jaw. The angles of him seem much more pronounced than when we left my village, proof of how much we have traveled and how little we have eaten.

As he closes the gray panels, I have a thought that as long as I stay where I am on this bed, he'll stay with me.

But then I force my feet onto the floor. I was always going to have to go it alone at some point.

At the door, I take the latch and slowly slide it over. As the bolt locks into place, I whisper, "Goodbye."

This is my journey, my life, after all.

Not ours.

## *Forty-One*

# A Problem Presents Itself.

"Sorrel. Open up."

The voice weeds its way through my restless sleep, and I jerk awake. The first thing that registers is the rain. Before it was falling. Now, there are torrents of water hitting the roof over my head—

*"Sorrel—"*

There's a thunderous rumble, more of the storm—no, it's Merc, slamming his shoulder into the door, the latch nearly giving way from the impact.

"I'm coming! Don't break it down!"

My legs are stiff and uncoordinated as I hit the floor and scramble over, and as soon as I throw the bolt, the panels rip open. The whiff of cooked meat and spice is very pleasant. The expression on Merc's face is not. He's tense and hostile as he comes in with a tray so laden with food and drink, I wonder if he hasn't held up the kitchen with his broadsword.

"Close the door," he orders as he sets his load down by the lamp.

I comply readily, because my stomach is very much interested in all he's bought, even though my mind couldn't care less.

"What happened?" I ask as I go back over to the bed.

"I got us a meal." He picks up a bird leg and bites into it. "Come on, then. Don't be shy."

"Is the girl all right? She was supposed to bring it up."

"You need food." Merc walks across and gets my earlier plate, which I set on the floor by the cup that held the lemon drink. "And sleep. We both need sleep."

Back by the tray, he puts the leg between his teeth, and the way he transfers bread, greens, and meat, it's like he's stabbing something with the fork. When the tower starts to lean, his boots grind into the floorboards as he takes two steps over to me, and while the plate is shoved forward, I look up at him.

"Talk to me."

"I have nothing to say," he counters.

When I merely stare at him, he shrugs and takes what he's gathered over to the window seat. He lowers himself down facing away from me, his knees bending so the length of his legs can be accommodated as he braces his boots on the opposite side. The orange lightning flashes. Thunder comes and goes.

"Days," he mutters as he works his way through the meat. "No rain lasts that long."

I want to remind him that he can leave anytime. But I'm afraid he'll take it as an invitation.

"Are you all right then." He doesn't look over, and his tone is matter-of-fact. "Was that collapse really just about hunger and thirst? Or was it something else."

I get up and go over to the tray on a surge. Serving myself, I murmur, "What else could it be?"

"You were looking at that girl. Right before . . . whatever that was happened."

Abruptly, there's no hunger anymore for me, but I put things in my mouth, chew and swallow, because he has a point. This interlude has to be about recuperation and planning for me, and I've never seen rain last days, either. I'm not going to feel as safe as I do with him, so I might as well take advantage of his presence while I have it.

"She reminds me of myself, back at the Gauntlet." I'm back where I was again, and the food is good, even if the meat is greasy compared to the lean *balas*. "Trying to survive in a hard place, all alone."

"You're still in that situation."

"Thank you for the reminder."

We eat in silence, him sitting by the whistling shutters, me at the bed—thinking that we're going to have to extinguish the lantern at some point to conserve oil. When my stomach absolutely can't fit another morsel, I excuse myself to the water closet.

Merc grunts from his perch and puts the plate down under his knees. He's avoided the bread and greens, no doubt because he views them as sustenance for the weaker sex. I'm surprised he didn't bring mead back, but then again, the Outpost is not like my little village. Even a man such as himself should keep his wits here.

I mostly close the door, needing some light to find my way around. What I see is . . . unlike anything I've ever found in a loo before. The little room is dominated by a porcelain basin big enough to recline in. There's some kind of piping system above it . . . that appears to offer a raining upon the head? There's also a chamber pot–like setup with a similar network on a smaller scale behind it, and a sink, as well.

I test out the former, finding a handle that rushes a quantity of fresh water into the bowl. After a quick swirl, things all disappear into a hole in the bottom.

"Genius," I murmur as it refills. And so much better than the latrines of my village.

At the sink, I turn on the faucet, and the effort requires both hands due to corrosion. Though I expect what comes out to be cold and foul, as I test the stream with my fingertips, the rush is warm and sweet-smelling. No dirt or minerals taint the supply, just like the river out in the flats.

There are no cloths to dry off with, so I wipe my palm on my hip, and then I must inspect the big basin. The water release is a tiny wagon wheel on a vertical pipe, and there's a squeak as I turn it to the left. A spray of warm droplets falls into the tub, and gets me right on the head with the same clean rush as the sink.

"I'm having a washing?" I call out.

I think I get a grunt in return. I can't tell with the water coming down.

After I use the chamber pot and try out its fancy processing system for real this time, I pause and look to the crack in the door.

"Merc?" I go over and peer out through the aperture. "I said, I'm going to . . ."

My voice drifts as I push things open.

Across the way in the window seat, Merc has crossed his arms over his chest, like he's activated his own latching system, and his chin is down on his sternum. With his pack still on his back, his surcoat, too, and his weapons all holstered, he's ready to respond to any threat, and I wonder if he ever truly rests. Those black and white eyes of his may be closed, his lashes down on the summits of his cheeks, and his breathing may be slow and steady . . . but I have no doubt that if I so much as whisper something, he'll be on his feet with that broadsword in his hand.

I also know I shouldn't watch him like this.

But when I close my own lids briefly, I see only the burned houses, the bloodstains in the children's beds and the symbol markings, the *S* and the *P* intertwined by the doors that were still standing.

Salvation and Protection.

Innocent people slaughtered because others thought they were cursed by demons. Whole families gone out of the same fear that hunted me.

Glancing over to the door, I realize Merc hasn't followed his own rule.

In silence, I pad across the gray floorboards and bolt us in. Then I go back into the water closet. It's easier to undress knowing he's sleeping, and as I start to undo the fastenings on the navy blue coat, I can't help but think of where I was when I put these borrowed men's clothes on me. That glen of trees and Julion's request feel like it happened to someone else, a lifetime ago—

The first hint of the problem that's developed reveals itself as I try to pull my right arm out of the sleeve.

Pain lances up my forearm and I hiss a curse.

Persisting through the discomfort, I have to grit my teeth to keep from crying out, and when my outer layer is off, I catch my breath like I've been running. As I put the folds down, I see the ragged tear through the silver detailing.

I don't know if I have the courage to inspect what was done to me by that giant black bird. But like I have the choice?

The inhale I take is rough, and then I look down at the red cloth that Merc wrapped the injury in. The makeshift bandage is damp. I tell myself it's from my dip in the stream, except in this dim water closet, I can't tell if I've just been slow-bleeding for hours. Heart pounding, I begin to unwrap things, and when I'm done, the room is spinning. Trembling, I step over to the slant of lantern light that pierces through the crack at the doorjamb—

"Oh . . . *no*."

The periphery of the jagged slice is already turning red and puffing up, and the inside is heading for purple. It's a deep cut, nearly to the bone in places, and very long, running from my wrist bone nearly to my elbow. If it looks like this now? By the morning, I'm going to have a fever.

I look longingly at the tub. And turn the water off.

Going back out into the room, I rewrap things as I clear my throat. "Merc? I have a problem."

*Forty-Two*

# The Herbist.

I've never seen water fall from the sky horizontally before. You'd think that's impossible, but current conditions prove the contrary. The storm's pour is traveling parallel to the ground, like a herd of horses on a bolt. Sheets of droplets peel my eyes back, push into my nose, and muffle my ears even as I have the wrap around my face. I do what I can to protect myself, putting both my arms up, but nothing seems to help—

Merc shifts me in behind him, his big body offering a lee. I grab on to his broadsword holster, and hang on, but the deluge seems to be falling up from the ground, too. By the time we've crossed the muddy lane where the pair of drunken men fumble-fought, I'm soaked all the way through—and we still have to go down a couple of buildings.

When we finally arrive on the shallow porch of the store with the HERBIST sign, there's little shelter to be had beneath the overhang. It's so dark inside that I expect things to be locked up tight, but when Merc tries the door, the entry opens readily, a little bell tinkling.

We bring the storm inside with us, and Merc cuts it off by putting his shoulder into the door, like he's keeping out a rude guest. For me, the instant I take a proper breath, the smell of prepared roots, leaves, and bark returns me to my home under the stairs and my eyes water in a way that has nothing to do with everything that's dripping into my face.

"We're almost closed," comes a male voice out of the back.

Forcing myself to focus, I feel instantly at ease. It's a small shop, but there are so many glass jars on the counters and the shelves, I can't count them. I do recognize some of what's in the containers, however, even though the signs are in a language I can't decipher.

A man enters from a door behind the counter by the register of cash. Taking one look at us, he shakes his head. "I said, we're closed."

He's on the young side of maturity, with dark skin, a shaved head, and a set of silver spectacles perched on the end of his long nose. Dressed in the brown felt of a villager, he has a white apron tied around his waist, and the way he's wringing his hands together makes me think he's either washed them or compulsively wishes he could.

Merc turns to him with a glower. "No, there was an 'almost' in there. And now, we're in *here*, we're going to buy whatever she needs."

As the shop owner sizes up Merc, he becomes noticeably more agitated. "What do you want. And do be hurried about it."

That's when I hear the muffled sound. It's somewhere off in the rear of the little building, and when the shopkeeper wrenches around to the noise, I have sudden paranoia he's holding someone captive.

I step around Merc. "I need to make a poultice of *purpa*, *turtine*, and *roships*, with a binding of local honey."

The man rubs a spot over his brow. "I don't know what you're referring to—" As the sound repeats, he glances over his shoulder again. "I'm closed—"

"Here. This." I walk down the aisle, and point to jars on the second shelf. "This. And . . ."

I continue down the way—

The shopkeeper steps in front of me, those palms of his rubbing together, his eyes darting about. "I'm sorry, I'm closed—"

Merc materializes beside him, and puts his sword hand onto the other man's shoulder like an anvil. "And I said, you're going to give her what she needs. You don't want us in here for much longer, right? Because you're closed? So how 'bout you set us on our way with what she requires—and lock the door behind us so you don't get inconvenienced by paying customers again."

Unspoken is the last part of his message: *And if you don't comply, I will take what I want and ruin the rest.*

I want to tell Merc to back off, but I can't escape the condition of my wound. "I'm very sorry about this, but I'm injured and I desperately need to treat my—"

The sound repeats. Like it's timed.

Narrowing my eyes, I watch the sweat bead over the shopkeeper's upper lip. But then he shuffles away and goes to the counter, where there's a stack of folded bags. His restless hands jerk and tremble as he takes three—and then he has to double back to get a metal scoop because he forgets it.

"Are you staying at the pub then," he says.

"Aye," Merc answers.

"Then you get the honey there."

In the back of my mind, I start to count as the shopkeeper goes to one of the jars I pointed out. As he takes the glass container down, he fumbles it, and I jump forward to help. The weight hits my palms and I duck his eyes just in time, focusing on the white line around his mouth—

The sound comes again as we straighten, and I don't let go of what connects us. "Take me to your wife."

The shopkeeper freezes.

Even though it's the last thing I want to do, I have to help. "Please, I can hear her. I can . . . help her. Maybe."

His breathing changes, as if he's been forcing his composure and it finally breaks. He begins to take short little puffs of pure fear.

"It's her first."

"Okay." I glance down at the jar that links us, the glass as invisible as the threads of fate that tie strangers and intimates alike. "Give me the jar, let go. And then you're going to take me to your wife. The time's already here."

Outside, there's a holler from the storm, and the very rafters of the store groan. And then the soft moan of agony repeats, a woman bringing new life into a hard world, walking the line of death all by herself.

The shop owner looks warily toward Merc—

I put the jar aside and step between them. "Don't worry about him. It'll just be me. He'll stand guard, but he won't come into her birthing room."

When there's still a hesitation, I lower my voice. "This is not the first time I've attended the bed."

"How . . . many, for you."

*Hide.* "Too many to count."

The counting of moments resumes in my head, and abruptly, I've had it with the men. I push them both out of my way, and I follow my sister's laboring voice behind the counter, through a door, and into a living space that is the opposite of the farrier's. Here, everything is tidy, especially with the herb station. All its tools, as well as the plants, leaves, and roots that are in mid-preparation, stand at the ready in a neat order, no doubt for the healer who is in labor.

No dirty plates, rotting food, and scared children in the kitchen area.

There is a single door in the far corner that is cracked open.

Going over, I place my hand on the gray wood. "My name is Sorrel. May I come in?"

There's a weak groan, and I close my eyes briefly. I truly do not have the energy for more loss, more pain, more—

I push open the door. "I'm here to help you."

*Forty-Three*

# Into Battle I Go.

The beautiful woman on the bed is black of hair, dark of skin, and thin of limb. Her face is drawn in pain, and she has braced herself into a sitting position, her upper body curved around her big belly. A white shift is covering her, and she has sweated through it from her laboring. White blankets and sheets drape her shoulders and waist, and I'll bet she has bloodied what's under her already. Her weary eyes lift to meet mine, and the fear in them is something I sense, even though I do not look into them.

To make sure she can see me properly, I take the wet cloth from my face, and then I go to her. "Let me feel your belly—"

Her hand reaches out and grabs on to my own. "There's something wrong—"

Though she has a deeper accent than her husband, I can understand her words.

"Let me check."

With my free hand, I splay my palm over her distended stomach, and just as her husband appears in the doorway, I catch the ripple of the contraction that racks her. I go lower down, and am relieved to feel the baby's head. At least it's not a breech.

"How long like this?" I ask her as I kick off my shoes and move onto the bed on my knees. "Stalled, I mean—"

The woman's head falls back and she flashes her white teeth as her body attempts to force out the bairn.

"Lena . . ."

Over in the doorway, the shopkeeper switches to what must be their native tongue, his words a river of syllables spoken in a pleading voice. And then he just stands there, lingering on the periphery as they always do, scared and helpless. Though men are most often the protectors, in this sacred time, we women are the warriors, fighting for the territory we take, for the lives that we must defend against death's jealous grab.

I twist around to him. "How long has she been like this, at this frequency."

"Two hours," he mumbles. "At least. Before the storm started."

"And when did the pains start."

"Yesterday morning."

Not good. "Has her water broken?"

"Yesterday noon."

I close my eyes briefly. "We have to get the baby out now or they're both going to die."

As I go to move the blankets off of her, I already know what I'm going to find, and yes, the blood pool is tremendous. She doesn't have much time, and I'm aware of this without looking into her eyes.

"You're going to have to help," I say to her husband. "You're stronger than I am."

When he stays where he is just inside the room, I snap, "Do you want her to die while you watch? Get over here. You put the seed in her, and now you're going to have to help her with what you've both created."

This casts him into movement, and he follows my instructions, setting up at his wife's side in a kneel. As he stares in horror at the blood that's come out from between her legs, I have no patience for his shock. It's time to act. But first I must—

There's a basin on a little table, and I have a feeling it's exactly what I need. Sure enough, as I lean my nose down, I can smell the pungent bouquet rising up from the clear liquid. I plunge my hands in and scrub them vigorously.

They are dripping as I bring them out of the washing, and I leave them that way. To wipe them off, even on what appears to be a clean sheet, would compromise the cleansing.

Holding them away from everything, I position myself at the end of the bed and look up at my sister, focusing on her sweat-soaked throat. "I'm going to find the baby, okay?"

But she's gone. Though she retains consciousness, she isn't aware of anything except what's going on inside her body.

Going between her bent knees, I am gentle, yet firm, as I find her birth canal—and I can feel the baby's head. I shift my eyes to the husband.

"Let's lay her back. We need her flat. Help her now, to lie back."

As he just stares at me, like I address him in a language he can't understand, the urge to scream at him is nearly irresistible. It's just not helpful, though. The calmer I am, the calmer he'll be, and the more he'll listen to me.

"What's your name," I say, forcing my words to be slow and even.

"R-Ronl. This is my wife, Lena."

"Ronl, I need you to please lay your wife back. Gently. Do this now."

The fake patience unlocks him and he does as I ask—and though I'm easily frustrated in moments like this with the male proclivity for freezing at the birthing bed, I cannot fault the way he is with her at all. The love is there, between them, in him, as his careful hands settle her flat and her face turns to his touch with trust and acceptance. In spite of my impatience, a welling of gratitude warms my sternum, especially as I think of dear Ellyne back in my village and everything she was forced to endure.

I've almost forgotten how it should be, for all the examples I've seen on how it isn't.

"That's good, that's right." As he looks in my direction, I nod down to her belly. "Now I need you to put your strongest hand on the top of her swell, just under her heart and lungs." I expect him to hesitate, and he does. "Ronl, you're going to put your palm flat, and then cover it with your other. Right under her breasts."

He kisses her forehead and then moves into position, doing as I instruct.

"We're waiting for the next contraction." I get braced with my own hands. "I'm going to tell you what to do, and you must put all your effort into it. You will not hurt her, I promise you. But this is the time to get the baby out, and we will work together. On my command."

I look at Lena's long, dark braid, focusing on the curl at the end. I don't trust myself in the moment to stay away from her eyes and I can't know that this isn't going to work.

Because I cannot bring her or the bairn back.

Not here. Not at the Outpost.

Having already been chased out of my village, it's simply too dangerous with these strangers. The ban on magic most certainly extends to the Badlands, and I can't think of a place to escape to if I have to leave here.

"Lena, I need you to push," I tell her, even as I worry she can't hear me. "I know—I know you're tired, but we're going to help you. When the next contraction comes, you're going to push as hard as you can, every bit of you goes into it. Can you do that? For your baby?"

Abruptly, she seems to focus, as if the word unlocked something within her.

"Yes," I continue, "for the bairn. Take a deep breath with me—that's it. That's right. You're going to do this. You are going to—"

Just then, her womb contracts, and I feel her body tense.

"*Now.* Push, you must push the baby out—" I look at her husband's hands. "Ronl, push with her. All your weight, all your strength. Drive it in and down. Push the baby out of her. *Push.* If you want them to live—push!"

He does, bearing into his palms, arching his shoulders into the effort. And Lena does the same, her legs shaking, an animal sound roiling up and out of her.

The baby's position moves.

Closing my eyes so I can concentrate, I join the effort as well, but I am going in, not out. More of my fingertips make contact with the tiny skull, and I know what has happened. The baby is not face down. It's oriented to the side. So the shoulders are not passing through the wide part of the hips, but rather they are stuck on the pelvic bone.

"Harder!" I have to yell over Lena's growling. "*Harder—*"

The woman lets out a horrible scream, but it's not about pain. It's anger. It's a warrior's howl of fight.

"That's it, that's what we need!"

Another round of growling from her starts up, low at first, growing in volume. And then she screams again as her husband abruptly repositions himself, straightens his arms, and tilts all of his body weight into the downward thrust of his palms.

And then nothing happens.

No matter the effort we all do, no matter the woman's heroic straining or her husband's determined force, the baby stays where it is. Even as a fresh wash of blood hits my hands, and I begin to shake from the force I am putting into trying to grab on to the slick head, nothing seems to help—

The infant explodes out of the blockage with such velocity that its warm, slippery little body skates up my arms. I catch it in time, and immediately drag some of the sheets over to cover the tiny thing.

There is no cry. There is only floppy limbs and a still body.

I am not gentle. I rub the sheeting over the fresh skin with vigor.

"My baby . . ." Lena says weakly, her head lolling to the side.

"What is wrong?" the husband begs. As if he's confusing the question with a prayer. Or maybe for him, it's both.

"My baby, my—"

The piercing cry of the bairn is so loud, my ears ring, and yet never, ever, have I heard such a beautiful sound in all my years.

Life has won. Death has lost. And neither were my doing.

Instantly, the gray flesh becomes flush with a pink, healthy glow.

Tears come to my eyes as I turn to the woman and her husband, and lay the gift upon her breast.

"Here she is," I choke out. "Here . . . is your daughter."

*Forty-Four*

# Sunshine at Night.

As I watch Ronl and Lena marvel at what they created together, and what she brought into the world with his help, I fall back and catch my breath. When I go to wipe a strand of hair out of my face, I catch sight of the blood on my hands and glance down. The afterbirth has been passed—but the bleeding is like a faucet running out of her.

We are not finished, and we still have no time.

After I quickly cut the cord with the knife by the basin, I scramble off the bed, and plunge my hands back into the basin. When the husband looks up with grateful tears, I hold my palm out to stop the emotion so clearly welling within him.

"You must trust me to get the herbs she needs."

As I nod sharply between her legs, he looks down at the red sheets and shudders with fear.

"Go," he croaks. "Anything, take anything."

I'm nodding as I hit the floor running. Breaking out of the bedroom, I'm only vaguely aware of Merc standing in their little kitchen, as out of place as any mountain would be indoors. As his eyes pass over me, he mutters something under his breath, and I can guess my clothes are covered with blood.

"I don't have time to explain." I rush past him, and push my way out into the shop. "I need, I need . . ."

My eyes bounce around at all the jars, and instead of seeing what's in them, the signs in the foreign language are the only things that register. Panic tightens a grip on my throat as I blink and remember all the blood on that bed. This is not a success if the bairn lives, and the mother dies—

"What can I do?"

I wheel around to Merc. "I . . ."

Our stares meet, and then he asks, "What do you need."

I can't answer him. I just stand where I am, frozen like Ronl was, my breath getting short, my—

"You can do this," I hear him say as if from a great distance. "Sorrel, you've made it this far. What do you need to do."

"Stop . . . the bleeding . . . I need to stop . . ."

"And what here will do that for you?" he says calmly.

It's just the way I spoke to Ronl, and as I got through to the husband, Merc gets through to me: All at once my brain kicks back into gear and I glance to the shop entry.

"Lock the door. We don't need anyone else in here."

"I already did."

Wheeling around, I locate the three bags the shopkeeper was going to use for me as well as his scoop and the jar he almost dropped. My eyes then circle every container in the place, assessing their contents, sifting through what I know with surety, what I guess with some certainty, and what I do not recognize at all. Once the cataloguing is complete, I go into action.

"I need you to bring that down . . . and that down. Please get me those, and . . . that. Bring it all into the kitchen—"

The husband frantically appears in the doorway. "I can't rouse her. I don't know what to do. This is her shop, these are her medicines—"

"Help him bring me the jars I asked for." Grabbing the scoop, I squeeze his arm in reassurance as I rush past him. "*Hurry.*"

Back in the kitchen, at the herbist station, I find a mortar and pestle of good size, as well as a bowl and some string. The men deliver exactly what I've asked for, and I scoop out the various dried leaves into the bowl, trying not to spill them.

"Crush one of those roots," I order, not caring which of them does it.

"How much?" Merc asks.

"The biggest one in that jar there." I turn to the husband. "Go back and be with her and your daughter. Talk to Lena, try to get her to wake up with your voice and keep her with you."

"How much longer—"

"*Go,*" I cut him off.

Merc and I work side by side, and the pungent smell that rises from what he is crushing calms me down. The scent is right. And when I mix up the leaves with some water, I feel further in control. The aroma takes me back to—

My head stings with a sudden pain.

*Hide.*

I drop whatever memory tickles underneath my consciousness and the pain at my temples fades like a yell descending into silence. I stay resolutely in the present as I finish the preparation by adding in the root that Merc has, no surprise, crushed into a pulp.

"Cut me six lengths of the string. They need to be as long as your forearm."

He does so readily as I finish the preparation. Then I bring the bowl and the string with me into the bedroom. The wife looks very bad. She's cradled in her husband's lap, her mouth slack, her eyes closed, her lips drifting into the gray color her bairn was right before it roused. On her chest, the baby is nuzzling for her breast, and she does not respond.

Moving fast, I order Merc to wash his hands and then rip me up some bedsheets. He hesitates at the door for only a moment before jumping over to the basin and then grabbing a folded pile of sheeting I didn't see.

"Not strips," I tell him. "I need squares—this big."

As I air the dimensions with my hands, the sound of the tearing mixes with the bairn's cries, the newborn's struggles for its mother an instinct as ancient as time itself. After I wash my hands once again, Merc is by my side, holding out what he's done as he averts his eyes to the ceiling.

"More?" he says as if he wants a job.

"Yes," I return, even though there's a sufficiency. But it's the kindest thing I can do for him.

Taking the squares, I pack them with damp wads of the herbs and rooting, close the corners, and tie them up while leaving long strings. When I have six prepared, I move back into place between the woman's legs.

"I'll be as gentle as I can," I tell her, though her eyes are closed, and she does indeed seem to have lost consciousness.

The fact that she hasn't responded to those cries tells me she's well gone. Yet she is breathing.

With careful hands, I push the knots of damp cloth into the birthing canal one by one. I imagine them going deeper and deeper, until they reach the internal womb entrance; I picture the blood source constricting, the flow slowing, the flesh healing.

None of my visualizations will have any effect. But as with the stack of squares Merc is furiously making over at the bureau, it helps me feel a little better.

I glance up into the lovely dark face of the new mother. Her lids are still down. Her ashen color is . . . very bad.

What else, what else, what—

"I'll be right back," I blurt as I scramble off the bed.

Leaving the bedroom on a bolt, I careen back out into the shop, moving through the spaces as if they are my own. "Where are you, where are you . . . where—"

The leaves I'm looking for are up on the third shelf, the highest one. Using the ledge of the cabinetry below, I swing myself up and stand straight. As I stretch onto my tiptoes, I fumble the jar and I think of the husband as I grab it out of its free fall and clasp the container to my chest.

Jumping back down, I flash to the kitchen and knock over some mugs as I get one off a little rack. At the sink, the water comes readily, and I put too many of the leaves in. I force some out, and then mix with a spoon as I go back to the bedroom.

"Hold her up so she can drink," I say as I come in with the mug.

The husband shifts his wife higher, and wastes not a moment angling her lax head into better alignment.

"Take the bairn." Except if he lets his wife go, there's no way I'll be able to get any liquid down her throat. "No, wait—stay with her."

Like a trained dog, he snaps back into position, and I twist around to Merc. "I need you to hold the baby. If this works, there will be agitation."

The stillness in him seems to seep out through the room. For all his command, for all his strength, I have, with the simple request, utterly disarmed him.

"*Merc*, I need you to hold the bairn. *Now.*"

I nod sharply at the newborn who's at her mother's side, and that seems to bring him back to attention—but he moves half as fast as I'd like, and not at all as he usually does, his body clunky and unsure. When his hands reach out, they tremble as he gathers the small, crying bundle up from the bedding. With that settled, I lean down with the mug, and in my peripheral vision, I see him stepping back with the baby like he's cradling a broadsword pointed at his chest.

Refocusing on Lena, I put the tincture to her lips.

"Drink." I put some more volume in my voice. "Lena, you need to drink."

The husband breaks in, speaking in their language, and thank the crescent moon, that gets Lena's attention. She responds on a mumble, her lips parting.

I take advantage of this, tilting the mug. Most is spilled, but I can tell by the way her throat moves that she swallows a little of it. More, she needs more. I try again.

"Tell her to drink, in your language."

The husband offers another trill of syllables, and I wait for the response. As the wife opens her mouth, I take her chin, force it down, and pour most of what's left in the earthen mug into her. She sputters and coughs, speckling my face with the cold tea—

But then she swallows in a gulp.

I sit back and look at the damp brown leaves that are left in the bottom. As I put the mug down on the floor, I tell myself I can make more, but if she takes too much, she'll go into seizure and die from—

The wife's eyes flare open and she gasps. Then her face flushes with color, and she heaves a deep breath. And another. The animation that follows is restless and uncoordinated, her hands and feet twitching, the muscles in her legs spasming. But she's breathing, deep and often, dragging in the air she needs as her heart no doubt races from the concoction.

We all watch her. Her husband, right by her head. Me, at her side.

Merc standing over the bloody bed with the couple's daughter in his massive arms.

"Get me a belt," I order Ronl as the trembling rises even further.

Ronl reaches down for his waist, and paddles through his clothes. But then twists around. "I don't have—"

There's a *snap*!

"Use one of mine."

Merc holds out a black strap that's part of one of his holsters. As I take it, and put the length between Lena's teeth, she immediately clamps down on the strip of hide. The guard is just in time: She goes rigid, the shaking coalescing into a straining as all her muscles lock up.

I glance down at the mug once again. Fates, if I've given her the wrong dose . . .

It feels like hours, yet the seizure lasts probably no longer than a minute, and the first sign the stimulation is backing off is the easing of her feet. The next is her legs and arms, the straining stiffness relenting. And then she inhales more slowly.

The storm passes as fast as it came, but in its wake, the revival lasts. Her eyes flutter open and she looks to her husband first—and then to the mercenary dressed in black who is holding her precious daughter.

And that's when I glance back at Merc.

He's staring down at the bairn, his black hair falling forward, the twin braids with their beads swinging freely. The baby is quiet, but not because anything is wrong. He's taken his pinkie and offered it as a pacifier—and it's been accepted. He's also rocking back and forth on his boots, his weight shifting just enough to find a rhythm.

The incongruence of him with the tiny infant is like the night being interrupted by a bolt of sunshine, and my gaze locks on the hilt of that broadsword, rising up over his shoulder as if the weapon, too, is looking down on the bairn.

Merc's expression is utterly remote.

And I wonder how many children of his own he's lost.

*Forty-Five*

# Only One of Me.

"No, no, you stay with your Lena and the baby. We will be all right."

I'm standing by the shop's exit, and I'm in a set of red felt women's clothes. The bell skirt and jacket are surprisingly soft and lightweight, but the warmth I expected. There's even an inner pocket for the gold.

With all the blood on my own clothes—Julion's, rather—I couldn't go back to the lodging house without attracting unwanted attention, and we've bundled everything in a sack. The hospitality doesn't want to end there, however. Ronl is worrying over us, trying to press food in our hands.

"No more," Merc tells him as he puts a hand on that shoulder in a very different way. "Worry after your wife and daughter."

It's the same gesture we started with, but the four of us have become intimates of a sort. I will say that Ronl's obvious gratitude is nothing I'm used to, and my guarded heart reminds me that tomorrow, neither he nor his wife will know me again. That's always the way with my efforts, whether I use my illicit gifts or not.

So I drink this favorable regard up, and hold it close.

"Wait, wait, you needed something." Ronl motions about his shop. "You came here for a reason, you asked for things. You must take whatever you require. Please."

I cradle my injured forearm to my chest, and take a last glance around. I used all of the *purpa* and *turtine* on Lena, and the *roships* does nothing if not in concert with the other two. The rest of what's on offer I'm not sufficiently sure of, and I can't take risks of poisoning myself.

"What may I get you?" Ronl goes to the folded paper bags by the register of cash. "There is much here—I could ask Lena—"

"No, no, you let her rest." Then something occurs to me. "Although . . . I don't suppose you have any soap—"

"Yes! Yes, for to clean the skin?"

Ronl wheels away and all but runs back for his kitchen. He returns in a moment with a full bar that smells like the poultice I was going to make.

"Lena uses this on wounds." At the main counter, he puts the soap in a wax bag and folds the top over. "Please, take it. She washes times three a day—I wish she could advise you. She's a healer of some note—are you all right? How badly are you hurt?"

"I'll be fine," I lie. "Thank you."

Ronl presses the fragrant gift into my hands, and holds his own palms to my own. "If you hadn't come in—"

"It was meant to be." I pull the hood of the felt jacket up over my head, and not just because of the storm. "Now worry no longer and go be with your family."

"And lock the door behind us." Merc steps over to the bolt and points at it as if the shopkeeper might forget it's there. "I won't leave until you do."

My eyes prickle with emotion, and I lower my voice. "He's like that."

Merc opens the door, and we're quick about the exit. The storm's only gotten stronger somehow, the rain riding the gusts of wind and lashing at us with such ferocity, he puts an arm around my waist to hold me on the ground lest I be swept off.

And he waits. Until the bolt is thrown.

Then we are off, into the horizontal rain, the bracing gale, the deep muddy puddles. Merc is undaunted. The way he moves against the fury, how solid he is, how strong, is a reminder that both sexes have their utility in the harsh world. Without him, I would become a tumble that is carried away.

I also stay dry. So this is the why of the felt, I reflect, as the water beads off as it would the back of waterfowl.

When we get to the first of the entries into the pub and lodging house, Merc tries the doors and they're locked. He goes to the second set, with the same result—and I begin to worry. At the final entry, he releases me, and puts both hands on the grips, clearly prepared to rip open the panels if necessary—

They open just fine. And he all but throws me inside. As he jumps in behind me, he shuts things—

So many eyes upon us.

Though most of the chatter in the pub continues, and I avoid all the gazes, I can feel the attention like I'm too close to a fire.

*Hide.*

Except I would have hunkered down anyway. Merc, at my side, does the opposite. Instead of skirting the edges and ducking the pub's patrons as we head for the stairs, he tucks me into him with an arm around my shoulders, and he walks us right through the center of it all, as if there aren't easily a hundred or more roughheads, ne'er-do-wells, and gamblers measuring us for opportunities and weaknesses.

He doesn't care. Then again, he's used to this, no doubt. Me? I look around furtively, assessing the place for spots to take cover behind—which is more reflex than anything I'm going to act upon.

Staying with him is the very best course.

Similar to the Gauntlet, a bar runs down the far side, the difference being this establishment and everything in it is three to four times the size of Mr. Lewis's ale emporium. Round tables fill this space, barmaids deliver food and drink, and ladies who make their money upstairs drift around and sing in low-cut gowns that are not made of felt, but rather of proper, colorful silks that are fitted beautifully to their bodies. Lanterns hang from the low rafters, lighting it all—except for a stretch against the back wall, which is so dim, I can't see what is there.

A warning tingles up my spine as I focus on that darkness, and as my eyes adjust, some details emerge. It seems as though a single trestle table runs parallel to the rear of the building, and all its chairs face outward toward the open area with the patrons. The group of men sitting along its far flank have arranged themselves such that their heads are secreted outside of the dim glow of a couple of black candles.

There's a single man at the head of the group, and he's in an armchair.

That's when I see the hat. A top hat—

As if he senses my regard, the king of them all leans forward, only the bottom half of his visage entering into the flickering light, the rest hidden by the hat's edge. It's the rider, from the refreshing stream—and he's looking in my direction.

Touching that brim, he gallantly tilts his head . . . and smiles in that way he did when he told me the water I was in was poisoned.

I look away quickly, and trip on something.

"Watch it, wench—" The angry patron shuts himself up as Merc stops short. "She—um, she hit my chair."

The bearded man, who's not in felt clothes, goes back to his mead with a wince as the two others sitting with him also stare down into their tankards. After a moment, Merc keeps going, although I suspect, were I not with him, there would have been conversation.

If not more.

All I want to do is make it to the stairs in one piece and get away from the crowd. There are too many chances already being taken here, and I don't want to be rolling any more dice, literally or figuratively.

I've already won the pot tonight—

Fate is not done with me. We're nearly to the steps when I see someone bursting out of what appears to be the kitchen. It's the short-haired maid with the lovely singing voice—

"Oh, hello," I call over to her.

She ignores me, dropping her head and putting an empty tray up on her shoulder like she wants to hide underneath it. And it's then I see the man in a dirty butcher's apron who props open that swinging panel.

My blood runs cold and my feet halt. The image of him raising that heavy iron skillet above his shoulder, with his sweaty, red face carved in rage and his swollen body shaking, explodes into my mind's eye.

"Sorrel?"

I hear Merc say my name from a vast distance, and I'm too locked in to respond to him. I can tell by the way the cook stays put and tracks the maid through the crowd that he's staked possession of the girl. It's as if she's a dog, not a person, and he's checking to see if she follows her training. On her side, she constantly refers back to him with her eyes as she gathers used plates and empty tankards from tables full of men who tug at her felt skirt and laugh too loud.

"Come on," Merc says as he takes my elbow.

Abruptly, the man in the dirty apron stares at me with a glower on his ruddy face, and I imprint his appearance. He's ill-shaven, he has pockmark scars on his fleshy cheeks, and his thinning hair is combed over a bald spot. I can't tell whether he's of twenty years or forty, and I do not meet his eyes. Not the place or time—

"What're you lookin' at," he demands before spitting on the floor.

"You want to try that again."

Merc's voice cuts through the din, and the man looks up, way up. His surprise suggests he was so busy tracking the maid and then glaring at me, he somehow failed to notice the man who's with me, and I can tell the cook is going to fold and disappear back through that door even before he moves: It's in the way his bluster crumbles, his shoulders cave, his posture sinks, nothing but a paper monster who nonetheless can kill.

Right before he ducks out, his nasty, beady eyes go to that girl, and I'm terrified she'll pay for the mood he's in and the interruption of my presence. The bastard. He's the kind of man who only feels power when he makes someone smaller than him cower—

"Let's go," Merc says as the kitchen panel flaps shut.

As I'm drawn onto the steps, I look for the girl one last time. She's all the way across the pub, balancing what should have been an impossible load of tankards and plates upon her frail shoulder. And then my view is obscured by the stairwell wall.

At the top landing, Merc glances at me. "I'm not going to let anything happen to you while you're here, don't worry."

It's the maid I'm concerned with, not me.

We start down the corridor to our room, passing by the doors of the working women. Even though my body is beside him and I'm walking, I am far, far away, back in my own past. As I was an orphan, I've always felt like the women I've helped on the birthing bed are my family, my sisters, even though they never could or wanted to acknowledge me afterward—and I wish now, as I always have, that I'd be able to protect them all, the pregnant ones, those who toil under cruel masters, the sick, the infirm, the unfairly accused and the terribly abused.

But there are just too many . . . and only one of me.

## *Forty-Six*

# For the Best.

As I step into the water closet once again, I feel as though weeks have passed. I shut the door most of the way, leaving the same crack I did before, and go to the sink, where I set the clothes I was wearing during the birth to a soaking. If Julion the golden nobleman knew where his fine togs ended up? No doubt he would have kept them in his saddlebags.

Then I head to the big basin. Dipping my hand in the water I had planned to sit in, I find it cold and pull the plug in the bottom.

Exhaustion settles in as the gurgling rises into the silence, and it's only concern over infection that motivates me to start another run. Before I undress, I take a glimpse out into the bedroom. Merc is back where he was in the window seat, facing away from me, his legs bent, his boots once again pressed against the alcove's wall. His pack is on the floor beside him, however, and a lot of his weapons are with it, the cluster of deadly metal objects arranged with the grips facing him.

His elbows are on his knees, and his hands are out in front of him. He's flexing his fingers open and closed, and then he's staring at his palms.

I wonder if he's remembering the bundled bairn and I want to talk about the experience we shared. All of my previous near misses and dangerous saves have been nothing I could speak with anybody about.

As if I had anyone other than Mare?

And her I only had for a year.

Merc has not said one word since we returned to the room, though, and he is certainly not looking like he wants to chat.

Leaving him to his brooding, I back away and undress. The skirt stands up on its own, forming a cone of red, and the hooded jacket fits on top of the point as if designed to do so.

"Odd, but rather handy . . ."

Back over at the sink, I unwrap the soap, and though the level is not very high in the tub, I get in and sit down. The water falling from above is warm, and a balm to every ache and chafe I have—and there are a lot of them. Sinking into the pool I've created, I let the overhead rain dapple on me like fingertips. As I'm eased, my lids drift down and I put the soap to my nose—

The sensation of constriction on my forearm reminds me I haven't unwrapped again the injury yet.

The pain is too great to be good news.

I'm quick with the undoing, knowing that drawing things out is just going to hurt more. In the dimness, I can't tell much, but I know from the throbbing that the wound is even worse than it was as I left.

"That's what the soap is for," I say out loud.

Working the bar in my palms, the suds come as they're called, and I hiss a curse at the first pass over the injury. That talon was not clean, for certain, and I pray my raw flesh isn't a breeding ground for some kind of disease as well as the infection.

The latter is bad enough.

After three cleaning rounds, I can't take any more attention in that tender area—and given the amount of scrapes and rough spots I have in other places, I pass the bar over the whole of me, even my hair. At some point I have to stop and release the drain, for the water level is too high, and when it's time to rinse, I unplug things entirely and stand up.

As I tilt my head back to the fall of warm water, I think of the rain outside. There's got to be a cistern on the roof collecting what's falling from the sky.

Whatever the Outpost can be criticized for, one cannot fault its bathing facilities.

When I finally turn off the faucet and step out of the tub, I feel quite a bit refreshed in spite of the thumping pain of the wound, and I don't want to put the felt outfit back on—

"Here." Merc's thick arm comes through the gap between the door and the jamb. "Dry off and wrap up with this."

It's one of the sheets from the bed, that he's evidently stripped off.

I slap a hold across my breasts, and my other hand goes to the juncture of my legs. But it's not as if he can see through the gray wood panels—and he comes no farther inside.

"Ah . . . thank you." I take what he's offering like it's going to bite me. "That's most kind."

The sheeting is soft and fragrant, and after passing it over my body and damp hair, I wind it round and round. Then I tear off a piece and wrap up my forearm. After that . . . I stay where I stand, very aware of my nakedness in spite of all that covers me.

Except I'm not about to sleep in here.

Squaring my shoulders, I open the door as if I'm fully clothed and step out—

Merc is back in the window seat, his arms crossed over his chest, his chin down, his eyes closed. His dark hair is already drying, and I think of how grateful I am to be out of wet, constrictive clothing, all clean and warm. Doesn't he want the same? Then again, we are not the same. Nothing about his circumstances ever seems to discourage him.

"Take the lantern," he tells me without looking over. "To the bed. And then turn the flame down until it's almost out."

"All right."

I go over and pick up the source of light by its handle. Before I pivot back around, I notice that he has followed his own rule this time. The bolting to our room is well latched.

At the bed, I see that he's remade that which he no doubt messed up getting the sheet free.

"It's quite big enough for the both of us," I hear myself say. "The . . . bed."

"I'm fine over here."

"All right."

My cheeks are flaming with embarrassment as I mount the mattress—and I find that there's a hook driven into the wall right by my head. The lantern hangs from it readily, and I take a last glance at Merc before I turn the little lever and the illumination is strangled down to just a blue and yellow nub at the crown of the wick.

With the glow all but gone, sounds swell to fill the void: I hear the rain still falling with ferocity on the roof above, and the whistle of the wind in the shutters, and the distant notes of a piano. Voices crest and fall in volume and number, but they are far off.

"When are you leaving?" I ask into the darkness as I lie back on top of the covers.

There's no reply, to the point where I assume he has fallen asleep. And then Merc clears his throat.

"Soon," he says. "I'm taking another job."

Curling onto my side, I give him my back, and tell myself it's because I always face the door when I sleep. That's not it.

I need to leave him first, and not just for my pride's sake.

The sooner I get used to being on my own again, the better—

"I don't want any payment." His voice winds its way to my ears. "For getting you here."

I close my lids and shrink in my own skin. What happened to the man who kissed me by the stream, I wonder. "Not even money?"

"I've never been motivated by coin."

"Isn't that the point of being a mercenary?" When he doesn't reply, I feel churlish. "Well, I got a deal then, didn't I."

The silence between us presses down on me like a weight, and my lungs burn. I want to prod him into telling me the things he's hiding. I know they're there—if I have secrets, he does as well. But something changed again when he went down for our food earlier, though I doubt I'll ever know what it is.

And then came the baby.

Perhaps it's for the best.

Too bad it hurts.

*Sorrel! Wake up—*

I am in a maelstrom, my body lashed by a furious, swirling current that stings. But the male voice is urgent and close by, and I use it to orient myself because I can't seem to see anything. Sand. I taste sand in my mouth and feel the grit of it go down my throat as I gasp. The coughing fit that comes next—

I jerk upright on a bed, and the next thing I know, the mattress beneath me is tilting and a heavy arm is around my shoulders. As I pant in fear . . . I smell cedar. And that's when everything comes back into proper focus.

Merc. The lodging room. The Outpost.

"It's just a dream—shhh, woman." He pulls me into his lap. "That's all it is. Only a dream . . ."

My heart is pounding, and I am more aware, yet nothing much changes. I'm still surrounded by sand and I can't understand where it's coming from. The gritty abrasive is on my skin, and it's in my hair, too, the fine particles—

The Fulcrum. Somehow, the Fulcrum has come to find me.

As I tremble, a big hand circles my back. "Sorrel, easy there, it was only a dream."

Merc's voice is soothing, but I have no idea what he's saying. So I repeat the syllables over and over until they have meaning: "A . . . dream. It was a dream. A dream—"

"That's right. You've been thrashing about like a fish on a line."

Hazy images I can't decipher taunt me, even though my eyes are wide open and there's a flicker of orange lightning that chases away most of the shadows for a moment. The nightmare is just out of my conscious reach, the horror nothing I can grasp, yet it lingers inside my body, in shocks of anxiety and a pounding heart.

Recognizing that Merc is my way out of the realm I was in, I twist toward him and grab for his surcoat. The folds of leather are warm and soft, and I curl my hands into them.

"It's okay." He cups the back of my head and urges me into his chest. "I've got you."

The darkness is so dense, and the sound of the rain so loud, if I didn't have this physical contact, I'm quite sure I would be floating off into the night, into the storm, never to return again. Instead, Merc's scent, and the feel of his hair on my cheeks, and the way I'm held, anchor me.

He's murmuring something, the rumble in his chest transmitting into me, the brush of his chin against my temple as intimate as a kiss. The next thing I know, I'm releasing the hold on his surcoat and passing my hands inside. I feel his ribs and the ropes of muscle that run up his torso, and remember being on the horse and having to duck under to avoid being seen.

He pulls back a little, but I follow him—and when he tries again, I stay with him still.

"Sorrel . . ." His tone is firm, a fence line.

I have no choice but to let go—and it's as I retract my arms that my hand passes over something that is not muscle, is not bone, is not his leg or his arm . . .

But is long and hard.

His inhale is sharp and he jerks back.

He does not leave the bed.

"I know what you want," I whisper as I stay where I am, my body tilted into his.

"No, you don't." His hand touches my hair, though, his fingertips lingering on the white waves, before moving down onto my shoulder. "Not really."

"So leave," I counter softly. "Go back to the window seat, or go out that door."

He won't, though. In the same way I'm certain something changed for him earlier, I'm also clear that nothing has—at least not in this darkness, in this bed. In this moment.

Even though he's trying not to, he wants me.

"Sorrel."

There's an entreaty behind my name now, but I'm not inclined to help him out of his struggles. That's his journey, and I can guess what it's about. A woman he's come to have some regard for is an entirely different proposition for prostitution than someone he just wants to have a round with.

On my side, I want him. And as devastating as the consequences will be when he leaves me, right now, I don't care about them.

*"Sorrel."*

And there it is, the sexual craving that threads through his deep, low voice.

I move my hand back where it passed over, and as I feel the contours of his arousal, he groans and arches into me, his hips pushing forward. Immediately, he falls into a rhythm with my touch, his pelvis retreating only to come forward again, the length of him too much for my hand even as I splay my fingers wide.

Nuzzling into his neck, my lips brush the beating pulse at the side of his throat. I'm well aware that I'm testing his self-control, but I've made my decision. He needs to make his—

Merc is on top of me in the next breath, and his mouth on mine is not gentle. As his weight pushes me down, I split my legs so that he can come between them—and he does. I feel the hard ridge of him pressing into the sheeting that separates us, searching for the core of me.

He's riding me now, the thrusts as if he's already inside my body, and as his tongue enters my mouth, I moan at the thought of a penetration down below. Heat gathers there, and flows throughout my body, turning me liquid—

His lips leave mine and I can suddenly breathe easier as he sits up. It's not what I want. My desperate, fumbling hands reach up to bring him back.

As if our passion has called to the storm, lightning flares in a double strike, and the orange flash breaches the closed shutters to illuminate him. He's peeling off the leather surcoat, his chest expanding as he removes it. Then as the thunder comes, he strips off the mesh armor underneath, and there's a thump when the heavy metal links hit the floor.

Merc is coming back down to me as the next strike happens, and the orange flare dances through his midnight hair and his fierce features. He doesn't lie on me, but reclines on his side, his hands going to the top of the sheeting that winds around me, his fingertips traveling the makeshift bodice and the skin that's begging for his touch.

Stretching my arms up, I'm aware of a prickling ache from my wound, but it's so easy to ignore. The headboard is made of wooden slats, and I grab on to them as I curl my spine and offer him what he is going to take. What he must have. In this night, we are alone not just because there is no one with us, but because this feels as if we're out of any earthly timeline. We're swirling in a mutual dream, even as we're awake . . . the fantasy becoming a shadow reality that the daylight cannot grow, and the darkness harvests with abandon.

His fingers dip under the roll of the sheeting, and I feel him loosen the constriction. What covers me melts away, exposing my breasts to his hungry eyes as the lightning comes again. In another flicker of orange, I watch his head drop down to me, and then feel his lips on my nipple. As I cry out, the thunder consumes the sound of his name leaving my lips.

He knows what to do.

His hair spills around me, and the beads at the ends of his braids are smooth and cool against my collarbones, while his mouth latches on and sucks—and then his sword hand is on my body, traveling down my shoulder and onto my other breast. He owns me, playing me as an instrument, his callused palm sweeping to my waist, my hip, traveling back up to cup me and stroke me.

Crescent moon, he knows . . . exactly what to do.

Releasing the headboard, I dive into his hair and pull him hard to me. I think he chuckles, I'm not sure.

The thunder comes again.

Merc's back lying in between my thighs now, and I'm rubbing myself on him, the core of me hungry—and getting hungrier—as the lightning flashes anew and I see him, I see what he's doing to me as I feel it—the licking, the plying, the tugging. And his thumb, on the other side, going back and forth over my other—

The hand leaves my breast.

His weight shifts away once again, and I start to protest—but then his palm skates down the curve of my waist to the swell of my hip. Now it's on the outside of my thigh.

Merc breaks off kissing the tip he's so diligently applied his attentions to and returns to my mouth . . .

As his touch goes to the inside of my leg.

Slowly. Slowly . . . he rides up the soft skin . . .

And finds the even softer flesh that is wet for him.

He palms me, the heel of his hand pushing into me, and his fingers probe, but do not enter. For a split second, my rational side separates and tells me to be prepared. I've heard Sallae Mae talk to the new girls about how the first time can be painful. I wish I were better prepared. I wish I'd had sisters who could have told me how to do this, how to make it good for him as well when I touch him—

The lightning flickers yet more and brings the contours of the ceiling out of the darkness for a brief second. In the lull before the thunder, I'm aware that I sound like the women behind the doors at the Gauntlet, behind the doors at the head of the stairs here. I'm breathing hard and making soft plying sounds. I moan again—

"You will come for me," he says against my mouth. Then he puts his lips by my ear. "Sorrel . . ."

He issues the command by the way he says my name in a growl and by the way he starts to stroke me down below, the friction licking into me like the lightning, bringing an electrical charge to the very heart of my body that doubles and redoubles.

Outside, the storm swells to a terrible intensity, the rain lashing even harder, the wind clawing at the lodging house, as if it's trying to batter the whole town down.

Inside, I become the lightning. What he's called up within me unleashes, the great power let loose such that it shatters me apart with a pleasure so great I—

All at once, the room is alit with stars.

Though it makes no sense, white sparks flow across the ceiling to the four corners, skittering along the beams before they free-fall to the floor. For sure, this is all in my mind—

No, it's not.

Merc's head jerks up, and he looks around with wide black and white eyes as the beautiful display twinkles, a galaxy come to us—except unlike a clear night sky, whatever it is isn't eternal. As the sensations in my body begin to fade, the light show does as well, all that was released dimming until once more, the darkness consumes us and we float in a void.

Tethered only to each other.

And the storm.

## *Forty-Eight*

# The Departure and a Summoning.

When next I wake, I am alone and it's daylight.

Though the rain still falls, a lonesome gray dawn seeps into the room through the cracks in the window shutters, and the sallow illumination brings out the contours of the empty window seat, the table where the lantern was at first, and the bed I lie upon.

Pushing the hair out of my face, I look down at myself. Covers have been pulled up over me, and beneath them, my body is rewrapped in the sheet.

My eyes return to the window seat—but as if Merc could be there and I've missed him? Gone too are his backpack, and his weapons.

Fates, he's left me.

Putting my hands to my face, I try to piece together the night before. I don't get far and give up fast—and as I lower my arms, I look up at the ceiling and wonder if what he did to me in the darkness wasn't all a dream.

A beautiful, impossible dream.

Whether real or not, Merc left as the stranger he was, anonymously and in silence. His departure makes me think of when he first came through the door at the Gauntlet. Everyone stopped what they were doing and stared—just like they did last night downstairs. He's the kind of man you notice, and I can't help but wonder who's watching him walk into what room now. Where is he going, especially in all this rain?

Not here. That's all I know, and probably all I'll ever know.

As a piercing pain wracks my whole body, I have only myself to blame. I knew all along this was coming, and I made it worse last night. Still, I'd been hoping that if it was raining I'd have more time with him. But as if any storm is strong enough to stop him?

Though the room is not completely dark, I hunger for illumination to make me feel less alone. Reaching for the lantern as it hangs on the hook, I fumble around to find the crank—

The strangest thing happens.

The tiny glow on the wick flares to life before I get to the lever to raise the oil-soaked weave. And then when I go to take my hand away? The flame re-lowers itself.

Frowning, I try again, moving my fingertips forward—and the same thing occurs. The flame rises toward them as they get close to the clouded glass of the lamp, and when I move my hand around, the glow follows, the little teardrop-shaped flare tilting as if it's reaching for—

A creak of floorboards jerks my head to the water closet.

As my heart pounds, I grab for my waist out of habit, for the little knife used to be holstered there—

Merc steps out. His hair's wet, but he's fully clothed and armored, with weapons on—and he's as compelling and masculine as ever. Even more so to me now.

He stops and looks down at himself. "What?"

Treacherous relief threatens to flatten me, even as I'm not on my feet. And then I realize he's asked me something. "I . . . ah, I'm sorry?"

"What are you looking at? Do I have something untucked?"

The absurdity of the inquiry stalls me—like he's worried his britches are on backwards? And as he waits for a response, his brows rise, and his head tilts to one side.

"Have you gone daft in the night, then?"

"Yes, I have," I whisper to myself. Then more loudly, I say, "Nothing untucked, no. I'm just surprised you're still here."

"Where else would I be in this storm." He strides for the door. "In any event, I'll be back in a couple of hours. You rest."

"I'm not tired—"

"Then you'll stay here because you're not stupid and you know it's the safe thing to do." With a quick twist of his torso, he glances back at me. "Did you really think I'd left you? Without saying goodbye."

I clear my throat. "Oh, no. Not at all—"

"I won't leave without telling you." He taps the heavy metal bolting mechanism. "How would you be able to lock yourself in?"

As if that's the only consideration. "Well . . . thank you."

Our eyes meet, and I find myself holding my breath for some sort of . . . anything from him. No, that's a lie. I want something specific, some proclamation that what happened between us is the sort of rare thing he'll hold in his mind, too. When he says nothing, I think now would be a good time to tip his proverbial hand by dropping his gaze down my body or giving me that knowing half smile of his. Or saying . . . something, anything—

Merc pulls back the latch and taps it again. "I don't leave till I hear this get thrown."

He's out in the blink of an eye, closing the door behind him.

Only the thought of him waiting on the far side gets me to move, and I shift my legs to the floor—

The door opens again, and he brings in a tray of food. "She brought this for you. From the kitchen—"

"The maid who sings?" I make sure the sheeting stays wrapped around me. "Is she out there?"

"No, she hurried off." Merc puts the food on the table. "But she told me to tell you she tested this all. It's safe."

The same bread, carefully torn into bite-size pieces, the same refreshing drink—but there are two tankards and enough of everything for both him and me.

"There's some for you here," I point out.

"I'm not hungry. And anyway, I'm more of a meat eater." His eyes skate around the room, and then linger at the ceiling as if he's trying to measure the rainfall by what it sounds like on the roof. Finally, he nods at the latch. "Remember."

"How could I forget," I mutter as the door closes once more.

Standing there, I wait for another delivery from him. A second tray of food and drink. A stolen pony.

Nothing.

I go over to the latch, and shove it back into place. "Happy now?"

He doesn't reply to me, but I hear his heavy boots walking away. Pent up, I do some striding of my own, taking a little pass around the room. I end up back in front of the tray, and I picture the young maid scurrying up here with the nourishment, perhaps because she waited until that cook either passed out or went after someone else.

I eat not because I'm hungry, but because of the risks she took to bring me the food.

At least the bread still tastes good, and the drink sizzles through me, waking me up properly. The latter carries a complication as a side effect. I already sense the walls closing in on me, and the extra energy makes me feel even more trapped. But then I think of the man in the top hat, and all the others like him or worse. As much as I want to rail against Merc and his stupid bolt rule, he's right, this is a dangerous place—

*Knock. Knock.*

"Now what." I glare at the door. "Have you forgot something—"

"Sorrel?" A male voice—not Merc's—brings me to instant attention. "Sorrel, are you—"

Without thinking, I undo the bolt and yank the panels open. Ronl, the new father, is on the other side, standing in the corridor in his brown felt suiting, his eyes behind his glasses shifting over his shoulder, as if he's anxious he was followed. When he refocuses on me, he flushes and looks at the gray floorboards.

Oh, he's not anxious about what's in his wake. Of course he doesn't want to be caught anywhere near me.

The warmth and hospitality he offered as we were leaving was him overcome with emotion. But he's returned to his senses now—as they all do.

I pull the sheeting up higher. "What's wrong?"

"It's Lena," he says urgently. "She needs you."

## *Forty-Nine*

# Sister.

As I make my second trip through the rain to the herbist shop, I'm back in the red felt outfit and I have its hood up to protect Ronl. He's leading the way, and all I can say is at least what comes out of the gray sky is no longer horizontal and most of the orange lightning has stopped. I've never seen a storm last this long, and feel compelled to express this, but between all the water falling and the wind that can't seem to choose a direction, there's no conversation between myself and Lena's husband. Not that he's looking for any.

There's much mud, however. So much mud.

Felt shoes would be nice. Or maybe a rowboat.

When we get to the shop after what feels like quite a trek, Ronl jumps ahead and unlocks the door with a big key.

"Is she in the—"

"She's in the—"

As if she'd be anywhere else but the bedroom.

Rushing down the aisle, I skip around the counter and the register of cash, and see nothing of the kitchen on my way to the open doorway—

When I get a view of the bed, I stop so fast, I trip and nearly fall on my face. Across the gray-boarded space, sitting up against the headboard, Lena is smiling as she cradles her infant to her chest. Ronl's beloved wife has freshly braided hair and is in a clean white shift. Likewise, the bedclothes have all been changed, and there's a smoking dish of incense sweetening the air with the scent of *phosies* and *trill.*

"My sis—" I stop short, remembering my place.

For all we shared the night before, I remind myself that we are but strangers in the light of day, only my inner loneliness linking us now—

Lena holds her steady hand out to me. "Come, see what you helped into the world."

For a moment, I'm not sure I've heard right, and I'm vaguely aware of Ronl stepping in behind me. But then Lena sends her husband a radiant smile and holds out the bundled bairn to me.

"Come, see."

An utterly unfamiliar feeling of warmth and friendship envelops me, all of it coming from her. In response, it's like I'm on a cloud as I go over to the bed, and when Lena pats the mattress beside her, I sit down.

After which I find myself holding her precious child.

I hate that I must avoid the eyes of the little girl, because the face staring up at me is so perfectly formed, I want to take note of each and every feature. As it is, I linger on the tiny little mouth and the button chin, the chubby dark cheeks and the dusting of fine, dark curls.

I want to believe this precious gift will live forever. So I cannot bear to meet her stare.

"Oh, Lena." I glance over, keeping my eyes just above the new mother's head, on the tight braids of her dark hair. "She's so beautiful."

"She is called Gloriana, after my mother." Lena's voice chokes up. "I lost her just a year ago."

Closing my eyes, I shake my head. "I am so sorry."

"Thank you. I will honor my mother's memory by raising my daughter to be a healer, like us."

"Your mother was also one?"

"No, like you and me. We are healers."

I go very still. I suppose the word fits, but I can't say as I've ever known what I am. Refocusing, I glance at the bowl of astringent that still sits on the table nearby. It, too, has been changed, the water clear, no longer bloody.

"Ronl said you needed to see me?" I look at the stitching on her bed dress's bodice. "Are you having difficulty?"

Lena shakes her head. "You did what the mistress who taught me would have done. I'd have helped myself in just the same way, but I didn't have the strength." She reaches out and touches my knee. "I cannot thank you enough. If you hadn't come to the shop when you did . . ."

"It was fate." I run a forefinger across the bairn's chubby cheek. "And sometimes the invisible ropes that link strangers can be kind."

Lena's smile is luminous. "Yes."

And then she gets serious: "But you came into the shop for your own reason, and Ronl told me the three things you asked for. You referred to them by different names, but I know what they're for—two of them you used for me. Who is hurt, you or your husband?"

"Husband? Oh, he's not my . . ." As I flush, I take a deep breath and nod at my forearm. "I was . . . scraped. And I know that some things must be treated. But Ronl gave me soap which I have used to good effect."

I say this more out of gratitude to her than any examination I did this morning. There was no time to check under the wrapping before I left.

"Will you let me take a look at it?"

I blink. A couple of times. In all the years I've treated others, never once has anybody asked after my welfare—much less cared enough to do something about it.

"Ronl?" Lena smiles as her husband reappears in the doorway. "Will you please take your daughter?"

The herbist's husband is right and ready for the job, happily coming in and accepting a transfer. He is clearly enchanted with the infant and I contrast his warmth with the farrier's disinterest in progeny of the so-called fairer sex.

On his way out, he closes the door most of the way, and it's then I feel Lena's full attention. The way she looks at me, with steady, clear-eyed regard, tells me more than any explanation involving words that she has, in fact, come through the birth well enough. She's certainly of sufficient strength to direct her own care from this point—strong enough, too, to direct mine, apparently.

She sits up higher in her bedding. "Where are you hurt?"

Inhaling a deep breath, I undo the fastenings on the felt jacket, and I can't hide the wince as I remove my outer layer.

"Your forearm, then?"

I nod and pull up the sleeve of the under-shirting. With care, I begin to unwrap the sheeting I'd bound it in after my bathing last night, and I have to stop halfway through. Closing my eyes, I will the pain level down so that I can continue, acutely aware that this woman beside me knows even more than I do about physical agony.

Compared to labor, this is nothing. I need to toughen up—

"Take your time," she says softly.

Am I nodding again? I don't know. What I do know, as I get back to the unwrapping, is this is all a very bad sign. And I can feel the heat already.

Lena lets out a gasp as the binding finally drops away, and I glance around the bedroom to avoid looking at my arm.

"How did you do this?" she asks.

"I . . . ah, I fell."

"When."

"Yesterday."

As I risk a glance at the wound, all I can do is curse under my breath. The swelling has made the outer ring around the injury form a valley, and like the Lake of Lost Souls, the flesh in between is bad news: An infection has not just burrowed in, it's spreading, the redness no longer localized, but running the length and circumference of the lower part of the limb.

Lena's voice gets very no-nonsense. "You must be honest with me, if I'm to treat this properly. How did this happen?"

What does it matter, I think with exhaustion. There are lots of travelers that come through here, why would my identity be sussed out? And if it somehow were, and word traveled back north and east, would my village really have the resources to come find me?

Although Julion might. If he decided he needed to force that service he wanted from me.

Still, I tell her what happened.

"We crossed the Lake of Lost Souls yesterday." I shrug, trying to be nonchalant as if that will have any effect on . . . anything. "A big black bird of prey came out of the sky and attacked us—"

The gasp that Lena lets out is loud enough so that Ronl reenters the room. "Are you okay—"

"A skystalker?" she grits. "You survived an attack by a *skystalker*?"

Ronl tucks the infant closer to himself and covers her ear as if the bairn can understand what we're saying. "A skystalker? No one lives through such a thing—thank the moon your husband was with you—"

"Oh, no. He's not really my husband. And actually, I had to draw the bird away from him." I focus properly on the wound. "He was fighting the bird off with his broadsword, but then he found himself on the ground. So I got the bird to chase me—"

"You did *what*—"

"*What* did you—"

I shrug again. "They like flashes of light so I held my knife over my head and spurred our horse. The bird—skystalker, I guess—went after me."

There's a strained silence, and I glance at them, thinking perhaps they believe I lie? But no. They seem utterly dumbfounded.

"How did you get away?" Lena breathes.

"I ran it into a boulder."

Ronl is squeezing his infant so tightly to his heart, the little one lets out a squawk. "I do not understand? You did what . . . ?"

"I threw the knife." When I go to mimic the motion, my forearm contracts with pain and I wince as I bring the limb back down. "It wanted my knife. I galloped the horse toward a boulder grouping and I . . . when we got in range, I threw my blade into the rocks. It went for the flash of light." And fates, I wish I still had the weapon, if only for nostalgia's sake. "Anyway, yes, I ran it headfirst into a rock. And my injury happened just before that. One of its talons scored my arm as it came down at me."

Lena glances at her husband. Then she rubs her face as if she's collecting herself. "I have never met anyone who has lived through one of those attacks."

"Nor I," Ronl echoes. "And there are many who come here from the Lake of Lost Souls route. In fact, I know many who have lost members of their traveling parties out in that territory to those birds of prey."

The awe they show me is nothing I'm used to, but at least Lena moves on fast. "Such a wound is very dangerous. They carry disease because they are necro-eaters, and they use those feet to gather the dead that are their meals."

With that, Lena falls silent, but she's not looking at me, her husband, or her newborn. She is staring into the air before her, her mind clearly working.

It's a while before she speaks, and when she does, it's in that language I cannot understand. And "speaking" is the wrong word. She's barking orders at Ronl, and he's nodding. Then she holds up her arms and he puts the baby into her outstretched hands.

Ronl has proven to be a gentle soul, but there's none of that as he turns away for the door. He's going to battle, under the instructions of his wife . . . for me.

"I don't want to be a bother," I say in a small voice.

"You helped me keep my life and made sure my baby survived. I pray that I am not returning that mortal favor unto you, but I worry that I am." She shakes her head. "This is very serious, this wound—and you know it. I will do all that I can."

Abruptly, Lena sits farther forward, even though she grimaces as she does so. Taking my hand in her own, she says, "Do you always cry when people are kind to you?"

"I'm sorry?"

She reaches up and brushes my cheek, turning her fingertips around so that I can regard the tears she collected.

"Do you cry when people are kind to you?"

I wipe my eyes and try to hide how I tremble. "I wouldn't know."

She squeezes my palm with her own. "You are family to me now. What is the word in your voice? 'Sister,' I believe it is."

Lowering my head, I watch as my tears fall on our entwined hands.

"Sister," I repeat roughly. "Yes, that's the word."

*Fifty*

# Doors that Open . . . and Close.

It's quite some time before I return to the lodging house, and Ronl sees me back through the rain. I have been well and truly treated, my forearm cleansed, packed, and rebandaged properly, and I have been strictly informed to return the following day for a reexamination. Things are quite sore after all the debridement, and whatever Lena put in the wound's deep, angry core is stinging, but the care I was given warms my lonely heart to such an extent I barely notice the discomfort.

As we arrive at the first of the lodging house's three entries, Ronl holds things open and then steps inside with me.

"Oh, don't worry." Pushing my hooding back so he can see my face, I smile at him as I focus on his chin. "I'm quite safe here."

He buys the lie with a bow. "You must return on the morrow, or she will send me to gather you again."

Putting my hand on his arm, I give him a squeeze. "I promise not to make you come get me."

Ronl bows again and then glances around. He nods at a few people, then says his goodbye to me and ducks back out into the storm.

It's as the door closes that I hear the singing. My first thought is of the maid, but that's not who is vocalizing. It's two of the working women. They're over at one of the round tables by the bar, their legs extended and crossed on empty chairs such that their stockinged ankles show beneath the hems of their skirts, their corsets loosened so that their décolleté is not quite so obvious. The pair of them are harmonizing with such purity and ease, I'm a bit in awe, their voices so high and lilting, like birds in the spring. I'm sad that such gifts are squandered for the life they have been forced to live.

Given the morning hour, the pub is comparatively empty, and I glance at the trestle table in the back. Even Top Hat, as I've come to think of him, is not in residence. I'm guessing he owns the place. Perhaps the whole town.

The henchmen-like entourage that was with him is also absent.

Behind me, the doors open once again. It's a man, not dressed in brown felt, and I move out of his way before I find myself in the kind of trouble I can't easily solve—

He takes one look at me and jumps to the side. He's clearly drunk—I can smell the alcohol on him, plus his balance is such that it's as if the floor under him is unreliable—but avoiding me is clearly important enough to cut through his addled brain.

That's when I notice the other men who are dotted around the tables. They're not looking at me. At all. Their eyes are locked on their tankards with such studious nature, it's as if they're going to be tested by a schoolmarm as to the froth that awaits their numb tongues.

I tug the hooding back into proper place so that my features are fully hidden.

Obviously, Merc's presence precedes me, and this gives me a depressing shot of confidence: Even after he leaves, I suspect I'll still be considered his woman.

After last night, I certainly feel as though I am.

Heading over to the stairs, I stop—and then I reroute to the kitchen's flap door. Some sixth sense spurs me on, and I put my hand on the sticky panels to give them a push.

The cooking facility is bigger than I thought, as dirty as I feared, and empty of staff. The counters are oriented in a square around a central stone hearth that vents up a chimney that is big as a barn. Multiple oven entry points circle the heat source, and there are cords of chopped wood stacked by each one. Courtesy of all this, the dominant smell is not of food, but of fire and ash, and I'm taken back to the settlement.

Countless loaves of bread are cooling on floured racks, hunks of meat of unidentifiable origins are left out to flies, and vats of stew sit on the floor. Clearly, people survive on the food that's prepared like this—and I'm one of them. But my stomach turns at all the grease, grime, and debris. I've never seen so many discarded grain sacks, although the rat population is no doubt grateful for the sloppy pours into the grain grinder—

A door opens from the back, and I hear a squeak.

As I turn, I catch the short-haired maid making a U-turn to duck back into the half door she came out of.

I speak up quick: "Wait, stop."

She halts immediately, but doesn't pivot to look at me. As I trace the trembling of her shoulders with my eyes, I reach out my hand, even though there's no way I can touch her from all the way over here.

"I just wanted to thank you for the food this morning," I say gently. "And yesterday."

"You're welcome." She speaks to the wall. "If you'll excuse—"

"Hold on."

"I have to go—"

"Why." I stride across the kitchen, rounding the great oven. "Please, don't leave—"

"I have to—"

It happens so fast. I come up to her, just as she's trying to go back through the half door, and she stumbles in such a way that the side of her face becomes visible to me.

My breath catches in my lungs. "Crescent moon . . ."

The maid hides her bruised cheek with both hands. "Please . . . just let me go."

"He's going to kill you."

As the words jump out of me, she twists around and looks up at me in horror. Instantly, I make a catalogue of the bruising pattern. It's the exact match to what I saw yesterday. My stomach drops.

"What say you," she whispers.

"You heard me." I brush some of her hair back, checking another wound on her temple. "And it's going to be soon."

The timing is in that red on her cheek, and the knot on the side of her forehead. It's also in the rash around her throat, and the cut on the side of her mouth.

My voice is grim. "You need to leave, now."

"Please, just let me go—"

I put my hands up. "I'm not touching you. But I'm telling you, he's going to finish this. You need to take your things—"

"I have nothing, and there is nowhere to go—"

"—and I'll help you."

The maid stares up at me with such confusion, I nearly meet her eyes again. "Why would you do that?"

We've been speaking in hushes, faster and faster, and suddenly crash into a silence.

Now I want to take her hands in my own, as if that will help my message get through, but I fear that if I make contact with her, she'll spook and run.

"Because I am you." I have to clear my throat. "I've worked as you are, and

I've been alone, and I've been convinced nothing can or will change. Let me help you."

She looks away from me, and I study her profile.

"You can trust me."

"You can't help me." Her hand lifts to her cheek, the fingertips skipping along the surface of where she's been hit. "It's always thus with him. Since he bought me from my parents five years ago."

I smoother the urge to scream that she was bartered for. "Don't you want something else? You make the bread, don't you? And you clean. Wouldn't you like a position in a safe home or an inn?"

I think of the dead cows outside of my village and of the Fulcrum. Some savior I am, promising things I fear cannot be delivered anywhere in Anathos.

I place my hand over my heart. "I will help you."

The maid looks over my shoulder toward the massive hearth. "He needs me to work herein."

"You owe him nothing, and you shouldn't feel bad for saving yourself—"

"No, he's not going to kill me because he needs the labor. He's careful only to correct me so far as I can heal from."

Lowering my head, cold despair washes through my whole body . . . as well as a hot fury. "There are others who work here. I beg of you, fate is offering you an exit—"

"He'll go after my sister." The maid rubs the back of her neck like it hurts. "She was part of the brokerage, but she was bought by the stable master. He's a kind man, and he and his wife have treated her well. She needs to stay with them."

Frowning, I speak of strangers as if I know them. "So they'll protect her—"

"He tells me that will not matter." Her hands tangle in front of her chest, as if her heart is skipping beats. "She'll be forced to fulfill both obligations. He says that is the way of twins in the law here. We are indivisible, and so he will do what he's done to me . . . to my sister." There's a pause. "All of it."

Those hands pull the collar of her undershirt closer together at the base of her neck.

There's a thump and a rustling in whatever room is beyond, and the maid begins to tremble. "You must go—"

"Let me help you—"

*"No."*

She slips back through the portal, and I feel as though I've just watched her disappear into her grave. My first and only instinct is to go in after her, but I know if I'm caught here by the cook, there's no doubt what the consequences will be.

My seeing her death and trying to do something about it . . . will cause her to be murdered.

I hurry out, hating every step that carries me away. I wish I were as physically strong as Merc. I wish I could wield a broadsword and behead that cruel, bullying ogre.

As I emerge into the pub proper, I can feel a dark energy flowing through me, and instead of being horrified by it, I find myself embracing the wrath and anger. I don't know where it comes from, and I don't care as I round the base of the stairs and start my ascent. With every step, I imagine a different demise for that bloated drunk who's terrorizing that innocent girl—and doing more than just beat her.

I'd kill him with my bare hands if I—

My feet come to a halt halfway up, and an odd tunneling of my vision occurs. As my sight dims, my hearing becomes more acute, and I look down.

Through the loosely nailed boards of the steps, I hear the voices, back and forth. The low, slurred deep one, the meek, higher-pitched one. The cook has roused, maybe because of my interruption. Closing my eyes, I pray that I'm wrong about what I've been shown.

Even though I know I am not.

Every instinct in me tells me to go down there and put myself between them, bodily. But that will just put her in more danger—

"Get out," he bellows. "You worthless whore—get the grain!"

There is a scampering and a door closes.

I exhale, even as I know this is no reprieve for her. Just a pause in the destiny that's coming like a reaper.

From out of a part of me that I don't recognize, a conviction takes root and begins to grow. I tell myself it's wrong, on so many levels. When you can't live with inaction, however, you don't always get to choose the trail you're set upon.

As I lift my foot up and place it on the next step, I'm aware that I've made a decision, and I spend the rest of the stairs trying to find a way around it. The time is now, however.

Just as I reach the top, the door of the room before me opens—

Merc steps out and is pulling his surcoat back on. Behind him, in a bed draped in bloodred satin, one of the working women is lying back in an indolent sprawl, her long, flaxen hair waving over the pillows, her naked breast exposed, her painted nails trailing down her cleavage as if she's recalling what he did to her.

And being very satisfied with their interlude.

As his head comes up, he sees me and freezes. His face shows a brief flash of emotion, but then he puts a mask in place.

He recovers faster than I do. "What in the fates are you doing out of that room."

Kicking up my chin, I arch my brow as I've seen him do countless times. "I'd ask you the same about being in there, but that's self-explanatory. At least your pants were done up before you opened things."

As I stride off, I find it incredible—in a bad way—that for someone who's never felt jealousy before, I take to it with such facility.

*Fifty-One*

# Limitations.

"I asked you a question. *What are you doing out of that room.*"

Merc is tight on my tail while I march down the corridor to our room—*my* room, I mean. As he repeats his demand, he's keeping his voice low, but he might as well be yelling. On my side, every time I blink, I see that bed . . . and all that's in it. The wrinkled sheets, too. And those painted nails on the woman's—

With a lithe jump, he gets ahead of me and shoves open the door, staying in the jambs so that I have to push by him. I'm more than happy to give him an elbow, and as he closes us in, I continue to walk as if I have a destination somewhere, anywhere, other than here. With him.

"You are not supposed to leave!" He jabs at the bolt. "I told you, you have to stay here—"

I walk right up to him and peg him eye to eye, even though I might as well be trying to meet a mountain in the summit. "No, I don't."

The fact that he's positively gobsmacked is satisfying in a perverse way. But he recovers quickly. "Yes, you do—"

"Why."

Merc tilts in to me. "Are you joking? You think all those nice men downstairs who are drunk want to be your friend?"

"No, why do you think I have to do what you say." I motion around us. "I'm not your wife, your sister, your child, your charge. We had a professional arrangement that you fulfilled, and having discharged it, we're done—considering you said you won't take money from me."

Or take my body properly, I tack on to myself.

Something that is not happening for so many reasons now, given that his needs have obviously been attended to, and I got to see the aftermath.

"Listen to me." He sinks down on his thighs so our faces are on a level, planting his hands just above his knees. "You're going to get yourself killed—"

"Only forward, never back. That's what you said to me in the tunnel. So go forward, Merc. The door is right there."

As I swing my arm and point at the exit, I think about what a gift it is that others cannot read our own minds. The fact that he's just been with another woman curls me with rage, even though I have no more right to that than he has dominion over me.

"I'm only trying to help you," he grits out.

I open my mouth to hit that platitude back at him—except then I realize that, in some ways, he's in the position I was downstairs with that maid. And thinking of her makes me want to curse.

Breaking off from him, I walk about the room, staring at the floor as I'm torn between what's happening up here—and what I know is happening down in the kitchen. On his part, Merc takes the opportunity to go into the water closet. I hear him mutter, and when he reemerges, he has his backpack in his hand. For a moment, I remember his warning to the woman who showed us this room. So of course all our things have remained exactly where we've left them.

Merc thumps the weight down on the table, jerks open the throat of the shouldering bag, and rifles through the contents like he's checking that nothing is missing. When he closes it all back up again, I take it things are okay—in his current mood, I have to wonder if he wishes theft had occurred just so he could do something about it.

I expect him to walk out. Instead, he plants his palms on either side of the pack and leans into his arms. As the muscles bulge, I trace his bent back, narrow hips, and strong legs, and imagine him naked between that other woman's thighs. Did she relish the way his hair fell around her, too? Did she like what he did with his mouth—

"Where did you go," he says roughly.

I'm so caught up in my head, there's a delay as I realize he's spoken to me. It's only as he looks around his shoulder with expectation that my mind decodes his words.

"Ronl came. He said Lena needed to see me. I had to go."

Merc opens his mouth. Closes it. Looks back down at his pack. As the tension in his strung-bow body gradually eases, I resolve not to be impressed, one way or another, with the fact that my explanation has placated him.

What does it matter.

Turning to me, he levels his black and white stare. "Is she all right?'

"Yes." I cross my arms and feel the bandage that the woman wound around my injury. "She is."

I would mention what she did for me, but it's best to start the separation now.

"Sorrel, listen to me, you shouldn't go out alone here—"

"Sooner or later, I have to take care of myself. Whether it's now or when you leave after this incessant rain stops, you're not going to be looking after me forever."

There's a long pause. "It's not that simple anymore."

"Yes, it is."

"No, it's not." Merc shakes his head and snatches his pack off the table. "And you're going to regret this. Soon or later, you're going to need me in this town, but it's going to be too late."

The truth of the statement makes me more angry because I do need him. Just not in the way he's thinking.

Maybe this is a sign.

I point to the door. "Go forward, Merc. Take your own advice—and don't lay upon me any lingering on your part. You're less important to my destiny than you think."

There's another tense pause. "Fair enough. Fare thee well."

And that's where and how it ends. Merc just walks out, and there's no slamming of the door, either.

Left to my own, I start to shake, so I go back to pacing, thinking of more things I should have said, want to say—none of which are conciliatory, all of which revisit me kicking him out. But then I move beyond myself.

I can't get the maid out of my mind. And even if I have to let Merc go eventually, I can't do the same to her.

I need him one last time.

With a curse, I march back over to the exit and yank open the door, prepared to hunt for him—

Merc is standing right outside, his pack on the floor at his feet, his body leaning against the gray wall. If his brows were down any lower, his belly button would be glaring, and as he turns his head and stares over at me, I don't know what I'm feeling.

No, that's a lie. I don't like anything that I'm feeling.

"You don't have to wait for the latch anymore," I mutter.

"Habits die hard."

As he bends over and picks up his pack, I can see down the corridor—and at the head of the stairs, the woman with the red bed has stepped out of her room. She's wearing a low-cut, black silken robe that reminds me of the color of Merc's eye, and it brings out her long, pale hair. Her lean against the doorjamb is an invitation if I've ever seen one, and her attributes are as obvious as mine feel invisible.

She's turned toward Merc—to us, now—and she's clearly prepared to catch him on his way out.

"You're right," I say.

My words stop him as he starts to walk away, and I find myself staring the other woman down—even as I remind myself I have no right to any of the aggression I'm feeling toward her. Too bad that logic is utterly irrelevant as I remember him coming out of her room.

Opening my own door wider, I step to the side. Merc narrows his eyes on me.

"What," he demands.

Swallowing my pride, I say in a low voice, "I need your help."

"What's changed. In the last three moments since you kicked me out."

There are so many ways to answer that, many of which are anger-based and will only drive him away, the rest of which I don't want to say out here.

"I've decided . . ." I clear my throat. "As much as it pains me, I have to be honest about my limitations."

His brows lift, and I expect him to gloat. Instead, he just nods once. "Fair enough."

Merc's big body moves by me, and I look down the hall.

The working woman smiles slowly and then inclines her head, as if she's deferring to me and the claim I've staked. I wait until she's disappeared back into her room.

Before I turn away and go into mine.

As I close the door and lean back against it, I remind myself of how far Merc and I have traveled and all the things we've battled and bested by working together. These memories fight for the forefront of my mind against the image of that pale-haired woman in her messy bed—but neither the things Merc and I have shared nor what he did with her matters.

"It's not about me," I hear myself say.

Merc stares down at me, and I swear I can feel his exasperation. And the confirmation of his annoyance is the way he tosses his pack on the table.

"I thought you said Lena was all right."

"It's not her, either."

"So are we going to just play roulette with the names of strangers—"

"It's not your woman." Before he can respond to that, I cut in, "And if you can't help me, I understand. This is . . . beyond the normal course of things."

Well, for me it is.

That black and white gaze narrows. "What do you speak of, then. Out with it."

His sword hand rests on the pack, as if he's fully prepared to pick it up, strap it on, and resume the exit that was paused out in the hall.

"Go on," he prompts. "What about it."

And that's when my voice fails. At first: "I want you . . . to kill someone."

The chuckle that comes back at me is the last thing I expect. "My woman?" he drawls. "As you referred to her."

"No," I snap.

Instantly, he changes. "Who hurt you. What happened."

The fact that he's willing to come to my defense so readily is a balm I don't want on my hurt pride. "I told you, it's not about me."

With a stumble of syllables, I explain everything except the vision that started it all, and as I hear myself talk, I have to look at the floor because the enormity of what I'm suggesting begins to fall on my head. Except I'm taking none of it back.

Lena called me a healer, and I think she's right about that. But there's another side of me, too.

"If we don't help her . . ." I clear the lump out of my throat. "And we don't do it now? She's not going to live to see tomorrow."

Merc's hand leaves the pack and pushes his long hair over his shoulder. As he stands in silence, I catalogue the weapons I can see on him, especially the broadsword that's currently riding his hip as opposed to his shoulder.

"How certain are you it's the cook?"

"She, ah . . . she told me it was him. Just now. I went to check on her and thank her for the food, and he's . . ." I motion around my face. "He's beaten her, badly. I'm pretty sure it's because she brought that tray up to me yesterday."

"Okay."

I wait for him to continue. When he doesn't, my heart pounds with worry. "So what else can I say? Do you have questions or—"

"No." He turns to his pack, opens it back up, and roots around once again. "It's fine. I'll take care of it."

There is a metal-on-metal shift as he unsheathes a strange dagger. The weapon's sharp end is narrow and very short, but the hilt is nearly as long as his forearm. He tucks the latter up into his sleeve and locks a grip on a bar that rests right about the seat of the blade.

It's easy to imagine him punching into someone's stomach and dragging the cutting surface upward.

"There's going to be a certain amount of cover-up required," he says. "So it might take a little while. But I'll handle everything."

"Merc—"

"And given the nature of this request, will you *please* stay in here as I go to work? I don't want to worry about what in fate's name you're doing."

"Yes," I whisper. "And I'll throw the latch."

With that, he leaves, and I immediately bolt myself in—and do it loudly. Then I back up until my legs hit the bed's footer and I fall into a sit. Clasping my hands tightly in my lap, I stare at the gray floorboards as if they are glass and open up a view into the kitchen. My blood is humming as it does before my panic gets away from me.

And yet I am not scared or anxious.

I feel something else.

Vengeance.

I think of every time I huddled and ran from a man I met in the lane back in my village. I think of the mob who came for Mare, and Elly's death on the birthing bed, and the maid downstairs and her twin sister. I remember those cruel boys taunting the dying dragon, and the top-hatted man with his cadre of dark-hearted guards. I tell myself I should be horrified by what I've set into motion. Surely this will be a contamination on my soul, for I've behaved no better than any of them.

Except I don't care and I have no regrets. The only thing I feel in my heart is a disappointment that I'm not the one striking down the maid's tormentor.

Overhead, the rain continues to fall, and as I close my eyes, I see it as blood spilling from a body. I should be horrified. I'm not. Opening my lids, I look down at my palms, and swear I see red all over them. I tell myself I should be shocked. I'm not.

Yet in my core, I know I've added another violent layer to all the other wrongdoing of the situation. The cook is an abuser, but am I really any better than him? And what if Merc is caught and killed afterward for the crime? Then I've saved the maid and doomed him.

This is bad. What I've done is a kind of evil.

A feeling of disquiet animates me, so I set once more to a pacing, and it's as I make another round of the room that my pack catches my eye. Before I can comprehend what I'm doing, I go over and pick the weight up, taking it to the bed. The tie all but falls free for me, and getting a hand inside is like pouring water it's so easy.

The box comes out as if it's moving on its own.

When I go to free the little hook, it's already been released, and the lid comes up as if blown open—

A flash of lightning flickers around the room and the circle of black crystals catches the illumination as if breathing in the energy.

An uncontrollable urge to take the object out stirs in me, but I'm not about to cut myself on it again, so I'm careful about how I reach in. This time, it doesn't feel cold, and there's no sharpness as I take the circle of—

A crown.

It's . . . a crown.

As the contours emerge from the box, my eyes skip around. Curls of black metal seat the spears of black crystal that rise up at different levels, all of them capturing the lantern light and going rainbow. The detailing of the workmanship is like nothing I've ever seen before, and what I think is just an abstract pattern of waves turns out to be the depiction of an army of warhorses and weaponed men. I turn, turn, turn the circlet in my hands so I can inspect each individual figure, their swords and musket guns, their forward leans over the necks of their galloping, furious steeds, the many deep of the ranks.

It is a crown of war made of shadow, and Mr. Lewis's voice enters my mind as if he's speaking right to my ear.

*One is a compass that will guide you on your quest, the other is the point of it all.*

For some reason, tears spear into my eyes—

"Sorrel, it's me."

I jump to attention and look at the door. Has Merc acted this fast? "Coming!"

My hands are sloppy as they return the royal jewel to its velvet seat, and it's as I get the box back into the pack and then jump forward to unlock things that I revisit my resolve: That object is not my journey.

I am at my destination.

My fingers fumble with the bolt on the door, and I'm shaking as I open things up for so many reasons.

Merc enters and shuts us in together. "Not the right time."

As he goes over to the table and puts the strange knife away, I struggle with a cowardly relief and a surging frustration—and when he turns to me, I feel even more unstable. He's *so* calm, but then again, this is his business. He's unbothered because this isn't a shocking situation for him to be in.

I remember him saying he wanted to kill the cook himself.

"There are workers all around him in the kitchen." Merc nods as if I've asked him a question. "Yes, she's there and surrounded by others. They're in preparation for the evening meals. It's better to wait until the pub is full and the drinking is well on. The chaos will be to my advantage, and the night will make the after work much easier."

This is a sign, I tell myself.

Maybe I should call off the murder and find another solution.

Merc goes over to the window seat and settles in. Crossing his arms over his chest, he lowers his chin and closes his eyes.

"Get some rest." He exhales and shifts his shoulders as if getting more comfortable. "I know night is a while off, but we both need it after the travel."

Then again, with the incessant storming, it might as well be after dark already.

I turn to the bed. Then look up at the ceiling and think about the night before. "Merc."

"Mmm . . . ?"

There's a creak of leather as he looks over at me. Then on an abrupt surge, he's back on his feet, and coming across.

As our eyes meet, his callused, scarred hand reaches out and brushes at my hair. I think of him and the blond working woman and feel sick to my stomach.

"It shouldn't come easy," he says.

"I'm . . . sorry?"

The black side of his stare reminds me of the crystals rising out of the crown's beautifully wrought black metal. "Killing something, even if . . . you're doing it for the right reasons. It shouldn't be easy."

That's when his mask falls away, and I'm leveled from the pain and the regret in his soul. It's as if I've entered a dark, deep cave of torture and I'm staring into an abyss of pain. And still his eyes roam around my face, my hair, my shoulders.

"You are a rare light in this world, Sorrel. Fearless and brave, strong and true—"

"I am no such thing."

"You need to acquaint with yourself, woman." His exhale is ragged. "You're all that and more."

"I'm a coward who's asked you to commit murder."

His shrug is so offhanded, we might as well be talking about the weather. "The cook has it coming. And don't let him bother your conscience. He's not worth it."

"Murder is wrong."

"And you're only feeling like this because it's your first time." Abruptly, his tone grows weary. "It's the hardest."

"It's my *only* time."

In the silence, I think of the speech that Sallae Mae always gave the new girls, about how the first time . . . was always the hardest—and I try to find the farmer in the mercenary before me, the man beneath all the weapons and the scars.

"Was that true for you? Was your . . . first . . . the hardest."

It's a long while before he shakes his head. "I thought so for a long time. But as fate would have it . . . I was wrong."

Riding a desperate wave, I gather his much bigger hands in my own, and squeeze to try to get through to him. "You can stop. You can get out of this life. I see what's inside of you—"

"No, I can't." He separates us and goes back to the window seat, resettling his body in a determined pose of repose. "And . . . you don't."

*Fifty-Three*

# Belt and Suspenders.

It happens again.

As I come awake, there's grit in my mouth and down my throat, and the sensation of the sand is all I'm aware of—that and an urgency gripping my mind and body. Some kind of dialogue is happening when I sleep, but I don't have any conscious memory of what was said or by who—

Sitting up with a jerk, I seek Merc across the room. He's where he was, in the window seat, and he's got a journal open in his lap. He's brought the lantern over, and in the golden glow, he's writing something with a lead pencil.

"Why didn't you wake me?" I shift my legs off the bed. "How late is it—"

"Late enough." He makes a couple more notes, puts the journal aside, and gets to his feet. "The crowd is full downstairs. It's time."

I don't hear anything but the maddening rain and a screaming in my head. How many hours have passed—oh, fates, maybe it's too late and the girl is dead.

"What are you going to do?" I ask roughly.

"Do you really want to know."

As I fall into silence, Merc stretches his arms over his head, his powerful body arching like a bow. Then he goes to his pack, and I know what he's taking out of it. He tucks the oddly bladed weapon up his sleeve and pulls things back into place.

Opening our door, he glances over at me. "I don't know how long I'll be—"

The sound of men laughing and women cooing draws both our attention. Down the hall at the head of the stairs, there are charges coming and going out of the working women's rooms, a nonstop carousel of arousal and satisfaction the velocity of which suggests Merc's very right about the crowd down below. They're drunk and very distracted.

"Lock up," he orders in a grim voice.

Things close behind him, and I go to the latch. After I bolt myself in, I turn my hands over and expect to see red upon my palms. That they're flesh-colored is a surprise. Meanwhile, all that vengeance I was alight with earlier has faded, and so too the moral qualms. The clarity I have in the aftermath is a cold, empty logic.

The maid's death. The cook's death. One of the two I must live with, and I know which is the easier of the curses.

And that's my decision.

As for Merc? Well, he's a professional, isn't he.

As the din of the crowd rides another swell in volume, I go restlessly into the water closet and run the sink. Bending down, I part my lips to drink—

There is sand on my tongue. Actual sand.

My fingers tremble as I bring them to my mouth to clear the particles, and I go to the slice of light that penetrates in from the bedroom lantern.

Black grains of sand.

Rushing back to the sink, I try to rinse them out of me with great swooshes of water, but no matter how many times I draw from my cupped hands and spit things into the drain, the sand refuses to clear.

Convinced I'm going mad, I prowl around the bedroom, and my pacing takes me over to the window seat. What I find there is the only thing that could distract me: Merc's left his journal open, and in the light of the lantern, the graceful strokes of lead pull free of the pale paper and form something with depth and breadth, as if the page is a window and I'm looking out at an actual landscape.

It's a gate, between a pair of stone pylons, and the wrought iron is curved into a beautiful design of hearts and flowers.

I run my fingertips over the drawing, marveling that someone with such brute strength could have such a delicate hand with a pencil.

I shouldn't go through his other drawings, but I do, starting all the way back at the first page. It's landscapes, one after the other starting with a mountain range. Then it's a verdant valley. And another set of mountains, but this time from the perspective of a trail. A lake. A road. A village center. A meadow . . . and then, finally, the gates.

Frowning at the design of the barrier, I want to know what's on the other side, as if it's real and I'm standing before the thing. But from what I can see between the curls and strokes of lead, there only appears to be just more meadow.

I go back to the beginning again, and as I make a second pass through . . . I realize it's a journey. Not ours, but perhaps one he took once.

Or maybe it's the way back to his home.

I return the journal to where it was, and think about how he's going to move on. And then I consider the maid's future. Even if he saves her from the cook, what awaits her next in this harsh place? How much help can I be to her—when I have to keep my own self alive? There are so many dark alleys, dark corners, dark nights here at the Outpost.

And that's assuming the demons don't come—

In the hall, I hear arguing, and I go to the door. Slipping the bolt free, I crack the panel and peer out. Down at the stairs, two men are shoving at each other, their bodies banging off the corridor walls. A third one sneaks around the rumble, and slips into the room of one of the women with a sly smile, as if he intends to take what they're fighting over.

I focus on the face of the working woman who welcomes the interloper into her bedroom. She's not afraid of the fighting—or the men. And I think of the pair who were singing as they sat together earlier. And the others I have seen.

The one who Merc—

I shake that vision right out of my head.

For all the drinking and the violence, for all the rough and the tumble, the women here have not been bruised or handled roughly that I've seen. More than that, they've never shown any fear, or flinching, which means what little I've witnessed is in fact the way of things: They're protected in this establishment.

That's why they're unafraid—and untouched except for when they choose to do what they do for the coins they keep.

And with a sudden clarity, I know who watches over them.

## *Fifty-Four*

# An Offer Made.

I leave the room with my head uncovered, and as I walk down the hall, the men who are dallying around the doors by the stairwell sober up and look away or become busy with their mead-soaked clothes. The women who linger in the doorways with them watch me. The blond one that Merc was with—

Well, she's nowhere to be seen. And I have a stupid paranoia that they're together again, but of course that's ridiculous.

Because he's killing someone for me.

I'm cursing myself and Anathos in general as I descend the steps. The din in the pub reminds me of the Gauntlet, but I feel no nostalgia. I'm too busy practicing what I'm going to say. When I reach the bottom, I turn toward the flap door into the kitchen. Then I look out into the crowd. I don't see the short-haired maid with the bruised face and the beautiful voice.

I worry all this is too late. In the event it isn't, I have to press on.

A feeling of disassociation overtakes me as I walk into the sea of patrons, the smell of sweat, mead, and mud dimming along with the sound of the voices. The brief looks of surprise I get are as if from a great distance, and when chairs are shifted out of my path, I judge harshly the gamblers and degenerates for their pathetic need for drink and sexual distraction. They're nothing but a herd of cattle wandering their pasture of short-term pleasure.

And I hate them.

I proceed all the way to the back, to the trestle table, and the hard, sober men who line its far side, facing out at the patrons, the working women, the barkeeps, and the maids.

Top Hat is there, presiding over everything at the head of the group.

I can't read his face, of course, on account of that brim. All I see is the unforgiving cut of his jaw, and his dark sideburns.

"This is a pleasant surprise," he says in a low, smooth voice. "But where is your husband. Busy?"

His attention seems to go out to the floor, and I have a thought that he knows Merc went to see one of the women—and is taunting me on purpose.

"If that's why you've come," he drawls, "I'm afraid I can't help you. I'm a businessman, not a preacher to address the morality of husbands gone astray—"

"I need to speak to you. Alone."

Top Hat leans back in his chair, which is bigger than all the others. A throne, for a despot who rules by the fist, no matter his fine clothes.

"Now, why would you want to do that? Speak to me." Then he drags out a last word, as if it's the final line of a song: "Alone."

"I have a favor to ask."

The chuckle that comes back at me reminds me of his smile at that stream, a warning. Like a snake's rattle.

"This should not surprise you," he counters, "but I am not a man who's inclined to charity."

"I have something to offer you in return."

I feel his eyes travel down me slowly, and I wonder what he makes of my borrowed outfit, the one that matches the clothing of those who live here. I do not meet his gaze. Instead, I'm focused on the diamond tiepin that secures the cravat at his throat. It's the size of a marble. And then my eyes move to the pinkie ring on his right hand. I don't recognize the blue and green stone, but I'm sure it's very valuable.

His crew of men are silent and still, and given that I'm used to the masculine urge to pile on when it comes to grinding down something inferior, I'm surprised none of them taunt me. For sure they are soldiers of a sort, and like any regiment, they have a uniform: They're all dressed in versions of what Top Hat is wearing, the finely tailored suits in dark colors accented with waistcoats and golden pocket watches that are obvious—and undoubtedly, weapons that are not. The one closest to him, who sits at his right elbow, has a beard. The others have mustaches or muttonchops.

"I am intrigued—to a point," the man in charge says. "What of you, then."

"I will meet with you alone."

"These are my men." As he indicates the assembled, his pinkie ring glitters in the low light. "There is naught which they do not know."

I don't believe that for a moment. "What I have to offer is only for you."

"Are you trying to get your husband killed, then?" Top Hat drums his fingers on the table as if he's getting bored. "For what he did upstairs with my *daline*? As I just told you, domestic disputes are not something I am interested in entertaining, and if you try to put me in the middle of one, I warn you, I may well settle things."

"This has nothing to do with him."

I can feel his stare hardening on me, and hold my ground at his tiepin.

"If we are 'alone,' I do not believe that will be his opinion." Top Hat rises out of his throne. "Suit yourself, though. Far be it from me to turn down a lady's request."

Bending to the side, he lowers his voice and speaks to the bearded one. Then he indicates for me to come around to the wall behind the table. Something is triggered, perhaps by where he puts his foot, and a section slides back to reveal a shallow hall lit by a single lantern.

"After you."

The gallant way he indicates forward is nothing to be fooled by, and I shouldn't be as composed as I am while I step into the hidden hallway. I'm not frightened of him, though, for I know what I have to offer is invaluable, even though he thinks it's just something as irrelevant as my body.

The panel slides back in place with a thump, and when he stays where he is, I turn around to face him.

"It's customary for me to search for weapons." He steps in close, and he smells clean and fresh, nothing of mead or sweat upon him. "You understand that women get no dispensation from this."

His hands move around my waist and proceed upward until he meets my underarms. Then he leans in very tightly to reach around the small of my back and go up and over my shoulders.

"Nothing yet," he says in a seductive way. "But let us see what we have here."

I am without the red felt coat, wearing only a small white blouse that buttons up to the throat. He takes his time with the fastenings, revealing my camisole bit by bit.

Pulling apart the shirt's two halves, he lifts up the lace and stares down at my bare breasts. "No weapons, yet. But we have to be sure."

His fingers skate over what only Merc has touched, and I can't keep my grimace to myself.

A chuckle ripples through his chest. "What did you think was going to happen with this offer of yours?"

I shove his hands away and pull the camisole back into place. "You are checking for weapons, remember."

There's a pause. "So I am." He sinks down to the floor. "Spread your feet. Please."

As I do so, he kneels before me and goes under the red felt skirting. I focus on the panel and breathe evenly as he feels the outsides of my ankles, my calves, my knees. He continues up to my hips before returning to the floor and repeating the ascension. On the inside of my legs.

He goes all the way to my sex, and he lingers with his hand there. "Oh, look. I've found something."

When I stay silent, he frowns. "If you have a favor to ask of me, you'd do well to provide me with an enrichment worthy of the request."

"My body is not what I am offering."

The hand between my thighs retracts and he straightens to his full height.

"I am not the kind of man you want to toy with," he says in a low, threatening voice.

"I have something else you need, something far more valuable than what you can easily find elsewhere. With a woman who holds enthusiasm toward you."

There's a pause. Then the man stomps on the floor and a different panel opens beside me.

Clamping a hand on the back of my neck, he all but throws me into the black hole on the far side. I stumble, but catch my balance, and as my eyes adjust, it's obvious that these are his private quarters.

With another stomp of his boot, he shuts us in and then strides over to a side table set with crystal decanters and delicate glasses.

"Care for a drink?" he drawls. Then he glances over his shoulder. "Before we get down to business?"

There's a bedding platform in the center of the space, and the padded handcuffs that hang off the headboard gleam in the light of the lanterns that simmer from various hang points. On the far wall, a wardrobe is locked up tight, but has a line of top hats resting on its top, and beside the monolith, a fan of swords is mounted on a freestanding wheel.

"No?" he says as he pours himself some whiskey and downs it in one swallow. "How ladylike of you."

The man leaves his glass behind and comes at me slowly, like a cat with a mouse. When he stops, he reaches out and touches my exposed collarbone, running his finger back and forth.

As he continues down the lace to my sternum, I straighten my spine and say, "If you think you can shame or intimidate me by another fondling, you have the wrong woman."

That chuckle rumbles out of him. "I can do anything I want with you in here. No one will hear you scream."

"You don't strike me as a man who considers being endured a compliment. And if you kill me, then you won't know what I have to offer, and you will miss out on the single most important piece of information someone such as yourself can possess."

He taps between my breasts, right on my heart. "You have an overinflated opinion of your value."

"No, I don't. I know exactly what I have to offer."

As he assesses me, I continue to stare at the diamond on his cravat, and in the silence that follows, I think of the number of times I have run from people back at my village. I'm not running now—or hiding. And with this other part of me awakened, I don't believe I'll ever run away again. From anybody.

His finger continues downward, to the waistband of the red skirting. "Tell me, what is your name."

"Sorrel."

"You may call me Thale." He drops his hand to his side. "I'm curious, what is this favor you're willing to risk your life for."

I start to do up the buttons he's released. "I want your protection."

The top hat tilts to the side. "I would think your husband does a fine enough job of watching over you."

"It's not for me."

"Interesting." He indicates himself. "So you come here, to a man you do not know and should not trust, and offer yourself in exchange for protection for somebody else."

"I told you, I'm not offering myself."

"Oh, that's right. Information." More of that chuckling. "Tell me, fair lady, what can you possibly tell me that I don't already know—"

"How you're going to die."

*Fifty-Five*

# The Acceptance.

Thale freezes for a moment. Then his laughter rumbles around the room and he breaks off from me, returning to the decanters.

"You know, I was surprised when your husband visited one of my ladies earlier today." He looks over at me as he pours himself another measure. "But I am getting a very clear reason why. You are beautiful, but delusional—and tedious with all this misplaced self-possession."

He drinks some of his second whiskey, and comes back with the glass. "I doubt sex with you is very much fun."

I think of Merc leaving the bed we shared and choke up that this stranger may be telling the truth. But now is not the time to fall into my own emotions.

When I make no response, he shakes his head. "You are serious, then."

"You have heard of me," I say softly. "I am whispered of in the darkness, the one who knows when the time for dying comes, the one who brings the bairns back from death, the girl who can harness the magic that should not be used. *You know who I am.*"

This time, as Thale goes still, he doesn't even breathe. I know this because that diamond that's twinkled even in this low lighting to the beat of his respiration offers no flashing. Then he jerks the glass to his lips and throws his head back.

"I don't believe you." He goes to the bar once more and puts the glass down. When he turns back around, his right hand is tucked in close to his hip. "There is no such female."

"Then why do you have your hand on your firearm."

Gone is all trace of joking in him now, as well as any sexual impulse: He becomes utterly serious. And I truly know I've put my life on the line.

"You're smart to have this lair to retreat to." I glance around the room.

"With the amount of money and power you have? You're the king in this den of iniquity, but you're also the prime target. If you know what your death is, you could prevent it. Protect yourself. And I'm the only person who can provide you with the how and when."

Abruptly, he leans back against the bar and crosses his arms over his chest. "I'll say it again. I don't believe you."

"Then meet my gaze." I shrug. "Whatever do you have to lose? A big, strong man such as yourself, surely you're not afraid of a little woman like me."

"Of course not."

Except he comes no closer. He stays where he is.

He will not be able to resist, however. He will have to know—or at the very least, hear what I have to tell him, even if he thinks it's a lie.

With an elegant flourish, Thale takes off his top hat and puts it aside by the decanters. His hair is black and wavy, but has a white streak in front. Pulled back and tied with a black thong, his hawk-like features announce exactly what he is.

A man who rules by the fist and the firearm.

"Nothing will come of this," he announces.

"So there is naught to worry over, is there. Meet my eyes."

"You are the one dodging mine."

"Are you saying you're ready?"

With three long strides, he plants himself before me and bends down so that our faces are on the same level. In a derisive voice, he says, "Should I brace myself."

"No, that's what I must do." I put my hand out to shake. "Have we a deal?"

"You're a trusting sort."

"Not at all. The working women here are very well cared for. They're healthy, comfortable, and confident as they move around. Given your clientele, I know this is because you protect them so—"

"I am done talking. The time for games is over."

Taking a deep breath, I shift my eyes up and meet his—

The gasp explodes out of me, and I go for my throat as I taste copper. Staggering to the side, I put my hand out as the air going down into my lungs bubbles through the blood that rushes out of the open slice running nearly from ear to ear. As I suddenly pitch forward, I head for where the decanters are, to the table. Slapping my hand down, the glass he drank out of goes flying and shatters as my fingers shove to the edge and seek a specific spot under the top.

Where there's a hidden latch.

Still gagging and weaving, I free it, and a drawer shoots out from under. Without looking inside, my palm locks on some kind of grip and I pull out a silver pistol. Swinging the heavy weapon around, my legs splay out and I fall back against the table, the bottles rattling—

It's the man with the beard. He's standing over me, but what's in his hand makes no sense. I guess it's a knife, but it's unlike any I've ever seen before. An icicle? Like the ones that form on the roof edge in winter?

Surely I'm not seeing this right—

The bearded man's mouth is moving. He's taunting me as I struggle to hold the pistol up. My strength is declining fast—the silver weapon drops from my grip, and I put both my hands back up to my throat. I look down. The diamond pin on the tie is a ruby now from my blood, which is puddling under me.

"You bastard," I hear myself say in Thale's voice.

The bearded man kicks the silver pistol out of the way. Then he straddles my legs—

I groan and try to put an arm up to defend myself. He slaps it away, and lifts his fist over his shoulder. The wound across the front of my throat is deep enough to be a mortal one, but the death occurs when the man plunges his arm down.

The pain is so sharp, but it doesn't last.

Or rather, my inability to breathe becomes the only thing I know. I can't draw a breath, and my lungs are burning so badly, I retch to try to clear the blood out of my mouth. The bubbling froth that erupts from my lips is hot, my skin feels cold, my chest goes numb.

The last thing I see, as my vision recedes to a pinpoint, is the man leaning down and plucking the blood-soaked diamond from my tie—

All at once, the vision is over.

The death is done.

I come back into my body, and have a moment of confusion as I realize I'm on the floor and there's broken glass shimmering all around me.

Looking up, I expect to see Thale standing over me. He's not.

He's stumbling back from me, and when he bumps into the bed in the middle of the room, he lands in a bouncing sit.

His face is drawn into a mask, and he is pale as milk. "Get out. Get . . . the fuck out."

As I go to rise to my feet, I must be careful with all the glass, and when I'm standing, he shrinks away from me and covers his eyes with his hands. Like a child.

Then he reaches down and touches something on the side of the footboard.

As the panel we came through slides back and reveals the dim hallway, I look at him. "Where is the other release? To get me all the way out."

He curses.

Then he surges to his feet and marches out past me into the hall. In a low voice, he says, "Don't ever come anywhere near me again."

Thale stomps his boot in another place, and the first panel we went through retracts to reveal the trestle table and the group of men. I walk out alone, and things are immediately closed up behind me. He's smart. He needs time to recover from the shock, and he can't be around anybody who knows him well until he has.

I'm very aware of the eyes that follow me as I step around the empty throne. Before I disappear into the pub proper, I glance back. The bearded one, the one who will murder him, is the only member of that private guard who isn't looking in my direction.

He's turned around and is staring at the wall.

Walking into the crowd, I weave my way in and out of the round tables, heading for the staircase. The entire time, I focus on the kitchen door and wonder how I could get in there and check to see if the maid is still alive.

It's as I decide that I can't, at least not without endangering her, that the cook himself comes out.

In a bloody apron that's marked just like it had been in my vision.

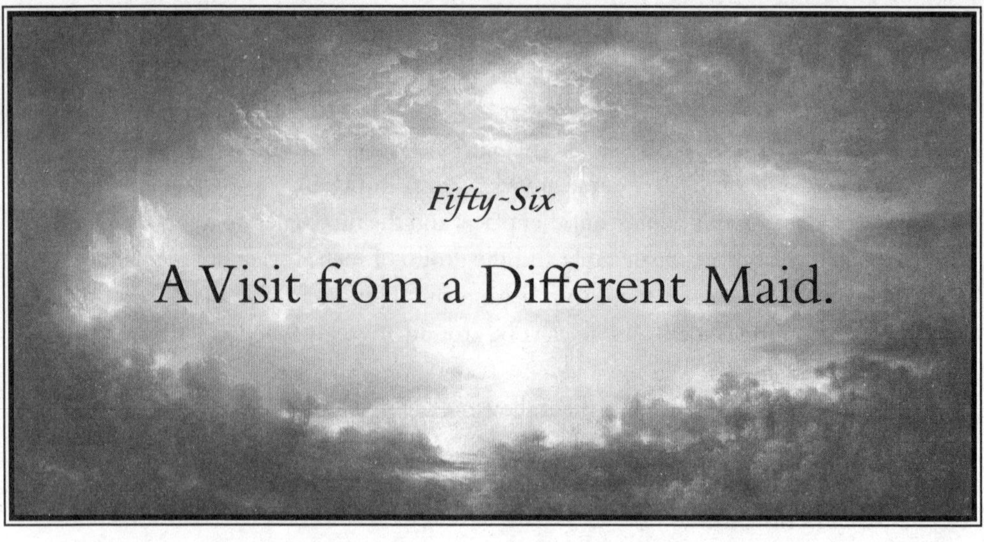

*Fifty-Six*

# A Visit from a Different Maid.

I stop short, then look around for Merc. He's nowhere to be seen, so I refocus on the cook.

The man is counting something in his cupped palm. Coins, it seems? Whatever it is, he's consumed by this effort, his fleshy brows eclipsing his eyes, his jowls pulling forward from his weak chin. That apron absolutely terrifies me, and I tell myself that maybe he's just been breaking down sheeplings or cows?

As he pilots a distracted course for the nearest exit, he seems agitated, his free hand passing over his greasy hair repeatedly.

And then he's gone.

The door flaps shut, and I wait for Merc to appear out of nowhere, anywhere, and follow him. When this doesn't happen, and the cook doesn't make an instant reappearance, I bolt for the kitchen entrance. My heart is pounding with anxiety as I worry that we are too late—

Things open again and I jump back. "Oh, sorry!"

A red-haired maid swings around with her tray of food—and then reaches out to steady me. "Pardon, miss. Are you all right then?"

I wish I knew the other maid's name.

"Ah . . ." I try to see over her shoulder. "No, but thank you."

As she bows and goes about her job, I have to enter the kitchen. I need to know.

Pushing the panel wide, I peer in—and get nowhere. Smoke from the chimney's various hearths clouds the air, and there are so many maids circling the oven, I can't track them. Brown hair, she has short brown hair . . .

So do most of them.

"Miss, do you need something?"

I turn around. It's another young girl, who's just come in from the floor. She has a huge load of empty tankards on her tray, and her exhaustion drags down the line of her shoulder and stoops her back.

"No," I say roughly. "Thank you."

She bows to me, just as yet another young woman with another tray, this time with plates, approaches to enter. With a sense of futility, I back up and turn to the stairs—where I catch sight of one of the maids who's out in the tables. Drunks paw at her and tweak her skirt, trying to pull her into their laps. To their credit, the working girls who are treated with better respect defend her, slapping at the patrons' hands and glaring, but there's only so much they can do. Coupled with the low pay, the cook's hard hand . . .

I hate it all. I'm filled with rage.

And still I do not find the barmaid I'm searching for.

As I go to the stairs and head upward, I feel no better when I reach the top and see all the men gathered around those rooms. I'm hoping one of them gets in my way, but they step aside to allow me passage. When I arrive at the end of the hall, I disappear myself into my room, and the first thing I do, after I enter, is throw the bolt.

But it feels like I've locked myself in, rather than made sure no one gets to me.

I go over and sit on the bed. My hands want something to do, but as the felt skirt settles itself with a bend at my knees like a kink in a branch, there isn't anything to smooth. Glancing down, I see that I messed up the do-up with the blouse, and as I yank the buttons out of their stitched holes, I think of all the things I've wished I could try again—

*Knock. Knock.*

*Knock.*

My head lifts. And then I rush for the door and unbolt it. "Merc, what happ—"

It's not him.

I instantly focus on the diamond that is centered on that cravat.

Behind Thale, the corridor has gone absolutely still and quiet. Neither the working women nor their patrons are saying a word, and their bodies are frozen in what I'm guessing were the positions they were in when the big man himself made his appearance.

I step back and indicate the way inside.

Taking off his top hat, Thale enters wordlessly, and I shut the door.

"You left this behind," he says roughly as he focuses on the floor.

From out of the interior of his fine jacket, he takes a silk handkerchief embroidered with golden thread.

"That's not mine."

"Then perhaps you'd like it."

"You didn't need a pretext to come up here."

Putting it back into his pocket, he walks around, checking the shutters, and the corner where there's evidence of an old leak at the ceiling. He leans into the water closet.

"You need more oil in your lamp. I shall see to that."

I just wait. Soon enough, he turns to me.

"Which maid," he says gruffly as his eyes remain at my feet.

My exhale of relief is audible. "The one the cook is beating."

"That hardly narrows it."

Flattening my mouth, I pray that the death is happening, right now. "She has a twin who works in the stables."

Thale nods once. "I know her. Consider it done."

I take a step forward, focusing on his face as if I am staring down the barrel of a pistol I know how to use. "Just so we're clear, I will know whether you live up to your side of things. And there will be remedies if you do not."

Now he frowns, even as he continues to stare at the floor. "My word is bond, no matter what you think of me."

I hope this is true, because I know I'm lying. I can't do anything about it if he fails to uphold his vow, but the bluff is the only leverage I have.

Fates, I don't even know if the girl still lives.

"And now you need to tell me," he says quietly. "You showed me a lot, but I need the one piece you kept to yourself."

Opening my mouth, I realize I'm condemning yet another man to death—and yet my words are smooth on my tongue. "The bearded man. The one who sits next to you." Now I'm frowning. "I don't understand the weapon, though."

Thale closes his eyes as if he's bracing himself. "Tell . . . me."

I hold out my hands about twelve *nics* apart. "It was a blade, but it looked like a piece of ice, about this big. But there was no dripping as if it was melting? I can't say I've ever seen anything like it before."

Thale breaks off from me and paces around again. He holds his top hat with both hands, and his brows are drawn so tightly together, they seem to curl his upper lip, his white teeth making an appearance.

"What kind of knife is it?" I ask.

He stops and stares at the closed shutters. "It's made from a chip off the Crystal Gate."

Thale stares at those floorboards, as if he can see down through to the trestle table and who sits around it. When he finally glances in my direction, I note the way he avoids my eyes and wonder about all the people I've looked at thusly over the course of these many years.

"You do all this, just to protect a stranger?" he asks. "Or is there more of a story."

"The maid is being beaten and raped. Isn't that enough of a 'story.' In fact, all your maids need protection—and you're going to have to be more careful who you hire next for the cook position. You need to take care of the girls you pay, not only those who bring in money to you."

There's a beat of silence. And then his voice softens with incredulity. "I wouldn't have believed you, you know. If you hadn't . . . you knew where one of my hidden pistols was. You knew the latch—there's no way . . ."

"You will tell no one of this or who I am," I say in a strong voice.

Thale laughs in a harsh burst and puts his hat back on. "Not a soul. *Ever.*"

With the gallantry of a nobleman, he bows to me and then straightens to his full height. "It shall be done. For all of them."

I take another deep breath. "Thank you."

For a moment, he just stares at me without meeting my eyes, his head tilting in what I recognize is a habit of his. Then he nods once and goes to the door. With every step, he becomes once more the man I first met by the stream, his shoulders moving back, his jaw extending out, his air of unquestioned authority like a cape that he pulls on about himself.

He pauses as he puts his hand on the knob. Then he says slyly, "How do you know I will have to hire a new cook?"

"I see deaths, remember."

"And you have nothing to do with his demise?"

"I only have visions. I am no killer."

His eyes slant over to Merc's pack. "You know someone who is, however."

When I don't reply, that taunting smile returns to his lips. "You know, I think I shall let you in on a little secret. After all, someone as altruistic as you should get something for themselves every once in a while."

"What secret would that be."

Thale's chuckle threads through the rain hitting the roof. "When your husband went to avail himself of Miss Bethle's charms, he couldn't perform. And without becoming indecent, allow me to say that I am very well versed on how . . . inspirational . . . she can be. I reckon he picked her because she looked like you, her blond hair so close to your own color. But apparently, the substitute does not hold a candle to the real thing."

My breath catches. Is this true?

As the man just stares in my direction, I know it is, and there's an uncoiling of tension in me that I cannot deny.

Thale's half smile seems self-mocking. "Ah. It appears as though I have made good on something for once. I shall have to toast my virtue later—after I take care of a problem all my own thanks to you—"

A muffled voice cuts him off. "Sorrel. It's me. Open up."

"Speak of the devil," Thale drawls as he ducks his hand into his fine jacketing, no doubt to secure a weapon. "Or rather . . . your husband."

"Sorrel. Open up."

Before I can respond, Thale opens the door. "Worry not, mercenary. My business here is done so I'm leaving."

He glances back at me with that smile. "Isn't that right."

I ignore him. I'm too busy cataloguing Merc from the floor up. Is there blood on him? If Thale knows the cook's death is his doing, will there be trouble? The big man certainly seems like the type to take a pound of flesh out of anybody for even the smallest offenses.

Which making him look for a new cook could well be among.

When I reach Merc's eyes, they're not on me. And he's looking like he's ready to use that knife with the long hilt on Thale.

"Don't look so aggressive, friend," the other man says to him. "Nothing happened here. I do rounds and check the rooms when the storms last this long." He points to our lantern without turning away. "You are almost out of oil. That is the extent of things. Do not let your head spin away."

Neither man moves, and the standoff attracts attention. Down by the stairs, the drunks have noticed and they're pulling together, like an audience for a fight.

When Merc stays silent, Thale's voice drops even lower, to the point where I can't hear what he says. Then he steps around Merc, their shoulders knocking as if he intends the contact.

In the aftermath, Merc watches him go.

I brace myself for the door to be slammed, but he closes it quietly.

As he turns to face me, I blurt, "What happened—"

"That man did not come up here for the oil. He wouldn't do a woman's job. What was he doing in here—"

"We are almost out of—"

"Don't lie to me." Merc looms over me. "And before you tell me it's none of my business, I killed a man for you tonight. So you can bloody well be honest with me."

"The cook is dead," I breathe.

"Yes."

Rubbing my aching eyes, I shake my head. "I tried to find her in the kitchen. I don't know if we aren't too late—"

*"What was he doing in here."*

I drop my arms and lock eyes with him. "I asked Thale for help. For the maid. I asked him to protect her after you're gone and I'm . . . wherever I am."

I can't stay in the lodging house permanently, after all. Not until I can figure out how to melt down Mare's gold.

Merc's black and white gaze goes to the bed. "And what exactly did you give him in return."

"Nothing."

"You expect me to believe a man like him would provide anything to anybody for free?" He looks back at me, his stare raking down the front of my blouse. "You're lying. And do you have to bed every man you're around?"

I glance down. The buttons are all undone, my chemise showing. From when I'd intended to fix the buttons.

Merc steps in to me. "You know what, I think I will collect. After everything I've done for you, especially tonight, I want what we agreed to in the beginning."

His hands go around my waist, and between one blink and the next, I think back to being in Thale's lair, with that man touching me. I felt nothing then. But when it's Merc, now? My body comes alive, heat rushing to my breasts and in between my legs.

With a jerk, Merc pulls me against him, his arousal obvious.

"Will you deny me after you had him," he growls. "You're still in charge."

Leaning back in his arms, I turn my hands into fists as I grip his leather lapels. I do some jerking of my own, roughly bringing his mouth to mine.

Though I have battled death for what feels like centuries, tonight it seems to be prowling around, looking for a way into me, and I feel the futility of any mortal contest against the grave. I'm also tired of worrying over so many strangers, the ones here, the ones back in my village . . . even though they're all I've ever had.

And then there's the parting with this man right here.

There's nothing gentle in the kiss. Merc's lips rake over my own as he backs me up not to the bed, but the wall next to it. The waistband of my skirt is yanked at, my hips tugging this way and that, the hard length of him pressing into me even through the stiff felt—which promptly drops down to my feet after he undoes it.

Merc lifts me up with one arm and kicks the skirt away. I don't care where the thing goes, especially as his hands come between us. He's working at the ties on his britches—and then he's wrenching the top part of them down his thighs.

His mouth is still on mine as he paddles up my underskirts. I feel a cool draft on my legs, but there's no dwelling on that. He cups the back of me, lifts me up, and for the first time, there is a blunt probing at the core of me.

I brace myself for the pain, squeezing my eyes shut. But I will not stop this.

I want him. I want to know what this is—

Merc drives into me with a thrust, his arousal penetrating me in one hot branding. My eyes flip open and I see through the shroud of his black hair the window seat where he sits. The lantern is glowing, the journal open where he left it, the shutters whistling from the rain.

All of that disappears as the pleasure flows through me.

I look up to the ceiling. There are no sparks that fall, no stars twinkling to their own little deaths at the floorboards. But I feel like I did when that happened, whole and complete as I soar. In between my legs, Merc is pumping into me, to the point where our mouths break contact, and all I can do is hold on. I wrap my arms around his big shoulders, drop my head into the raven waves that fall all around, and squeeze my eyes shut. The wall behind me is hard, his body is hard . . . he is hard, inside of me.

I become nothing but energy, nothing but what he's calling from me. He's unleashed, wild and alive, as if he's killing me as he did the cook, his breath coming out in explosions, his hips pumping faster, the strokes shorter and shorter.

A growling sound vibrates into my ear.

And then I don't hear anything at all.

I'm flying free of my body on a rushing wave that turns my blood into sunshine as Merc pushes into me one last time and stays here, his sex kicking deep within me.

Forcing my lids open, I look to the ceiling again.

I'm breathing heavily. So is he.

The rain seems loud as our panting.

When he withdraws and puts me on my feet, I feel the cold again, even as something hot comes out of me. His seed, on the inside of my thighs. From where he left it inside.

Merc never stumbles. He does now.

He trips over one of his own boots as he yanks up his britches, and he turns away as if to spare me.

"Considering what we just did," I say roughly, "it's a little late to worry about modesty—"

"We're settled up now." He pivots back around, but not toward me. Toward the door. "I got you here. You gave me what I wanted. What was started between us . . . is finished."

Merc goes to the table and picks up his pack.

He doesn't look at me as he leaves.

The door closes as quietly as a last breath.

The pain is indescribable, a horrible counter to everything I just felt when we were joined, and if I weren't already leaning against the wall, I'm certain I would collapse. This is not how it's supposed to end. This is not . . .

Across the way, I stare at the bolt.

I go to the door and try to calm my breathing. Before I open it, I tap the latch for luck—

He's not waiting for me.

Leaning out, I look down the hall. Merc is nowhere to be found, and the next thing I know, I'm all the way to the head of the stairs. I expect to see his shoulders and that broadsword descending to the lower level. All I get is a pair of drunks bumping their way up the steps.

"He left."

I turn to the female voice. Through an open door, I see the blond. Bethle, I think her name was.

"Yes," I hear myself say. "I know."

"It's better this way." Her eyes drift down me, lingering on my underskirts. "Once Thale gets involved, if you have any regard for your husband, it's best he moves along."

Crossing my arms over my heart, I turn away and walk back down to my room. This time, as I close myself in, I throw the bolt even though I'm no longer worried about my safety here. Thale's authority, like Merc's, precedes me among the patrons and anyone else who might seek to harm me.

And my own reputation precedes me with Thale.

As I glance around the room, the whole of Anathos seems barren, and I can't believe it all happened so fast. The sex. Merc's leaving.

My return to solitude in a dangerous place.

That's my final thought as the oil in the lamp runs out and everything goes dark.

## *Fifty-Eight*

# My Solo Journey Begins.

When I wake up the following morning, I'm curled on my side facing the door, my hands tucked in at my heart as if I'm praying. The grit in my mouth abrades my tongue and the insides of my teeth as I try to swallow, and this comparatively small unpleasantness makes me feel all the big pains to an unbearable degree.

Forcing myself to sit up, I—

There's something in my hands.

His journal.

I glance back at the window seat and try to re-create why I have it. That's right, he left the thing behind, taking only his pack. So sometime during the night, I must have gone over and picked it up.

As I put the journal down on the bed-sheeting, the small, leather-covered folio opens to the last picture he sketched, of the gates and the meadow beyond. I touch the edges around the drawing, not intruding on the depiction of the stone pylons or the curling pattern of the iron . . .

With a frown, I look up. Listen hard to all the silence.

Shifting off the bed, I go to the window seat. There are a series of hooks securing the sash in place, and then the shutters have inner locks as well. I finally get it all open, and stare out over the gray sprawl of the Outpost's shops and homes.

The rain has stopped.

Overhead, the cloud cover remains low and thick, and everything is dripping, from the rooflines to the porch corners to the fences, suggesting that the cessation is recent. Maybe it will start up again, but surely all of the water in the sky is wrung out.

As I regard the town sprawl, I can't help but wonder where Merc is. I doubt he would have left in the night, and I have to wonder if he stayed with the blond. But with the storm moving along and daylight arriving, I'm guessing he's well departed by now. Did he take our horse, I wonder.

That is no longer my concern, though. And besides, I'm not going anywhere, so what do I need a horse for—

"No."

The word comes out of my mouth, but I check over my shoulder because it certainly seems like it was spoken by someone else.

When I turn back around, the clouds part and a beam of sunlight pierces through the congestion. As it zeroes in on me, shining like Mare's royal coins, I am swamped by a feeling that I do not belong here. And not just the lodging house, but this whole town. Even as the most reasonable side of me points out that this has been my destination, and maybe with people like Ronl and Lena, I could find work and a place to stay . . . something in my soul tells me otherwise.

This is not where I am to end up. I'm meant . . . to keep going.

"Not the plan," I say aloud as I look to the horizon.

But the protest doesn't matter now, and it's not going to mean anything later. As much as I want to fight it, I know that this is a way station to somewhere else. Something else.

My true destiny is calling.

It's as this conviction sinks in that the commotion starts.

The first of the shouting ripples through the still morning, and not long thereafter, a man comes running down the muddy lane toward the lodging house. Going by his brown felt dress, he's clearly a resident, and with that staff in his hand, I'm guessing he's a farmer or herder of some kind—and I'm not surprised when he leaps up onto the pub's porch and then I hear one of the doors slap shut.

A moment later, there are all kinds of feet pounding on the porch. A group of men emerge and take off in the direction the herder came from.

Dread chills the nape of my neck. Have they found the cook's body?

Exactly what kind of "after work" did Merc do—and where?

The doors to the pub open again, and this time there are voices right below me. My ear lends itself to the fast-paced talk—

"—demons! What else could do that—"

"Fates, they are here, too—"

"—parts of the sheeplings, everywhere."

Not long after, the group of men return. There's blood on them, on their hands, and on their clothes. Whoever all is speaking under the overhang go silent.

I cover my mouth with my hands and fall back.

Demons. Here—

There's a thud across my room and my head whips around. It's my pack. I'd put it on the table, and for some reason, even though the thing was set well enough back from the edge, it's fallen onto the floor.

Abruptly, I see what's in there, as if the sack and its strapping have disappeared. Then I feel the compass and the crown in my hands, sure as if I'm holding them. With another burst of strange clarity, I remember being in the woods, and the old instrument pointing me to the south in what surely was a flare of magic.

Lastly, I recall the unbelievable story Mr. Lewis told me and the charge he laid at my feet.

The compass to guide me. The crown . . . which is the point of it all.

I must go to the warrior queen who sees no one, and return the power to her.

My eyes return to the open window. It faces south, almost as if I was destined to get this room—and a strange calmness comes over me, especially as I touch my bandaged forearm. Lena and Ronl. If the demons are here, who will protect them and their baby?

And the sweet young maid. Even if we interceded in time, and even if Thale does what he's promised, who will protect her?

Against evil.

Thale, with all his might, can't summon an army to fight the Dark King. And what if word carries, and what was done at the settlement is done here? Fates, what if my own village is burned down because the demons have found it, and a mob from some other town comes to purify the population out of fear?

Anathos will not survive a second siege of the Dark King. I know this in my core. The stories that have been carried forward through history, and are recorded in the Book of Time—which are whispered of at the ends of the nights in the pub back home—tell of suffering unimaginable, of people subjugated by an iron fist of evil.

I still do not know if Mr. Lewis is right about me. What I cannot deny is what is in my pack . . . and what is stalking now this Outpost in the Badlands.

And what the Fulcrum looked like, with all those black bands.

Lifting a trembling hand to my mouth, I remember the taste of the sand, the black sand, and filigrees of my nightmare tease the edges of my consciousness.

If the Fulcrum is failing, perhaps this queen can beat the demons back?

"Oh, what am I saying . . ." I moan.

But nothing is keeping me here. And as I lay out my reality, everything is telling me to go—

*Knock. Knock.*

Shutting the window up, I go over to the door and unlatch the bolting. "Merc—"

"Mistress? I brought you some food."

I just stand there and blink. It's the maid, with the short brown hair and the beautiful voice, the one I've been so terrified for. Dressed in her red felt, she is carrying a tray laden with bread and drink, and there is a small, worried smile on her lips.

"Food?" she repeats as she lifts the load up a little, like she's thinking I haven't noticed it.

I take a step back, my eyes bouncing around her face without getting near her eyes. "Crescent moon . . ."

"Are you well enough?" The girl comes in and puts the tray on the table. "You are very pale. Here, sit, sit—"

I don't mean to. But I throw my arms around her and hug her.

"Mistress?" The embrace is tentatively returned. "Do you need a healer? Lena has just given birth, but—"

Easing back, I find myself double-checking that the maid is real. But I still don't look into her eyes. The answer I need was given to me last night by what Merc did, and I don't want to know anything else.

"M-mistress?"

"You're alive," I choke out. "You're okay."

Her head lowers. "Forgive me for the way I behaved yesterday. I—"

"There's no need to apologize. I shouldn't have gone in there in the first place. I just . . . I've been worried over you."

The maid lifts a hand to her bruised temple. "I am well enough. This morning has been . . . very quiet. It has been a blessed change."

"I think things are going to get better from now on for you." I put my hand on her shoulder. "You don't deserve to be under a man like that."

As her eyes tear up, she shuffles away and makes a show of going over to the tray. "I know it is but bread and cheese, yet I made both with my own hands."

"It is a feast for me before I go, and well timed indeed. Thank you."

She glances back at me. "You are leaving then?"

The image of her in her traditional dress, her pale hands twisting in front of her, the bruising on her face still so painfully obvious, burns into me. In posing the question, I feel as though she's a culmination of something that has been coming ever since Mr. Lewis sat me down, something I have been trying to shut out and deny.

I wish Merc were here.

But he's not. So I answer for myself: "Yes, I'm going."

Fates, am I really doing this? Am I really heading south? And how will I travel, especially if Merc took our horse . . .

"Soon, or today?" When I don't answer, she takes a deep breath. "I shall pack some provisions for you and your husband."

"Just for me."

In the periphery of my vision, I note that her brows rise. "You will be returning home then?"

"No, I go to the Kingdom of the South."

There's notable relief in the way her shoulders ease of their tension. "Oh, you cannot go south. The flooding will stop you at the valley pass for at least as long as the rain fell."

Dimly, I recall her saying something about all that. "There's another way, though. Isn't there? The barrier, you referred to it as?"

"Oh, no, no one goes through the Crystal Gate. It's impossible."

"Why?"

"It's a barrier impenetrable. For centuries, people have tried, to no avail."

I go over and look out the window. "Can you show me the direction of the pass?"

The maid comes over and points down the lane. "You follow this all the way out to the travel roading. It will take you to the pass, but there is no reason to go. Three days, at least, for the runoff to clear."

"What about the—Crystal Gate, is it?"

"It's the same way. The trail to the gate breaks off from the main way."

"Is the trail marked? Or overgrown?"

"You cannot miss it. There are ancient pavers that show the way. But that will waste your time as well. Mistress, I'm telling you, best to wait here in this comfortable room before you attempt any travel to the south. What difference will three days make?"

I think of those men returning just now, all bloody. Like Mr. Cavenish back in my village.

"Thank you," I say.

She smiles and bows. "I shall continue bringing you food."

The maid backs out of the door and gives me a little wave before shutting me in again. I stare at the gray panels for a time, and then go back over to the window and listen. There are many voices now, talking fast and urgently below me, but there are others now. People are also running between houses, and gathering on porches.

Glancing over my shoulder at the food, I have absolutely no appetite, but

I'm glad there's a sufficiency for two. After I eat a portion of the bread, and down both mugs of the refreshing drink, I take the case from the pillow that has not been used, and put the rest of what she baked for me in it. The cheese makes my stomach revolt—not that there's aught wrong with it. But then I remember Merc saying to eat up in the tunnel before we made our swim.

That feels like a lifetime ago.

As I force myself to consume the cheese, I count the nights we've been here—*I've* been here, rather. So few. It feels like a hundred, and all I can feel is sadness and dread over what's ahead.

Except there's no help in wallowing in emotion.

And the truth of it is that this decision, this choice, has been coming since we first arrived. I need a purpose, other than doing what I did in my own village for people who will eventually betray me to their own superstitions and the reality that the Fulcrum is failing. I was only thinking of staying because I can't face what lies before me if I keep going.

But Merc said it best.

Only forward, never back.

*Fifty-Nine*

# A Death Comes to Pass.

After I have a wash-up in the tub, I re-dress in Julion's outfit, which I've managed to clean to a fairly good standard. Covering my face with a new layer of the turban, I put the bread in my pack, and then also Merc's journal. The latter is like a ghost creaking across the floorboards, a physical manifestation of all that haunts me, but I cannot leave it here just to be thrown out.

At the door, I pause. I'll never see the inside of this room again, and I focus on the wall next to the bed . . . where Merc held me up off the floor and pinned me with his body. Underneath my sadness, something flares in the back of my mind, but I haven't the strength to tease it out under the pressure in my head.

I can't believe I'm going. On my own.

Without him.

Feeling the weight of my pack, however, I become even clearer about what I must do and where I must go. And that's all that can matter. What did I think was going to happen with a mercenary, anyway? As Merc said, our arrangement has been met on both sides, and it is over.

The last glance is toward that window seat. I can still see him sitting there by the lantern, sketching in his journal.

Looks as though they'll be refilling that lamp with oil for the next people who stay here.

Out in the hall, I close the door, and as I walk forward, I hear the voices. There are many, talking fast and loudly, down in the pub. When I get to the bottom of the stairs, I glance toward the knot of men who are so furiously addressing an audience. They're the ones who went off together. The herder, who first came running down the muddy lane and shouted the alarm, is at the bar, emptying a tankard down his throat.

A couple of the men glance in my direction, but the way they disregard me is a good thing. I continue on, leaving through the door Merc and I came through that first night—

The brightness overwhelms me and I put my arm up to shield my eyes. After they adjust, I lower the brim of my hand and squint at the sky. The clouds have broken up even further, and the sunlight is a resplendent shock after all the gray skies of the storm, and the gray wood and dingy oil lamps of the lodge.

The lane is an absolute swamp, and I slog along, keeping to the side for there's a depression in the center that's collected runoff and turned into a pond.

I recall the stables being among the first of the buildings as we entered the Outpost, and as I continue on, my slipper shoes are not just muddy, but become mud itself. The sound of neighing and the smell of fresh hay announce I've arrived.

And that's when it happens.

Off on the far side of the lane, a fenced pasture of grass rolls down to a beautiful solitary realm tree that seems as big as my village. The sun pours over its bright green leaves as well as the horses that are galloping round and getting out their energy after having been cooped up for days. None of that is what captures my attention.

It's that I've seen the bucolic scene before.

In a trance, I cross through the depths of standing water to the fence line. Bending down, I thread the space between the parallel boards, and continue through the meadow. A magnificent golden stallion thunders past me, his white mane and tail flowing, his ears pricked, his body sleek in his powerful strides. Though he holds my eye, he's not the one I'm coming for.

The one I need to see is going to be down by the tree.

As I descend, I tell myself I have it wrong.

I do not.

I find the village mayor's chestnut gelding lying in the soft grass. His eyes are closed, his nose deep in the fragrant blades, his body at ease.

It's as I saw when I looked into his eyes in the Lake of Lost Souls.

Falling to my knees, I bury my face in the springy mane and wrap my arm around his neck. He's still warm, but he is no longer living, and I pray that he's gone somewhere where there are no more saddles, no more bits and reins, no more burdens to carry. I feel responsible for this, for driving him so hard when that skystalker came at us, for making him cross that stark, waterless landscape in the heat, for taking him so far away from everything he's ever known.

I cry for other reasons, too, and it all blends together—

"Oh, no. Oh, mistress, I am so sorry—I just let him out."

Sniffling, I wipe my face and look up. Then do a double take. It's the maid—except . . . not. The dark hair is long and braided on two sides, and there are freckles dotting her face. Instead of felt skirting, this girl is dressed in work pants that hitch up over her shoulders and barn boots that come to her knees. Her voice is different, too. Deeper.

"It's all right." I run my hand down his still side. "It was his time."

"I swear, mistress, I cared for him as my own—"

"I know you did." I offer her a smile and then glance around, watching the other steeds run. "And what a beautiful place for one's heart to stop. Surrounded by what a horse loves most . . . freedom, sun, grass."

The girl clears her throat. "I accept responsibility. I shall make this right—"

Putting up my hand, I shake my head. "Not to worry." I feel for Mare's coins, which are back in their travel pocket, as I've come to think of it. "Are there any horses for sale, then?"

Not that I know how to use the gold. At least I have it, though.

As the girl looks out over the pasture, I continue to stroke the gelding. Even though he's gone and he wasn't really mine, it seems beyond disrespectful to arrange for his replacement with his body still warm, but with what happened in the night, there's an urgency I must operate under.

"We sold your husband the last of the ones available earlier. He told us to leave the chestnut for you."

Ducking my eyes, it's a moment before I can speak. "That was very kind of him—"

"Oy! What are you on about!"

A man comes rushing down the slope. He's older than middle-aged, and has the ruddy complexion of either a drinker or someone who works outside. Perhaps both.

Before he can go after the girl, I get to my feet and stand off at him. "My horse was old and too well used, which is my fault. There is naught that she did wrong, and I shall not have an accusation in that vein."

He stops by the girl, and in the pause, my heart cannot take any more cruelty—

The stabler removes the wrinkled hat from his sunburned, bald head, and he puts a craggy hand on her shoulder. "Aye, she would sooner hurt herself than offer ill care to any animal."

My eyes sting and I have to blink in double time. "He was a very good horse."

"I'm sure he was." The stabler glances around the field. "We'll see that he gets a fitting burial."

"I have money to pay for his board and grain—"

"Your husband already took care of all that plus the next week, so we shall owe him recompense. Where is he now, then?"

"He's departed ahead of me." My chest feels so hollow, especially as I lie, "I, ah, I'm meeting up with him. I need to buy a horse, too, but I understand there are none for sale—"

The girl turns to the man and starts to speak in a language I'm not familiar with. His eyes grow large, and when she goes quiet, he puts his cap back on and looks out across the field.

I glance in that direction.

That beautiful golden stallion is galloping along the fence line, and the speed with which it travels is breathtaking.

"Can you come back in an hour," the stable man says gruffly.

I think of Lena and Ronl.

"Certainly." I look over at the maid's twin sister. "And I'll figure something out, somehow. Don't worry about me if there's none to be sold."

The stable girl is staring out over the field, her eyes on the stallion.

"You come back then," the stabler tells me. "We just need a little time."

"Again, it's not your worry—but I will take his tack." Glancing down at the gelding, grief pierces my heart. "Please treat him well. He was very good to me."

"We will," the girl says. "He'll be buried here, right beneath this tree he chose."

Lowering my head, it is all I can do to walk away, my sodden slippers trudging up the incline, stepping through the fence rail, and carrying me back to the muddy lane. I was going to stop by the new parents anyway, and seeing that infant in all its vitality is what I need right now. As I go down the thoroughfare, there are all kinds of people out and about, their voices stressed and fast, their bodies overanimated—but that's not just because of what they're talking about.

I think of the horses, cantering and free in the sunlight.

Animals and people are not so different sometimes. But the humans here on Anathos are aware of what's coming. The horses are just enjoying the sunshine and feel of their legs stretching.

When I arrive at the herbist shop, there's a woman exiting with a small paper bag. She seems harried, her hair askew, and she bumps into me in her rush. Catching the door, I go inside—

There's a line of talking women, and all of them look as though they've just rolled out of bed. They're speaking in the language the stabler used with the girl, their rushing syllables covering the air like layers of fallen leaves, everything a jumble. Down at the register, Ronl is trying to get them to calm down, as he points at an empty glass container next to him.

I'll bet whatever they're looking for is to ward off evil. In an instant, I'm back at the burned-out settlement, looking at those markings by the doors . . . and the bloodstains on the floors.

Even though I'm scared, I'm doing the right thing in trying to go south, I tell myself.

As I catch his eye, he gives me a wave and nods at the door behind him. I hustle down and give his arm a pat as I scoot into the back.

"Lena?"

"In here," comes the quick reply from the bedroom.

As I pass through, there are some swaddling blankets soaking in a tub by the water faucet, and a partially made breakfast on the counter of hens' eggs, and a bread wedge.

Edging open the door, I smile at Lena as she feeds her precious daughter. Then I point over my shoulder. "It looks as though Ronl was making you something to eat and got interrupted. May I finish the job?"

"Oh, would you? I'm almost done with her, and I'm still a bit sore."

"Just a moment."

It feels very good to do a simple task, cracking the hens' bounty over a cast-iron pan, and taking it over to the hearth. Sinking down onto my haunches, I go to put the—

The flames that curl up from the core of glowing embers bend toward me, their orange and yellow peaks tilting forward.

As I jerk back with a curse, Lena says with worry, "Sorrel?"

Shaking myself, I glance back at the bedroom door. "Yes?"

"Are you all right?"

I put my hand over my mouth. Then shove the pan onto the cooking grate and jump to my feet. "Oh, fine. Just fine, indeed."

Rubbing my eyes, I tell myself that there's a draft coming down the flue. A draft from the shop outside. A draft from the open window because the temperature outside is finally warming up.

By the time I deliver the plate, I'm recovered enough to trade the breakfast I've pulled together for the baby she birthed.

"Good morning then, little one . . ." I stroke the soft cheek and turn a finger over the downy sprinkling of dark hair.

Abruptly, I frown as it dawns on me Lena isn't eating. "Have I burned the eggs?"

The new mother doesn't appear to hear me. She's staring at her baby, her brows down, her mouth in a tense line.

"Are you not feeling well?" I prompt as I go on high alert.

"There was a slaughter last night." Her voice is soft, the words murmured absently, as if she's speaking to herself. "In the sheepling pasture."

"Ah . . . yes, I heard that there was a badness with some animals—"

"It was more than that. There was a death, of a man."

Putting the bairn up on my shoulder, I try to keep my expression neutral. "Who was it?"

"The cook." Lena shakes her head. "From the pub."

When she goes no further, I prompt, "What happened?"

She looks away from her daughter when she answers. "The men who went down to look at the body said . . . it was a demon."

*Sixty*

# Goodbyes.

"'Field-dressed' is the term, I believe." Lena rubs her eyes, and drops her hands into her lap. "One of the herders found him and the sheeplings in the morning when he went to let his animals out to pasture. The cook's stomach . . . had been cut open—torn. Desecrated. In life, that man had a horrible reputation, but nobody should die like that."

I picture Merc as he came into our room last night. No blood on him. No bruising. He wasn't breathing hard. Whatever "work" he performed to prevent things from being traced back to him certainly did not include staging a messy body to look as though it had been savaged by evil.

Assuming Merc caught the cook somewhere outside after I saw the man leave . . . a demon must have come along afterward.

Fear tightens the back of my neck as I imagine Merc out there, in the darkness . . . with one of those things.

"There have been attacks in other territories," Lena says. "We've had travelers in the last weeks come here with such reports. And a settlement was burned up north, we heard."

"Yes," I whisper. "We saw it on the way here."

I don't want to go into the symbols and what really happened.

"What world have I brought her into."

Lena's eyes seek my own, but I dodge them and stay focused on the plate I prepared for her. I can't bear to know what awaits her, not just because I don't want the bairn I hold to be left an orphan as I was. The truth is, I was hoping what I saw of the horse's future was evidence that everything in Anathos would be okay. I thought the chestnut gelding had years until its peaceful end and that meant we were all going to survive somehow; the farrier and that maid might have only had days, but our steed . . . he promised me a horizon.

Or so I thought.

"That's why all the wives came." Lena shakes herself and brings the plate onto her lap. "They're looking for *astra* to ward off evil."

"What is that?"

"Just folklore. There is naught real to it, but if the lie calms them in the near term, let them buy what I have of the weed."

"I believe you've sold out of it."

"Ronl should just give them something else. They won't know any different." Lena sighs. "Sometimes, the only way we can help people is by reassuring their minds, even if it changes not a thing. As healers, we must do what we can."

"Yes."

We are silent as she starts to eat, and then she pauses between bites. "You have come to say goodbye. I can tell by the way you look at her." She reaches out and clasps my hand. "You mustn't go. Even if the flooding lets you pass in a couple of days, even with your husband, it's not safe."

"I must. I am . . . needed elsewhere."

"Once, the demons were to the north, far off, but every week, they close in. Sorrel, it is far too dangerous to leave—and consider I am saying the Outpost is the better option." When I don't respond, she puts the plate aside. "At least let me see your arm again, then. And allow us to provide you and your husband with some basic supplies."

"Oh, you do not have to worry about us—"

"You will take everything as gifts for your aid unto me. There will never be a way to repay you, so you must allow us this heartfelt exchange."

I take a deep breath. "Can you and Ronl leave?"

"This is our home. Besides, Thale protects us because he needs us to care for his women and their . . . complications. He will let no harm come to us."

In the silence that follows, I know we're both thinking the same thing: Can the man protect anybody from what stalks the night?

And then all I can think of is this town burned to the ground after everyone, even this beautiful baby, are sacrificed to superstition even though they are no more contaminated by evil than I am.

"Put her in the bassinet, and let me see your arm."

I follow the orders because that's what one does when given a reasonable command, and Lena is efficient: The cloth bandage is removed, the healing inspected, and I'm told where to find the herbs I need to bring her from outside in the shop proper.

As I reemerge from their private quarters, Ronl's still dealing with all of the women, and it appears as though he's found the solution Lena came to as well. He's filling bags from various containers, and refusing to take money, shooing off the fearful customers' coppers. I make motions over my arm, and point to the three glass containers Lena told me to bring to her, and he nods me along.

When I'm back in the bedroom with everything, more quick work is made. Though Lena remains in recovery, her hands are fast and she mixes and reapplies the same poultice that she put on me. The wound is so much improved that I feel certain of a full recovery, and she makes sure I have enough for two more applications, which is as much as I'm allowed to have of the components.

She then insists that I go to her dresser and take a skirt and jacket, as well as some blouses and clean underthings, and put it all in a traveling saddle pack. When she tries to give me shoes, I draw the line.

"Lena, you must stop." I cover my face with my palms because my eyes are getting misty. "It's too much—"

"You have nothing, don't you." Her voice grows soft. "You have lost all that you had."

"But that's not your fault."

"It will be if I do not give some of what I have to you now."

I shake my head. "No, you need these things—"

"Sister, remember? And what sister would I be if I let you leave with no change of clothes." She motions impatiently to a freestanding wardrobe. "Now go in there. Go on—Sorrel, if you do not open those doors, I shall be forced to get up and do so myself."

Turning toward the gracefully carved wooden expanse, I pull the latch on one side of the double doors—

"No." I glance over my shoulder at her. "We're not taking any of Ronl's suits."

"Oh, I know better than to suggest that husband of yours wear anything but the leather that protects him. No, it's up on the shelf, there. In the back. Sorrel, let us not argue."

Capitulating, I rise onto my toes, and stretch my good arm as far as it will go.

"It's in a sealed fold." Lena nods. "A little farther—you can get it."

My fingertips make contact with something soft and square, and I pull out a stitched bag that makes an odd chiming sound as I take it down.

"Put that in the bag." Lena nods impatiently. "And yes, you must keep it for a special occasion. Some night, when you want that husband of yours to bow at your feet, you will put it on."

"That's really not going to happen," I mutter.

"I've been saving it for a festival, but Ronl and I have already served its purpose." She looks lovingly at her daughter. "Besides, I think it's perfect for you. Now put the herbs for your arm in there, tie the top, and let us say goodbye—"

Her voice catches at the end and she clears her throat. "Forgive me, I am a little emotional these days."

After I do what she says, she puts her hand out to me, and as I lay my palm in hers, I sit down on the bed.

"Thank you," she says after a minute. "For not lying to me."

"About what?"

"That you might be coming back."

We embrace, and as I hold on to her, I look over her shoulder at the gray wall. I can't bear my thoughts, but closing my eyes would just add terrible pictures to all my fears. So I stare at the grain of the wood and pray to nothing I believe in that she and Ronl and their daughter will be spared.

"If I ever do come back," I say, "I will repay you somehow."

She shakes her head. "You will always be a part of our family, no matter where you are—and in my culture, there are no debts between those of blood."

I wipe my eyes. "I'm unused to being claimed."

"It was meant to be, then."

When I stand up to go, I know I'll remember her sad smile and her beautiful baby for as long as I live.

"Goodbye, sister," I whisper before I leave.

## *Sixty-One*

# Lavante.

As I walk out from behind the register of cash and wind my way through the wives, Ronl pushes his glasses back into place and gives me a wave—but then loses his smile as he sees the saddlebag I'm taking with me. At the door, I lift a hand to him, and after a moment, he does the same. He seems very grave, no doubt because he's thinking about the very same thing his wife told me about.

Demons have come to the Badlands. So now is not the best time for anybody to leave.

Outside, I take a moment to enjoy the sun, and then walk back down to the stables. As I arrive, I look out to the realm tree. The chestnut gelding has been covered by a lovely white drape with a pattern on it, and I watch the other horses nibbling at the grasses, drinking from the stream, and standing together in a herd—

"He's all ready for you, mistress."

"I'm sorry?" I murmur absently. Then I turn around.

And don't know what else to say.

The magnificent golden horse with the white mane and tail is saddled with the gelding's saddle, but not the bridle, no doubt because of the size difference.

I immediately shake my head. "I cannot take this horse—"

The girl keeps her voice low. "I know what you did. Last night."

Going absolutely still, I say levelly, "I beg your pardon."

"The cook never left the pub kitchen. Ever. Not for an errand, not for a wander, not even for a breath of fresh air. Except for last night, when your husband came down and the two of them talked."

"I don't know what you speak of—"

"My sister told me you approached her and begged her to let you help yesterday. That you saw what that animal did to her and so you were compelled—" She has to collect herself. "For so long, I've tried to get her to come and stay with us. The stabler and his wife are very kind and good people. They would have taken her in in a moment. She wouldn't leave though."

Because the cook had threatened to take her sister in her place, I think to myself.

The stable hand continues, "I never understood why he picked on her the most, but I was certain that one night, he was going to . . ." She looks away. "My twin is the other half of me, and the guilt I feel that she's lived with what she's had to and I have everything so safe and contented with the horses—it wasn't fair. But you changed that—"

"I'm afraid you're mistaken. I did talk to her, yes, and I asked her to allow me to—"

"I know what you both did for her." She presses the reins into my hands. "And you must take him. He is the only thing I possess in this world other than the clothes on my back. I raised him from a foal, and though I have been offered money enough to live on my own . . . I haven't wanted to let him go. Until now."

"And you must keep him—"

"Tell me you did not put your own lives at risk to save my sister's. Tell me, and upon your honor, do not lie."

I open my mouth. Close it. "You don't have to do this."

"You didn't have to save her." The girl brushes the tears from her cheeks and then looks at the horse. "I always had the sense that I was just holding him for his real destiny. I feel as though this is all working out the way it was supposed to."

I look at the horse properly, although not in the eyes, of course—

Oh, he is even more magnificent up close. And I am struck with the conviction that this big, strong stallion, with his intelligent head carriage, and his long, powerful legs, might well be the only thing that can get me where I need to go.

"I will come back," I hear myself say. "And I will return him to you."

This is a terrible vow to make. I can no more ensure I can make the journey, much less swing back through here as a war is started.

"He's very smart." The girl runs her hand down his gleaming muzzle. "He'll pull his head if you let him. And watch his back left shoe. He throws it when he gets bored."

Then she winds herself around his neck and squeezes. I want to tell her no, just as I tried to stop Lena, just as I wished the maid wouldn't cook anything special for me. But these gifts that refuse to be denied are filling a place in me that's so broken, I can't bear to look too closely at it.

In the village where I spent all my days in service to others I was a pariah. Here, at the Outpost, among strangers, I'm embraced and taken care of.

So much of this destiny of mine has been unexpected and difficult to bear or believe, but this . . . is a lovely surprise.

The girl smiles even though her heart is clearly breaking. "I would have wanted to give him to you, even if you hadn't lost your horse. I couldn't have you leave with what you both did without paying you back in some way."

"Thank you."

Though I duck her eyes, I draw her in for an embrace, and I feel her tremble as she holds on to me. Then she pulls back, and straps the pack full of Lena's clothes behind the saddle.

Where I used to sit.

The enormity of what I'm about to do hits me. Merc was my sword and shield. Now I'm on my own.

The girl offers me a lift up, and the instant I am in the saddle, I feel as though I've been astride this horse already. Beneath me, he prances and tosses his head, his platinum mane like a spray of water, but he doesn't buck and he doesn't bolt.

Maybe he's just minding his manners for the moment and all the misbehaving comes later.

"What's his name?"

"Lavante. In my language, it means wind from the east." She steps back and crosses her arms over her chest. "He'll eat anything, by the way. No worries there."

As she looks out to the pasture, I can feel the energy coursing through the stallion, and he minces his hooves into the slop.

"I'll take very good care of him."

"I know you will." She glances back in my direction. "It's your nature. And when you find the way impassable and have to return, come here and I'll check that back shoe while you wait for the water to recede."

Her sister must have told her my plans.

I'm not coming back, though. And I don't know what awaits me, but there's no more time to waste.

"Thank you," I say again.

Upon the signal of my heel, the stallion—Lavante—surges forward, plunging his hooves into the mud. As we head off in the direction the maid told me to go in, his stride, even with the lousy ground, is smooth as a breeze, and my seat takes to him with such facility, I can't believe it's my first time on his back. He also seems to behave himself, listening to the signals of the reins.

I don't intend to stop again, but as I come up to the pub, the maid is out in front and she has a bundle in her arms. She starts waving as she sees me, and there's no way I can pass her by. The stallion comes to a halt as she steps off the shallow porch, and given his nicker of greeting, it's clear they know each other.

"Emma told me she was going to give him to you," the maid murmurs as she strokes his muzzle.

"I tried not to take him . . . but she insisted and I am very grateful."

"I have this for you." The maid holds out a cloth-wrapped weight. "There are utensils, more bread and cheese, and bladders you can fill for water."

"Oh, I have half of what you prepared—"

I am roundly ignored. The maid secures her gifts to the saddle by rising up on her tiptoes. When things are settled to her satisfaction, she steps back.

"You will return," she says, "when you see for yourself that the way is impassable. I shall save your room."

There's nothing else to say on that front, as far as I'm concerned. "Please take care of yourself."

The girl looks down at her hands. "I . . ."

I want to hug her. "It was never your fault. You did *nothing* wrong. The problem was him."

"Emma says that your husband . . ."

"You know what I've found helpful, in life?" I wait until she glances up at me, even as I don't meet her eyes. "Only forward, never back. Your future is ahead of you."

And indeed, I'm trying to heed my own words as I contemplate leaving here without Merc.

"I shall do my best." She takes a step back. "And I will see you soon."

*No,* I think to myself. *You won't.*

In the heartbeat that follows, I know it's time to go. I know I must nudge my heels into the stallion's flanks, and loose the reins, and—

The center double doors open.

And Thale emerges.

*Sixty-Two*

# The Promise of an Overlord.

The Outpost's ruler is dressed in another one of his finely fitted black suits, and he has a top hat with a purple band above the brim pitched on his head. When the maid sees who it is, she ducks her head and scurries for the other entrance, clearly terrified that she's been caught outside when she needs to be at the oven.

"Lalah," he says sharply.

She freezes in mid-step—and I realize I've never known her name. I should have asked—

Abruptly, he switches to that other language and I'm surprised. I don't know what he's saying, but his tone is gentle and the tension in the girl's body dissipates like the stormwater that is even now evaporating in the sunshine all around us. When he's finished speaking, she glances up at him from the side, and as he nods a dismissal, she takes a deep breath, and continues on at an easier pace.

Well, what does one know. It appears that he intends to keep his word.

At least in front of me.

Thale saunters over, his tall hat accentuating his height. "Nice horse. And I see you've been well provided for. Those packs are quite full, are they not."

Across the muddy lane, people loiter and glance over with curiosity that they cannot hide.

"In spite of the Outpost's reputation," I say roughly, "I've found the people here to be quite kind."

"Hmm. That is more a commentary on you than this place, I suspect. You have a way with others."

I recall the mob who wanted to kill me in my village, and decide that's one word for it.

"I hear you're heading south, then." He glances down the lane. "You'll be back soon when you see the flooding. You're the type of woman who must experience things for herself, however. We'll hold your room."

I glance to the entrance Lalah used.

"That wasn't just a show for you," Thale says softly. "I will protect her. Worry not."

"And the other maids."

He slides me one of his sly smiles. Then touches the brim of his top hat and inclines his head. "The others as well."

"Thank you." I have to clear my throat. "For being honorable."

"You sound surprised." He places a hand in the center of his chest, right below the diamond tiepin. "I would be insulted, if I were not aware of my, shall we say, well-deserved reputation."

He steps in close to me just as a number of pub patrons peek out of the doors on the porch—and that's when I notice that windows on the second floor have been cracked open as well. It reminds me of when Merc and I arrived here.

As if Thale reads my mind, he murmurs, "I do not know where your husband is." There's a pause, as if he expects me to fill him in. When I don't, his lips press into a tight line of disapproval. "He should take better care of you."

Before I can respond, he snatches my hand and I feel something so cold against my palm, I recoil—

The only reason I don't drop the ice is because he forces me to hold on to it.

"Take this," he says quietly. "Sneak it into your pocket. Use it if you need to."

I open the grip he's curled my hand into. It's not ice. It's some kind of octagonal crystal that's been fastened into a—

I know exactly what this is, and my eyes nearly meet Thale's.

"You grip the blade this way." He pushes the shank part through the fore and middle fingers of my hand, then secures a right-angled hilt into the meat of my palm with my thumb. "Lightweight, very deadly. I believe you've seen it before."

Yes, indeed. It's the weapon his bearded guard was going to kill him with.

"There are a lot of ways to use a dagger like this, and as I said, you're going to keep it in your pocket. If you need it, you're going to grip it out of sight, and use the element of surprise in your favor. You're going to drive it in like a punch to the gut and put your shoulder into the stab when you do it. It'll cut through a man's stomach like a piece of fruit."

The sunlight gleams through the transparent stone. Each of the angles of the crystal core are sharp as a blade, but the flat faces fit perfectly against the V of my fingers—and the tip rivals any knife's point.

"A gift, to you." He points at the beautiful weapon. "Very expensive. Worth as much as a house—you can also sell it if you have to."

"I . . . thank you."

"It is, quite literally, the least I can do." I feel his eyes traveling over me. "And you . . . you will call on me. If you get into trouble, you send a messenger for me and I will come. No questions asked, and I'll even pay for the courier."

Frowning, I find myself wanting to meet his eyes, but I stop at the hard line of his jaw. "You don't strike me as a man who's interested in being a savior. Why would you—"

"I am in your debt." Thale steps back. "As long as my heart beats. And we can discuss this further when you return after you assess the flooding with your own little eyes. You aren't going to get far, but I'm sure you'll enjoy the ride on your new horse—"

"What about the other way? The barrier . . . the Crystal Gate. Everyone talks about it, but no one's told me what it is?"

"Ah, now, there would be another trick for you to pull off. In all of known history, no one has ever been able to get through it." His smile is wide—and were he a different sort, I'd say it's warmly fond. "Go see for yourself. The cutoff is quite clear. And then tell me what you think when you come back here."

I give him a nod, and gather my reins.

"Sorrel." His tone becomes urgent. "Be back well before dark, yes. Your husband isn't the only deadly thing out in the night around here. Unless you already know your own grave?"

"I wouldn't want that information, even if I could have it."

He chuckles a little. "Care to let me in on mine own, again? It has for sure changed."

I shake my head. "You don't want to be on that carousel. Besides, your wits and strength have kept you alive this long. They're the only second sight you require."

"That's not what you first told me, is it. And I did need you, as it turned out."

"I think you would have figured it out." I shrug. "In any event, you go forth from here. As do I. Goodbye, Thale."

"Call on me. Anytime."

Mindful of the sun's position in the sky, I give the stallion only the most minute of cues and we are off at a jog. As I proceed down the muddy lane, there are many more open shutters with faces staring out at me, but they are not hostile.

They seem . . . mesmerized.

Just as Lalah said, the lane takes me away from the Outpost and into rolling fields similar to what Merc and I encountered after we came out of the Lake of Lost Souls. I'm grateful that I can see in all directions, but I feel like I have a target on me and there are weapons of unknown descriptions and far-off locations trained on me as if I'm a threat.

Or a meal.

The hollow space behind my sternum is howling for Merc like a dog abandoned, and you'd think there wouldn't be room for any other emotion. Fear, however, is also riding with me, and I think of the other times I've had waves of anxiety. This seems worse than all of them combined.

There's no shaking, no sweating, no head spins or panting, though. I'm a frozen block of nothing but instinct on the back of this spectacular horse. Oddly, he seems to understand that I need him to keep track of where we are. He scans from side to side, his tail swishing with impatience, his hooves light in his quick, smooth gait. At least the roading, with its two tracks for carriages, becomes drier and easier for him. Out here, in the flats, the storm fall has already been consumed by the ground and the persistent sunshine.

Then again, with his energy, I'm not entirely sure this stallion couldn't trot on air.

Off in the distance, a mountain range looms, and given where we are proceeding, I know it's the Rozars. The jagged peaks are not high enough to bear snow on their summits, but they'd still be the perfect nesting grounds for dragons, so the point about staying off their inhospitable flanks is sound. Approaching them, it's as though I'm closing in on a gate constructed purposely by nature to keep the Outpost on one side . . . and the Kingdom of the South on the other.

The inhabitants of the former were not wrong about the flooding, though. Over to the west, a rushing waterway—that might well have been the sweet, apple-tasting stream prior to all the rainfall—is covering a swath of meadow that's ten times as wide as my entire village. Including the moat. The river parallels the road, and the current is heading for the Rozars. Assuming that the passes between the peaks are narrow, there will indeed be no chance of me getting through.

But Thale is right. I need to know myself, and it won't be much longer.

I measure my progress by the trees that ring the bases of the elevations. Thanks to the stallion, we are making fast work of the distance to the forest, and soon enough, my eyes can sort through the various types of leaves and boughs.

I tell myself it's going to be a little safer when I get there.

I'll have some cover.

Of course, so will anything that might hunt me.

This is the back-and-forth my mind is trapped in as I come to the fork in the road. I pull up on the reins, and the stallion jogs in place.

The way to the right is well traveled, the road packed into its twin tracks, no weeds in the center. To the left, pavers that are weathered enough to be ancient are choked with tufted undergrowth and brambles.

"Shh," I murmur as I look to the right. "Lavante, settle, please."

The stallion tosses his head as if in argument, but then his hooves go still—and that's when I hear it. The roar of water.

Staying focused on the right, I follow with my eyes the traveled lane into the tree line, and though I can't see the flooding, I know that somewhere, up ahead, there's an intersection between the road and the river. And going by the sound? There will be absolutely no passage.

But what of the other way. The barrier.

The Crystal Gate.

Reining the stallion to the left, I send him onto the other route. He doesn't care a bit about the weeds, and seems to like picking his feet up high to get over the hairy green seams of the old pavers. When we reach the tree line, I pull him up again and stare into the forest. The darkness that lurks there, even in the bright daylight, chills me, and the enormity of what I'm doing rushes up from all directions.

I am alone. With a bag of royal coins, a priceless weapon, and a horse that any thief would like to steal.

I glance over my shoulder. The Outpost seems so far away as to be on the other side of Anathos. All I want to do is return there.

"Always forward, never back," I whisper as a mantra. And yet I can't go any farther.

Even as I order my heels to give the signal, as my hands churn against the reins, as I lean forward in the saddle . . . I remain stuck in the mud, even while my steed is fully capable of continuing on the stone beneath his shod hooves.

I need help, though. I need . . . courage and help and—

My hand moves on its own, going up to the straps on my shoulder. The next thing I know, my pack is in my lap, the reins are tucked in under my knee, and I'm opening the neck.

As I reach inside, the compass finds my palm as if it has taken control, and when I draw it out and remove its satchel, there seems to be a glow about the object that has nothing to do with sunlight hitting the gold. My thumb strokes over the cover and finds the release on the top.

When the lid pops open, a whoosh of energy comes at me, and the horse feels it, too. He rears up and stomps the ground.

I gasp, and not because he surprises me.

Before I can even focus on the plain dial, the map that does not exist jumps out at me—

The stallion whinnies and rears up again. Settling him, I see what I was shown before, the outline of Anathos . . . except everything has reoriented itself to my position now, in the Badlands, a distance south and west from the Outpost.

The red arrow is pointing resolutely south.

Which happens to be directly in front of me.

It's as if the instrument is telling me to go forward—

Abruptly, and without warning, the compass closes itself up, the cover flipping over on its own and clicking into place, as if the request I put no voice to has been answered and our business concluded.

I can only stare in disbelief at its gold contours. Putting my thumb back on the release, I push it. Push it again. Push the little release a third time.

When nothing happens, I feel as though it's refused me a dialogue, and a strange gut instinct tells me that if I keep trying to force another audience I'll be considered rude. And considering this inanimate object—that nevertheless moves itself—is my only ally outside of my horse, I return it to its satchel, put it back in the pack, and remount the now-familiar weight onto my shoulders and spine once again.

In a sudden panic, I look at the sky, worried I've lost time. But no. This has all happened in just an instant. I have a thought that the hours that lapsed before were for another reason . . . maybe because Merc and I had to wait for the intersection of the mayor, his sons, and our lovely, loyal gelding.

Or perhaps it was something else. Fate only knows.

Meanwhile, shadows are lurking in the forest ahead of me, the great unknown waiting in and among the trees. It's as if I'm peering into the mysteries and peril of destiny itself, and I have an innate urge to turn back. Still, the direction from the compass is as good a portent as any I'm going to get—and besides, this is where I must go. If only I could see more clearly the path ahead—

A shimmering coalesces before me, like heat waves upon a roof, and it's as green as emerald and as reflective as a silver plate. And then a breeze comes from behind me, the tops of all the grasses and weeds bending away with a part down the middle, as if making way for us.

The mysterious effect travels forth to the forest, and that's when the creaking and snapping starts. For no reason that makes any logical sense, the trees are arcing to the sides as the grasses did, their tops turning outward until their trunks prevent any further bend, their branches giving way more easily until some even snap off and fall.

Magic.

This is . . . no dream. This is actual magic.

I exhale in disbelief and awe—and have the sense that I am not alone, after all. Something is with me, taking Merc's place as a protector.

Except then I remember the black sand in my mouth, and I wonder if this is a trap. There's no evil that I can sense, though. And the horse isn't balking.

"Always forward, never back."

Gripping the reins, I urge Lavante forth, and he leaps at the chance to get back into motion, his hooves clapping over the ancient pavers toward the forest. As we proceed, I glance over my shoulder. Like two pieces of fabric knitting back up, the grasses resume their density in our wake—and now I am in the trees. Courtesy of their bowing away, I have plenty of light and there are no places to hide from my eyes.

All around, a subtle green sheen sparkles, swirling and twirling on invisible currents as if the energy is what is holding back everything for me. And after I pass, the forest rights itself. This continues as I go deeper and deeper into the woods, the way before yielding to me, the path in my wake sealing back up. Is this the compass? Whatever it is, I'm struck with a suspicion that I'm being led somewhere by a force outside of my control.

And I'm not sure whether it's benevolent.

After some distance, the road starts to curve and continues to do so until there's a convergence with the Rozars, the trees on the right-hand side giving way to throngs of ragged rocks that protrude from the ground at gradually increasing heights until they tower over me. This is like no range I have ever seen, less mountains that rise above than something pushed up from a place deep underground. The peaks are black with brown horizontal veining, and certain faces have faded from sun exposure. As we sidle up on them, I'm astounded at the sheerness of elevations, and soon enough, I have to throw my head all the way back in order to see what I can of their flanks.

I remember Merc saying that any mountain can be traveled in the rain, but these things couldn't be scaled in any kind of weather.

The trail takes a sharp jab to the right. Doubles back on itself. Makes another hook. Narrows down tightly. As the rock walls close in, Lavante's hoof strikes start to echo—and gone goes the sun. Though there's plenty of light to see by, none of the rays reach down here, and the warmth fades quickly. I think of the water rushing through the other section of the mountain range. With these vertical rises, and the narrow passages between them? Assuming the other way is similar, the storm runoff would be deadly in these snaky canyons, and likely to come up quickly—

A sound vibrates through the tight trailway, bouncing off the planes of rock and amplifying with every angle. The stallion hears it, too, and comes to a stop even as I'm about to pull back on the reins.

It's a rhythmic strike . . . that has an odd resonance. Like someone—or something—is repeatedly hitting a surface that has some metal in it—or maybe that's just the acoustics of the passageway?

Urging Lavante forward, the stallion treads even more lightly than usual, as if sneak attacks are a trained skill for him. I become prepared, too, for all the good it will do, by putting my hand in my pocket, finding Thale's gift and recalling how he told me to use it—

Without warning, I come out of a turn into a clearing that's broad and deep enough to allow the sun to penetrate down to the packed ground. But the slanting rays and return to warmth are not what I notice.

It's not even the bizarre, towering barrier I'm confronted with.

All I see is the raven-haired man in black leather who has his boots braced and is hauling a broadsword over his shoulder again and again . . .

At a milky pane of glass as tall as the sky itself.

## *Sixty-Four*

# The Crystal Gate.

Merc halts the momentum of the sword in mid-backswing and wheels around, putting the weapon out in front of him. The tip lowers and he straightens. He's breathing hard, and behind him there are chips out of the extraordinary barrier—

Lavante jumps in place and then starts to mince around, pawing at the dirt and tossing his head. I have to sink into the saddle and gather his mouth, and even so, he refuses to settle. Then again, there's a disquieting gleam to whatever Merc is battling.

"Nice horse," he says between inhales. "You decide to go for a ride?"

I soak in the presence of him, all of his weapons and his black surcoat, his long, black hair and his beautiful black and white eyes. And as he speaks, the sound of his voice goes into my body, not just my ears—

I tighten myself up, just as I would my pack. This is not a reunion. This is an intersection.

"Our gelding died," I hear myself say.

I don't expect him to have any reaction, but his brows lift. "I didn't know."

I want him to be sorry. To feel what I did.

"The stabler's girl felt responsible even though it wasn't her fault." I stroke Lavante's neck and resent my emotions. As well as Merc's lack of them. "I see you got yourself a mount."

A dark-colored, stout-rumped horse is standing off to the side, one of his back feet cocked at the tip as if he's taking a nap in spite of the noise and the new arrivals.

"His name is Snooze. I believe that started out as a descriptor."

Merc turns back to the barrier, putting his hands on his hips such that the broadsword is pointed at what he was trying to strike down.

My eyes drift away from him and up the expanse of the anomaly. Never have I seen anything come close. The translucent, smooth plane extends up from the ground to the height of four or five houses stacked foundation-to-roof, and given its reflection, I can make out Merc's face, his horse, my horse, me—but it's not a mirror. And though it can't be man-made, I can't see nature creating this, either. It's too precise: Incredibly, the seal against the cliffs and across the ground is tight and total, without gaps, and there are piles of crystal shards at the intersections of the mountainsides. It's as if the topography has closed in over time, and the shift has shaved parts of the thing.

"So this is the Crystal Gate," I murmur.

Then my eyes return to Merc as if he's the dominant fixture in the landscape. And I resent the weakness. "Do you know what it's made out of?"

"No." He reaches up and runs his palm across the place he's been driving at. "It's most . . . extraordinary. Nothing seems to weaken it, and I'm not the first who has tried."

That's when I notice all the musket balls that cover the dirt. I'd assumed they were pebbles, given the layers of them. There are also objects of various extraction—axe-heads, hammers, arrows—that suggest many people over many, many years have tried to break down that which has stopped their way forth.

Though Lavante remains agitated, I swing a leg over and drop to the ground. Tightening the reins around one of the saddlebags, he stays put, but doesn't like it, his hooves stamping at the loose detritus, kicking up musket balls and shards. I walk over to the barrier, and feel the smooth expanse with my fingertips. It's cold, ever so slightly bumpy, and has a pearlized effect that prevents me from seeing anything but shadows on the other side.

Leaning into my hands, I push against it. There's no give, and as I go over to where it meets the elevation on the left, there's a tinkling sound at my feet. The shards that have fallen are octagonal in nature, and as I drop down on my haunches and pick one up, it's Thale's weapon.

Or rather, the bearded man's—

*Gong! Gong! Gong—*

"By all means," I call out over the din. "Let's continue that approach as it's worked so well."

Merc halts in mid-swing again. "Have you any better idea? Or is commentary all you have to offer."

The crystal falls from my hand, refinding its like. "I'm surprised you went this way. To the south."

His expression remains remote. "I take jobs when they come to me and go where they take me. So I am here. What about you."

I open my mouth to suggest we could have traveled together all along, but that's like a declaration of failure on my part, isn't it. Besides, I haven't told him about my change in plans, and I don't want him to think I'm just following him. I wonder where he spent the night? Somewhere in the Outpost? Or the bed of another woman, maybe this time someone he could finish with—

Well. I might as well stab myself at this rate.

Returning my palm to the barrier, I sweep it up and down as I walk over to him. It occurs to me, as I examine the height and breadth of the gate, that the unevenness on the surface is concentrated in a band that is somewhere between the chest and the upper arm reach of a grown man. Clearly, efforts to break through have focused in this area, though there are pockmarks farther up, too.

"What created this," I murmur.

"It's ancient." He puts his own hand on the pane. "And there has been plenty of trying."

"So you're in a hurry, then. To go south." When he doesn't reply, I glance over at his grim profile. "What about heading around the other way?"

"I already attempted that. Rushing storm runoff, and a mud bog that if it were water could be boated across, but as it is, everything's impassable at least for days."

He nods to his horse, and that's when I notice the muddy hocks.

"Then you'll be returning to the Outpost?"

Merc shakes his head. "No, I shall be getting through this."

"By will alone, I presume."

"As I said before,"—his tone becomes sharp—"if you have a better idea, by all means, woman, have at it."

He bows and sweeps his arm forth with mocking gallantry, and then he walks off for his horse, stabbing the broadsword into its holster on his back. When he arrives at his saddle, he shoves the various rolls and packs around, and takes off a bladder. After a stout drink, he turns to me, and doesn't meet my eyes.

In fact, he hasn't looked at me properly since my arrival.

"And if you don't get through it." I glance around. "Were you camping out here?"

He glowers at the barrier. "Is that your plan?"

"I hadn't thought that far ahead."

"I figure you'll be wanting to get back to the pub."

"No, my way is only forward—"

"Your friend in the top hat must be heartbroken."

My brows go down, and the next thing I know, I'm marching over to him. "Hit it for me, will you?"

When he seems confused, I point at the gate. "I'd like to see you fail at something. It will cheer me up, and be far more fun than arguing with you over a man I haven't touched."

Now he looks at me properly, and we just stand there, glaring at each other.

"Let me guess," he mutters as he's the one who breaks the eye contact. "You want me to use my head for the job."

"Certainly would give it something to do for once." As he slants a look over at me, I shrug. "Or use your sword. The sword will be less painful, of course."

"Will it," he mutters as he unsheathes his weapon once more. "There are advantages to concussive events, loss of consciousness among certain company, for example."

"Must you flatter me. I'm blushing."

Merc curses his way back to where he was when I arrived. Through gritted teeth, he says, "Step back, sometimes there are shards."

Sinking down into his thighs, he winds back with the broadsword over his shoulder, and I can't help but admire the form of him. He ripples with muscle and power as he bends back and then hurls the razor-sharp blade at the milky white—

*Gong!*

All my concentration focuses on the barrier as I look for any changes in the surface. After the sound fades, I nod toward him.

"Again." I step forward and put my hand on the pane. "Please."

Merc winds up and brings the sword to the gate once more. *Gong!*

Closing my eyes, I feel the nearly imperceptible vibration in the . . . whatever it is. And then I look up, way up, at the pearly expanse.

"I think if I had some explosives," Merc announces. "Or a cannon—"

With a snap of cognition, my mind takes me back to Mr. Lewis's pub.

"I know what to do." I stride over to Lavante. "I have to return to the Outpost. They have what is needed there."

As I'm swinging up into the saddle, Merc goes over to his horse and likewise mounts. The sight of him urging his slowpoke toward my stallion fills me with a relief that I refuse to acknowledge.

"Coming back with me?" I ask.

"Unless you think you can drag a cannon back by yourself, you're going to need me."

I could tell him that's not what I'm going to get, not even close. But then he might change his mind, and I want him by my side.

Even if it's just for a little longer.

Merely for safety, of course.

Nothing more.

*Sixty-Five*

# Recruitments.

"You cannot be serious."

We're stepping out of Thale's establishment as Merc makes the announcement. And follows it up with: "And he believed you."

"It's going to work." I have no idea if this is going to work. "Trust me."

"You're mad." He gets back on his horse. "And he's mad for listening to you."

One of the sets of double doors opens, and Thale emerges with two of his working women, and I try to avoid looking at the one on the left. It's Bethle, the lady for hire Merc was with, her long blond hair flowing down her pink gown. A quick glance at him and he doesn't seem to notice her in any fashion—and she doesn't seem to mind. Linking arms with her cohort, who is in turquoise, the pair of them are like fancy birds in the bright light, their bodices rippling as they giggle and preen.

"I must say, this is a new approach to an old problem." Thale looks down the lane impatiently. "But it's a lovely day for an outing in my coach, isn't it, my dears."

"Wait." I glance at him. "There's a third."

"Oh? Does she have blond hair?" He smiles in Merc's direction. "One fair-haired maiden seems to be more than enough, no?"

Merc's glare is sharp as his broadsword's blade. "You *really* don't want to address me right now."

I step in between them. "Just hold on a moment."

Praying that the pair of them don't get into it, I race back inside and pass the stairs. Pushing open the kitchen door, I scan the maids who are about, kneading bread dough at the counters, doubling up to roll in extra kegs of mead, stocking logs by the oven's side doors. Everything is cleaner, and fresher smelling, and the pall that seemed to affect all the staff has lifted. Talk is relaxed, cheerful—

"Oh! There you are." I go over to Lalah. "I need your help—"

"You're back!" She smiles at me. "Your room is ready—"

"I need you to come with me."

Her brows rise, but she immediately wipes her floured hands on her apron. "Of course."

In my haste, I almost trip over a bag of grain, and she helps me catch my balance. As we head through the kitchen door, she turns to go up the stairs.

"No, out here."

"Oh, you need help with your pack." She smiles as if in apology. "Allow me to take Lavante to the stables and bring you your things."

Though she tries to get to the pub's exit first, I'm the one that opens it for her—and we both stop as we see the black carriage that has driven up to the porch. With a matched pair of gray horses, and footmen in the back, it's like a royal visitor has pulled up—except for the lack of a coat of arms.

Its passenger entry is opened by one of the uniforms, the red velvet interior like a hearth. But Thale is the one who gets the working women settled, helping them inside with a chivalrous hand.

"May she ride with you, too?" I ask.

He pivots back around, and raises an eyebrow. "Yes, she may." He gets in and extends his hand to the barmaid. "Come now, Lalah."

She glances up at the driver, who's stationed on top. It's Emma, her twin, who motions for her to get in—yet still, she remains frozen.

Aware that there's now a crowd around us, I clear my throat. "Would you prefer to ride with me—"

I barely get the offer out before Lalah scurries over to Lavante. There's a chuckle as Thale shuts himself and his women in together, and then a pounding on the carriage roof. With a snap of the reins and a smile to both of us, Emma sets them off.

Putting my foot in the stirrup, I saddle up, and then Lalah does the same, pushing a toehold in where my slipper was and hopping high. There is more than enough room for the both of us in the cradle—a good thing, because with my supplies and clothes secured where I once sat, there'd be no way to accommodate anyone behind me.

Merc waits until I give Lavante the go-ahead before spurring his own steed on, and we must canter off to catch up to the stagecoach. It turns out that his horse is better as a follower than a leader and now regularly keeps up, whereas when Merc was on his own, he had to constantly urge the gelding forth. Still, I feel the need to check on them—

There's a parade in our wake.

As we head out of the Outpost, all kinds of townsfolk gather their horses and their carts and fall in with the procession. How they have scrambled so fast is a surprise—then again, given where they live, they're no doubt prepared for all sorts of eventualities.

Seeing them snake along the road makes me anxious.

What started as a possible solution has turned into a spectacle, and everything's resting on my silly idea.

"Are you okay back there?" I ask Lalah.

"Oh, yes. My sister and I used to do this bareback."

The trip through the meadow is a blur, and as the rushing of the floodwaters grows louder, and we approach the branch in the travel road, I find myself terrified that the grasses and trees will bow to me again.

Fortunately, nothing unusual occurs. And I can explain that no more readily than I can explain what happened before.

When we close in on the cliffs, and then are closed in by the cliffs, our speed slows and the cacophony of so many people and horses and carriages in the narrow passages creates a din. After what seems like no time at all, we cram into what previously seemed to be a sizable clearing, with people wedging themselves tight for a view of the Crystal Gate.

"You dismount first," I say to Lalah.

But she's already slipping off and taking the reins to hold Lavante.

Merc is also already boots-on-the-ground, and when Lalah offers him her hand, he gives his horse over to her as well.

I shake my head. "No, Lalah, we need you, too—"

"So!" Thale's voice ushers in a silence so quick, so complete, it's as if no one was talking at all. "It's time to see what you want to do with these beautiful women."

The smile he gives me is indulgent. The look he gives Merc is self-satisfied, as if needling the other man's obvious hatred of him is such a bonus to the adventure.

"And if you are wrong," Thale continues, "no matter. I have enjoyed my time with . . . dear friends."

The black-haired woman dabs at the corners of her mouth with her fingertips, then licks her lips as if she's tasted something she enjoyed. Next to her, Bethle laughs in a throaty fashion and leans into Thale, draping her arm on his shoulder.

"What would you like us to do," she asks me with a bold smile.

I clear my throat. "I would like you to sing."

As the women frown, Thale cracks a laugh. "Though I have many abilities—"

The ladies offer an affirmative chuckle at that. "—I'm afraid carrying a tune is not among them."

"Not you." I nod to his working women. "The ladies. Please."

As a twin set of surprise comes back at me, I indicate the barrier. "You have strong, high voices. I believe that if you get the pitch up enough, the vibration will—"

Conversation explodes around me, people laughing and shaking their heads. Even Thale, who's been readily enough going along with this, gives the idea a hearty shout of mirth.

"Like with a glass." I speak louder. "Haven't you seen someone sing and break a glass before?"

"There are many broken glasses at my establishment," Thale counters, "but such a note has never been the cause of such a shatter."

"Please." I glance back at Merc, who's frowning at me. Then I refocus on the women. "I heard you singing together the first day I came into the pub. You have pure, soprano voices, and I think the acoustics will help amplify them—"

Thale bends down and picks up a palmful of musket balls. "All these projectiles, over all these years? And you think song will do what these have not."

"They're the wrong tool for the job." I glance up at the gate. "We must try, at least. A concert, for all these people who came this far? And surely you're willing to share your gifts if they might open this more direct trade route to the Kingdom of the South? And I know I'm right, this is a better way down there."

Thale inclines his head. "It's true. It would be much faster."

"And we are used to sharing our talents," the raven-haired one says with a seductive smile. "If you want us to sing at this wall, why not."

She takes the hand of her blond friend and saunters forward. There are some soft words between them and then they nod at each other. With the sunlight streaming down, and the pink and turquoise dresses, they're like part of a rainbow come to rest in the midst of all the lead shot, axe-heads, and iron hammers.

They take a couple of deep breaths. Then there's a pause filled by the restless crowd chattering.

I glance at Merc once again. He's staring at me, as if two beautiful women in bodices that accentuate their assets are not standing a length away from him—

The women start to sing, their voices rising and falling to a tune that is chipper and lively. The harmonizing skips along the cliffs and redoubles, until the song comes alive as if a hundred voices are carrying these words I do not understand—

"No, no." I cut them off, waving my hands. "It's lovely, but—"

The women fall silent and glare at me.

"One note." I wish I could look them in the eyes to make my point. "Just one. As loud and high and long as you possibly can."

I remember how Sallae Mae used to do it, focusing her voice on the rim of the glass, singing in a prolonged, steady way until—

"On three," I tell the women. "One . . . two . . ."

As I get to three, I point at them.

There's only annoyed silence. Until Thale orders sharply, "Do as she says."

"One," I repeat. "Two . . . and *three*."

On my command, they both strike a note, high and loud and clean. "More!" I yell over the sound. "And project it at the barrier!"

I slap my hand on the pane, and I can feel the vibration. "Yes! It's working! Keep going—"

They run out of air almost as soon as they start, and take deep breaths to recover. All around, the crowd shifts on their feet.

"We need to try again." I look over toward my horse. "And we need one more voice."

*Sixty-Six*

# Breaking Barriers.

Leaving the Crystal Gate, I approach Lalah. "You must join them—"

The girl's eyes bulge with fear and she clasps the collection of reins close to her heart. "Oh, mistress, no—"

I lower my voice, so that only she can hear. "You sang, outside of my room, right after we checked in. It was beautiful, and higher notes than the two of them reach now. Please. Sing—not for them. Sing for me. I must get to the Kingdom of the South, as soon as I can—this is the only way."

Her head lowers and her shoulders slump—

From behind, her twin appears, and Lalah looks over at the girl. Some kind of wordless communication passes between them, and then Lalah's shaking hands transfer the reins of the horses to her sister.

The maid retracts into her red felt jacket, and she approaches the ladies as if they have weapons pointed at her.

The black-haired one looks her over. "Come on, then." She reaches out a hand. "It'll be all right. We just sing. One note. The three of us."

The smile that is offered Lalah is nothing like the ones the woman gives anybody else. It's a gentle, natural expression, without any pretense.

Bethle does the same, leaning around and nodding with echoing kindness. "Just one note. And she'll tell us when. Big breath, okay? We do this, together."

Lalah looks back at the crowd with fear.

I step in with them, trying to block out all the people. "Don't worry about them, Lalah."

She glances over, and in a meek voice says, "For you."

I exhale, hating that I've put her in this position when she's so clearly uncomfortable with the attention. But then she takes a deep breath. And another.

"I think we're ready?" When I get nods all around, I start again. "One . . . two . . ."

Lalah takes an inhale with the other pair.

*"Three."*

The women start off high and loud and lean forward as if they're pushing the sound at the barrier, and as I tilt in and put my palm upon the crystal pane, I can feel the vibration start again. They hold the note harder and longer than before—

The raven-haired woman gives out first, her face flushing, her cleavage heaving as she recovers. Then Bethle has to stop, and she's clearly dizzy from the effort, throwing her hand out to catch her balance.

As the echoes dissipate, I can feel Lalah looking at me.

Everything goes into slow motion as she opens her mouth. What comes out is a rough, strangled sound.

"You can do this," I say quietly as I focus on the bruise at her temple. And then the ring around her throat. "You can bring down this wall."

She stops. Reaches up to her battered face . . . then lingers her fingertips at the banding red mark across the front of her throat. As her eyes darken with pain, I nod gravely.

"Bring down the wall, Lalah," I say in a stronger tone. "Bring . . . him down. All those years. All of it."

I point at the wall. "Send the pain there."

After a moment, the maid draws in a tremendous volume of air.

Then she opens up her mouth.

And screams.

The sound is hoarse, and it is ugly, and it gets uglier as the rage breaks out of the girl. Closing my eyes, I hear the suffering, shame, and fear leaving not just her body, but her soul. It's all in there, the era of torment and agony, the cruelty endured, the helplessness of her life.

It's hard to tell when exactly the tone changes.

But as I reopen my lids, the scream shifts into a something else. Lalah is singing now, higher and higher, the cliffs doubling and redoubling the sound. Louder, higher, louder, higher, louder—

Tears are streaming down her face, and as beautiful as the sound she's now making is, she's in terrible pain as she creates it. Next to her, the two working women have their hands over their mouths, their expressions full of regret, as if they knew what was going on with her and had had no idea how to handle it.

And wish they'd done more.

I am only dimly aware of the crowd around us, but one thing is certain. Lalah's voice is finally getting heard, by all of them—

The first crack appears right in the center, where Lalah is standing. And then there are others, spidering in from where the barrier connects to the rock spires on the sides, weaving up from the base, coming down from the top.

"It's going to shatter!" Merc yells. "Watch out! It's going to—"

At that moment, there's a great explosion, and I jump in front of Lalah and hold on to her, shielding her with my body as I'm pelted with shards of whatever the gate is made of. All around, there are shouts and screams, the horses rearing back, the carts being ground into the mountain's flank, Thale's beautiful grays jumping and trying to dart with their carriage still attached.

It's the loudest thing I've ever heard, my ears registering it not even as sound, but as a penetrating sting that goes into my head. Musket balls and shards come at us in a wave, swamping our feet like a tide coming in, dust blooming like a sandstorm, debris landing and making both worse.

And then it fades.

Well, at least the sounds and the falling crystal splinters and the ground cover settle. The fine particles in the air hang around—

As Lalah's legs go out from under her, I hold her slight weight as best I can, easing her onto the ground. Immediately, her sister is by her side, talking to her in their language.

I brush tears off her cheeks. "Just breathe . . . Lalah, just breathe . . ."

She turns her head to the side. "I . . . did it."

Easing back from Emma, she sits up and stares at the great, gaping hole that's revealed as a new wind enters the clearing from whatever is on the other side. This ushers some of the dust out, and I look at what has been exposed: It's just more of the same, a trail, through high jagged mountains.

I expected there to be a treasure on the far side.

But as Lalah struggles to her feet, and holds on to me for balance as she looks straight ahead, I know that what she's gained in this is better than any gold. This will have repercussions for her future. She is now more secure, and not just because she's under Thale's protection.

She has herself now, too.

"Let me take her back."

I don't recognize the voice at first. But then I see the top hat. Thale.

"Ride back in my coach," he says softly to Lalah. "Your sister can sit with you. I shall drive the horses."

With a careful hand, he draws her away with the other two women, and her twin stays at her side—

Lalah breaks off and bolts back toward me. I know she's looking at my face fully, but I can't . . . I can't meet her eyes. I just can't know that she'll die by a demon some night soon after having survived so much.

What I can do is get to the Kingdom of the South as soon as I'm able.

And deliver the crown of war and shadow to its rightful owner.

The arms that are thrown around me are strong. "Thank you," she says roughly. "For everything."

Then she runs back to her sister.

I stay where I am as Thale helps the four women into his carriage, shuts them in, and mounts up to the driver's seat. As he takes the reins of his grays, he starts barking orders for the crowd to follow him back to the Outpost. The men and women who witnessed it all are talking in excited voices, and I'm sure a number of them want to go forward and see what's around the next corner.

But Thale's in charge. And they will not defy an order.

Glancing over my shoulder, I see that Merc has both our horses. Thank the crescent moon for that. Although his might have stayed, I'm not sure Lavante would have.

I look back at the coach.

Thale is staring in my direction. And then he takes off his top hat, and bows low.

With a last nod, he hauls his team around and disappears, taking the crowd with him.

After which, it's just Merc and me.

"How did you know she had it in her?" he asks in a quiet voice.

I turn to where the unbreakable barrier used to be. All that is left are mounds of crystal shards, the way forward clear for passage.

"How could she not," I reply grimly.

*Part Four*

# The Kingdom of the South

Destinations.

*Sixty-Seven*

# Not Here, Not Now. Not Ever.

The way ahead is as the way behind.

As the echoes of the crowd's departure fade, I look to beyond where the Crystal Gate was and see the other half of the clearing we're in—and am unimpressed. The continuation of the cliffs, and the hard turn out of the open space is just like all the other twists and curves we went through to get here.

"I thought the Outpost was your destination," Merc remarks.

So did I. "I changed my mind."

"The only thing after this is the Kingdom of the South."

"Yes. That is where I'm going."

"We ride together then," Merc announces as he holds out Lavante's reins to me.

I look over at him. The collapse kicked up dirt on all of us, and like my own togs, his clothes are dusty. He even has a shard hanging in his hair, and as my eyes catch it, he raises his hand and picks the crystal out.

His face is a mask of his features, neither his expression nor his black and white eyes giving anything away. For a moment, I'm tempted to suggest that he go first and I give him a half hour. But that's just being petty.

I mostly keep my bitterness to myself: "Another new job for you, then."

"Don't sound so surprised."

"Disappointed, more like it. I still think you need to stop running and go back to what you love to do." I take my reins and saddle up. "But we all have choices to make, don't we."

Lavante is very excited about what just happened, and he paws at the shards that sparkle on the ground at his feet. The majority of the crystals blew outward from the maid as she broke down the wall, so the debris field is in front of us.

I'm worried about the horses' hooves.

"Is it safe for them?" I ask.

"We don't have a choice," Merc tosses back. "So neither do they."

He throws a leg over his saddle and spurs his steed forward—

His horse shies away from the crystals, rearing up while backing away and shaking its head. Though Merc gets control and prevents a full-on bolt, when he tries a second approach, the same thing happens, only with a buck or two thrown in for good measure.

"Let me go first," I say as I give Lavante a little head—

My stallion prances over and kicks up his hooves, the shards spraying around him as he dances through the light show he's deliberately creating. As I glance back, Merc is giving me an annoyed look.

"I'm not asking him to do this," I call out over the tinkling sounds.

At least his horse falls in line, the instinct to stay with the herd greater than its fear of the strange ground covering. Soon enough, we're through the beautiful mess and onto solid dirt. I'm not surprised there's no vegetation here, as there wasn't previously on the trail, but as I look up at the stone cliffs, something is different . . .

I just can't figure out what my instincts have picked up on.

"No spent musket balls on this side," I remark as I look down. When Merc doesn't reply, I glance over my shoulder. "I said, no balls. On the ground—"

"I heard you."

Pivoting back around, I bristle in my seat as only the landing of hooves and creak of tack fills the silence. "Guess only the Outpost wanted out."

I lead into another turn, and glance up again. The rock faces rise so high I cannot see their tips, and as before, the stark, steep verticals are black and brown. But there's an odd rippling I can't explain—

"You know," I say to try to calm myself, "I find it hard to believe that a kingdom wouldn't have at least tried to break it down."

Again, I wait in vain for an answer. So I continue, "Especially given how long the barrier was in place. Although perhaps they don't care because it's far enough from them, and there is the other way through."

"As long as it hasn't rained for twelve years straight," he gripes.

"It was only three days."

"Just felt like years then—"

I haul up on the reins and pivot in the saddle as our horses go side-by-side. Before I can open my mouth, he cuts me off. "Is this the second time you're going to tell me to leave you? Or the third? I've lost count at this point—and survival is more likely with us together. So let's just stop the bickering, shall we."

My brows drop low. "Good point about survival. Without me, that skystalker would have had you for luncheon in that gray stone wasteland."

"And without me," he snaps, "you would have been eaten by a *balas*. Or even more likely, murdered by one of your own villagers before you even got the chance to try to escape. Tit for tat with mortal boasting is going to be a losing game for you."

"I'm not the one with the attitude problem—"

"Oh really? Whose voice is raised now?"

"*You're* the one who got upset." I lower my volume with determination. "Just because Thale was in our room."

Merc laughs to the stone spires around us. And then leans in with a glare. "You want to repeat that? Just so you can hear how ridiculous it sounds."

"Yes, I do. Because it's what happened. When you came in and saw Thale, you got upset and—"

"I can assure you that Thale's presence has nothing to do with anything—"

My disbelief echoes upward: "You wanted to kill him!"

"And that has *nothing* to do with where he was. The man sells women for profit, takes money from gamblers, and has the gall to parade around in a fancy suit and a stupid hat thinking that means he has authority. He is a common bully with a fortune from misbegotten gains, nothing more. He is utter shite."

"And yet you didn't get upset until he was in my room."

"*Our* room."

I arch a brow. "Were you really just worried about your personal property."

In the silence that follows, I study every minute thing about Merc's disapproving glower.

"You went to one of his women," I say softly. "I'd hardly say that gives you the right to be critical."

"A man has needs."

I think of what Thale told me. "And out of all the ladies for hire there, you picked the only one with pale hair. Like mine."

"Was she fair? I hadn't noticed." His lids lower. "What was on her head was less important than what was below her neck."

I think of what we did, up against the wall, next to the bed. "Why don't you just admit it. You were jealous."

For a moment, he seems dumbfounded—or pretends to be. And then he begins to laugh without smiling. "You know, you're reminding me of why I travel alone. You truly are—"

"I was jealous when I saw you coming out of the blond's bedroom. It just about killed me, even though I have no right to feel that way." I kick my chin up. "There. I said it. I'm brave enough to be honest with you, but I guess the same cannot be said of a mercenary who *drips* with weapons and aggression."

Merc's gleaming black eyes narrow. "May I remind you that I killed a man, at your request. Before you go around with your judgments, you might recall the very bloodthirsty favor I did for you."

I swallow through a dry throat. "I saw the way you looked at the bruises on Lalah's face. You would have done it yourself."

"No, I wouldn't have." He jabs a finger at me. "I did that for *you*."

"Why." I arch a brow. "Why was my request so important."

Merc tosses up his free hand and sets to muttering. "I've had enough of this conversation. Follow me or don't through this maze of cliffs. But I'm going ahead and there is going to be no more talking—"

"Why can't you say it!"

"Say what!" he hollers back at me. "Are you looking for some declaration of love? Just because we had sex? Once? Surely your experience in your chosen profession tells you that it doesn't work like that between men like me and women like you—"

"You are the first man I have ever been with."

There's a heartbeat of silence. Then with the way he rolls his eyes, it's as if someone is trying to sell him a dead horse. Instead, I'm clearly beating one—and yet I cannot seem to stop.

"It's true," I protest as my head begins to pound. "I'm untouched. Or . . . was."

Now he seems bored. "You forget I saw money changing hands between you and a man old enough to be your father the first night I met you. Are you suggesting all he was paying for was holding your virginal hand? And I'd also like to point out that it was a well-plowed field I slid into last night, smooth as silk."

I open my mouth. Close it.

Rubbing my temple, I remind myself that this is neither the time nor place for this confrontation. In fact, we are two people who should never have such an intimate conversation. At all.

We're more than incompatible. We're strangers in a foreign land, set upon different, if for the time being parallel-once-again, courses.

Abruptly, Merc blows out a tired breath, and looks to the way forward. "I urge you to stop wasting energy on what you think about me, and get down to the job of traveling to our destination. And if you insist on pressing the issues of your good friend and lantern tender, Thale, I assure you, I am utterly incapable of jealousy."

"And why is that."

There is but an instant's pause: "Because I am utterly incapable of love."

A cold spear goes through my heart. Yet I shake my head. "That's a lie."

His head cranks in my direction, and his eyes are so bleak, they are like pits. "Don't confuse our proximity with who I am at my core."

"I saw you cry when you looked over that field at the settlement." When he goes absolutely still in the saddle, I question why I'm saying any of this. And then press on with, "And you left your journal open in the window seat. What's on those pages showed a soul-deep yearning. The picture you drew of that gate was—"

"Shut up."

His voice is no longer angry. It is dead.

And that is when we hear the grunting from above.

*Sixty-Eight*

# Into a Battle.

We both look up at the same time—and see the shadow that's affixed to the vertical slant of the spire on the right. Except . . . it's not a dark spot thrown by a cleave of the stone or a discoloration in the vein of rock. It's a creature that's the size of a horse, with skin that has the texture of bark on a tree. With its splayed hands and feet, it sits in place as if it's on the ground, and as it shifts its position to stare down at us, a strange fluctuation in coloring makes it blend in perfectly with the bands of black and brown.

This is what I sensed, but did not see.

The predator has been with us all along, and as its black tongue comes out and licks around jagged black fangs, lunchtime appears to be nigh.

"Ogre," Merc says softly. "I've heard about them. That skin is nearly impenetrable—but they're slow."

The beast's flanks are puffing in and out, and though it's hard to track the precise position because of the chromatic phenomenon, I think the back end of the thing is quivering. Like its muscles are engaging.

Because it's going to jump on us.

"We need to go," Merc warns. "*Now*—"

Just as he gives the order at a shout, the ogre goes airborne. I have a brief impression of skin flaps puffing out, the way a flying *squirrelle*'s might—and then everything becomes a blur. Lavante is not going to stand still as that thing tries to eat us. The stallion bolts and Merc's horse follows suit, right behind us. As the wind streaks back my hair and I hear only a roar in my ears, I have to look over my shoulder.

I can't see much of anything behind Merc, just the pale sandy dirt and the black-and-brown cliffs. Fates, if the ogre can camouflage itself, it's nearly impossible to tell whether it's on the ground chasing us or still on the vertical.

At thunderous speed, we jog left into a turn, flash to the right, then dodge straight through a smaller clearing. After that, it's a blur of more curves and sharp corners. I lean into Lavante's neck and do my best to follow his tilts, especially as the trail gets narrower and narrower—

A strange call, like nothing I've ever heard before, echoes around.

It's like the howl of a wolf crossed with the cry of a bird of prey. As the sound ripples out—

"They're closing in!" Merc yells over the din.

"'*They're*'?" So that wasn't just an echo. There's more than one chasing us. "Go, Lavante! *Go!*"

I give my heel, not that it matters. The stallion is flying as fast as he can in the increasingly cramped chute, given the number of directional changes and rerouting. But at last we finally hit a straightaway with a decent amount of width—

Lavante turns his head to the side and whinnies in fear, his great long legs suddenly surging. Taking his cue, I look up at the cliff wall.

One of the ogres is not only right by me, but getting ahead of the stallion.

"I thought you said they were slow!" I holler to Merc.

"Keep going!"

"Like I'm going to stop—"

*Flames.*

All at once the cliffs are gone as we thunder out of a turn and break into a red landscape that's unlike anything I've seen before. Bursts of blood-colored flame flare up out of fissures in the red dirt, the fires like burps from deep under Anathos's surface. Red, leafless trees with tangled branches and twisted trunks dot the flat plain, and immediately, Lavante surges around one. Dodges a second. Leaps to the side to avoid getting burned as a blast of fire explodes.

I do what I can to stay in the saddle—

It happens so fast, I couldn't have done anything, even if I'd known what was coming: An ogre lands in a crouch right in our path.

Lavante lets out a scream through his nostrils, his hindquarters digging in and kicking up the loose red dirt so that it splashes all around us. His lunge to the left is so violent, I feel myself go airborne, and as I tumble into a hard landing, I try to keep an eye on the ogre.

Its bark-like skin turns the exact red of the ground, only its beady red eyes showing.

And all those black teeth.

My breath gets sucked out of me, and I swallow dust that tastes like sulfur as I roll. During one of the rotations, I catch a brief glimpse of Merc and his horse blasting out of the cliffs at a dead run, a rippling overhead as more ogres leap free of their rocky roads and sustain flight with their wings of flesh.

And then I hear the grunting call.

Scrambling onto all fours, I square off against the ogre that is lowering into a crouch in front of me. Its tail rises like a scorpion's over its back, and the way the beast quivers just before it jumps tells me that I'm going to lose this ground fight.

Crescent moon, there isn't even going to be a fight.

As the sound of pounding hooves is still too far away for Merc to help me, I brace myself for the attack while the ogre leaps into the air, front claws ready to finish what the skystalker's talons started. The image of it silhouetted against the sky is right out of nightmares, and I bring my arms up to cover my—

Flames. Everywhere.

Sure as if I conducted them to do so, two columns of fire explode up from the ground, and the pair of them cross, just as my arms did, at the exact moment the ogre's trajectory carries it forward.

The creature lets out a shriek, and I smell burning meat. The next thing I know, the thing lands on top of me, one of its feet digging into my hip, another crashing into my shoulder. I hold on to my head and curl into a tight ball, expecting to be bitten.

But the beast has other problems.

Half of it is on fire, the red flames spitting and hissing as it paddles with its squat legs and changes colors randomly, black, brown, red, yellow—abruptly, it stumbles off me. Drops to its side. Shrieks again. As the stench of burning flesh mixes with that sulfuric odor, I, too, have other things to worry about.

Merc is weaving around the base of the mountain, and he has a stream of the ogres behind him, all of them transitioning from black and brown to the red—

Another shriek.

I wrench around on the ground. There's a second ogre flying at me, those wings that aren't wings out to guide its trajectory, the angle perfect to land on me, the black teeth bared, the black tongue lolling out as if it can already taste me.

But I put out my hands, palms forward.

And I call to the flames, an intentional command borne out of what unintentionally happened first with the lantern and then with the hearth at Lena's.

There are three nearby holes in the ground, like sockets, and as if the fire is something I can pull like a rope, I yank at the air—

Flames explode to life, sure as if I conjured them, and I throw my hands forward, pushing the blast of heat at the ogre in the air. It's the lantern's attraction to me amplified a thousand times, not the little glow of a wick seeking me, but so much, so very much, more.

I don't understand what I'm doing, or how, and in this it's just as I battle death.

But I do it.

The shriek stings my ears as I fall back and brace myself for another fiery trampling. The thing stomps over me, roaring in pain, that cooked-meat stench all that's left behind as it tears off for a length and then drops to the red dirt. I don't waste time tracking its death writhing.

Jumping to my feet, I search Merc out. He's making a circle and heading for me from the west, as if he intends on picking me up off the ground.

Behind him is an army.

The camouflaged bodies of the ogres ripple over the ground like a heat wave, and there is a sea of them—that are closing the distance.

And that's when I see the second lot explode out of another chute in the cliffs, the color shift to red happening as they fly off their perches.

I start yelling. It's a waste of effort, but the rage in me won't be tempered—and as if I am conducting musicians, I wave my arms wide and then bring them in again, calling the fire to attention.

And command it to do my bidding.

A wall of flames appears in a semicircle, and I hear the screeching on the far side, a couple of the ogres spinning up into the air as they burst into heat and smoke.

But then in horror, I realize what I've done. I'm protected. Merc and his steed are shut out—

Like a wraith, he jumps through the line of red fire, his horse's wild eyes and flaring nostrils nothing I can track, for I only have eyes for him. With his black leather–clad body and his flowing black hair, he is vengeance with that broadsword in his hand, the inferno parting for him only long enough for him to get through before it recloses.

As he and his steed land, he thunders right for me, smoke rising from his surcoat, the backlight of flickering red and roaring heat like he's come out of the very depths of evil.

And then he thunders past.

Spinning around, I see for the first time the ogre that was coming up on my rear. If there had been so much as a delay of just a moment or two, I would have been dead. But Merc takes care of me. He lets out a battle cry, reins his horse into an interception, and then leans so far out of the saddle to the side that he nearly takes the steed to the ground.

With a fluid stab, he drives the broadsword's vicious tip into the head of the ogre that's two lengths away from jumping on top of me.

The creature starts to spin around, faster and faster, tighter and tighter, until it yells in pain and spasms into a contorted, color-changing curl.

Yanking my head over my shoulder, I measure the wall of flames. I still want it to be up, and for no reason that makes any sense, I feel like it will stay there as long as I need it to.

This can't be happening.

"Thank fates it is," I hiss as I look around frantically.

Merc is yanking his horse into a circle and doubling back to the dead ogre. As he leans down and puts out his hand, I know he's going to reclaim his weapon.

Where's Lavante?

From out of nowhere, I hear a whistle—and then realize I'm making the call sound—

The answering whinny comes from the left, and there my stallion is, careening around a stand of red trees, barreling across the lengths that separate us, leaping over a sprout of flame that I have nothing to do with.

He's going fast as the wind, the flickering light making his beautiful golden coloring glow like the sunset, his white mane and tail flowing pink from the wall of fire's unholy illumination. And in spite of the heat and the creatures, he's coming for me.

I sink down low.

Just as he sets upon me, he digs his hooves into the red dirt and sinks into a halt—and as if we have done the move a thousand times, I leap back into the saddle with perfect coordination, throwing my leg over the packs that are still tied on. The instant my butt lands, I grab fistfuls of that mane, because I know what's coming.

Just as Merc locks a hold on his broadsword's hilt and rips it free of the dead ogre, Lavante surges forward with so much power, I feel like I leave a couple of my teeth behind. The stallion is impossibly fast and monstrously strong, his head extending straight out from his surging body, his spine becoming a rope that runs from the tip of his nose to the last strand of his tail.

As if he'd been waiting all along for me to signal for my pickup so he could do his part.

Flattening myself on the side of his neck, trusting him to pilot us through the holes that spit fire, I can only pray that Merc and his steed are staying with us.

That wall of fire can't last forever—and even if it did, those ogres are smart enough to find a way around the length of it.

We are not safe.

This battle is not over.

## *Sixty-Nine*

# Ask and Receive.

It turns out I'm wrong.

Merc and I let the horses run for what feels like an entire season of exertion, and though Lavante seems to have the stamina to gallop the length of Anathos and back, the other one begins to flag. Eventually, we have no choice but to slow down to a canter, and finally, at least on Snooze's side, an exhausted trot.

I spend most of my time checking in our wake.

Eventually, I cannot see the wave of fire and not because it's extinguished. We're far into a flat plain of the red, flame-spitting landscape now, and though the spires of stone remain fairly close by to the west, there's nothing to the east except the horizon. Having seen the compass's map, I know the ocean is somewhere in that direction, but the topography and the red trees make it impossible to see it.

The sun's placement is still very high in the cloudless sky, and this is reassuring. With the way the topography is looking, I'm not sure where we could find a good place to bunk down for the night. And I have no idea how much farther we have to go.

Or how much farther we *can* go.

Merc pulls up on his reins, and both horses stop, sure as if he has control of Lavante's bridle as well.

Before I can ask him what's wrong, he eases to the side and takes something out of his saddlebag.

"I bought a map," he says gruffly as he unfolds a parchment square. "Back at the Outpost."

Lavante goes right over to the other horse, as if he wants to check where we are as well. I lean in, and see all kinds of lines on a creamy background.

"I can't tell one from another on that," I say, staying silent as to what the compass has directed.

Because really, how could I explain it.

"You needn't bother." He turns the map to me. "It only shows the way from the main route that was flooded. It offers nothing for where we are."

Merc circles the lower part of the page that's blank. "Our location is somewhere here."

A quick glance over the rest of the map and I see all kinds of details up above where we are, from what I gather is the Outpost's group of buildings to the road we followed to the beginning of the jagged rises . . . to the flooded pass we couldn't get through and its route that continues onward until it reaches a massive, bordered territory marked *Kingdomg daSouse*.

"We need water for the horses." I shift my focus back to our blood-colored landscape. As if taking another look around is going to help somehow. "I'm worried about them."

"Agreed." Merc puts the parchment away and points at the mountains. "We better hope there's an access point to the Kingdom—and soon. The one thing I can tell is that that range curves right into the ocean. I don't know how we're going to get through it, and there will be no swimming. The surf is very high this far south. We could get trapped."

Trapped? Try "eaten by ogres." Winning one skirmish is very different from battling hordes of them for the rest of our natural lives.

As my mind spirals into anxiety, I know I must reconnect with the immediate issue at hand. We need water—

And that's when it dawns on me.

"What is it?" he says, as if I've mumbled something.

"I . . . ah."

Taking off my pack, I pull out the compass in its satchel. As I reveal the golden instrument, I can feel Merc staring over at me, and I'm glad he makes no comment.

Even though I have no idea why this would work, I picture water, clean, cool, fresh water that's safe to drink. When the image is so clear in my mind that I can smell the bracing scent, and see the shimmer on its surface, I flick the top open and hold my breath.

There's no reason to think this could help our situation. But I just manipulated fire, for fate's sake. Asking this old instrument for directions like it's a native to the territory and can communicate, can't be any more unreasonable—

After the map pops free of the face, the center arrow begins to spin, faster and faster, and the direction markers likewise start to move, in the opposite way. A vibration registers in my hand and travels up my arm, tingling my wound on its way to the center of my chest. From there, the energy is sent out in all directions, through my body—

All goes still.

I have to blink my vision clear: The arrow has oriented itself forward and to the right, and the directional markings show the *N* to be at the base of the instrument and a little to the left.

I point forward and toward the cliffs. "We go that way. For water."

As I put the compass back in the satchel, return it to the pack, and swing the weight onto my shoulders once again, Merc just keeps staring at me.

"What is that thing," he says in a remote voice.

Gathering the reins, I meet him in the eye. "Would you believe me if I told you I don't know?"

There's a long silence. "Yes, I think I would. But what I do know is that these animals just ran too hard for too long, and if we don't locate a water source and some shelter before dark, we could find ourselves in another . . . situation."

As I focus on the direction I was given, I feel an echo of the vibration reenter my palm and my arm.

And then I utter hoarsely something I never imagined I would: "It was left to me by my mother. It is very, very old."

*My mother.* The words feel as strange on my tongue as they do entering my ear.

"Is it magic, then."

All I can do is shrug. "I don't really have to answer that, do I."

Merc releases a slow exhale. "No, you don't."

When he glances back at where we came from, his eyes narrow and I wonder how much he noticed about our escape from the ogres. Nearby, there's a fire flare, and I glare at the flames as if they're a child I'm telling to pipe down. I don't understand what I did any more than I can explain the compass—

"Okay, we go that way," he announces gruffly. "And maybe we find some water."

I'm nodding in agreement as he urges his horse forward, and Lavante follows without any heel from me, though he tosses his head and stamps his feet because he hates not leading the way. He will go too fast for the gelding, though, so the weaker horse has to be first.

More red trees. More fires that spontaneously appear out of holes in the red dirt. We avoid the latter with a big margin, but at least the horses are no longer reacting to the blasts of heat and light, either because they're used to them or they're just tired. Actually, it's more like Lavante is no longer threatened, and Merc's steed is too exhausted to care.

I continue to scan the landscape, and Merc does as well, as the cliffs we were chased out of get closer and closer. We're as yet too far away for me to spot any ogres blending into the rock faces, and I worry that we're being tracked and just don't know it.

"The soil is changing," he remarks.

Sure enough, the red color is dimming because it's being diluted, its replacement the normal brown of the ground I'm used to—and soon, I catch little sprigs of green. The trees change as well, new varieties coming in and choking out the ugly, knarred red ones, the leaves becoming green. And no more fires, either, as we presently enter a forest—

Merc draws in a great breath through his nose. "I can smell it."

"What?"

"The water."

I try out the sniffing routine, but all I can scent is the sulfur and the burning flesh, as if it's stained my sinuses.

"There." He pulls his horse to the right and points. "Through the trees. Hear it?"

Leaning forward over Lavante's pale mane, yes, I do see it . . . a river that's flowing with a brisk current. The horses pick up on the stream, too, nickering and trotting faster through the low-hanging branches.

The trees by the rushing current are green, leafy, and packed in close together, and as we break through the congestion, the sight of the river is a huge relief. And it's big, the shore seeming to be overrun, no doubt because it's swollen with runoff from the Badlands' storm.

"Hold up," Merc orders as he hauls back on the reins. "Look."

Sure enough, there are a variety of footprints along the edge—as well as one big disturbance that's marked with a bloody trail that leads off into the trees. My fear immediately labels it as a demon attack, and I search downstream for a bloated animal corpse that has its stomach open and the meat ripped from its bones.

As Merc continues to scan the area, neither horse appreciates the delay, but I would rather wait, too. Thirst is not an issue if you're eaten alive.

"Hold him here," he says as he dismounts. "I'll test out the water."

I take Merc's reins, and he goes over and kneels down. He keeps his broadsword in his right hand, and makes a cup out of the left one. Though I need to stay aware of my surroundings, I focus on the dried gray blood on the blade and remember the fury on his face as he thundered by me and stabbed that ogre in the head.

To make sure I lived.

"It's clean," he announces.

As if the horses understand him, his breaks free and goes over to drink, and

Lavante impatiently stomps forward. I barely have a chance to dismount before my stallion wades in up to his armpits.

Merc captures the reins of both horses and nods at me to follow their example. Lowering myself down, I wash my hands first to get the red dirt off, and then I rinse off my hot face. The water tastes different than what was in the stream that led into the Outpost. It has a bite to it, no doubt due to the mineral deposits it's flowed through to get here—

"Sorrel."

Anxiety prickles and I glance around frantically. "Yes?"

Merc's scanning the trees behind me, his sword at the ready—and I realize I'll never get tired of staring at him. There's always something else to notice, whether it's the gleaming waves of his hair, or the strength of his hand on that hilt, or the way his thighs bunch up . . . he's a vista all to himself.

"Don't lose that compass."

It takes me a moment to decipher his words, even though they're well and clearly spoken. And then I have to look down and resume drinking, my eyes stinging.

There's a lot I don't want to lose.

"Never," I say roughly.

*Seventy*

# Whereupon It Is All My Fault.

"Stop here. While we're still in the trees."

As Merc mutters the words, we both pull up our horses. It's about an hour after we all had our fill by the stream, and though our trajectory has remained south, we've piloted a course through the forest with an easterly angle in an attempt to stay away from the stream—and whatever's taking meals at its shores. Overhead, the sun has begun its tilt into the horizon, and because of the density of trees, it's remained cool.

"What's wrong?" I say softly.

"There's something up ahead."

"Like what—"

"The trees end in about seven lengths. But I don't hear the ocean. I don't know what we're going into."

And that's when I see it as well. Up ahead, there's just sky through the trunks and branches . . . almost as if we've reached the end of this part of Anathos. But that can't be. Unless the Kingdom of the South has broken off the continent and been swallowed by the sea.

"Again, I don't hear waves," he mutters. "So it's not the ocean."

When we restart, I notice that the wind increases as we press forward, and the closer we get to the forest edge, the more my instincts prickle. Something is very different, and all I can see is the horizon—

We break through the trees all at once, and I gasp.

As Merc's horse throws its front hooves into a stop, and even Lavante shies back, I can't take my eyes off the vista that unfolds below.

We're on the lip of a steep slope that drops down to the ancient ruins of a city made of marble. Set within a crumbled wall of the creamy stone, there are the bare bones of columned temples and buildings, and statuary set on plinths that are missing pieces, and obelisks that are laying on the ground, not standing upright in the air. The layout of streets is set at right angles, and everything appears oriented around a tremendous center statue of some kind of goddess. It seems a miracle she's still vertical on her massive base, as there's debris everywhere, blocking off whole sections of the—

Abruptly, the aches and pains that have been plaguing me since I fell off Lavante coalesce in between my temples.

"There's no way around so we must go down there," Merc says.

I force my tired eyes to focus again. On the far side of the metropolis, there's another rise, just like the one we're on the precipice of, but a fog—or maybe it's low-lying clouds—prevents me from seeing what might be on it.

At least the view to the east is clear, and it takes my breath away—

"Fates," I breathe. "I've never . . . seen the ocean before."

It's the most beautiful thing I ever have set my eyes upon. The vastness, the slight arc where the water meets the sky, the tremendous waves that crest and fall against the shore—so big they're obvious even from this distance. I can imagine the sun rising, pink and peach rays stretching out overhead and coloring the blue-green expanse with flashes of precious gems.

As I trace back to the ancient city's grand, decayed entry, my eyes scan a vast plain of vegetation. It's not hard to envision grazing fields and herding pastures linking the ocean to its walls, and I can almost hear the chatter, the music, the lives being lived in what once was surely a peaceable kingdom.

"We don't have much light left," Merc remarks.

He's right. The jagged peaks of the western mountains are already cutting off the sunshine, and as I measure the claw-like shadows that are thrown across the ruins, I feel like I'm witnessing a death that transpired long, long ago.

"What happened here," I murmur. "And I suppose it's been forgotten, cut off by the Crystal Gate and the mountains—"

"We have to keep moving."

We urge the horses into a zigzag descent that is steep enough to require them to engage their hindquarters and for us to lean far back in the saddle, but not so angled that footing is lost. Though Merc is on the lookout all around, I'm consumed by the metropolis.

And my headache continues to worsen, until my heart starts to skip from the pain.

To distract myself, I focus on the ground—and that's when I see the footprints. In and among the low ground cover, pressed into the earth, there are lines of markings too numerous to count. That they are like no animal foot I've ever seen is no surprise. I haven't recognized any part of anything in the landscape for a good while now.

"Keep sharp," Merc says, as if he's noticed the same thing.

Though we're still a distance off, trails in and out of the ruins become obvious, the snaky paths through the collapsed marble border trod by many, many crossings, with dirt tracked in. I try to see where whoever or whatever go after they leave the confines of the ancient remains. There's no way of telling. And inside the abandoned city? I can see no one and nothing moving along any of the lanes or the toppled architecture, some of which seem to be draped in some kind of white cloth.

I'm not reassured in the slightest by anything I'm seeing.

I do start to notice the inscriptions, however. The stone pillars and columns are etched with pictures as well as writing in a form that's unfamiliar to me. The images are beautiful, even from a distance, and if I squint, I can make out—

"Are you okay, then?" Merc asks.

I come to attention. "I'm sorry? I mean, yes, of course."

"Thought I heard you groan. Like you were in pain."

"It's been a long day."

As my temples thump, I tell myself it's because I haven't eaten enough, and maybe because when I fell off Lavante, I hit my head.

But that's not it. And I don't think I want to know what it is.

I feel surrounded by things I can't explain about myself, and the further into this trip I go, the more that is revealed.

As we approach the bottom of the slope, we cross into the shadows cast by the mountain spires. They're extending so much farther than they did when we were at the top of the descent, and with the prevailing wind coming off the ocean, the cold goes quickly through my clothes. Tucking into my saddlebags, I retrieve the red felt skirt.

Turns out it can double quite handily as a cape.

Predictably, Merc shows no reaction to the chill. Then again, given how the broadsword is up by the mane of his horse, it's clear he's most worried about us getting ambushed.

We continue along the very edge of the flats, moving parallel to the ancient city in the crease where the land accommodates both the slope and the flat land that serves as a base for the marble constructions. Once again, I have the eerie sense that we're being watched, and my eyes dart around. The spreading eclipse in the lee of the elevations is unsettling, almost as if a pall has come across the land as opposed to it just being a lack of sunshine.

And things are only getting darker.

With every footstep the horses take, more and more of the sun is cut off, the hard line now slicing across the whole of the city, even the goddess statue in the middle. I watch as the shadow extends out toward the sea, as if a force is claiming the land. Glancing behind me, I tell myself it's just an effect caused by the alignment of cliffs and summits, that as the sun continues on its journey to the western horizon, things will realign and light will shine for a little longer—

Movement. By the wall . . . ?

Or is it just the uneven surfaces of the fallen blocks of rock and toppled obelisks.

"We have to cut across now," Merc announces. "I don't want to get too close to the marshland as fates know what's in it."

Oh, so it isn't a meadow for grazing. At least not all of it.

I nod and follow along, even though Lavante is still not happy with being second in line. The trajectory Merc sets takes us across the front of the ancient city, while the darkness strides out ahead, extinguishing the light toward the ocean length by length. It appears as though we're chasing the night, but what I feel is that it's trapping us—

Lavante stops.

"Go on then," I say softly, giving him a little encouragement with my heel.

When he just jogs in place, I look down—

For some reason, my hands have gripped the reins and pulled back.

I command my fingers to loosen, and they do not.

And then as Merc continues ahead, my head turns on its own. I'm precisely aligned with the entry of the ruins, the two towering statues on either side degraded to the point where there's no identifying what they once were, the main thoroughfare that leads down to the enormous central temple congested with crumbled—

Between one blink and the next, the gloaming and the decay are gone.

What replaces them are a vision of prosperity and grace.

All becomes bright and sunny, and suddenly, I see a painted wooden gate big as the mountains. The two panels are well fortified with copper bands and rivets that wink pink, and against a creamy background, there are rows of pictographs showing people wearing draped clothing offering alms to the poor, and tilling crops, and making mead, and reading books. And on either side of the entry, the statues repopulate and I see them as they once were. On the left is a beautiful woman, with long dark hair spilling down her draped gown, her face toward the ocean as if she's greeting the rising sun.

On the right . . . a man in a high-collared sheath. And he's looking at her with a dark expression—

*Hide.*

As the old familiar command blares in my head, the imaginary gate opens. The effect is so real, I hear the creak of the great hinges, feel the whoosh of air, smell scents of flowers and incense. On the other side? No ruins or crumbled statues, no partial buildings where only the strongest supports are still upright.

Everything is pristine, the marble columns like beautiful trees with their ornate headers and bark of pictographs, the lane clear of debris, the structures solid and welcoming.

The goddess statue around which all is oriented gleams with beauty. She is standing with one foot slightly in front and the opposite hand stretched high over her head. Her hand is open, her palm flat, as if she's receiving something from the heavens, her resplendent face staring out over her city to the sea.

But no one is inside the walls.

The streets are empty of pedestrians, and somehow, I know that all the buildings, homes, and temples are vacant as well.

This is . . . a mirage, and not just because my mind has imagined something. In fact, the vision has replaced reality—

"Sorrel, come *on*."

Everything instantly disappears, and I jerk to attention. And I mean to go catch up to Merc, who's a length ahead on his slow-poke horse.

That's not what happens as I release the pressure on the reins and urge Lavante forward. Instead, my hands steer him in between the crumbling statues of the man and the woman. As we hit the chipped pavers of the lane, his hooves sound out and echo into the fallen blocks and degraded columns. The going is slow because he has to step over white marble tile piles that have fallen off roofs and exterior walls, and all the statues that have been knocked over and shattered into chunks and pieces. And then there's the "cloth" I saw from farther away. The draping turns out to be some kind of frothy spun fiber, and there are pods of it, here and there—

Merc pulls up beside me, and I know he's speaking, but I can't hear what he's saying. My mind is ricocheting between the present I am not feeling clear on and a past that I shouldn't know anything about.

I've never been here before.

And yet I swear I have—

Merc pulls in front of me, blocking my way with his steed. His arm slashes in frustration, as he frowns at me and no doubt keeps yelling.

"I'm so sorry," I cut in hoarsely. "I just had to see. This place is—"

The streaming attack comes out of everywhere.

Giant black spiders with bulbous hairy bodies and legs that terminate in red knobs flow out of crevices and corners in all directions. The wolf-sized insects are the stuff of terror in the gloaming, fast as a horse, numbered like a herd, their racing progress tapping over the paving stones. Red, angry eyes lock on us, and mouths with great black pincers open and hiss as they close in.

The first of the silk ropes shoots out and captures my waist. The next comes from the opposite direction and latches on to Lavante's front leg.

As Merc swings his broadsword to avoid being captured, the horses panic and rear up, but it's far, far too late. We're caught fast, tied up in sticky balls of webbing that hinder hands and feet, bodies and hooves. The fact that our attackers keep our heads out and the horses' nostrils free suggests they'll hold us alive as they feed on our bodies.

And still the spiders keep coming, mounting roofs and swinging down from obelisk tips, the incessant sound of their scurrying process something that I will remember forever.

Not that we have that long.

Trapped in the cocoon that locks me in, I strain to look over at Merc. He's fighting against his own confines, his broadsword sticking out of the white silk that imprisons him.

"Fates," I croak out, "what have I done."

"You've killed us," he snaps as more of the arachnids close in.

## *Seventy-One*

# An Admission, Long Awaited.

The spiders make a clicking noise with their mouths as they come at us, their fangs gnashing—and one of them comes right toward me, separating from the pack. Lavante whinnies in desperation. He cannot see, for the web has been spun up over his head, but I know he smells them. He jerks under me, his frantic, fruitless movements transmitting into my own body through the saddle. I'm wrestling around and not getting anywhere either, pushing against a million gossamer threads that lock me in.

The spider who takes special attention with me mounts the base of the cocoon from the rear, its bright red feet making deadly time. Something is dripping out of its mouth. Venom? It must be.

Higher, higher still, as he comes up Lavante's rump, and I start to hyperventilate as I strain to keep my eyes on him. I take one last glance over at Merc. He's dealing with the same, one among many now up almost to his chest, staring him in the eye. The fact that that spider uses the blade of the frozen broadsword as a toehold is a testament to how useless the weapon is in this situation.

*Clickclickclickclick—*

That's all I hear as my breath rips in and out of my chest, and my vision goes wavy as my fear translates into tears—

From out of nowhere, a piercing red light sweeps in a circle, bathing the ruins in ruby illumination that's so bright, it's as if the metropolis is awash in blood.

The most incredible thing happens.

The spiders freeze. All of them. Then they rise up with their front legs, as if the mysterious illumination is calling to them.

As one, they turn toward the source, and begin a pilgrimage to the temple in the center of the metropolis. The statue there, which has weathered the eons better than anything else, is the bearer of the beacon that summons them . . . way up high, where the goddess's hand reaches for the sky, is the seat of the unearthly light. For a moment, I think it is magic at work. It's not. The red wash is an optical effect created by a beam of sunshine passing through a juncture between two of the Rozars' jagged peaks. As the hour has arrived, a precise alignment has occurred, and something in that stone palm is providing the refraction.

And it will not last. The sun will continue along its course, and the other side of the V will cut off the beam.

Plunging all into shadow once more, and releasing the spiders from whatever hypnosis has occurred.

"I'm trying . . ." Merc grunts. ". . . to get loose . . ."

For a moment, I'm frozen at the sight of all the spiders gathered around the base of the temple, their front legs risen up and spindling at the goddess. If a hundred came after us, then a thousand surely live within the ruins, and it's as if they have one mind that connects them all—

Lavante lets out another terrified whinny and I snap back to attention.

I try to move back and forth to make some room within the webbing. It doesn't work—just like it didn't work before. There's a give and take to the wrapping, every forward *nic* compensated by a corresponding constriction. And I have nothing of the brute force that Merc does. He's straining as if attempting to lift his horse off the ground—and getting nowhere, even as he tries to seesaw his broadsword.

Glancing up to the statue, I follow the sunbeam to the mountains in hopes of finding we have plenty of time. We don't. Already, the darkness is returning up at the top of the slope we came down, and soon enough, it will streak through the city and eclipse whatever is in the statue's palm.

This is a torture—

*There are a lot of ways to use a weapon like this, and you're going to keep it in your pocket.*

Thale's voice enters my head like a command, and I suddenly become animated with purpose. There's not a lot of room to spare, but the red felt skirting I'm using as a cape is the savior. Somehow its stiffness resists the cloying compression, and I'm able to force my left arm across to my opposite hip. My fingers claw into the pocket there—

And promptly get caught by Mare's bag of coins.

The crystal knife is under them. I can feel the slick tip, but I can't seem to get it around the bag because every time I move, the coins shift into the space I make.

I glance at the slope. The darkness is a quarter of the way down.

Next to me, Merc is still getting nowhere because he's so bulky, he can't maneuver to reach any of his other weapons.

Closing my eyes, I try to picture me gripping the crystal knife, my fingertips threading past the velvet bag's clingy exterior—

The coins drop out of my pocket. I hear the jingling fall and ringing impact somewhere on the ground inside the webs that tie Lavante's legs together.

My eyes shoot in fear to the spiders. But the sound is soft enough that it doesn't call any of them back.

And now I have the knife.

Wielding it as Thale instructed me to, by gripping the cross-hilt and allowing the main shank to extend out between my fore and middle fingers, I stab forward.

The webbing breaches immediately—and continues to do so as I wrench my arm upward. I'm relieved to find the blanket of silk readily falls away, as cutting it releases the tension that is tied to its grip: The more I slice, the more I'm free to continue stripping it off me.

"I'm coming for you!" I hiss as I measure the dark line's progression on the slope. "Just a moment more—"

I'm talking as fast as I'm ripping the strange knife around, and then all at once, my upper body is free. Beneath the saddle, Lavante is twitching, as if he knows he's about to be released. I can't continue on to his legs yet, though.

I pull my own free of the saddle, and leap to the ground. "I've got this, I've got you, I've—"

"Sorrel."

At the sound of my name, I freeze for a split second and look up at Merc.

He's staring down at me, wrapped like a mummy atop his encased horse, only his black hair and the steel of his chain mail showing.

"Get your horse free," he says softly. "I'm okay here."

"Are you mad?"

I go to jump up to the broadsword and he jerks his head back, like he'd step away if he could. "Sorrel. You keep going . . . don't waste time on me."

As his voice drifts off, I find myself unable to move. There's a haunting quality to him, to the way he looks at me, an almost wistful expression on his harsh face.

"I'm not leaving you—"

"I am telling you to."

"And when have I ever listened to you." I wield my crystal knife and start into the web by the broadsword. "I'll be careful, I don't want to cut you—"

The cocoon starts to fall away, but as I glance over my shoulder, the line of the returning darkness is moving with increasing speed. I check the spiders around the temple, and they remain enthralled, but I picture them coming back as fast as they first arrived as soon as that red illumination is snuffed out.

“There’s no time,” Merc says sharply. “You’ve got to get Lavante free, and start running. Head for the slope with the mist. You can hide in the clouding there—”

I look about once again. He has a tragic point. The spiders move fast, and all those pathways over the crumbled wall prove they have no trouble getting in and out of the ruins. Even if half stay to consume him, some of them will set into a chase.

“*Go.*” His voice gentles. “But before you do, I want you to know something.”

Brushing my eyes, I make a couple more slashes around his sword arm, just so he can have a chance to defend himself. “What’s that?”

“You were right,” he murmurs with a small, wry smile. “I was jealous of Thale.”

*Seventy-Two*

# The Race Is On.

As Merc makes the admission, my eyes search his. It seems so totally within his character to choose to be vulnerable at the end of his life, when it's too late.

"You are such an *aspinhaul*."

As I borrow a word from Mare, Merc throws his head back and laughs. Then he narrows his eyes. "What are you doing—"

"Shut up."

I'm back at the cocoon, slashing with the crystal knife, its blade gleaming red. "I'm giving you a chance to save yourself—if I didn't want you to die before, I definitely don't now that you're finally being honest."

The more I do, the more he can do with his own blade that is so much bigger, and the next thing I know, the weight of the web is peeling free of his leather surcoat, and falling from his waist. And then he has a dagger in his other hand and is able to go to work himself.

I rush back to Lavante. I have to be so careful to not cut into him—and the way he throws his head as I go up his neck doesn't help. Grabbing the reins, I try to control him as he begins to thrash his back legs and buck.

We are all but out of time. The darkness is about to reach the easternmost wall. From there, it will be a matter of moments before the eight-legged congregation is no longer hypnotized.

"Hurry," I demand to Merc.

As if that direction is necessary. He's making even quicker work than I could have, the sharp edges of his dagger and his broadsword flying around as the web falls farther and farther down his horse's legs. Just as Merc arches up and peels his steed's neck with one slice, Lavante breaks out with a violent, all-body explosion.

I barely have time to grab the reins.

The stallion gives me only a heartbeat of no-motion, his wild eyes swinging around to my own, as if to tell me that should I not get on his back this very instant, he's leaving without me.

There's no hesitation. I stuff my slipper shoe into the stirrup and throw myself up into the saddle—

He doesn't give me a chance to get settled. And good thing. Lavante bolts down the pavers at a raucous dead run, his hooves hitting the stone with such force, the echoes among the broken statuary and cockeyed columns are like the roll of a drum. Without any direction from me, he dodges around fallen boulders and marble tiles, and I know better than to try to interfere. He's a far better judge of what his footing can handle than I am.

I look back.

Merc is out of the saddle, but still working at getting the web free of his horse's head—and the line of darkness is closing in. If he doesn't get moving now, it will be too late. That dooming eclipse is traveling across the crumbled rooftops and the lanes now, moving so fast that it will reach that temple within moments.

"Hurry!" I holler over my shoulder.

When Lavante reaches the great entrance, he leaps as if there's a jump before us. As he lands on the sandy dirt, I rein him to the right, just as the darkness wheels over us. He's as fast as ever as he takes us toward the other slope, with its cap of dense fog.

"Merc!" I yell into the wind.

Twisting around, I can't see him. Fates, he's run out of time. The spiders must be coming back into awareness by now, and there's no way they're going to forget the two riders and horses they'd been ready to feed from.

I want to go back. I need to go back—

Merc and his horse burst free of the entry, and in spite of his horse's name, they're going like the wind. I have a moment of relief, but then I see the why of its speed.

Spiders.

A thousand of them spill out of the entry between the statuary, and when there's a jam, they split up and flow over the disintegrated wall, forming a river of black legs and red, hungry eyes.

A sudden shift underneath me makes me refocus. Lavante has brought us to the slope and hit the incline hard. The stallion is grabbing at the ascending ground with his front hooves as if he's climbing a ladder, great pulls keeping us going even as our speed slows. I want to look back at Merc, but if I fall off, I'm not going to be able to outrun the horde.

I get down low on Lavante's neck, and hang on to his white mane, giving him all the head there is. The higher we go, the slower the pace becomes, and I hear his heaving breaths. But he doesn't give up. He keeps going, fighting for every length. Yet the top seems only to be getting farther away.

Higher. Higher.

When Lavante starts to slip and then tumbles down to his knees, I have to guide him to the left so his angle is not as extreme and he can get more purchase. Sure enough, he takes to the better footing and goes faster.

And then we're at the top.

The fog swallows us whole, and it's so thick that I have no idea what's farther ahead than Lavante's ears. He immediately slows to a walk, his sides pumping in and out as he recovers from his exertions—

Something slaps at my face and I scream.

Which causes Lavante to shy away.

I'm hit by another branch, and pushed at by a third. At least I think they're parts of trees. I can't see anything until it's right in front of my face. And the fog—or perhaps this is a cloud?—is so thick, it also swallows sound.

So I'm not going to hear the anguished screams of Merc's horse as they're overtaken down below.

*Seventy-Three*

# Into the Mist.

Moisture drips off my nose and clings to my hair, and I taste the sea in the back of my throat. As Lavante keeps snorting, I suspect he's experiencing the latter as well, the sound eaten by the fog. The trees are the same leafy variety as were by the river, and I have to hold my uninjured arm out in front of me to ward them off. My saddle creaking is the only thing I hear.

The disorientation is real and total.

This makes sense on another level. I'm still down on the flats, even as my physical body is up here. I picture Merc getting caught again, and he and his horse dragged back to become one of those pods that rest as coffins among the ruins.

Maybe some of the salt is from tears.

How could I leave him like that?

Anger curls in my gut as I want to go back and make another choice. I should have stayed in the Outpost in the first place. Then Merc wouldn't have been able to get through the Crystal Gate and none of this would have happened. And while I'm at it, why couldn't someone *else* have the destiny to bring this army to the fight with demons, why couldn't *they* be the one to have to pick a journey they don't want over the man they l—

I squeeze my eyes shut.

*Love.*

The man I . . . love—

Another branch wheels through the thick mist and slaps me in the face.

My eyes whip open. And I yell. At nothing, at everything.

And that's when I hear my name.

I snatch the noise I'm making back from the mist, and hold my breath. When what I thought I heard doesn't repeat, I feel like it was something I made up—

*"Sorrel . . ."*

"Merc!" I pull up on the reins and spin Lavante around. "Over here! *Merc!*"

My heart gallops in my chest and I put a hand over my mouth so I can hear better over my harsh breathing.

*". . . Sorrel."*

The ghostly sound weaves through the fog, and I turn Lavante around again. "I'm here!"

When nothing more comes back to me, I panic, thinking that those are his last words, traveling up from below, a condemnation of my selfishness and cowardly—

"I'm here."

Merc comes through the wafting cloud right in front of me, nothing but a big shape astride his horse. At least . . . I think this is really him. My visions were so vivid down below, I can't tell whether I've conjured him or he's actually found me.

I shove my hand out into the void. "Are you real?"

His strong arm penetrates the mist between us, and I grab on to his scarred palm, squeezing as hard as I can, feeling the calluses and the vital warmth and the unyielding bones.

"Yes, woman." He laughs a little. "Very real. You don't think I'd let that bunch of uglies keep us apart, do you."

"Fates, how did you get away?"

Merc leans forward, his face emerging, the specter made real. His black and white eyes search for mine, and as they lock on, his half smile is arrogant as always.

And like the ocean, so beautiful, I will not forget it.

"I just told myself your friend Thale was up here for the killing. The motivation was more than sufficient."

I'm shaking my head as I too tilt out of the saddle. He meets me more than halfway, our lips brushing before our horses fidget and the contact is broken.

"Now that wasn't so hard, was it?" I breathe.

"The spiders or the admission," he replies dryly.

The way he looks off into the fog shuts the door on all that. But my heart is singing for so many reasons, I don't even care.

"I think your compass should be helpful," he says. "We're all turned around—and if we so much as poke our heads out of this cover, those spiders are waiting for us."

Before he finishes, I'm already taking off my pack and going in for the instrument. As my hand closes on its satchel, a piercing sadness has me turning and looking back—not that I necessarily find the direction we came from.

It dawns on me that I lost Mare's coins. I had to drop them to get the crystal knife.

It's not really the intrinsic value—it's all they represented: Her last request, her attempt to take care of me, her kindness in return for my own. I feel as though I've left her behind in those ruins with those eight-legged predators, even though she's already died.

"What's wrong, then?" Merc demands.

"Nothing, sorry."

Once in my palm, the compass top flips open on its own and the map jumps out at me as it does. It's wheeled around once again, the landmarks that I now readily recognize oriented at a different position. Immediately, the arrow and the directional headers start on their counter-spins.

Spin, spin . . . spin . . .

As the turning continues, I worry that my disorientation has been transmitted into the instrument. Or maybe the fog is enough to do that on its own.

"No reading?" Merc says. When I don't reply, he curses.

I'm feeling the same frustration—

The halting comes not with the definitive stop of before, but more a sliding halt with the arrow pointing to our rear.

As I twist around and look over Lavante's rump, every instinct in me tells me it's the wrong way. That that is going to take us back to the ruins and to our deaths.

I glance down again, in case the compass shows me something else. It doesn't, and I try to take some confidence that the directional headings are south and a little west, just as before.

"What does it tell you?" Merc coughs as if the salt is in the back of his throat, too. "Where—"

"That way." I point behind myself. "But always forward, never back, so it feels all wrong."

"Back is relative, however." He reins his horse about. "And it took us to the water—besides, what else do we have to go on?"

Lavante swings his big butt around, as if impatient with the pause.

"True," I murmur as I put the compass away.

I'm not sure what exactly I'm agreeing with, but off we go, through the mist and the infernal, slapping branches. As a chill settles into my bones, I am grateful for the red felt skirting. It really makes for a terrific cloak, especially with my arms out through the pocket-holes.

Predictably, I feel like we go forever, and I wonder whether time, like our own senses of direction and even the compass's ability to see, isn't confused.

My brain continues to scream that we're going the wrong way, and I swear I can feel the constriction of the webs once again.

Still, I keep going, though blinded, and the parallel to destiny's path through a person's life is inescapable—

A glow up ahead. Otherworldly, as if something magical is coming for us. Surely, evil wouldn't be golden against the fog.

"Let me go first," Merc says.

"No, we go together."

"Why do you not listen—"

"You have no more idea what's up there than I do—"

"—when we have no idea what is up there—"

"—so we might as well both find out—"

We're arguing as the mist disappears as abruptly as I dove into it with Lavante, like the cover is a solid block we walk out of.

The horses stop without being asked. Then again, considering what's ahead, there's no farther to go. The mountain range has indeed curved around to the ocean, just as Merc's map detailed, but what confronts us was not shown on his parchment.

The gate is the largest and most fortified I've seen, and like the translucent barrier Lalah managed to break down, it secures the vast gap between two of the pointed elevations with utter surety: Running from the grassy ground up to the very sky, the flanks lock into every nook and cranny of the passage that was cut into the black-and-brown spires. And the pair of hinged halves lock against a great vertical pillar.

The whole lot of it drips with condensation, as if it's alive and sweating from the effort of keeping closed.

"Quite the construction," Merc remarks. "Why use boards when you have the tree itself."

That's when I notice what it's made out of. An entire forest has been felled and bound, countless stripped trunks lined up horizontally and stacked in dozens of rows. Secured by mortar, and bolted in groups by great metal bands, they form the cage door that locks whatever is on the other side out.

Except then I glance back, and decide that more likely it's keeping where we are coming from contained—and contained we be.

"There are hinges." Merc urges his horse forward. "So it opens. Or used to."

Testimony to the gate's age is in the staining down the exposed, weathered wood from the salt in the air corroding the metal banding system. The passage of time is also in the debris that's built up at the whole of the base—which seems to be a kind of sawdust? Perhaps the bark wasn't so much stripped as it fell off, the wear of the many years disintegrating the arboreal casing into a reversion back to the soil that once nurtured the roots of its very origin.

I let Lavante go on his own wander, and no surprise, it's to dip his head and suspiciously sample the grass. Whatever flavor it is, the green blades pass inspection, for he begins munching in earnest, putting one foot in front of the other as he chomps a trail closer and closer to the newest thing we must get through.

Exhaustion doesn't so much creep up on me as leap into my body.

It's as my head falls back that I measure the sky. That star is still up there, brighter than ever, looming like a portent that, considering the way things have been going, I know for sure is not good news.

And then I get a proper look at the top of the gate. There's a parapet that runs across the obstacle as if the builders knew with weight so great, framing reinforcement was required not just at the sides and center, but all along the height. It's also a prime defensible position.

Merc glances back at me. "No bell to ring."

"I don't know if visitors are welcome from this side of things."

"Can you blame them—"

The sound is like thunder, except it has a metal ring.

One side of the gate begins to vibrate, to the point where rain kicks off from the bundles of trunks, the drops falling on my face and hair, even as Lavante backs away. Just as I think the metal bands are going to pop and the forest is going to fall free to roll over us, there's an earthquake.

Lavante jumps into a splayed stance to stay on his feet, but Merc's horse has the opposite reaction. He bucks and tries to bolt, forcing Merc to sink into the stirrups and fight for control over the bit—

The seal breaks with a crack that resonates through my chest, and I exhale as a rush of wind comes at us through the small opening. That's when I smell something unbelievable: Flowers. I catch the scent of meadow flowers, and there's a beam of sunshine that pierces in, landing on the grass where Lavante was nibbling.

I once again palm the crystal knife, and Merc, who's gained control, points his broadsword in the direction of the aperture.

After that . . .

Nothing happens. The opening gets no bigger, nobody comes through it, and no hint is given as to who's giving us access or what we'll find on the other side.

"I go first," Merc says as he urges his steed forward.

I don't argue with him this time, mostly because I don't want either of us to be distracted. Lavante is ready to go, as always, trotting in place as we proceed at a cautious walk. When I finally get a look at what awaits us—

My delight knows no bounds. The undulating field ahead is just a profusion of blooms, the beautiful specimens possessing every color of the rainbow. And beyond them? A marble city, gleaming and white in the declining sun. It's four times the size of the one that lies in ruins in the ocean valley, the very picture of what that ancient metropolis must have been like in its heyday.

And now I am on the other side of the gate, standing in a chute created by a forest rim having been cut back and kept clear, no doubt for occasions such as this.

Immediately, the screaming metal-on-metal sounds repeat, and then comes the thunder followed by the earthquake, once again. But now there is something else. A squeaking.

Glancing over my shoulder, I see that a huge bar is being pushed into place, extending across the center vertical pillar. Surely it must be getting moved by men, but there is a cascade of ivy draping down the sides of the mountain, and whoever is working is underneath its extravagant fall.

There's a finality as the bolt fits into its socket, the stasis returned. But in spite of the beautiful field that unfurls before me, and the fragrance in my nose, I don't feel protected. I feel imprisoned—

The guards come from out of the trees. They're on horseback and on foot, the former with spears, the latter with swords. Their uniforms are dark blue and tailored, with gold details, and a crest over the left pectoral, and their caps are set on tightly shorn haircuts of various shades of brown and black.

We're surrounded before we can even attempt a getaway, and then no one moves. Not them, not us.

What clearly is an authority emerges down the wall of green ivy, as if he's descending from some kind of hidden facility there, and when he hits the ground, he strides over at a lazy pace, arrogance preceding him with the thrust of his narrowed jaw and the slash of his lips.

I gather he's in charge, for the guards part to accommodate his approach, and then close ranks in his wake when he nods at them with an arching glare.

His eyes pass over Merc . . . and lock on me. I hate the way he looks me up and down, the banked speculation on his face the last thing I ever want to see.

"You have trespassed upon the land of the Queen of Sudaland," he says in a deeply accented voice. "I am placing you under arrest and you shall be tried accordingly—"

Merc's voice cuts through the posturing. "You have no right to detain us—"

The officer takes out a pistol and shoots Merc in the chest.

As I start to scream, I hear the soldier say, "The woman is mine. You know where to take her."

## *Seventy-Four*

# Of Dungeons and Cells.

As I'm dragged along with my hands tied behind my back, there's a bag over my head that smells of *woodle* root, and the weave of it is tight enough to hamper my vision, but loose enough to let enough air in so I can hyperventilate without losing consciousness. I don't know how far I've gone or what's going to be done to me, but I know that Merc is dead and—

The shove pitches me forward, and I land face-first in a rancid puddle. There's a clanking that suggests bars are being locked into place, and then a rattling of keys and fierce conversation between two men. Footsteps recede, after which all I hear is the dripping of water somewhere close by and the squeak of a rat.

Lifting my aching head, I shake myself to get the wet patch of the bag away from my nose and mouth. With my hands immobilized, there's no way of taking it off. My feet are untethered, though, so I'm able to maneuver myself into a sitting position. I don't trust myself to stand up for so many reasons.

"Merc . . ." I whisper between heaving breaths.

I can still see him slump over in the saddle, his broadsword falling from his hand. I kept screaming until Lavante was caught with a lasso and I was dragged off him and struck on the back of the head. I came to in some sort of carriage or cart, and then I was yanked off and made to walk. I knew we were going underground by the tilt and the musty smell, but other than that?

Now I am here, wherever this dungeon is, and the way I turn my head to look around is nothing but habit, a waste of effort—

"There's no way out, I'm afraid."

I shuffle around on my bottom toward the taunting male voice. It's the ranking soldier, and he's very close by, so I guess he's locked us both in together. When I hear a creak of wood, I guess he's sitting down in a chair.

Sure enough, his words come to me from a slightly lower position, his accent making brisk work of the syllables. "What is your name?"

"Take off this hood," I say. "Release my hands."

"You're not in a position to make demands." There's another creak and I picture him leaning forward. "You could ask politely, however. Or perhaps even better . . . beg."

"Where is M—" I clear my throat. "Where is my husband."

"There is no reason to concern yourself with—"

"Where is my husband!"

There's a rush of movement, and then I'm slapped so hard, my torso twirls around and I land with my face in the puddle again. Inside the bag—inside my skull—I see stars, a whole galaxy spinning around me, and now there's a different taste in my mouth, not just the liquid rot and mineral deposits of the puddle.

Copper.

My lip is bleeding.

The chair accommodates the soldier's weight once again. Then there's a fabric shift, as if he's brushing off slacks he prefers to keep pressed and very clean.

"We are not getting off to a good start, you and me." He chuckles softly. "And I have plans for us. So many plans."

Instinctively, I retract my knees up. As a wave of nausea tackles me, I don't know if it's my head injury, Merc's death, or what this man wants to do to me.

The chair tells me again that my captor is moving, and the next thing he says is right in my ear. "You will tell me your name now."

When I don't reply, my head is yanked back so hard, my spine bends. As I grunt in pain, his voice remains icy calm. "I would much prefer you to resist. So please, indulge your urge to defy authority for as long as you like."

A hand moves to the front of my felt cloak, and I feel him fishing for access to the skin under my clothes—

"Sorrel," I grit out.

He stops. The chuckle weaves its way into my ears again. "I am disappointed with your compliance. But I am a man of honor—who also believes pleasure is better with anticipation."

The soldier drops his hold on me and I barely catch the weight of my head before it slams into the concrete floor. As I recover from the strain in my neck, I hear heavy boots pacing around at an even pace, and I use the rhythmic noise to get a sense of the confines of my cell.

"Where is my husband?"

"How did you get through the Forbidden Land?"

I swallow through my dry mouth and taste more of my own blood. "We broke down the Crystal Gate—"

"Liar." His voice is close by once again. "How did you get through the Forbidden Land—"

"We broke the barrier down and proceeded through a red forest—"

The slap shuts me up, my teeth humming. "No one can break down the Crystal Gate or survive the Field of Fire and all its contamination. It has been thus for millennia, and shall always be. Now tell me, how did you—"

"It is the truth."

"Do not play stupid with me. We have had spies attempt to infiltrate our territory before, none who have come the way you have, granted, but that is—among other reasons—why you are getting my special attention. You are a very lucky, lucky woman . . . Sorrel."

There's a hand on the ends of my hair, I can feel the subtle pull. And I brace myself for him to yank my head back once more.

"The red land with the fire," I whisper. "How is it contaminated."

The exhale is exasperated. "You are just my type, Sorrel. Anticipation, delay . . . by whatever means." The laugh is very nearly self-deprecating now. "You know how to pique a man's interest, but I am afraid teasing only goes so far. Thus I shall take what I want from you, and then send you the way of your husband. If you are good for me, I will make your death quick and easy."

There's a jerking back and forth—

With a whoosh, the bag is removed.

The soldier's face is right before mine, and before I can stop myself, I look into his pale, cruel eyes—

I gasp, and jerk at the tie that rounds my wrists. My stomach is on fire, the pain so intense, I feel a tide of blood coming up my windpipe. Gurgling now . . . a gusher coming out of my straining lips—

"What ails you, woman," the soldier mutters. "Are you diseased then—"

Moaning, I fall to the side, my mouth gaping as I suffocate and strain with pain. My eyes blink as I look up and—

I see myself.

Standing over me.

My clothing is wet and dirty, my hair in a tangle, and the expression on my own face is a combination of horror and vengeance.

In my hands . . . the crystal knife Thale gave me to protect myself with.

And it appears that I use it in the exact fashion he advised me to.

As I struggle to stay conscious in the midst of the death throes, I fight against the terrible conclusion that cannot be denied. This is the next evolution past asking Merc to do what he did to the cook. This is *me* as a murderer.

Except it has to be wrong. How could I ever get out of this cell if I kill him—and anyway, there's no way they left the knife with me. In addition to taking my pack, they must have searched me for anything and everything.

It's as I pass out that it occurs to me . . . I am far more concerned about how it will all play out.

Instead of the act of killing itself.

Then again, that bastard murdered the man I love. Right in front of me.

## *Seventy-Five*

# Walking and Talking.

When my hearing returns, so, too, does my vision. The latter is spotty, however, so I get fuzzy visuals of the soldier leaning over me with suspicion. Over time—though surely it only feels like hours are passing—I am able to make a full impression of the man.

Of my victim.

He is solidly built and rather tall, and when he isn't tilted toward me, he has the posture of a straight-backed chair. Not much of his face registers, then again, he has forgettable features that are on the rat-like side. His coloring is fair, his skin tanned as if he spends time out of doors, and for all the grime of the dungeon I am in, and however far we all traveled here from the gates, his navy blue and royal red uniform is pristine: Not a smudge or a streak, the slacks pressed to perfection, the riding boots polished to a mirrored shine.

There's no reason to ever look into his eyes again. Needless to say, I'm never going to forget those pale irises and black, malevolent pupils.

Or what was revealed to me.

He's muttering, seemingly to himself, and I use his distraction to get my bearings. My cell has a front face of iron bars with an entry that appears to slide back on runners, and the rest of the floor, walls, and ceiling are grungy stone streaked with mineral deposits. Oil lanterns hang in the aisle beyond, and across an open area full of tables, contraptions, and—are those buckets?—there are more filthy cells, all of which seem to be empty.

I was hoping to see Merc somewhere.

A chest wound is fatal, though. Surely he is dead—

A moan comes out of my soul.

"Oh, you are awake." The soldier smiles with all the warmth of a reptile. "I was afraid I'd lost you there."

As he puts his hands on his hips, I note there's a pistol mounted on each side of him, and I lock on to one of his ornate sidearms.

Forget the crystal knife. I want to kill him with what he shot Merc—

"Now, where were we." His knees pop as he drops down to his haunches before me. "Ah, yes. I was about to enjoy the pleasure of you begging me—"

The footfalls are heavy and urgent, echoing around all the dungeon walls. And then comes the shouting. A heartbeat later, a guard skids to a halt in front of my cell, and he speaks fast, in a foreign language—and even though I don't understand the words, I can tell whatever it is, it's urgent and important: His arms are flapping like he's trying to take flight and his eyes are so big, I wonder if they aren't going to pop out of his skull.

The soldier slowly stands up. "That cannot be."

The guard shakes his head. Points at me. Flutters his hands.

This time, when my tormentor looks down, his expression is remote, instead of lascivious. "Well, we shall see about—"

The figure who strides into the open area makes me think of the difference between power that is truly held and a person who needs to believe they have authority. Interestingly, it's a woman who's entered, and she's dressed in black robes that fall to the slick stone floor. Her silvery white hair is pulled back and plaited in a complicated way down past her shoulders, and her face is as hard and sharp as blade.

When she speaks, it is without emotion.

I don't understand her words, either, but going by the ugly red flush that travels from the collar of the soldier's jacket into his face, I guess she's dressing him down. Sure enough, he goes over to the cell entry—which was not locked, as it turned out—and steps through to stand just off to the side.

The woman stares over at me. And one would think the fact that we share the same sex would lead to clemency of some sort. Instead, I feel my situation has not improved.

And has possibly worsened.

She addresses the soldier tersely, and there's only the most subtle of pauses before he bows in a deference he clearly does not feel, and then strides past the front of my cell. His head tilts in my direction as if he's glaring at me. I will not meet his eyes, but I don't doubt he looks at me with the promise of a rematch.

After his departure, orders are issued to the guard who ran in. As his eyes widen once again, it's clear he does not want to be anywhere near me or her. Still, he enters the cell, helps me to my feet, and frees my wrists. Then he salutes her with a brisk flat hand to the brim of his hat.

The woman doesn't so much leave as dematerialize: She's there and then she's gone, only her white plaited hair glowing in the darkness as she disappears on a float through some doorway.

"Follow me, missus."

Except the guard puts himself behind me and points over my shoulder. "This way, missus."

My legs are stiff, and one ankle is screaming, and I'm figuring out my balance as I step forward—only to stop short.

The center space around which the cells are set is filled with gruesome torture devices and stations. The buckets? They're to catch the blood and slop of intestines and organs, and several of them are half filled already. Fates, everything that is made of wood is stained red and brown, all the metal is sharp and tarnished, and anything that is leather has buckles and spikes.

"Please, missus. This way."

The guard points again.

As I shiver until my teeth clap together, I realize I'm soaking wet, and if I have any hope of loosening up, I have to get warm. Thank fates they didn't take Lena's felt skirt from me. The makeshift cloak is all that's keeping my body temperature up.

Am I in shock? I wonder.

"Walking, please. Missus."

Limping past the horrible display makes my stomach turn over again, and the drains in the floor with their congestions of gore make me gag. Trying to keep control of myself, I glance back at the guard. He's averted his eyes, not that I had any intention of looking into them, and as he points to a lantern-lit archway off to the right, he puts even more distance between us.

This allows me to discreetly pass my left hand inside the felt cloak and feel for the pocket of Julion's jodhpurs—

Thale's crystal knife is where I put it after I used it on the webs.

My gasp hisses through my locked teeth. How did they miss it? Probably the bulky red felt that covers me, I decide as I enter a tunnel marked with many more archways.

For a brief moment, I consider palming the weapon and wheeling around to gouge out the guard's stomach. But I have no idea where I am or how to get out, and I can hear the voices of what I'm assuming are other guards emanating from different offshoots of this subterranean maze we've entered.

This is a vast prison, and it's better to bide my time: I now fully intend to kill that soldier—but I'm going to need an escape plan.

And as long as they don't find the knife, I have a weapon. *The* weapon, as it were.

What I need additionally is information.

"Sir," I say, in my best subordinate tone, "may I please know where my husband is?"

When he doesn't reply, I glance back. "I beg of you. I know there is naught I can do, but I must know what has happened to him. Are you mated? Surely you'd feel the same if your wife was separated from you."

"Face forward, missus. Please."

I immediately comply, hoping he'll view the deference as—

"He is alive, missus, but gravely injured. Further, he has been found guilty of trespass with intent to disarm the court in the Old Laws."

I don't have to feign the weeping that overtakes me, and only the smallest part of what I feel is relief that Merc survived the bullet.

The consequences of the charge are obvious in the guard's tone.

"And w-what happens now?"

"He will be executed in the square tomorrow morning at first light."

I spin around, focusing on the low rank insignia on his lapels. "May I see him, *please*. Before he—"

"That is enough, missus." The guard puts his hand down to a sidearm that's the same as the officer's. "Face ahead and continue to walk. Now."

"Please." I want to grab him and shake him. "He's all I have—"

"Do not make me hurt you, missus. You must keep walking."

He's not cruel, not like the soldier. But he is very serious, and I remind myself that if I get myself killed here and now, I'm no help to Merc—and I also don't get my chance with the sadistic soldier. I turn back around and keep limping. The rest of the procession through this lower level is a blur as my head spins with all kinds of bargains, some with fate, some with the man behind me, some with that woman with the white plaited hair. But then we are mounting steps and coming to a double door that seems near the size of the gate that opened for us after the mist.

The guard barks a command or a password, and both sides are opened—

I recoil at the brightness, bringing my hands up.

"Go forward, then, missus."

He doesn't prod me physically, and his voice is surprisingly gentle, as if he feels sorry for me. I am determined to use this to my advantage when I can. If I can.

As soon as my eyes adjust, I continue forth into the blinding illumination, and promptly lose my stride. We've entered the head of a marble colonnade that seems to stretch as far as the eye can see to the left. Towering columns that taper to ornate headers hold up a lofty ceiling, and there are gold flourishes everywhere. Guards, too: Pairs of uniformed sentries are posted at regular stations all the way down the impossibly long expanse. Meanwhile, off to the right, there is a beautiful landscaped garden and then a high, high wall that clearly is intended to keep people out.

Torches are everywhere, and it is their flames that beat back the night, the fuel they use burning sweetly.

Or perhaps it's all the flowers in the garden.

"This way then, missus."

The guard yet again extends an arm over my shoulder and points down the colonnade. As we proceed, we pass by many doors guarded by many pairs of men, and my mind wanders to all kind of priorities, a positive catalogue of things I urgently need to know: Where is the compass. Where is Lavante. Where is Merc.

Then it dawns on me that I should be keeping count of the doorways. Glancing behind, I catch up thanks to the number of guard pairs we've passed. Five it would be, and we're approaching the sixth. I tilt my head back and check the ceiling for any markings that can orientate me. The roof is so high that the lanterns which dangle from golden chains are like suns in the sky, and coupled with the ones mounted by the sentries, their number seems more than I can count—

*Six.*

Beneath my feet, the marble tiles are so clean, I wonder if anybody has ever walked this way before. In other circumstances, I'd have been amazed at the scale of this building, and marveled at the ornate carved headers on the columns—

*Seven.*

Finally, an end appears, still quite a ways off, but there's definitely a wall that terminates this grand and glorious promenade. Statues are lined up down there, and in their graceful poses, they remind me of smaller versions of the goddess in the ruins. The female forms are depicted in draped gowns that fall elegantly to their bare feet, and they appear to be carrying different objects—

*Eight.*

A lute. A book. Something I don't recognize, but I guess is another instrument given the strings. The faces seem to be different, the individual features becoming clearer to me as I close in.

We finally reach the wall with the statuary after fourteen pairs of guards, and I'm surprised at the mammoth size of the female forms. They are twice my height, and the carving of the marble is expert to say the least.

"To the left, missus," my escort tells me as he once again points over my shoulder.

I swallow another gasp. The lineup of statues continues down a long expanse; there must be fifty of the female forms—or maybe it's even more. And unlike before, there is just one set of sentries up ahead, at a pair of golden doors mounted halfway down the processional. Unlike all the other men, these guards are dressed in red and there are two on both sides.

Our echoing footsteps drift off when we stop in front of the grand entry. My guard salutes and is saluted in return and then everybody looks at me.

I drop my stare to the polished white floor and try to look as small and nonthreatening as possible. Underneath the red felt skirt that I'm using as a cloak, I want to sneak a hand into my pocket and palm the crystal knife just to calm myself, but I can't risk its discovery—

With a coordinated set of ceremonial moves, the inner two guards in red step forward, unlatch ornate ivory handles, and open wide the gold panels—

What is on the other side takes my breath away.

*Seventy-Six*

# The Mural.

I step forward though I'm not ordered to do so, and just as I breach the threshold, I look back at my guard.

He shakes his head. "No, missus. I am not allowed in there . . ." He lowers his voice. "Do be careful."

Under the brim of his cap, he seems honestly concerned about me, and he stays where he is as the guards in red shut me in alone. As the golden doors are locked, I turn back around, and get my breath caught anew. The ceremonial hall is twice as long as the colonnade I walked down and easily four times as wide. With a ceiling that surely must touch the sky, and twin rows of towering columns to support the yawning expanse above, the space is everything I pictured a royal court to be. Yet that's not what captures my attention.

On either side of the columns that delineate the aisle down the center, there is a mounted army of statues standing at the ready, the uniformed warriors fully weaponed and astride horses that stand hands taller than myself.

"The warrior queen . . ." I whisper as I walk over to one.

The detail of the carving is astonishing, down to the buckles on the boots and the stirrups, the mane of the horse, the fierce facial expression of the soldier . . . it's all so life-like, I could swear they're breathing.

I wander down the lineup. There must be . . . a thousand of them. Set nose to tail, with four deep on each side, they face downward toward an ornate raised platform, and as I reemerge in the processional aisle, I focus on what's ahead.

The bejeweled throne sits up high on the dais, gleaming gold and sparkling with gems, and I cannot comprehend any of it. My eyes have never seen anything like this; even the whispered stories and exaggerated gossip from

Prosperitus don't come anywhere close to the reality of the royal court I'm in, the statues I'm surrounded by . . . the magnificent seat of authority down there.

The amount of wealth needed to build and sustain this is beyond my grasp, and so too is the power required to hold on to it all—

Something trickles into my consciousness, and my eyes go past the throne, to the semi-circular walling behind it. The bowed expanse is painted with some kind of mural, and even as my instincts prickle, I know I'm not here to look at the art, or get lost in the majesty. I need to get to Merc and free us both.

Perhaps that's how the soldier dies? In the course of the rescue?

"Hello?" I call out.

When I get no reply except the echoing of my own voice, I limp down for the throne, and think of the crown Mr. Lewis gave me. Assuming they've gone through my pack, they must have found the box—and maybe my journey is finished? If they turned that circlet of black crystals in to the queen?

As I pass by the stone warriors, I note once again how their faces are all different, just like the female statues in the hall. And it's as I continue along, looking at each passing row of fighters, that I have the unmistakable sense that I'm being watched. Glancing up, I look to the ceiling, and then down to the floor . . . and finally to the side. Through the forest of static men and horses, I see a set of doors. And another. And another.

Ah, so this is what's on the other side of all those guarded portals that I counted as we came down the colonnade.

I keep going, putting my hand in my pocket, palming the crystal knife, and telling myself that of course I feel as though I'm being monitored. There are thousands of "eyes" upon me.

Except I know it's something else.

When I eventually reach the dais, I stand before the throne and trace the gemstones with my eyes as my mind spins with all manner of what-nexts—

Until my attention is abruptly caught by something else.

"What even is this," I murmur. "This cannot be . . ."

Frowning, I go around behind the throne and inspect a mural that was painted on the curved wall. At first, there's almost too much to take in, but as I pace back and forth along the images . . . I realize that a story is depicted, and the narrative starts on the left.

I go over to where it all begins. There's a gleaming white metropolis, set close to a brilliant blue ocean, and surrounded by verdant fields full of flowers. The next frame is of what must be this hall, and there are people lined up with their arms outstretched . . . toward a woman in royal regalia who sits upon—

"That throne," I say aloud as I glance back at the ornate chair.

The Queen bears a heavy red and gold crown on her head, and she is addressing her citizenry, one arm outstretched with a bejeweled staff, the other settled in her lap, bearing an orb. She is young and very beautiful, with deeply colored skin and black hair, both of which are set off by her red robes, and the jewels that hang from her neck and her wrists. She's smiling serenely, as if she knows well her position and wields her authority with grace and fairness, as a mother would watch over her family.

But the next compartment of images is dire. There's darkness in this hall, everything empty, the Queen and her people gone.

"A tragedy." I keep my voice at a whisper as I reach up and run my fingers over this part of the painted scene. "Never to be the same again."

Except it doesn't detail anything about what happened.

I continue along, and see the Queen taking to her quarters, and crops that fail, and some kind of massacre happening in a wooded glen. Though the city's life seems to continue, none of it is the same. Time passes, as suggested by a pinwheel of seasons, the spring, summer, fall, and winter all represented with the Queen's closed door in a palace suggesting she stays hidden.

And then the next panel is curious. We're once again in this great hall, with an army of statues as they appear now, the only difference being that there is a single figure standing down by the throne—

I stumble back.

There's a squeak as I hit the dais and bump the back legs of the heavy throne, knocking it out of its precise alignment on the podium. Dimly, I rub my shoulder from the impact and cannot take my eyes off the painting before me.

Surely this cannot be true. And yet my eyes do not lie.

There is the great hall, and the whole of the stone army, and the vacant throne. The figure, though, tucked away in the back . . . behind the throne . . . the one that is facing away from the viewer because the person is looking at the mural . . .

Is a red-cloaked woman with long, colorless hair.

I put my hand up to the crown of my head, and bring some of the waves that fall past my shoulders forward. And then I glance down at the felt skirt that I have fastened around my neck.

The depiction of me. As I appear right now.

Numbly, I look to the final image that has been painted.

The Queen is once again seated on her throne, with her citizenry rejoicing, the statues removed from the hall, the sun shining outside on crops that thrive.

I look back at the depiction of the red-cloaked figure, then I rush over to the left and start the sequence all over again, lingering at the dark moment and then comparing it with the final square in the sequence. Something changes between the two compositions, and not just with the disappearance of the Queen and her people and the appearance of the army of statues. I don't know what, though.

I have to go through the narrative a number of times before I spot the difference between the first painting of the Queen and the one where the red-cloaked figure is standing . . . right where I am standing, now.

Stumbling around, I circle in front of the throne, and look up to the high back of the golden chair, following the curlicues in the metal, and the winking, twinkling faces of the gems—

To the gaping hole at the apex of the top.

My eyes shoot back to the mural, and I see that what rests upon the Queen's head is not a crown with a massive ruby, but rather a golden crown . . . in front of a ruby set into the flourished top of the throne she sits on.

A noise catches my attention.

Abruptly, I crane my head back so that I can look up, way up.

Above the mural, nearly at the top of the wall where it meets the ceiling, there's an oculus. The aperture is covered with a mesh curtain, and the subtle undulations in the metal links give it away.

"You, up there," I call out. "I see you."

The curtain stills. But whoever is behind it remains. I can see their outline as a shadow on the far side of the mesh.

A strange calmness goes through me. "You are the Queen . . . who sees no one."

When there's no reply, I put my hands up, as if I can stop her from disappearing. "I need to talk to you! I come with an urgent appeal! Please, hear me, I have your crown—"

The shape turns as if to depart, their profile striking a bold carve-out behind the mesh.

"Wait!" I yell desperately. "*Wait* . . ."

I look at the throne. Then the mural.

"I know what you're missing," I hear myself holler.

Pointing to the empty setting among all the gems, I cast my eyes back up at the Queen and talk fast. "I know where your ruby is! And I can return it to you!"

## *Seventy-Seven*

# A Declaration.

The shape resumes the position it was in behind the mesh.

"Please," I shout. "I . . . if I bring the stone back to you, will you hear me out and spare my husband? It's in the mural . . . I'm supposed to be here. That's why you had me brought to you—"

A hidden door off to the side opens and the white-haired woman in the black robing steps out. "*Enough.*"

I wheel on her. "No, it's not enough. It's there, on the wall." I jab my forefinger at the pictures. "That's me. I'm supposed to bring the stone back. But I'm not going to unless she agrees to speak to me and spares my husband's life—"

The woman calmly walks over.

And slaps me across the face.

"I am the *grande vizare* of this court, and you will arrest your tone when you speak to me." She tugs her long sleeve back into place. "And may I remind you that you are under criminal charges for trespass—"

"Your guards opened that gate," I grit out as half my teeth hum. "We didn't even ask for the invitation."

"—and that I will add to those offenses impertinence to the Queen."

Marching up onto the dais, I point to the empty socket at the top of the ornate back. "If you want that stone back, I'll get it for you. Unless you like things the way they are now."

She is so shocked at where I'm standing, she needs a moment to recover. But she doesn't call for the guards, which I think is interesting.

"We are doing quite well," she snaps.

"Not according to this mural, you aren't."

The woman's regal bearing goes downright imperial. "I've had quite enough of you—"

"You're not in charge." I look up to the oculus, where the shape is still in place. "*She* is."

Stepping back, I make sure that the Queen can have proper sight of me. "I need my horse and my pack. You already hold my husband here. There's no chance I will not come back as long as I know he's alive—"

"Your husband," the woman in black cuts in, "is a dead man. Whether you are here or gone will not change his fate—"

"He's no spy for another court and neither am I!" As I ignore the *vizare*, it hardly seems helpful to mention that Merc kills people for money. "He came with me to protect me on my travels to see you, Your Highness."

"And you hail from where," the advisor says in a bored tone.

Ignoring her, I focus only on the oculus. "I am from a small village outside of Prosperitus. I come bearing news that the Fulcrum is failing and demons are afoot. Anathos needs you and your army to save us from the Dark King—"

The woman in black barks out a command, and a flank of guards stream in from the hidden door.

"I beg of you!" I shout. "We need you to fight the evil before he grows too powerful to defeat! We are on the verge of a war that Anathos has no defenses to, and you are the only one who can save us! I have the crown of war and shadow you will wear—"

I am grabbed on all sides and pulled back.

"Please!" I yell up. "You know this is what has been foretold! It's on the very wall behind your throne—"

At once, I'm dragged through the hidden door, the panel closing with a finality I cannot live with. "Let me go! I have to talk to the Queen—"

The advisor steps in front of me, but talks to the men who hold me in place—in my language, no doubt so I can understand my reward for offending her: "Take her back where she was. And let the lieutenant know that she is available for his pleasure."

As she waves her hand in dismissal, the guards follow her order, picking me up by the armpits and carrying me over the marble floor of the antechamber.

*"Wait."*

The *vizare*'s voice stops them and they wheel me back around to her, my feet dangling.

"He is not to kill her," the Queen's advisor says sternly. "She is to be beheaded in the square with that spy husband of hers first thing in the morning."

The woman turns away, her plaited hair swinging like rope down her back as she glides away through yet another seamless panel.

The guards spin me round once again, and off we go, their grips biting into my arms, my stomach flip-flopping in fear. They proceed a different way than I was first escorted, heading through a doorway, into a corridor, down a set of stone stairs, and into another part of the dungeon below. The stench of fear sweat, damp stone, and old blood is the same however, and as I start to choke, I open my mouth to breathe in hopes of not throwing up from the stench—

The hooting and hollering starts as we take a corner and begin down a long, narrow block of cells. The men in them are dirty and wearing tattered clothes, their hair and beards grown out. Through the bars, they reach for me, yelling obscene things that I cringe and look away from. Just as we reach the final cells and are about to make a turn—

Merc is there on the left, sprawled out against the stone wall, blood oozing, glossy and alarming, from his shoulder, his eyes closed, his chin down on his chest. He's been stripped of his chain mail and all his weapons, and they've even cut off the beads from the ends of his braids, the pieces unraveling out of their weaves.

"Merc!" As I scream his name, his eyes open and his head lifts. "*Merc*—"

I renew my fight against the guards, and against everything that is logical, Merc somehow jumps to his feet and throws himself at his cell's bars.

"Sorrel!"

With a full-body yank, I slip free of all the grips and careen over to him. He's pale, and there is blood in his hair, on his throat, down his long black shirt and leather britches.

"I tried—" I start crying. "I tried to get us free—"

"Are you all right—"

One of the guards re-grabs my arm, and Merc thrusts the heel of his palm forward, catching the man on the chin. As the latter stumbles back from the impact, the other guard jumps in to pull me away—

The first man in uniform is caught by the inmates across the way, and he lets out a scream as they start to claw at him. His comrade has no choice but to release me and run to his aid.

Separated by bars, I search Merc's eyes. "I'm so sorry—"

He strokes my hair back. "No apologies. Not from you, ever."

Our lips meet, and then I say it, the words I have known in my heart for the longest time . . . maybe even that first night back at the Gauntlet when I smelled him.

"I love you."

The expression of pain that contorts Merc's face is something I feel in my own chest. I can't believe we end here, like this. After coming so far—

"Sorrel, I—"

The guards get free of their tangle with the prisoners, and I'm grabbed around the waist and hauled away.

I'm yelling Merc's name as the men march me around the corner.

The last sight I have of the man I love is him straining against the iron bars, his arms outstretched, his black and white eyes full of tears.

*Seventy-Eight*

# A Dreadful First.

After I'm thrown back into the cell, the bars are closed on me and locked this time, and then I'm left alone.

I spend the first couple of moments standing with one foot in the fetid puddle I landed in twice, tears streaming down my face, my arms wrapped around myself. And then I realize that the soldier will come for me. This is how . . . it happens.

And if the last thing I do on this continent is kill that man? I am all right with that. If I'm dying tomorrow morning anyway, I might as well make sure that he doesn't hurt anybody else.

I back up against the stone wall and wait.

And wait.

And . . . wait.

Wherever I am in the underground stone maze, there is no sound that travels to me other than those that are immediately about: There are drips from leaks in the mortar of the walls and ceiling, squeaks of the occasional rat, and the hiss and spit of the torches mounted around. And then there's my ragged breath.

But no voices from somewhere else, not a footfall or hinge of doors.

Then again, this is where they torture people. They don't want sound to travel.

My nervous eyes skate over those gruesome tables and the stained racks, those buckets, and the drains. I rub my face, and start to pace.

That lasts . . . for a while? I don't know how long.

When my legs begin to ache and my sore feet protest my weight, I settle down on the floor, and think of the position Merc was in as I finally saw him. Mirroring exactly the orientation of his limbs, I arrange myself as he was because it seems like the only way I'm able to be with him.

More time passes. I know this because it always does, and in my solitude, as the cold and damp seep into my bones even with my makeshift cloak, I think of how many days and nights have gone by without my noticing over the course of my life . . . how many times I awoke under the stairs, and scurried to work in the Gauntlet's little kitchen, and went to Mare's, and raced back, and cleared tables and cleaned up messes—only to go to bed and get up and do it all over again.

So many days and nights.

Countless, really.

And now here I am, with no outdoor lighting for reference, floating in an unknown sea of hours that may be going fast or slow, I have no idea . . . waiting for a man to come back so I can kill him. Having no watch or clock or rhythm of repetitive actions to ground me is a mental challenge. It's as disorienting as walking through a dark room, this time blindness, and the longer it persists, the more drowsy I become. Even though I want to stay alert, I can't seem to keep my heavy eyelids open and once they close, I . . .

"Leave us."

At the sound of the male voice, I jerk my head up. I'm lying on my side on the stone floor, my arm as my pillow, my legs tucked up close to my body.

It's the soldier, finally. And he's closing the two of us into the cell together as he keeps his eyes on a pair of guards who retreat at his command. After they disappear through the door across the way, he goes immediately for the front of his britches.

He smiles coldly. "I do not know what you have done to increase the ire with which you are held, but I commend you for your efforts on our behalf. I have been assured that we will not be interrupted. For however long I wish."

My lungs strain for air, and I struggle to my feet as the soldier comes at me—and then he's upon me, one of his hands gripping my throat and squeezing, the other shoving under the felt cloak to commence the groping.

I mean to be strong. I intend to fight. I tell myself to scream and kick and punch, and fulfill what I've been shown—

Instead, I freeze.

As his rough, greedy fingers start to tear at my clothes, my skin tightens all over my body in revulsion and my stomach thrashes in the cradle of my pelvis. I smell his breath and his sweat, feel the wool of his sleeve streak across my stomach and under my breasts—and then the jodhpurs are gone and he forces himself between my thighs.

He stops. Pulls back and frowns at me. "I expected more resistance from you. You were far more promising before."

The soldier yanks my arm up over my head and pins it to the wall. "Nothing to say? Are you not going to beg me to stop, *whore*?"

The word snaps me out of the numb place I retreated to. All at once, I'm threaded with heat: The surge starts in my extremities and zeroes in on the center of my chest as a sudden rage floods me—and I embrace this other side coming out.

From a vast distance, I hear my own voice, steady and calm.

"You want a fight," I say.

His horrible laugh is like his hands on my skin, something that I cannot abide. And will not.

The fury in me redoubles, and then explodes until I am shaking, not from fear, but from a pent-up energy that feels totally different than anything I have ever experienced—

"I told you before." His lips go to my neck. "I will hear you beg."

The soldier bites my collarbone, and as I let out a shout of pain, he laughs again. "Ah, more like it. Let's try that once more—and if you make this good for me, I'll ensure your death tomorrow morning is quick—"

The gasp he makes goes right into my ear, and echoes in my skull.

As he straightens, he looks down at me in shock. "What . . . have you done."

I pull my free arm back—and punch him again. And then I'm looking him in the eyes as I am punching, punching, *punching* him in the gut, over and over—with such strength that I'm pushing him back against the grimy stone wall.

"You want to fight," I growl as I plunge the crystal knife into him again. "You want to hurt me as I beg for mercy?"

I stab him another time, so deeply now that my whole fist is going into his abdomen—and now I'm twisting and forcing the weapon up higher. Blood speckles my face and throat, warm little flicks that surely stain my soul. I am unleashed though, and the act of killing feeds the vengeance within me—

Red sparks fall from the ceiling as the soldier collapses into the corner, still with a look of utter surprise on his face. Whether it's because of what glimmers and twinkles in the air or what's been done to him, I don't know. I don't care. As he coughs up blood, he knocks his hat off, exposing his balding hair and a mole at his temple that's the size of a coin.

Stepping over his hips, I stare down at him as blood drips off my fist and dapples the open fly of his britches.

I tell myself to leave him. The door to the cell is once more closed, but I see that he didn't bother to lock things behind him. All I have to do is slip out, and navigate the passageways and tunnels back to where Merc is—

There's no one around and no worry that sound will travel. I also have time because the soldier told the other guards to leave us alone and boasted he could take as long as he wanted.

As these thoughts occur to me, I don't know why I'm wasting time with them—

The dark wave of energy that flows through me overtakes everything. Even as I am horrified, there's nothing I can do to fight the urge that commands me.

Tilting forward, I take my foot and press it into his groin until all of my weight is on his crotch and he is writhing under me as he hoarsely starts to scream.

The moment his lips open, I bend down, draw my arm back—

And drive the crystal knife into his mouth.

The officer's whole body spasms, his hands and legs flopping on the stone floor, his eyes rolling back as he coughs blood and chokes on it. But I'm not done yet. I retract my fist, feeling his teeth on the back of my knuckles—and then I stab him one more time, in the seat of his manhood, in the flesh weapon he was going to enjoy hurting me with. All he can do is moan and writhe, his blood-stained hands going for the front of those britches which he was so hurried to open. After which . . . he no longer moves.

In the trembling quiet that follows, I hear harsh breathing and I'm surprised he's able to get anything down into his chest—and then realize it's me. I'm dragging in hoarse breaths.

As I take back my crystal knife from his privacy, the last of the red sparkles fall from the ceiling of the cell and my fury starts to ebb.

Standing over the soldier, my mind begins to clear and I am . . . mortified by what I've done, especially as I look down at his gutted torso: I'm no better than those demons, ripping into a man's stomach like that.

"He would have raped and killed me," I say aloud. "It was survival."

Maybe. Up until that last part—

The sound of a door opening spins me around. Out of instinct, I shove the crystal knife back into the pocket I took it out of under my makeshift cloak. Of course, the blood smudge I leave behind is a telltale that I have a weapon.

Like the messy corpse isn't?

And then stupidly, I put my hands up, both the bloodied one and the one that is relatively clean, as if someone is pointing one of those sidearms at me.

It's not guards. It is that advisor.

As she comes up to the cell, I keep my focus on her chin. It tilts down as she obviously looks at the soldier and then relevels as she regards me.

Well . . . I was going to be killed, anyway.

At least I took a bad man with me.

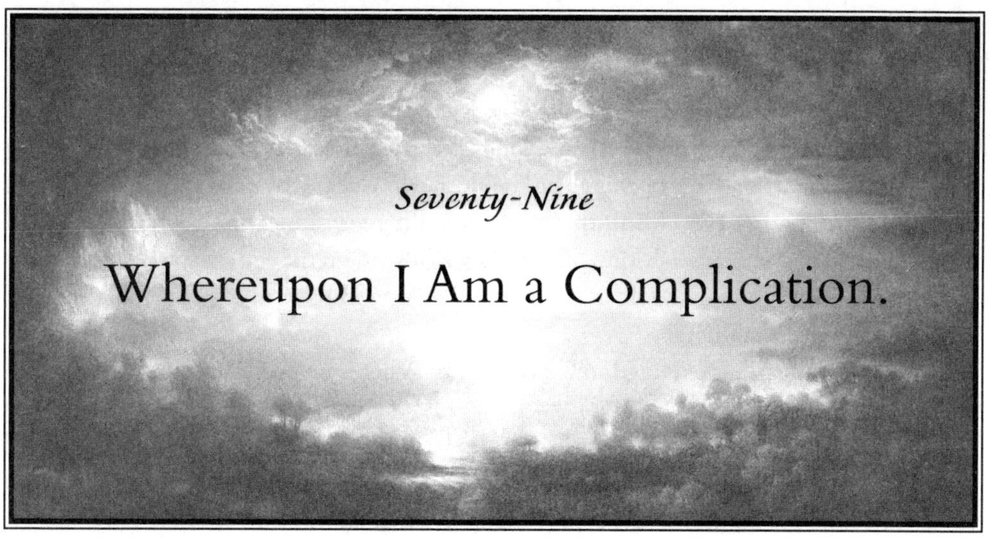

*Seventy-Nine*

# Whereupon I Am a Complication.

As silence stretches out between myself and the Queen's *vizare*, I can feel the blood of the officer inside my sleeve. What splattered up into my face is drying already, and my pores tighten as it evaporates. Stupidly, I wonder how I'm going to get the stains out of Julion's pants . . . even though it's not like I'm ever going to see him again, if by some miracle I make it out of here alive.

Which is not going to happen—

"Why must you be *such* a complication," the advisor snaps.

There's a bark of command from her, and guards come in. When they see the soldier in the cell, looking like something ate through his stomach and then tried to come out both ends of him, they unholster their weapons.

"Bring her with me," the woman in black orders.

Yet another pair of grips lock around my upper arms, and as I'm dragged out of the cell, I wish they wouldn't hold the exact same place. It's already bruised there. Like it matters, though.

I don't even try to walk. Part of this is exhaustion. Most of it is giving up. Yes, yes, they were going to kill me anyway, but now that I've taken one of their own? Maybe I'm going to face an even worse death than beheading.

And wouldn't I deserve that for what I just did? It started as self-defense—and ended with something else entirely.

Closing my eyes, I revisit the violence I wrought and try not to weep. Where is the healer in me? Where is the girl I once was and the woman I was becoming with Merc? Both feel lost in the ugliness I've found within me. I was never capable of murder before, and certainly never capable of cruelty.

When I set off on this journey, I knew the world was a hard place, but I still had all my humanity. Now . . . I don't know what I am, anymore.

The only good part of this is at least Merc and I will not live long enough to see the downfall when the Dark King is released from the Fulcrum—

I hear a set of doors opening and the smell that reaches my nose is a surprise.

Opening my eyes, I find that we're in a different tunnel, the terminus of which glows with a peach-tinted light. As we close in on the end, a vista unfurls of white buildings and golden sunlight, of lawns and flowers, of people off in the distance walking.

This must be the Kingdom's city square. Where the executions are going to happen.

"Merc," I moan in a forlorn voice.

We break out into the light and I wince and blink. To orient myself, I look to the sky and find the sun. It's once again at a low angle on the western horizon—

I've lost an entire day. All those hours, waiting for the soldier to return . . . added up to a full day. So they didn't kill us "in the morning," after all. Unless they've already executed Merc—

"Your husband is still alive," the advisor informs me with a bored drawl.

And then I hear a familiar nickering call.

I spin around just as a guard brings Lavante around a corner. The instant the stallion sees me, he rears up and paws at the man who's holding his reins, impatient to come over.

"You have until tomorrow morning," the advisor announces. "But if I were you, I would return posthaste. There have been certain . . . attacks that have taken place after dark of late. That is your concern, however, not mine."

By the tone in her voice, she disapproves of all of this, so I'm not surprised as she tacks on, "I make no representations about what shall occur when you return, even if it is with Her Sublime Highness's lost jewel. Especially after what you did back in that cell." She nods at a pair of guards who arrive upon their own horses. "These men will escort you to the gate, and you will be permitted back in, but none will enter upon the Forbidden Land with you. From there you will proceed alone."

I'm not listening to her. As the guards who have been bruising my arms release their holds, I shoot forward and drape myself around Lavante's neck. Breathing in his fresh scent, I want to weep.

Instead, I pull back and take the reins.

As I mount up, I cannot ignore the streak of blood I leave behind on his beautiful pale neck. But then I'm up in the saddle and gathering my stallion as he starts to trot in place. My saddlebags have been removed, and I infer from how sprightly he is that he's been fed and tended to properly. It makes sense. He is, after all, a stallion anyone would want to own.

Just as I turn to the advisor, she nods sharply at someone behind me. "Yes, yes. Your pack."

My shouldering bag appears and is given to me.

As I slip it onto my back, I feel that its weight is the same. The crown and compass are still with me.

"Again, we have your husband," the *vizare* says. "Remember that when you decide whether or not to return."

The guards cue their horses to walk off, and I glance back at the advisor as I set Lavante to follow. Though I do not meet her eyes, I can feel her glare on me.

Given the chance, I know she'd have me killed in an instant. Merc as well.

I have to hope the Queen who sees no one can nonetheless control her court.

The guards take me down a well-trod lane that is made of packed white shells. As we pass by citizens, the men and women stop and look up at us. They're in the midst of whatever lives they lead, the laborers coming home from the fields dirty, wrinkled, and tired, the aristocrats striding with their heads held high, the maidens scurrying in giggling groups. A keen eye catches the truth behind the momentary glimpses, however: The laborers look defeated as if their efforts are not producing enough, the aristocrats' clothes are threadbare, and the maidens are even sizing up the laborers, as if there are not quite enough men to go around for marriage.

Because they've been killed or died off.

And the buildings we pass, though whole and clean, are showing a loss of roof tiles here and there, a chimney that requires a repair, a column that is split and unfixed.

This Kingdom of the South is teetering on a fall. Add some centuries? It'll be what's down that slope, eroded back to the raw components from which it was made.

Everything is as the mural proclaimed.

When I and my escort of guards reach the edge of the city, we exit a border wall and proceed out into the meadow of wildflowers. The crop fields are off to the south, and I know from my previous foray into the compass's map as well as what Merc's map showed, that there's an ocean somewhere close by, but I cannot visualize the latter. I'm not concerned with the land's details, however.

It's the sun I am most focused on.

Now I thank fates for the passage of all that time in the cell, and I can guess the why of the delay. The Queen had given an order to let me go, and the *vizare* wanted to make sure her majesty was serious about her decision. No doubt that advisor was hoping that clearer minds would prevail in the morning. And into the start of the afternoon.

Obviously they didn't.

It's a relief to see the trees come up, because it means no more daylight will be wasted with travel, but I am filled with dread as the gate looms. While I look up and follow the walkway across the top of the great doors, a shot of fear goes through me. Over to the north and west, way above the spiky stone summits of the mountains, there are shadows riding the currents. They look like birds, but that's a misinterpretation because of distance. They are dragons, readying for the hunt as wildlife begins to move into its nocturnal hideouts. I imagine that those kings of the clouds live off of ogres and maybe skystalkers, in addition to the *dsteers* and *goatum* that roam the more habitable rises.

But they might well take a human if they were hungry enough. Or a stallion.

Soon enough, I am once again standing before the mighty gate with its banded bare trunks and its center split. The creaking occurs at the hinges as the side I entered is opened once again, and then I see through to the mist on the other side.

No one says a thing. But I didn't expect the guards to wish me well or help. Their job begins and ends at seeing me to this point, and I suspect they're relieved to discharge the responsibility. At least my stallion is sticking with me. Lavante is happy to go through and be in charge once again, no more horses he must follow. He has no conception of what we are in for, however, as we confront the fog . . . and the gate starts to close—

"Wait!" I call out.

I expect the closure to continue. When there's a pause, I wheel Lavante around.

"I need one more thing," I request. "Please."

## *Eighty*

# Spiders and Rubies.

On the far side of the gate, the mist is even thicker than I remember, and I'm battered from all sides as we go through the trees with their slapping branches. Lavante is just too good at weaving in and out of that which I cannot see, another game he likes to play. The torch that I got from the guards doesn't help. Flames flare and spit as I dodge the arboreal attacks, but all the golden light gets consumed in the thick humidity, frustrating me as I search for the drop-off down to the ruins—

We find the slope when Lavante's hooves slip out from under him.

As he goes into a topple, I'm nearly unseated, and grab on to his mane to try to steady myself while also making sure I don't light either of us on fire. Even with his superior sense of balance, he's falling sideways through the mist, his hooves digging for purchase, his grunts a testament to how hard he is working to recover.

I look back at where we were; then attempt to see forward.

If the mist persists below now, I worry that we'll not be able to orient ourselves at the bottom and sure enough, we finish the scrambling descent without notice, the ground underfoot suddenly angling sharply to the flat.

I can see absolutely nothing.

And then, as I cue Lavante forward, there's a sloppy sound.

Fates, I think we're in the marshes. I've gotten turned around without knowing it, distracted by conjecture, fear, and sorrow—as well as our sloppy, flailing nosedive—so I didn't check in with the compass. And now I'm certain we are much, much closer to the ocean than the ruins.

Pulling up on the reins, I squint as I look around even though that doesn't help. If we keep going in the wrong direction, we're going to get mired in, and that is going to be disastrous.

Arranging the torch under my leg, I mutter, "You need to stay still or that mane of yours is going to be the hair equivalent of kindling."

Shucking off my pack, the compass finds my hand as if it's ready to go to work, and I picture the ruins as clearly as I can recall them, with the megalithic sculpture in the center—

The top pops open, the map appears, and the spinning starts. My heartbeat redoubles as I try to imagine making this foolhardy attempt without the instrument—and I think of what Mr. Lewis said so very, very long ago.

"One makes it possible, the other is the reason for it," I whisper under my breath.

I think of the crown of black crystals and resolve that somehow I'm going to get that ruby, and then I'm going to force the Queen to accept her destiny.

I had to accept mine even though I didn't want to. And now here I am.

Her Royal-damn-Highness can do the same.

In the flicker of the torch, the directional notes on the compass face continue to go round and round, and the red arrow works in counter to that. As with before, it takes longer, as if the mist is a disorientator, but then the arrow settles and points behind us.

So I was right, we would have gone the wrong way.

"Thank you," I whisper as I return the compass to its satchel and the satchel to its place in the pack on my back.

Lavante is agreeable to the about-turn and off we go, trudging our way along until the ground becomes solid. It's right about this time that the mist thins out—at least on the ground. There's still heavy cover overhead, and I try to tell myself that's somehow an advantage. I don't know how, though, except for keeping dragons at bay?

But sometimes, we need to create our own optimism.

The ruins come up to us, it feels like, as opposed to my stallion and me approaching them, and I pull up on the reins while we're still a couple of lengths outside the walling. Though the diffused afternoon illumination remains choked by the fog, I remember enough about the layout to know where to enter between the crumbling statues and how we're going to have to go. I also see in my mind the web strands and cocoons that dot the lanes and pepper the collapsing buildings.

Like I'm ever going to forget being captured like that or the red eyes of those spiders.

Glancing at the torch, I know that the flame is going to have to do all of the work, and I can only pray that my foolhardy plan works. At least I didn't plan on using the red wash and their supplication to my advantage. With this fog? There's no sun to create the visual effect, no matter the hour.

"Faster than you've ever run." I look down and think of the pavers we're going to encounter. If there's too much condensation on them, Lavante's shod hooves will slip. "And fates, may you stay on your feet—"

With a shout and a strike of both heels, I command him to run.

Lavante is more than ready. The stallion tears off, making lightning speed over the grass. As soon as we get to the gates, his hooves hit the stone lane, and the sound is a blaring drumroll. With the wind ripping at me, I focus my attention on the torch, willing the flames to burn hotter and brighter—and just as the red fires that burst out of the red earth listened to my commands, so too does what tops the bundle of oil-soaked reeds.

If my flames go out, I'm dead.

If a lot of things happen . . . I'm dead.

Columns and broken statues fly by on both sides, and the salt in the air stings my eyes and coats my throat. I know that the spiders will come for us, I just pray that we are far enough along—

The first of them appears off to the left, eight-legging it out of whatever lairs they have. My instinct is to charter our course to avoid them, but I can't lose my concentration on the torch. All I can do is hold on with my knees, focus on keeping the flames going, and trust Lavante to carry me down the lane to the statue.

Just as with the entry to the city, the center statue jumps out of the mist ahead of us. By this time, we're leading a parade of spiders, so there's no time for an orderly dismount. I pull back on the reins, and Lavante fights me for his head, as if he knows that speed is our friend if we want to escape. But that's not what I need from him.

His velocity barely slows, however, and in the end, I just have to leap off. As I leave the saddle, I slap his rump so he carries on. Not that he wouldn't keep going without me, his survival instinct being what it is.

I land in a tumble, rolling on the slick, wet pavers—

As I go to jump out of the momentum, there is a spider right in front of me.

The beast opens its mouth and starts to send out a silken thread. Whipping the torch up, I send the flames forward, and there's an instant response to my mental command, a great burst of fire licking forth.

The spider squeals and backs away, but it's too late for him. The arachnid is done for, the stench of burning hair and flesh wafting over as the spindly beast tries to escape what's consuming it. There's no time for triumph. Another takes its place. And another. And—

I wave the torch in a circle, and will the flames to form a barrier around me. Somehow, this works and as I go forward, the webs that are sent my way sizzle into black smoke as they're consumed by the billowing barrier. I try not to think of how many are upon me, the whole of the colony called out, great, streaking lines of spiders flowing toward me, an evil tide.

When I arrive at the goddess statue, I see that she's standing on a temple that forms her base. The single-floored building is in tatters, all of its columns collapsed, as if it's given way under the great weight of the stone above. I'm going to have to find a way into it, and can only hope there's an access point somewhere, although I'm worried about whether trying to figure my way around will make me lose the coverage of my flames: The spiders are constantly testing for lapses in the fire field, their silk forays coming from all angles—and I pray they can't hop, because if one got on top of me, I'd lose my concentration and then for certain they'd all be on me.

Glancing up to the goddess's stained and cracked robing, I visualize her palm and remember the beam of red light.

The Queen of the South Kingdom's ruby is what sits there. That enormous stone is what catches that slice of sunlight that swings through the spires at a specific angle at a specific time, the refraction causing the temple and surrounding environs to change color.

And hypnotize the spiders.

I don't know how it got there, who put it there, or why. All I care about is getting the gem down—and for that, now I need to go up—

Through the licking, dancing flames, I see a better path to the statue's bottom. Starting off with care, instead of trying to navigate an interior that might well collapse right on me, I mount one of the fallen columns and travel up its tilted, ridged flank. The going is tricky because of the carved fluting and the fact that everything is wet and slippery from the humidity, but I keep my balance and link up with another one that's angled into an intersection. My soft-soled slipper shoes help, my toes gripping at whatever contours they can find to hold on to, my free arm out to the side for counterbalance.

The whole time, I pray that this pick-up-sticks arrangement is not disturbed by my weight. If any of the columns start rolling? I'm going to be crushed—if I'm lucky.

Except I'd rather go out that way than face the spiders.

It's not long before I reach the temple roof's decorated railing, and as I duck under it and look up, it's hard not to get defeated. The goddess's hand might as well be in the stars, and there's mist all around her, swirling on currents as water encircles a drain. Meanwhile, the horde is following my ascent like coyotes on a rabbit. Forced to keep their distance by my circle of flames, the spiders nonetheless stay right on me, and I have a moment of pure panic as I realize that even if I secure the stone, I'm going to have to get down, somehow.

And then get out of the ruins.

"Forward, never back," I grit as I look up once again.

That's when I see the staircase.

Through the marble spindles of yet another broken railing, inside a circular space revealed by more columns that have fallen from their bases, there are a set of marble steps.

"Fates . . . thank you."

I have to fight through debris—and a couple of the goddess's fallen toes, which are the size of my entire body—to get over to the stairway, and I'm careful to keep the biggest part of my brain occupied with retaining my fire wall as I go. Finally, I'm at the steps and I don't waste time assessing the ascent. I start running upward, or at least, trying to. In the enclosed, narrow space, webs are everywhere, the silken strands clinging to my shoulders, my hair, my feet, until I'm pulling them along with me like the train on a wedding dress. I have a worry that some of the spiders who are behind me will try to grab on and yank me back—

The staircase I'd planned on using to the very top of the statue ends too soon, the way up choked by an internal collapse at the first landing I come to. And with a quick glance over my shoulder, all I see in the flickering light is a tangle of spider legs and a thousand red eyes.

The panic comes fast upon me, especially as the temperature rises from all the fire around me. I'm trapped here, no way forward, no way back—sorry, Merc and your saying, the motivation is not going to work this time—

Except there's a wedge I can maybe squeeze through off to the side. Of course, the flames will consume me if I have to share the same space with them—but I have to try.

Projecting them to my rear, I keep a tight hold on the torch and crab-walk up the loose collection of boulders and stones. When the pile shifts some, I put the reed bundle in my teeth, and start clawing at the marble chunks, making more of a gap to force my body through. Behind me, the fire becomes a solid wall, and that gives me a chance to work—

It's like a birth of sorts.

After I shove the torch through, and some kind of interior space is revealed by its light, I squeeze my head and shoulders through the aperture. With a gasp and a strain, I force my way along. The felt of my makeshift cape protects me from scrapes, but it's a hindrance, too, adding bulk. I'm swimming now, through marble debris, dust getting into my nose, the flames behind me growing dimmer as I continue—

I pop out as bairns do, sliding free into a tumble that lands me on my face.

Lifting my head and the torch—

I'm in a little room, and I can smell fresh sea air.

Ah-ha. There's a cutout in the wall across the shallow space, and a grate covers the opening. That's where the mist is getting in from.

And at least there aren't spiders staring back at me.

Fates, I'm tired.

Closing my eyes, I picture Merc staring out of that cell as I'm carried away. This gives me the strength to stand up. The metal mesh has a latch, and I'm worried that it's going to make a lot of noise as I open it and my position will be given away—

Everything is so corroded by the salt and lubricated by the mist that there's no sound at all.

As I lean out, I'm shocked at how far up I am, and very grateful that the horde is concentrated on the entrance to the stairs and hasn't noticed me yet. But as the eddies of mist surge and retreat, I'm horrified by what's beneath me. The entire spider colony has rallied around the temple, packing every available avenue of escape. I'm going to need more than just a ball of fire around me to get through all that—and how has Lavante fared? Has he lived? Even if I get down there, I need a way to rush back to the gate before the darkness comes.

Besides, I've come to love that horse—

I can't worry about all that right now. Looking up, I find that I'm at ankle height, and it's hard to see past the flare of the robing's hem, and the rise of the bent knee.

Great. Now what.

I'm wondering how I'm going to drag myself up all that slick marble when I see the bolts. A series of huge metal hooks have been drilled into the stone, and given that they seem to go all the way up the statue, I imagine they were used to secure drapes of cloth to the goddess's body or maybe ceremonial flowers or fates know what.

I'm going to have to climb them like they're a ladder.

After a couple of deep breaths, I put the torch back between my teeth, crouch down, and emerge through the access point. Gripping the nearest cold, wet hook, I pull myself upward and go drawn-and-quartered, feet apart on two of the bolts, hands above my head gripping another pair at the same distance. I don't wait but a heartbeat before sucking the fire wall out through the hole in the collapse and surrounding myself with the flames. I'm dimly aware of screeching, like the spiders are frustrated they can't get at me, but they don't have to worry. Their brethren on the exterior have noticed where I am already and are rerouting from the bottleneck at the stairwell and around the temple base, to a collective mounting the statue itself.

"You can do this . . ."

I move one foot to a bolt a length up, push through my thigh and knee, put my other foot up, shift my hands' positions—and I'm a little higher.

Again. And again. And . . . again.

The going is slow and arduous, and my breath gets tight in my lungs from exertion. Then a gust of wind tests my ability to hold on, the whistling in my ears like a scream. Or maybe I'm making that noise—

Except . . . it's not the wind.

*Eighty-One*

# The Goddess and the Climb.

More gusts come, and the screaming call continues. It's not, in fact, me, but when I try to figure out the source, panic starts to strangle me. It's while I try to find my composure once again that I see the first flash of a dragon's wing. A blink later the whole beast appears out of the clouds, its scaled body and speared tail as graceful in flight as any bird's, its horned head and gaping, tooth-filled mouth exactly what I do not need in my current situation.

I flatten against the statue as the thing swings by, and the flames that protect me dim as they're hit with a downdraft that carries so much humidity.

Beneath me, the spiders are unaffected, dousing my hope that they might be scared off by the arrival. No doubt they're not enough sustenance for the predator to be bothered with. But a woman, such as myself? That's a different story. And just as with the skystalker, no doubt the fire that circles me was what called them from their summits. They came to check things out, and now they might get fed—so they're not going to leave.

Sure enough, the dragon disappears only for a moment into the mist, and then it comes right back for another pass. He's red and black—or maybe it's a she?—and I'm reminded of the old wives' saying: Be one dragon, there are three; keep thy light dim and in a lee.

I'm really sick of sky-bound creatures who are attracted by light.

As the air beast makes yet another pass, his great wings open up a column of visibility around the goddess—and I see only the trial ahead, only my impossible journey.

Up I must go.

With the torch still in my teeth, I ladder my way forth, and there's more swinging and worry over losing grip as the dragon creates its own weather system of gusts. When I get to the parted hem of the goddess's robing, I have to stop and catch my breath again—

The red and black dragon makes yet another pass, even closer this time. And the old wives are right. There's another on its tail, also coming to investigate, either because of the light or to see what its ilk is toying with. My body buffets back and forth in the breeze, and I desperately try not to think of how far I am from the ground or what waits for me below if I fall:

Hard marble or hungry spiders.

Spoiled for choice—

As if the latter want to protect their potential food source from the apex predators who've shown up, the red tips of some of the spiders' front legs appear directly below me. With all my distraction, my ring of protective fire has dimmed, and they've taken immediate advantage to close in.

Palming the grip of the torch, I send fire at them with my mind. "Get back!"

A fresh blast of flame bursts out and there are squeals of pain. I keep going because I have no other choice. My forearm aches from what now feels like an ancient injury, my palms are going raw from gripping the salted metal hooks, and my toes burn from grabbing on and being my body's anchor. Then there's my front teeth, which were not meant to be used as a third hand. As I pull myself higher and higher, the flames keep the dragons interested, but the spiders stay away—and I gather a third has joined the pair who've been swooping by. With every pass, I must flatten myself, which is hard with the bundle of lit reeds being so big and ungainly in my mouth.

I work my way up her skirt, and then over her bust on the side by her ribs, following the line of bolts, being followed by a line of spiders. I slip at her shoulder and nearly fall off, my damp, soft shoe going out from under me. But I recover and continue up to her arm, grunting, straining, sweating in spite of the cold. The mist is impossibly dense up here, such that I see only what's immediately above and immediately below. At least the dragons' wings part it from time to time, so that I can measure my progress.

How kind, really.

Finally, I am at the wrist. My hair is whipped around in the wind, and I am breathing salt water for all the droplets in the air. The temperature is much, much colder, and this presents a problem for my hands, but I force them to keep gripping even after I can't feel them anymore.

Now I must go slowly. Peering over the heel of the palm, I see the ruby. It's nearly the size of my head, and cradled in a depression deep enough to settle the gem in tight, but not so deep that the facets cannot be reached by the sunlight.

This is going to require two hands.

But what hasn't.

My jaw is getting tired and my teeth are sore from biting down on the torch's girth, but I'm nearing the end of this.

This part, at least.

Pushing my weight into the goddess's smooth wrist, I reach up and over the edge of that palm—

It happens so fast, I cannot track the sequence.

Just as my hands capture the smooth, cold ruby in a grab as if my life depends upon it . . .

The first of the dragons, the red and black one, explodes out of the swirling mist and we're face-to-face.

I stare into its mouth, rather than its eyes, those fangs a far more immediate threat than whatever death it's going to face. With perfect aim, it's come right at me, its great wings splitting the mist such that the waning light in the sky gives me perfect vision.

Of what's going to eat me—

Except it doesn't go for my head and shoulders. It plucks the torch right from my teeth with its stumpy forearm, delicate as a lady taking a tea cake from a silver platter.

Off it goes, into the clouds.

And with it, the swirl of fire I was using to protect myself.

*Eighty-Two*

# Falls of Choice.

The golden light thrown by the torch is sucked away into the mist, and the spiders waste no time. Their black bodies and those red-tipped legs scurry up at me. I clutch the ruby to my chest as they crawl over each other, zeroing in, silk already releasing into the wind where it's swirled away. That won't last. As soon as the next gust comes from the opposite direction, the webbing will be blown into me and I'll be caught.

I look down toward the street, so far, far away that I can't see it for the clouds. I think of the cocoons, and know that their prey is still alive in some, kept paralyzed but aware that sometime soon, they will be sucked dry—

A spider crawls up onto my feet and rears onto its back legs, revealing its bulbous, hairy belly. As I see the silk glands and know what getting trapped will mean for me, I make the decision just as the sticky web spins out to capture me.

I jump off the statue.

The free fall is a terror I'm resigned to. I'd rather go out on my terms, staring the bastards in the face, falling to the marble below for an instant death, than be kept as a meal for fates only know how long.

Tears spring to my eyes and my hair streaks up past me as the wind resistance on my back and legs offers a cushioning, but no real help. To have come so close, to have the ruby . . . but did I really think this was going to work? Did I honestly think I could pull this off?

And now Merc will die, too.

I had to try, though. Sometimes, all we can do is—

*Whooosh.*

All at once, and without warning, the rush of air hitting my body is stopped with a bump.

My first thought is that I have made impact before I expected and death is painless. But that's when the rhythmic rocking registers . . . and I see the tips of the wings.

Scrambling around, I find myself in the curve of a dragon's back, right behind the horned and horrible head. There's a divot at the nape, and just as the ruby was centered on the goddess's palm, so I'm cradled as the beast flies over the ruins. Through breaks in the mist, I see down below, the streets with the broken statues and the tumbled columns, the strings of webs, a stray spider here or there.

I twist around and look over my shoulder. The goddess's head is obscured by the mist, but her body is visible.

Her draping clothes are made of spiders, teeming in confusion.

It's as I turn back that my eyes catch the wing rising up.

Green and purple . . . with a tear through the base, an injury that has healed.

A numbing shock goes through me that has nothing to do with the fact that I'm freezing cold and lengths upon lengths above the ground.

Could this be the dragon I saved? The one whose eyes I stared into, whose throat I cut, whose life I returned to his body?

I think about the distance I traveled away from my village—so far for me, but I know for them it's but a coasting upon the airways: They're known to nest on the snowcapped mountains to the west of my village, yet travel extensively to mate or find food.

The coloring is right. The healed wound is right.

And he must . . . remember me.

Splitting my legs, I sit astride just above the shoulders as if on a horse as we soar out past the front entry with the decaying statuary and over the marshes. The dragon makes a big circle above the shoreline of the sea and then dips down close to the ground.

We're so close, I see the individual leaves on the water lilies rushing by.

And then we're over the meadow, heading back to the ruins. At the last moment, the dragon curls to the right and shoots down the long side of the ancient city, still close to the ground, running parallel to the slope Merc and I first descended.

I start to worry how I'm going to get off him and whether he knows I'm even on his back or if he's about to throw me loose into a rock, existential payback for what I did to that skystalker—

At first, all I notice is the movement against the ancient marble wall, like with the ogres and their visual tricks.

Then come the dark shadows, streaming around the far corner of the ruined city. Spiders in a horde, chasing after—

*Lavante.*

It's Lavante who's running at breakneck speed, his golden coat a match for all those pale stones, his snow-white mane flying like a flag behind his neck, his tail streaking out in his wake—and the dragon is on a collision course with him.

The two are going head-to-head, the dragon so low now, I could jump free if we weren't going this fast. Lavante bobs to the side at the last moment, the dragon not altering his line as we pass my stallion—

Fire.

So much of it, my efforts at marshaling the stuff are put to shame: Great balls of flame curl forth, exploding out of the dragon's mouth.

Aimed at the spiders.

There's such shrieking as the immolation occurs that it's as if Anathos itself is being torn apart, and there's naught the attackers can do to defend or protect themselves. In fact, the fire spreads from one to another, carried on the gossamer bands of silk that have been released, a chain reaction.

And then there is a swoop upward, the dragon riding the air as if it were solid ground it was running over. Around we go, and I squeeze with my legs to hold on, ducking lower behind the great horned head, holding on to the ruby as if it's the very beating heart within my chest.

The dragon sails ahead of Lavante as the stallion makes the turn in front of the entry to the ruins, and the horse is neither stupid about the danger nor lost in his surroundings in spite of the oppressive, milky misting.

He gallops straight for the slope he and I descended.

And thus the dragon carries me into a graceful landing, bringing the bracing journey to an end in the long grass with a running set of feet . . . until he stops.

I leap off and back away, being careful not to meet his eyes. And as the cold-blooded master of the skies turns to me, I hope I haven't just fallen into another mess.

He doesn't eat me.

And in the moments that follow, I wish I could communicate. He seems to know, though. For he waits as Lavante thunders to me.

I whistle, high and loud, even though the horse is already coming my way, and as he throws out stiffened legs and skids to a halt in front of me, I jump into the saddle while the mud is still kicked up in the air. One arm traps the ruby to my chest, the other grabs the reins, but not to steer.

My stallion is not the type of horse that has to be directed.

He takes off again, faster than ever. Leaving the dragon—my dragon—behind.

We're nearly to the slope when I look back through the sea fog.

The green and purple beast is still on the ground and facing away from our escape, scrummed down to protect our racing departure. No spiders come, however. He's not killed the colony of them, but he took so many out, and his presence is more than enough to keep us safe as we bolt back for the slope, and for the Kingdom of the South's gate . . . beyond which there are many, many dangers, just of a different sort.

At least none of them have eight legs and spin a web. And right now? That's the best endorsement for any royal court there could be.

As we hit the incline, the mist swallows us even more, and I take one last look behind. I expect the dragon to have taken to the sky once more. He still has not. He remains our guardian, his wings outstretched, puffs of flames coming out his snout as if anybody needs a reminder of what he's able to do.

Then, like so much else, we're swallowed whole into the land cloud, and the moisture on my face is salty as my tears.

Destiny has always struck me as cold and hard. But here, in the strange landscape and foggy weather of this foreign land, my act of kindness and mercy, that I made with no thought or expectation of ever being repaid . . .

. . . was returned to me at the very moment, and in the very circumstances, when I most needed a miracle.

## *Eighty-Three*

# So Close, Yet So Far Away.

When Lavante and I ride back through the city with our guards, I hold the ruby high over my head. I do this not in triumph, but so there's a public record of my having returned the gem to the court. And they all know what it is. Regardless of class, the citizenry stares up in awe as the last of the daylight plays in the facets, and then they drop to their knees wherever they are, whatever they're doing. Their bowed heads and tented palms suggest many prayers of thanks are being offered, and I'm glad so many people see the jewel.

Mural behind the throne notwithstanding, it's crucial that I provide no out for the advisor to manipulate any of this.

And upon further reflection, I feel like there has been some thievery on the Queen's part. That setting in the palm fit too well, and I wonder if maybe she stole it after the city down there collapsed. Someone took it back, however—and I'm not sure whether I'm delivering the thing to its rightful owner or not.

For Merc, though, I'm willing to become a robber—and much worse.

The guards take me right to what turns out to be an entry into the court's great colonnade and audience hall, and I recognize the one who takes Lavante's reins. He's the kind man who escorted me into the ceremonial hall yesterday, the one who took pity on me as much as he could.

As I dismount, he's staring at me like he's seen a ghost. I suppose I must look like one with all the spiderwebs still clinging to my hair.

"Take care of him," I say. "He needs to be cooled down before he eats."

The guard bows, his eyes locked on the ruby that I still have over my head. "Yes, missus."

I don't wait for permission to walk forward, and quite honestly, if any one of the men with the muskets and swords had gotten in my way, I'd have pushed him down. I ride a wave of exhausted power up a set of steps, and find my way into the colonnade I went down before—whereupon I drop my numb arm because the crowd can't see me anymore. The guards come with me, but stay in my wake, their boots echoing on the marble smartly. I am leading them, not the other way around.

Maybe all this changes the instant I am not holding the jewel.

I'm not going to worry about that right now, and I know the way. I make the turn at the corner at the lineup of feminine statuary . . . and now I am before the entrance into the audience hall itself, with the two pairs of red-uniformed guards.

It's not a surprise that the *vizare* is standing there, waiting for me. And I can look at her full face now because as with everybody else, her eyes are on the ruby in my hand as if she cannot believe she's seeing the stone.

Coming to a stop in front of the woman, my voice is rough, but strong. "I will be the one to take this in."

She opens her mouth as if she's going to dispute the carrying of such a sacred object by someone of no pedigree or standing in her community. Something in the way I stand before her changes her mind.

The advisor nods sharply at the red-uniformed guards, and they open both sides of the doors for me.

I enter the hall and hobble down the center aisle toward the throne and the mural. Up above, in the oculus, the shape is in place behind the mesh, the profile present.

As I pass by the marble soldiers on their marble steeds, I think of the ruins of the other city . . . and then the settlement that was burned out. People should never confuse the habit of days with permanence. Everything can die, anything can be lost . . . nothing is forever.

When I get to the throne, I look up to the oculus. "I have brought you back the sacred stone."

I mount the dais by the shallow set of steps off to the side, and place the ruby on the seat. Then I take off my pack, remove the box from the folds, and go to flip the hooked latch. The thing resists, until I nearly split my nail once again, but I get the top up and balance the ancient wooden container on the throne's arm as I take out the crown of black crystals.

Holding it up over my head, I put volume into my words. "This is yours. I was sent here to give it to you. Wear this and know that you can defeat the Dark King—"

"Leave us."

The voice that filters down is deep for a woman's, exactly what I would expect of a warrior queen. I notice this first, and then the meaning of her words filters through my broken brain.

Exhaling, I slump and take a deep breath. But crown aside, I will not—I *cannot*—leave unless it's with Merc—

"Your Sublime Highness, surely you need me as witness."

I twist around. The advisor is bowing at the waist, her long, complicated braid slipping off her shoulder and falling free. As she looks to the oculus, her face is drawn in tight disapproval, but her tone hides this.

Almost.

In response, the voice from above carves a single syllable out of the tense air: "*Now.*"

The hidden door by the mural opens and a pair of guards loom on the far side of the threshold, the implication clear that if the order is not followed, it will be promptly enforced.

"As you wish." The *vizare* bows again, and then walks out, head held high, back straight as one of the columns.

And then the secret entry closes up, as if it's a mouth that's bitten her off the tip of a fork.

I look back up at the portal.

"You killed one of my officers," the Queen says in clipped tones. "That is an offense against my authority and property, punishable by death."

"He was in the process of raping me."

"Yes, so I gather. His pants were open." There is a pause. "The corpse was quite messy."

"I was being held in your torture chamber. I'm quite certain that particular 'mess' is not the first of its kind in that section of your dungeon."

"Those torture tables were my father's."

"He's still alive, then?" Before she can answer, I cut in, "Because they've been used recently."

There is another pause, and I wonder whether I'm dropping news, or have stepped over a line that will get me put on one of those slabs.

"Given the extenuating circumstances with my officer," the Queen continues, "I believe I shall forgive your offense. From one woman to another, I too would have killed him."

I close my eyes in relief. "Thank you."

There's another beat of silence. "You have been through quite a trial since last we met."

Pulling at some of the cobwebs in my hair, I shrug. "'Trial.' That's one word for it—"

"One might consider accusing you of possessing the ruby all along, and then trading it for the life of your husband only after you both found yourself in an untenable situation. But given your . . . obvious condition . . . it would be impossible to dispute that you fought for what was taken from me by a common thief a long time ago."

"Was it really yours? Or did you do the taking first."

"Watch yourself." And yet there's a subtle mirth threading her tone.

"Well." I shrug. "The thief did not survive very long after the extraction. Trust me."

"Oh? And how do you think he was dispatched unto his grave."

"I believe it was a very sticky and binding end, Your Majesty."

A laugh ripples down to me. "Good. I hope he suffered. Now tell me exactly what you did."

The story spools out, not unlike the webs, and when I finish recounting everything, from our stay at the Outpost, to the breaking through the Crystal Gate, to the wash of red light that saved Merc and me originally, there's a very long period of quiet.

"I knew it was there," the Queen remarks. "But that gate is not something I am prepared to breach with my own men. Yet you were able to triumph, by yourself."

"I have a good horse."

Another burst of laughter. "You do. And you came all this way just to bring me that crown?"

"Yes." I hold up the circlet of black crystals. "This is yours."

"According to whom."

"I . . . it was what I was told."

That voice becomes a strident demand. "By whom."

I clear my throat, and edit part of the story, just so there is a chance I'll be believed. "My mother. And before you ask who she is, I can't answer that. The man who's tolerated me my entire life while I lived under his stairs said that I was to take this to you because that is what my mother intended all along."

The silence is long, so long, I would think she's left if I couldn't see her profile on the other side of the mesh. "Do you know what you are holding there?"

"A crown of war and shadow?"

Another period of quiet. "It is not mine. I have my crown, and now that you've returned my ruby, what has been missing is no longer lost."

I lower my arms. Return the circlet to its padded seat.

"Please. Listen to me." I suddenly feel cold down to my bones, though certainly it's a mild temperature in here. "Demons are escaping the Fulcrum because it's been contaminated. I've seen the dark bands myself, and your own advisor said that you're finding dead cattle after dark on your lands. The same is true for the Outpost and my little village, which is far, far north from here. This means there are a lot of them, and they're spreading out."

I don't care whether or not she takes the crown. I just want this woman and her army to fight for us.

"Anathos needs you," I say urgently, an energy, a presence, entering me as if from somewhere far above me. Though the voice is my own, the words come from a different entity: "If we do not fight, the Dark King will return, and a new era will begin, the likes of which even history will find unbearable. Come with me to the north. Prosperitus has also resources with which to battle. If you join with them, we have a chance to—"

"No."

My breath catches. "What do you mean . . . no."

"The answer is no."

I exhale a curse. "You have to believe me—"

"I do believe you. I send out scouting missions regularly to the north and the east. They have reported to me about the black bands which have formed within the Fulcrum, and they have found the savaged bodies of farm animals and wanderers alike. My guards have even stated that they have seen demons, out in the shadows of the night."

"What do they look like," I breathe.

"Nothing one ever wants to meet without being fully armed and without a backup of at least three."

"Please . . . you have to come fight with us."

"Us? You are going out, into the night, and hunting those things?"

The sensation of free-falling, from when I let go of the statue's palm, returns to me. "I would rather die battling this enemy of Anathos, than be slaughtered in the Dark King's victory."

"The Dark King does not slaughter." That hard voice goes hoarse. "It is so much worse than that. You would be better served to avoid such a battlefield."

"I brought your ruby back, didn't I."

"Let not one successful mission blind you to the realities of war. Especially with an enemy such as the Dark King."

"Are you coming . . . or are you afraid."

"Watch your mouth," the Queen snaps. "Liberties are granted at my discretion, and much more easily revoked."

I let my head fall all the way back and stare at the ceiling. "*Please*. We need you. Anathos . . . needs you."

There is a shifting, the Queen turning to go. "My people here are my first priority. I will not leave them to battle for others. They have suffered enough these past years—"

"There won't be a Kingdom of the South if the Dark King gets out of the Fulcrum!"

"The mural has foretold the prosperity that is our due—"

"*It is wrong.*" I step behind the throne and wave my hand around at the painting. "You are a leader who will not look any in the face, I have your crown and these are naught but pictures! The time is nigh for war, and we *need* you—"

"Our business has concluded."

"Wait!" Abruptly, I think of Merc in that cell, and rearrange my priorities. "My husband. Please may I see him?"

"He is already in your room and resting."

I blink stupidly. "We have . . . a room?"

"You brought me back my ruby, so yes, I am inclined toward proper hospitality. I have also had him attended by my personal healer."

"You did this before I even returned?"

"If he was dead and you were triumphant, that would have put a damper on things," the Queen responds dryly.

"And if I didn't come back with the gem?"

"I would have killed you both and been done with it all."

The casual way she speaks of death reminds me of exactly who I'm speaking with: A warrior who makes calculations with all the emotion of a broadsword.

"You are the only one who can lead us," I say as tears spear into my eyes. "I beg of you, please take your crown."

Maybe if she touches it or puts it upon her head . . .

There is a silence that lasts so long, I wonder again if she hasn't left. But no, her profile is still visible.

"I did not think you were real," she says in a different tone. "After all these years, I thought . . . surely you were dead."

I squint up at the mesh, trying to see the face. "Who painted your mural? Who knew I was coming?"

When she doesn't answer me, I remember Mr. Lewis sitting me down and telling me a tale I did not believe, assigning me a quest I could not complete. And yet here I am, standing before the Queen Who Sees No One, with her crown, having survived so much.

And still I failed.

The Queen speaks up one last time. "You may stay here until morning. Then you will take that cursed crown, get onto your horses, and leave my Kingdom, never to return again. Know this as an exercise of my will and authority—if you or your husband ever set foot upon my lands after tomorrow morning, you will be shot where you stand and buried where your family shall never find the body."

"I have no family!" I shout up at the oculus.

I wait for a response. I wait to beg some more, yell some more. I wait . . . because this was the whole point of it all, and the part of me that hasn't given up yet will not give up now.

But she walks off, the shadow behind the mesh no more.

And with her departure goes any hope of accomplishing what I came for.

*Eighty-Four*

# A New Lodging.

This is *no* dungeon.

Though I am tired, aching, and still covered with cobwebs, though all I can think about is seeing Merc with my own eyes, though I am stinging with how I've let the whole continent of Anathos down, I cannot avoid noticing the grandeur and the luxury I'm being directed through. The ceiling that arches over me is leafed in gold, the carpet under my feet is royal blue, and the walls of this hall are covered in a flowered silk that is as lovely as any meadow I have stood in.

In fact, I recall these flowers. From the fields after the Kingdom's gate—

"This way, missus."

Once again, I'm guided by the guard who's so kind. Our paths keep crossing somehow, and now he's in front of me, narrating the turns; no more pointing over my shoulder. I suppose I could look at the fact that we keep meeting as some kind of fate. I don't. I think it's an indication that the warrior queen doesn't have much of an army at her disposal anymore—and the further I mull that over, the greater my sense of futility becomes.

Stuck in my head, I float along this fancy corridor, and not in a good way—and the muffled sounds of music and laughter in the distance don't help with the disorientation. I gather that word has spread throughout the Kingdom about the sacred ruby's return, and I want to tell them to stop. The future is not bright, the reprieve of strife is only temporary, and it's all going to get so much worse for everybody.

As I pass by another window that looks out onto a courtyard, there are torches dotting and dashing in the darkness as those holding them spin and gyrate in glee, like fireflies in the summer. I worry this will call the demons to the castle, and see blood spilled all along the colonnade of white marble—

I almost walk into a floor vase full of flowers. As I jump back, I blurt, "How lovely."

Because . . . well, they are.

My guard glances back. "The Queen plants them. In memory of her mother."

"I am sorry for her loss." Continuing on, I think of the torture racks. "And . . . what of her father?"

"That I do not know, missus. But those fields of flowers are tended even when our crops fail."

"How . . ." Sad. On so many levels. "She must have loved her mother very much."

A familiar longing pierces my heart—

"Here, missus." The guard stops in front of a door. "Your husband awaits. Food has been delivered. You will see a bellpull should either of you require aught."

"Thank you."

My gratitude for him is real, yet I'm already forgetting his existence as I reach for the golden knob myself and open the door—

"Merc!"

Though I am a mess and covered with webs and limping, I launch myself across the golden room, over to the grand, golden bed on which Merc lies.

"Sorrel—"

He tries to sit up and collapses back against the satin pillows with a groan, but he is alive and I am alive, and really does anything else matter—

Does he pull me forward? Do I bend down? All I know is that our lips meet and his are warm against my own, warm and vital. Just as he is.

When we part for breath, he frowns, his black and white eyes traveling around my face and hair. "What happened to you, why are you covered in—"

He stops and tries to sit up again. After he's finished cursing from the pain, he barks, "You did *not* go back there to the ruins. Dearest fates, are you mad, woman?"

With a tired smile, I trace his face with my fingertips. "All that matters is that we are here, together."

"*Why.* What did you do there—"

"It matters not."

As he does some more cursing, I'm relieved he has the strength to glower and get worked up. He's dressed in black silk, the high-collared shirt up to the base of his throat, his legs covered in loose pants of the same flowing fabric. His hair is damp and smells of cedar and spice, and his braids are gone. All in all, he looks better than he ever has, and also worse: He's clearly as worn out as I feel.

"Are you well enough to travel?" I ask grimly as I back off and remove the webby cloak.

"I don't mind being comfortable at the moment."

"But can you."

Merc's brow rises, in that familiar way, and it feels as though it's been years since I have seen him. As my eyes prick with tears, I am so very, very tired.

"Yes." He goes to put his hands behind his head and grimaces. "Now tell me what's happened. What have you done to land us here? And mind you, I am *not* bothered by the improvements in our accommodations."

Haltingly at first, and then with increasing composure, I explain everything to him. Well, almost everything. I leave out what I did in that cell to the Queen's officer as well as the issue with the crown and the Queen and the demons. As far as Merc knows, it was only about bartering our freedom with that ruby.

I just don't have the energy to explain the rest, especially as I feel like this whole journey was a waste of time, nothing but mortal risks and failure.

"So we have to leave tomorrow morning," I conclude.

"Or we shall be shot."

Getting up from the bed, I nod grimly as I pace around, touching the heavy satin draping, the golden lamps that have blown-glass shades, the oil paintings of landscapes around the city. It's hard to know exactly when I make the decision, but I suppose, like so many of the choices I've come to along the way, what may appear to be quick is actually the result of much brooding under the surface of my conscious thoughts.

I turn to the bed and stare at him. "I must go to Prosperitus. Will you . . . come with me."

There is no hesitation: "I will."

"Why," I whisper, even as I am relieved.

Merc tilts his head, the lamplight gleaming in his black hair. "Why what?"

I answer him with a question I've wanted to know the answer to for a while: "When you left the Outpost, were you really coming here?"

"It's where I ended up, is it not." He smiles a little as he indicates himself atop the bed. Then he rolls those black and white eyes of his. "Are we fishing again, then? Fine. I thought perhaps you might need some help along the way. Note that I said 'need' not 'want.'"

"But why are you doing this for me," I say as I shake my head in wonder.

"I told you before." He grows serious. "After you helped birth that bairn, and then took care of the maid at the lodging house . . . I have decided that the world is very much better with you in it, Sorrel. I'm not much of a man for callings, and there are many things I have done that were I of a better soul I would undo, yet protecting you seems like the appropriate endeavor. At least at this point in time. So yes, I will go with you unto Prosperitus."

"Thank you."

"You're welcome." His eyes travel down me. "And while we're going on about confessions, I'll tell you frankly that the next time I see a spider, I'm going to crush him into oblivion with my boot."

We both laugh, and then his eyelids lower—and I know that he's no longer thinking about travel or fishing or eight-legged bugs . . . and I have a renewed sense of energy. Except when I go to take a step forward, I see a web on my slipper and curse in disgust.

Merc chuckles softly. "Just so we're clear, I'd take you any way you come, woman. But the water closet you'll be looking for is right back there. I took advantage of it myself in the hopes you'd come and find me in this big bed—and look, it worked. That basin is magic."

"Can we take it with us then," I mutter.

"Only if we put Snooze in it to make better time."

I'm smiling as I go over and kiss him. "I won't be long."

His face grows grim. "Don't rush. I do believe you have earned it."

I press another lingering kiss to his mouth, then I cross the beautiful carpet. As I pass by a dresser made from exotic wood, and check out the lineup of porcelain figures and silver brushes on its top, the luxury is such that never have I even imagined such things.

Mare likely lived like this at one point, I think as I disappear behind an ornate door.

After I shut myself in, I remember the coins I left behind in the ruins, and wish I could have retrieved them. Getting out with someone else's priceless ruby was the plan, but as this quest seems to always demand, I have to leave a piece of me behind.

Refocusing, I look around at the facilities. They're even more sophisticated than what we had back at the lodging house at the Outpost, and as I set the tub's water to running, I'm astonished to find I can titrate the hot with the cold. While the level rises, I remove my clothes, and when I step in and sink into the warm pool—

I start to weep.

It's impossible to define the precise emotions, the complex mix of gratitude and pain too much for me to understand—or control. Covering my face with my hands, I try to muffle the sounds as flashbacks from the goddess's sculpture twist my head and memories of the officer in the cell freeze my bones—

"Sorrel."

At my name, I drop my palms. Merc is kneeling by the tub, his beautiful black and white eyes searching my own.

"It's all right now," he says softly. "Whatever you see in your mind, that's the past. You've lived through it. You must let it go."

He brings a soft cloth into the warm water, and then he wipes my face gently. "Remember what I told you. Always forward . . . never back."

"Sometimes I can't help it." I wipe my eyes and wonder if they'll ever stop with the leaking. "The images come and I'm back where I was—and it's never good."

"You will train your thoughts away from all that just as you'd learn any other skill. With practice."

I reach out and take his hand. "Will you tell me something you run from?"

Merc strokes my face, and lingers with his thumb brushing my lips. Then he looks away with a defeat that is wholly inconsistent with all that I know of him.

"I don't run from what ails me," he says in a low voice. "Wherever I go . . . there I am."

*Eighty-Five*

# Reunion.

Merc stays beside me while I have my bath, stroking the warm, dripping cloth over my hair, over my freckled shoulders, over my arms, and eventually, my tears ease. With the crying passed, I lean against the side of the basin, and rest my cheek on the curved lip. On the inside, I continue to weep, but I keep that to myself.

I just feel so powerless.

"Would you like me to wash your hair?" he asks me.

When I nod with gratitude, he retrieves a bar of fragrant soap from a small dish. It's what he smells of, and he puts aside the cloth and lathers up his hands.

"Tip back for me," he says. "So that all is wet."

I'm grateful for the job, and focus my thoughts on getting my head all the way under the water. As the level goes over my face, I hold my breath and look up through the wavy pool of warmth at the black-haired man who looms over me.

If I saw the shape of him like this and did not know him, I'd swear he'd been sent to kill me. Instead, I have a sense of security and safety. He's already proven all that he's willing to do for me.

And I've done the same for him.

Thus we have fought for this peaceable moment right here, our reward this short time of communion which is so much more precious to me than any kind of material payment.

When I emerge from the depths, I come up chin-first, my breasts breaching the surface thereafter. His eyes go to them, and the stark hunger in his scarred face shifts the energy in my body away from the strange despair that's gripped me . . . toward something that is so much more preferable.

"Just look at you," he says in low voice. "Woman . . . you are a beauty in any light."

As I flush, I sit forward and brace my hands under my seat to hold myself as very nearly float. There's a fragrant explosion as he passes his palm over my hair a couple of times and then he's massaging the soap into my scalp and down the lengths. Suds form and propagate around me, tickling my nipples as they play hide-and-seek with Merc's hot stare.

"So we leave on the morrow and head north," he says.

It's hard for me to connect to his words when his voice has gone to that deep, low place that thrills me. But the translation filters through all the sexual charge.

"Ah, yes." I clear my throat. "Please."

"And when we get to Prosperitus, what then?"

"I shall have to speak with the King."

Merc's laughter is a balm to my nerves. "Good thing you ask for nothing much at all, woman."

"Well, I do believe in starting modestly." As our banter evaporates in the warm, humid air, I exhale with exhaustion. "If I can get to a Queen who refuses all audiences, surely I can find my way to a ruler who actually rules."

"And what would you be speaking to him about?" When I don't immediately answer, Merc says, "Would it be the demons, then, yes?"

"Yes."

"So that's why we came to the warrior Kingdom. You want to protect that village of fools who'd sooner have killed you from something that stalks them in the dark. And now that you're here, you see that there's only shadows of the past in this castle, and no one who's willing to help."

"Something like that."

"Fair enough." He nods down at the water. "Another dip then, shall we."

I indulge his command, dropping below the surface once more. When I reappear, he fills a separate bowl with clear water from the tap and rinses the soap out at the crown of my head over and over again—and after he puts the porcelain aside, he gathers my hair up and twists it into a knot on the top of my head.

"I think we can get to Prosperitus in a day." He sits back a bit. "Provided we leave early."

"Indeed?"

"Yes. All of our things were delivered by a very nice servant, and after I checked to make sure the contents of my pack were in hand, I consulted the map for want of anything else to look at. There's a northerly route that's far enough inland it avoids that mountain range we fought through altogether.

It does cut close to the Fulcrum, but it'll get us to well past your village in the daylight—not that I am suggesting we stop there, mind you."

"Best we do not, yes." I look at the suds that swirl about me on the surface of the warm water, obscuring and revealing my body by turns. "And if we can arrive at Prosperitus by nightfall that is . . . for the better."

But fates, why do I think the King will see me? A woman traveler, with nothing to offer him?

Maybe Julion can help me, though.

"Then we leave at sunrise," Merc says. "I was told to ring the bell if I needed anything and I'll have our horses brought around. Wherever . . . around is."

"At sunrise, yes."

His smile tilts one half of his mouth up. And yet his eyes begin to glow with a very different intent than that of conversation.

"Shall we do the rest of you then?" he asks huskily.

I can only nod as I suddenly don't trust my voice.

He comes back with the soft cloth and he soaps it up, before stroking the sudsy square down my back, my shoulders, my arms. And then he attends to my throat . . . and goes lower. At the first brush over my breast, I moan his name.

This is only the beginning. Soon, he is progressing even farther down.

As I split my thighs for him, I ease back until the tub catches me in a cradle. Merc is indeed very thorough, and soon the cloth is replaced by his hand, his fingers. The next thing I know, he rears up over the tub and we kiss until we're both breathless—

The pleasure peaks for me and I jerk, splashing water out onto the floor and getting him wet. But there's no stopping the release. I cling to him, to his mouth, his strong shoulders, his hand as my thighs clap together. And just before the energy starts to fade, I pop my eyes open and look to the ceiling.

The light show doesn't repeat, and I know, though I cannot say how I know, that once expressed, it doesn't come again.

A threshold being crossed. A journey made, and completed. And after it . . . a change in me that is permanent.

Merc eases back. "To the bed."

"Yes . . ."

With strong, gentle hands, he helps me from the tub, guiding me up and over the rim. As I step out, I am naked before him and suddenly shy. For all the intimacy we've shared, it's another thing to be standing like this—

"Sorrel . . ."

My name leaving his lips is a caress over all my flesh at once, and I'm shocked when he kneels before me. Running his hands up over my legs, he brushes his lips on my belly, on my hip, on my thigh. Gently, he urges my knees apart—and presses his mouth to the top of my sex.

I gasp and bend down. But not to stop him.

Merc goes lower, to my foot, and he puts my leg up so that my heel rests against the edge of the tub.

Then he leads with his mouth. And speaks the language of love to the very core of me. I'm shocked by the intimacy, and yet it seems so natural, especially as the pleasure peaks for me, the feel of his soft, wet mouth on my soft, wet flesh a match made in ecstasy.

The next thing I know, my knees buckle, and he catches me, stretching me out on the soft rug that covers the marble floor, joining me as he arches over my naked body. After I undo the buttons of his satin tunic, I pause at the bandage that has been applied to part of his chest.

"Are you well enough," I ask roughly.

"It'll take more than that to kill me. Much, much more."

Trying to stay in the moment, I push my unease away and slide my hands up his back—

I stop as I get to a pattern of scars that mar his skin, and squeeze my eyes closed with piercing empathy. "Oh, Merc."

"Do not think about it."

"Who hurt you," I whisper as I stare up into his eyes.

His expression darkens, but the anger is not directed to me. "It was a long time ago."

Except it's still with him, and not just in his flesh. My mind reels with all kinds of scenarios . . . betrayals, ambushes, attacks. Is this why he lives the life he does? Rootlessly going from aggression to aggression?

"Do you still fight them," I ask. "Whoever it was."

Those black and white eyes trace my face, and he strokes a strand of hair from my cheek. In a grim voice, he answers, "Every moment of every day and each night. Especially now."

"I'm so sorry—"

"No more talking. We have this moment, let us not waste it."

When he brings his lips down to my own, I move my hands to other places. And then his mouth, that talented mouth, is on my neck, on my collarbone, heading lower to my breasts. He is slow and deliberate with the way he pleasures me, his hands stroking my thighs and my hips, my core once again.

Our bodies move together, in perfect harmony, the satin pants he still has on offering no barrier at all, but rather an enticing slide to his hard angles. I'm the one who pulls down the waistband, and as I wrap my hand around his shaft, it's like holding a brand.

"I need you," he groans, coming up to my mouth again.

I guide him to me, and this time, the penetration is slow and easy. Smooth and hot. Deep and full.

He rides me with care, and I arch into him—just managing to catch my hands before they run up his back again. I agree with him. We have such a short time, and I can't waste it on things that are painful. So I hold on to his hips instead, and suddenly, he's moving faster and faster. A crest of pleasure comes for me anew, and then he joins me in the release, his body locking into mine as his sex kicks inside me, filling me up.

"Sorrel . . ." he says in a voice that cracks with emotion.

As he finally comes to rest, I wrap my arms around as much of him as I can reach, and smile at the ceiling far above us. There are ways of telling someone you love them without speaking the actual words.

And the way my name left his mouth just now is one of them.

*Part Five*

# The Start of the War of All Souls

## *Eighty-Six*

# Hide.

Just as the sun peeks over the eastern horizon, Merc and I are checking the tack on the horses. We're outside the royal stables, attended to by a couple of guards and some uniformed footmen. In spite of the hour, Merc and I are ready to go, and so are our horses. The others are a different story. Given their half-mast eyes and the wafts of mead that emanate from their very pores, the celebrations continued well into the evening.

Putting my hand on Lavante's silken flank, I walk around to his butt and sweep down to check his back shoes, remembering what Emma warned me. Both seem fine. Then again, if he only throws one when he's bored? This stallion hasn't had a moment's peace unless he was sleeping.

"Oh, I forgot," Merc says as he swings his pack off the back of his saddle. "I have something for you—"

One of the guards weaves on his feet, goes elbow over teakettle, and lands in a planter. His comrades, and the stable hands, immediately attend to him, and Merc shakes his head as he pulls something out.

"This is yours, isn't it?"

In his callused palm . . . is a red velvet bag I never expected to see again.

My breath catches and all I can do is stare. Mare's coins. "Where . . . did you find it?"

"I saw it on the ground back at the ruins, just as I was bolting out of there. It was so out of place, and right where you and the stallion were." He jogs the satchel, the muffled chiming that rises up sweet to my ears. "Heavy. Sounds of only one thing."

"Thank you." I take the weight and hold it close, closing my eyes. "Thank you so much."

He settles his pack back on Snooze. "I don't know what kind of coins are in there, but going by the weight? I'd say that's a fortune."

Glancing up at him, I wonder if he's thinking of payments and that I hid wealth from him at the start of all this. There's no bitterness on his face, no tension in his body, though.

"This was . . . a gift from a very dear friend. Upon her death."

"Then she must have loved you very truly." As a second guard faints, Merc steps around his horse—who is, actually, snoozing even with all the activity around him—and goes over to help with a curse. "Oh, for fate's sake, man. You're in uniform. Pull it together."

Turning in to Lavante's flank, I open the neck of the satchel and pour a couple of the coins into my palm. They gleam in the dawn light, as if bits of the sun have fallen from the sky. I remember Mare, and wonder what she would think of me now.

Only parts of my evolution would she approve of.

I'm putting the coins back when I stop and frown. Picking one up, I angle it this way and that, an eerie feeling coming over me.

"Julion . . ." I breathe with shock.

I'm staring at his face on the coin. It's the strike marking that's different from all the others, the one that features the unbearded young man . . .

He was no mere knight of the court. He is heir to the throne.

Yes, I think to myself. We go to Prosperitus.

I couldn't coerce the warrior queen with the crown, but maybe I can leverage a different throne if I do what its prince requested of me.

"So are we ready, then?" Merc asks.

I glance up, and have to shake myself back into focus. "Ah . . . yes, yes, we are."

Closing the tie, I put the velvet bag back in the pocket of Julion's jodhpurs—which have been laundered and pressed by the royal attendants and are just like new. They even cleaned the turban, although I left it behind.

Merc and I both saddle up, and then the guards—minus the two who are sitting on the ground with their heads cradled in their hands—walk us over to an exit in the back of the royal castle's protective wall. On the approach, as our horse's hooves clip-clop over the stone aisle, I think of the great gate, the one that opened up to mist and the ruins.

This one up ahead would be considered towering, if I didn't have the former for comparison.

As the oak panels open, a dew-laden meadow is revealed on the far side, the dawn's delicate, golden light drenching flowers and fruit trees alike. All around, birds chatter sweetly on branches and flit from post to post in flashes of blue and red and yellow, blooms in the air itself. Taking a deep breath, I'm reminded that the scent of nature feeds the soul, and I miss my herbs and potions.

Can I call myself a healer anymore? Or did my actions in the torture dungeon taint what I always thought was my calling to the point where I am like the Fulcrum, contaminated and no longer serving a higher purpose?

"You'll be wanting to just follow the road—" The guard's instructions are cut off by a burp that is obviously sour in nature given his grimace. "That would be, go north and north anew. Few travel this way, so you should be fine, but keep sharp."

Merc inclines his head. "I will."

"Thank you," I say to the man. "And thank you for caring for our—"

All at once, the guards remove their hats, place them over their hearts, and bow low to me. As they speak in a quiet rush of words I don't understand, I think they're praying for our safe travels. Certainly as they straighten, I can feel their warm regard, even though I don't risk meeting any of the eyes that rise up to me with open reverence.

As soon as we are outside the wall, the gate is closed and I can hear the echoing of a sturdy bolt as it's thrown. I glance over my shoulder. Though this is the rear entry to the Kingdom, it is still grander than any I have seen, but the luxury falls away quickly as we start forward.

So many abandoned homes.

Beyond the lee of the great court and all of its acres of protected, tended, marbled finery, out here to the north and the west, there's nothing but vacant property and overgrown fields. It may be because everyone is crammed into safety inside the palace walls, but you couldn't fit this populace into that space.

No, this is a decline in citizenry.

And the guard who spoke was right. The carriage lane we're on is not well tended at all, a reminder that the Kingdom isn't looking or caring for visitors in any fashion: Weeds grow up on the shoulders, choking out a series of marble plaques that bear the profile of the Queen, and the median in the center has a cultivation of curly green grass and tiny blue flowers. The tree line that stands in sentry on both sides is sloppy with suckers invading what was certainly once a maintained allée, and there are rusted-out pieces of farming machinery decaying here and there.

And then we're reminded of just how bad things are.

As we round a broad turn, Lavante's leisurely trot gets choppy, and he tosses his head, his nostrils flaring and then releasing on a worried whinny. Snooze likewise shies away—

The dead cow is lying on its back in the center of the lane, its hooves lax, its belly exposed. Between one blink and the next, I see the officer I killed in a slump against the corner of the cell, his abdomen as open as a window in the summer.

As I cover a choking sound with my hand, Merc curses. "We deviate."

I have no idea what he's talking about, but then he directs his horse into the ground cover along the road's shoulder. Lavante is more than happy to avoid the carcass, and he bounces through the undergrowth as I try not to dwell on the desecration.

And then there's another one seven lengths farther up. This time, without a head as well with that stomach.

"We must hurry," I hear myself say.

And hurry we do.

The route we take is over flat land, with plenty of fresh streams to keep the horses and us properly watered. Though the sky overhead is blue and dotted with fair-weather clouds, the wind only the kind that keeps a rider in the sunshine comfortable and cool, I can feel a storm coming, every instinct in my body calling for me to take shelter and hunker down.

As noontime arrives, we are no longer in the Kingdom of the South, but I have no idea what territory we've entered. Merc checks his useless map and I confirm our trajectory with the compass, and that's all we know because the former offers no name and the latter doesn't speak. Whoever took care of the horses also packed us some food, so we stop briefly to eat and relieve ourselves. Then we take another pause at a river to water everybody, and we continue going. The road takes us over bridges that are ancient, and we pass by settlements that haven't been lived in for eons. There are also so many fields that used to be tended, but have since reverted back to forestland, only the low stone walls indicating property lines left.

And still we press on, neither of us saying much. Merc, because he is hyperaware, his broadsword in his hand, his black and white gaze scanning everything we go by in search of threats. Me, because the sense that I'm heading into something on the horizon consumes my every heartbeat.

Going by the angle of the sun, I'm guessing it's around three in the afternoon when I first hear the roar off in the distance. I've noticed that any mountains are strictly to our east and mind what Merc said about where this route takes us.

Some twenty lengths later, the forest to our left thins out, and not because some other kind of topography takes the place of the trees.

Everything is dying. The leaves on the branches have shriveled up and dropped off—and not on account of any change in season. Though fall is certainly coming as we continue north, and temperatures are dropping, it's not enough to kill what grows. No, these leaves haven't gone through their normal cycle. They're blackened and deformed as they lay fallen on the ground, their crumpled twists mixing with strips of bark that have peeled off due to blight as well. Even the root systems are affected, the arboreal legs mangled and protruding from the dirt.

Which is riddled with black contamination.

That's when I see it, off in the distance . . . the Fulcrum.

All of us stop, Merc, myself, and both of the horses.

The containment is nearly all black now, and the strange flakes that float off from its churning circumference swirl around as evil snow.

Beneath my saddle, Lavante churns at the ground with his hooves as if he's looking for permission to bolt.

"We must keep going," Merc says grimly.

And I agree, but I find myself hypnotized by the slowly turning mystery—

"Sorrel? What ails you?"

"Nothing. I just—" A tickle in my throat prevents me from going any further.

Putting my hand to my mouth, I taste grit and spit out black grains of sand—and that's when it happens. The nightmare that's been haunting me finally reveals itself.

Just as before, a face comes forward, pushing out of the Fulcrum's swirling sand, the features at once completely foreign—and terrifyingly familiar: They're not only what I know I have seen in my tortured sleep . . . they're something I have stood in front of.

It's the statue.

From outside the ruins. The man whose face was turned to the beautiful woman. The man who looked at her with possession.

"What is it, Sorrel?"

"Do you see that," I moan helplessly.

"See what?"

And that's when my inner village wall, the one that's protected me all these years, the one that's been crumbling and disintegrating with increasing decay, falls to the ground. Except instead of keeping things from getting at my mind and my marrow, it releases everything it's been holding in.

I know *this* man. In my soul, I recognize who he is, and who he is to me. Though my conscious thoughts reject the shattering conclusion, my soul cannot deny it—

*Hide.*

The step-by-step journey from who I thought I was to who I have always truly been is suddenly completed. It started with the story of my birth, the one that I repeated as if it was programmed into me, the lie that I told others and believed myself . . . and continued with my ability to know and dance with death . . . and kept going with Mr. Lewis's revelation . . . and then kindled further and further with the compass, the crown, my first sexual experience with Merc, and finally with the fire and the trees parting . . .

As well as the way I wanted the cook dead and how I killed that officer.

With my vengeance.

It was in the visions that I saw with such clarity as I looked down the lane of the ruins.

It was especially in the nightmares that have stalked my sleep.

It has been with me all along, driving my urgent need to keep my face covered . . . so that those around me, who were born and matured and died in the normal course, wouldn't notice that there was an immortal in their midst, stashed in the pub of their little village, overseen by generations of the same family until the night came when fate was a tide that could be dammed up no longer.

And here and now, the beast of truth within me is released, no more mental wall to hold it in. With horror, I realize that I've had it wrong all along.

*Hide.*

That voice, which I have always minded, to the point where for years and years I have covered my face and kept to myself in spite of my loneliness, wasn't warning me about other people.

It was keeping me away from *him*, from this face that emerges out of the black sand, the contamination.

That voice is not mine. It is my mother, the Savior, who has spoken to me.

And she's commanding me to stay away from he who she imprisoned within the Fulcrum she created . . . from the other half of me, the half that has always simmered below my surface, powerful, vengeful, and angry.

The Dark King.

The source of all evil, the commander of demons, the scourge who seeks to be free, once again.

Who we must battle to survive.

My . . . *father.*

*Eighty-Seven*

# The Beginning and the End, at Once.

The rest of the trip is a blur. I do what I can to respond to Merc in a way that's appropriate, but he's not stupid. He knows I'm somewhere far off from him, even as I travel in his wake. Except I cannot speak any of this to him. The implications are too epic and awful, and maybe he wouldn't believe me.

I know I didn't. I know I still try to mount pathetic, hedging excuses.

But now I know the why of me, and having seen the truth, who I am cannot be buried in my mind once more.

So caught up in my own head am I that I fail to notice that the landscape is becoming familiar, that we're entering the trees I grew up with, and passing by the plants I foraged for, and crossing the streams I visited back when only my daily life was complicated, not all of Anathos and my legacy, too.

What finally brings me back and grounds me in the present, as the afternoon light tilts well toward the horizon, is the smell of burning wood.

It's subtle at first, but gathers increasing saturation, until the insides of my nostrils tingle and I sneeze. Through my relentless, crushing introspection, a warning registers, but it's not before I feel wrapped in the stench that I realize there's only one thing that could be causing this.

I glance around in a frantic twist, and recognize our precise location.

"Stay sharp," Merc mutters. "There's something wrong—"

And that's when the trees part and the horror is presented.

My village has been burned to the ground.

I release a primal scream and heel Lavante forward, as if I could do anything, as if it weren't far, far too late.

Plumes of gray and black smoke rise out of the protective wall, as if the whole of it is a chimney. The bridge is down, but even the great planks of that crossover have been cindered, and indeed, dead, bloated *balas*, boiled by the heat, float on the fetid surface of the moat, which is much, much lower than it has ever been.

A stew cooked down by an unholy stove.

Lavante balks at my attempt to get him to go across the bridge, so the next thing I know, I'm dismounting and leaving him there, without regard to whether he'll run off or where Merc is. I stumble down the planks, jumping from solid part to solid, while keeping my eyes on what's ahead.

Ashes. Ruins. Cinders still smoking.

Bodies.

As I break out into the village proper, I pass the two large *SP* symbols that have been painted in blood on either side of the archway, and skid to a halt in front of the Gauntlet. The pub and lodging house is a burned-out shell, and still I step into the charred remains, reconstructing out of the destruction what once was, overlaying the memories of the bar and its crabby tender, and the working girls, and Mr. Lewis holding court at his table up by the door.

I even remember how it stood just as I left, the chairs upturned as I was searched for, Mr. Lewis sitting with a satchel and a box, untouched ale at his elbow and a lantern in front of his drawn, pudgy face.

I cover my mouth to keep from screaming, to keep the stench out, to deny everything that I'm stepping over, the tankards and plates, the silverware and nails, all that remain, but for the biggest of the support beams and the heart of the stairs.

Even though it makes no sense, I shuffle forward, tripping and falling, catching myself until my palms are black from ashes, until I get to where my little home was. Or about where it was. Some of the second floor has fallen down on the first, so I can't really get close for the still-smoking ruination.

Tears are flowing down my face, for I know my connection to all of this now—and it's not as a banished member of this village I grew up in.

My father is coming to find me. That's why the demons are stalking the night. He's looking for me.

It seems somehow fitting that this truth resonates as I come to the stairwell that's collapsed down into a tangle so dense, it couldn't completely burn, but certainly managed to destroy all of my personal effects. Not that any of that matters.

I have to keep going.

Spilling back out into the lane, like one of the drunks that are no more, I continue on to Mare's. The old shoemaker's shop is utterly disintegrated, and I think of the blankets I stole from the public house for her, and the tea I made her to ease her pains, and how she hated when I made a fuss over her, and loved every moment I spent in her company.

When did this happen, I wonder as I put my hand out and feel the heat still emanating from a metal hinge.

Last night. It happened . . . last night.

As I continue on, I realize I'm retracing the steps I took the evening I tried to run from the farrier, the evening Merc arrived, and everything started—

"The girls!"

Racing down the lane, I spill out into the village square. The farrier's shop is destroyed, nothing left except for his forge—

"His death . . ." I whisper.

When I looked into his eyes, and saw him aflamed, in the throes of his final miseries, I got it wrong. I wasn't seeing an accident at his work. I was seeing . . . *this*.

He was burned, like all the villagers were, good and bad.

What about those girls, I think desperately. Is there any chance the eldest one, who took care of the others, got them out? Had the way she kept them from their father all those years helped her survive when the purifiers came?

I picture those children cowering in that filthy kitchen, with all those chicken bones on the table.

I keep going, although really, what for. The marketplace is obliterated, the stalls the vendors would cycle through nothing but ash, the central gazebo where the mayor would make his pompous announcements just a partial roof and some singed steps.

The *SP* symbols have been painted on the lane, on what's left of the shops, on those few row houses which have partially survived—

The sound of hoof falls precedes Merc's arrival in the village square, and he's as grim as I've ever seen him as he strides over to me, leading both horses along.

Before I think about it, I run to him and he captures me against him, holding me tight.

"I am sorry," he says into my hair.

I pull back. "It came from Prosperitus. Only the royal court there has enough manpower to do . . . this."

Breaking away, I pace around, seeing only details I cannot abide: Part of a burned hand clawing its way out of a cluster of blackened boards, the skeleton of a young child held by the remains of a parent, someone's shoes kicked off, perhaps as they tried to run from palace soldiers riding fast horses with sharp swords and torches over their shoulders.

"They would have killed the men first," I say hoarsely. "And then moved to the women and children."

I cover my eyes. Then rub them. Neither helps get the images out of my mind.

"And then they burned it all to the ground . . . and left the symbols of salvation drawn in the blood of innocents."

There's great evil in the Fulcrum. But at least one can fight that front and center.

Pernicious superstition is a beast made of shadows and smoke.

"They might have lived." I look at Merc. "If we had fought the Dark King last night, they might have lived—"

"Sorrel—"

"—and they could have stayed here. They could have lived their lives with their children, in their homes, behind the wall—"

*"Sorrel."*

The way he says my name gets through to me and I wheel around. As I look at him, I know that I'm receiving another lifelong memory of the man: The way he stands there, the reins of the horses in one hand, that broadsword handle peeking over his shoulder, his boots planted like certainly, if *he* had been here, the attack would have gone down differently . . . is something I will never forget.

At least I'm no longer worried he will leave me. We're in this together.

Whatever it may be.

Whatever may come.

## *Eighty-Eight*

# Whereupon Losses Are Tallied.

"You cannot go to Prosperitus."

As Merc speaks, I close my eyes and still see everything that's around us, all the death and destruction. Like my lids are nothing but windowpanes.

"I know," I whisper. "After they did this, how can I fight alongside them. But what choice do I have—"

"You cannot fight, Sorrel."

Frowning, I wipe my tears and straighten my spine. "After everything we have been through, how can you say that."

"The Dark King is inescapable." He glances around. "Look at the power he has. It's all around you now, and not just about the demons. He infects people . . . takes their souls through the fear and hatred and vengeance he spawns. You need to leave, and I can help you. We can find a place where you'll be safe, away from all this."

*Hide.*

I see the face emerging from the Fulcrum, looking at me . . . and I'm chilled to the soul. I was terrified by the implications, but in truth, the entity wasn't threatening toward me.

No, my father is beckoning me.

He's inviting me to join him.

Merc's voice weaves in between my thoughts: "Do not even attempt a fight. He'll get into your brain, and he'll see your deepest fears and your deepest desires. Your safety is in disappearing. You *have* to trust me."

"It's not about trust, Merc." I motion to a burned skeleton a mere length away. "You're right. The Dark King's demons didn't do this, but his presence caused everything that happened here—people losing their humanity because of their fear of him, doing horrible things out of superstition."

I go over to those charred remains of someone I undoubtedly knew and want to weep all over again. "And that's before he gets free and claims us all. If we don't fight, we lose not just our lands, not just even ourselves . . . we lose every future generation and all their freedom, too. The only thing to do is defend Anathos—and if the great warrior queen won't join us, then we do it without her."

"So that's why you went to the Kingdom of the South."

"For all the good it did." I look to the sky and see only the smoke that rises from everything I once knew. Well, that . . . and that fates-forsaken star. "And now Prosperitus attacks my own village. If I hadn't wasted that effort going down there, maybe I could have stopped this."

"No," he says with finality. "You'd have been part of it. You would have been claimed, too."

Helplessly, I cling to his eyes and cannot speak what I know of my truth. Besides, once again, it all seems too unbelievable.

"If we go now," I counter, "Prosperitus is but a three-hour ride. We can get there before dark."

And courtesy of Mare's coins, I know that Julion is not just any aristocrat—and I have something he wants. Desperately.

Maybe the hard things he doesn't want to do without his true love are about the Dark King and the army of demons.

Merc shakes his head. "I don't know what you hope to accomplish there."

"The prince, Julion, he asked a favor of me, back in that wooded glen. Remember?"

"You want to go to him even if you think he did this?"

"But maybe it was by townspeople from the city. Maybe this wasn't a royal decree—"

"You're one of these villagers. You go to that royal court and say you're from here, and they'll have to kill you."

"They don't know who I am—"

"That golden knight does. He got you out of the goddamn moat as you were escaping a mob that was already after you. Besides . . ." Merc lowers his voice. "You say the nobleman came to you for a favor? What's a member of a royal court doing showing up to a village this far out of his city, looking for a 'favor' from a civilian woman. Tell me what I'm missing here."

I open my mouth. Close it.

After a moment, he says, "I saw what you did with the fire, Sorrel. When we were chased out of those passes by those ogres. And before that, I was there when you met that maid for the first time—and then asked me to kill the cook who was beating her. That compass? That's not right, what happens when that instrument sits in your palm. I took it out myself when you were sleeping. It won't even open for me."

His black and white eyes travel around the smoldering ruination of my village. Then return to my own gaze. "I meant what I said. This world is better with you in it and I can keep you safe. But we need to get up north, way up north. Where I can keep you hidden."

As I exhale, my breath leaves my lungs on a curse. "If you say Anathos is better with me in it, how does that work if I'm not fighting for her, fighting for her people? To protect them, and keep them safe."

"Exactly what do you think you can do for them."

Lowering my head, I put words to my deepest terror. "Merc."

"Tell me."

"I think you already know." I cross my arms over my gut. "The Dark King is inside of me, Merc—"

"*Stop it*, just stop it." He covers his ears with his hands. "I won't hear that—"

"I killed a man." As I bark at him, I meet Merc's stare straight on. "Back in the dungeon. One of the officers. He came to me with . . . intentions."

Merc's mouth thins to a slash and his brows sink so low, he looks positively evil himself. But I don't let him speak. "I took a knife to him in the cell."

"Good—"

"No, it wasn't. I didn't stop. I couldn't . . . stop. The anger in me was so violent, so undeniable, so . . . powerful, that I was overcome. And what's worse . . . " I close my eyes and want to scream. "When it was happening, it felt . . . good. I liked the pain I was giving him, the vengeance I was taking. So you have to understand, the reason I must fight is also for myself. I don't want this inside of me."

Merc's head slowly shakes. "The Dark King is not within you—"

"*He is*." I cannot bear to speak the words, but I know they're true. "I am going to Prosperitus, I am going to find Julion, and I am going to do the favor he asked of me so that he will take me to his father, the King—"

"He's just a knight—"

"That's what he said, but his face is on one of my royal coins. You think they throw anyone on those things?"

There's a heartbeat of silence. Then Merc shakes his head.

"Sorrel, you *have* to listen to me. I know more about the evils of Anathos than you ever will. If you go to that court, I don't care what you believe about that man. He and his royal sire, if he actually is the prince, will do exactly what every ruler must and protect their people—and *only* their people. You're just putting yourself in danger to no avail."

I think of the warrior queen who sees no one. That was her reasoning, too.

Merc steps in close. "Word about what happened between you and those boys by the Fulcrum will have traveled. You'll be hung in the gates of the city as an example of how they handle purveyors of unlawful magic. And if they eventually decide to fight on their own accord, they will lose and their soldiers will be claimed—which will only increase the power of the evil one. Every soul that's taken makes the Dark King stronger."

"If what you're saying is true, then we'll all just be consumed. Eventually. Do you really think a change in scenery, even if it's an isolated place, can save us?"

When Merc doesn't respond to that, fear floods my veins once more: Even though I disagree with him, I want him to be right. I wish there was a place we could go and shut out Anathos's fate.

In the tense silence, I throw up my hands. "So fine, no fighting. No trying. I guess I'll just walk up to the Fulcrum and get it over with. Submission strikes me as far less painful than waiting around for months, seasons, *years* until the Dark King finds me as the last remaining soul—and takes what he was going to have in the first place."

"There is nothing but pain that comes with submission to evil and its dark deeds," he says roughly.

The starkness in his voice tells me more than he ever has about all the regret he carries for the killings he's done for money, all of what he keeps inside.

"Let me take you away from this, and keep you safe," he says, one last time.

I slowly shake my head. "No. I'm not hiding anymore."

## *Eighty-Nine*

# The Worst Truth.

We're on foot outside of the village wall, having circled around to the rear where we got free of the moat. In fact, we're in the clearing where Julion gave me his clothes and tendered his request, not all that far from the road where Merc stole our gelding.

Who died peacefully under a realm tree, just as I foresaw.

I want to go straight east, and I can tell by his stiff body language Merc still wants to take us somewhere, anywhere, else. Neither of us is saying a word. We've both spoken our pieces, found no agreement, and yet the newest arrangement between us hasn't changed.

Whither I go, goes he.

And yet I'm terrified that he has a point. What if I get to the court and Julion must make an example of me? My reputation does precede me, even though I kept my face hidden.

It brought the Kingdom of the East's prince to me, didn't it?

"I think these two need some water," Merc says. "Is there a stream nearby?"

I try to remember where we are, in woods I have known all my life.

"There is a pond over that—" As I swing my arm around, I wish there was a place I could go for some clarification. "—way."

"Let us go then."

"I'll meet you there," I murmur as I remove my pack and kneel down. "Can you take Lavante?"

"Yes, but be careful with that compass."

"What do you mean?"

Merc shrugs as he starts to walk off with the horses. "You're assuming the energy it reads is always the good kind."

"It hasn't been wrong yet," I grit out as he disappears into the forest.

The tension between us is not helping, and yet I want to run up to him to argue the point. If it weren't for the compass's guidance, getting around that fog would have been impossible—

The instrument's top pops off as soon as I bring it out of its satchel, and the dial is already spinning under the magical map, as if there is an urgency to its message.

And then it stops. The orientation is north and slightly west—which is not where Prosperitus is located. In fact, there's nothing but more woods there, for as far as the eye can see. Or cannot see, as the case may be—

"Fates," I whisper as I realize where it wants me to go.

Closing the compass up, I hesitate for a moment, and as I consider the suggested course, I'm reluctant and doubtful. But all choices seem fraught.

Navigating through the branches and winding around the occasional boulder, I search for carcasses, and when I smell a bank of rancid sweetness on the breeze, I know that whole herds have been slaughtered. Whether they're sacrifices in the name of mistaken purification or the result of demons, it doesn't matter.

Aren't they the same thing, in a way?

As I break out onto a small sandy beach, I find Merc standing next to the drinking horses with his hands on his hips and his troubled eyes staring out over the still water of the oval pond. The sun is still high enough to top the crowns of the trees that grow on its opposite shore, and the rays are beautiful as they stripe their way over, seemingly in supplication to Merc.

His weapons are on him, his long hair flowing down his back.

And always that planted stance of his, as if he's ready to fight.

"You look like you want to take a swim," I say.

He stares over his shoulder, his face a mask. Yet he smiles. "And you look beautiful in this light."

Flushing, I push at my hair, which I have left down and loose. "I, ah, I want to go check and see if the Sooths are alive. Their temple is not far. Will you wait here? They're recluses and may not even let me in. I don't even know why I'm going."

But I'm sure they most certainly will not grant a man who looks like Merc any audience.

"Yes, I'll stay here." He turns back to the water. "There's enough daylight to get us to Prosperitus, but not much to spare. Be as quick as you can."

"I won't be long. I just . . . have to know whether the Sooths were burned down, too." I hesitate. "You should have that swim. You look like . . . well, I won't be long."

Merc nods like he's lost in his own thoughts. Yet as I turn away, he says, "Do you have a weapon?"

I push my hand into Julion's pocket and feel the smooth, sharp contours of the crystal blade given to me by a noble outlaw. "Yes."

"Good. Keep smart, and if you need me, I can be to you in a moment."

"Okay."

The trees are dense, and I fight my way through them, ducking and bending, crunching on the leaves that have fallen already. It doesn't escape me that there are the beginnings of the black blight here and there, and evidence of the black flakes I saw when I found the dragon, when we passed the Fulcrum today. The contamination is spreading, the Dark King growing more powerful.

It's a while before I see the telltale red roof of the temple, and much to my relief, the structure has remained untouched behind its wall. The building is two-storied and about the size of Thale's establishment. It has no windows, in keeping with the Sooths' belief that they must remain free of outside influence, and there's a little extension out to one side, like a short hall that pierces its protective barrier.

I've heard that's where people go to ask for help: No one is allowed inside the temple itself, but they will grant you an audience of conversation there, if they choose, with them staying behind their screening.

Underfoot, the ground cover crunches, and I can tell as I close in that my presence has registered because the smoke drifting out of their chimney changes from black to white. Perhaps it's the noise I'm making. Maybe it's some other monitoring I can't begin to guess at.

White smoke means they will see me. And the fact that I'm going to them, when I've never respected the so-called truths they pronounce, is not lost on me.

Any port in my storm of confusion, I suppose.

Rounding my way to the querent door, I slide a panel back and step into a cool, dark space. For a split second, I can't catch my breath from suffocation, especially as I contemplate shutting myself in here. But this is how it goes, I guess?

I slide the panel back into place and then I sit down on the bench—

A bell rings, my weight triggering the thing, and when I hear footsteps on the far side of what I guess is a thin wall, my heart jumps. In fear. With hope. In sadness.

I'm like a lightning rod attracting all manner of bolts.

In my head, I practice what I'll say and just come up with jumbles. I'm not even sure why I'm here, and explaining my presence with "my magic compass told me to come" isn't going to help.

And then nothing happens. There are no more footfalls or voices. No welcome of any kind.

As I continue to wait, I wonder if some of them haven't abandoned the facility. They're so close to my village—

There is a sliding noise and a thump, and suddenly the glow of a lantern, diffused through a metal screen of symbols—as well as a person draped in red from the crown of their head past their shoulders.

I'm reminded of the oculus and the Queen who didn't only refuse to see me, she refused to be the warrior all of us need.

And then I'm not thinking about anything except the presence on the other side. It's the strangest thing . . . it feels not like a whoever-it-is, but a *what.*

When I'm not addressed, I clear my throat. "I . . . ah, I am from the village. But I wasn't there when . . ."

"I know who you are." The voice is female, and surprisingly melodic for the power that seems to pulse out of the form. "And I know everything about you."

Tightening my hands on the lip of the wooden bench, I whisper, "Everything?"

"Yes. And you wish to be advised where you must go. I am to tell you that it is here. You are where you need to be."

Frustration makes me fidget. "Well, yes. I suppose I must be *here* right at this moment to get advice. But I need to know where I go next—"

"Your village, you just went there." The voice is so soft and hypnotic. "And your heart is broken."

"Yes." But come on, that's no revelation. "And what I need to know is what I should do next—"

"It shall be broken further."

Dropping my head, I resist the urge to yell. "I don't see how that's possible after I saw all those people who were sacrificed for nothing—"

"That is not how they died."

I look at the delicate weave of the screen. "Yes, it was. I saw with my own eyes what was done to my village in the name of purification. They were slaughtered, in their homes, and everything was set afire—"

"We know. We heard the screams, and smelled the smoke."

Fury licks into my gut, and I shake my head. "And you did nothing? Maybe if you'd gone out there, you could have stopped them. You who are here, in your little sequestered temple, who are supposed to be giving advice from some sacred source, could have actually *done* something for once!"

Getting to my feet, I turn away. "This was a waste of my time—"

"If you walk out that door, you will not get what you came for."

"I'll figure out for myself where to go next—"

"You came for the truth, not for direction."

Something in the tone of her voice stills me and I turn around. In a bitter voice, I toss back, "I know my truth, it's advice I need—"

"The villagers were not killed for purification."

I throw up my hands. "I saw the symbols, drawn in the blood of the innocent, all around the ruins of where I have lived my life. Do *not* try to argue with the carnage I just walked through—"

"And what did that symbol look like."

The fact that the Sooth remains so calm infuriates me further. That she asks such a stupid rhetorical question makes me positively volcanic.

"It's the joining of *S* and *P. Salvatore ute Protecficitrae*," I snap at her. "In the old tongue, Salvation and Protection. Now, if you'll excuse me—"

"That is not the meaning of that symbol," the Sooth says evenly. "And you have come here to find out its truth."

"I know the truth."

"No, you do not. Now *sit* down, and receive what you seek."

*Ninety*

# The Symbol that Changes All.

As I slowly lower myself back onto the bench, the little bell rings again. It's as the tinkling sound drifts into silence that I focus on the screen as if my stare could burn away its delicate weave . . . so that I could look properly on the Sooth, who, I suddenly fear, holds an answer that I do not want.

"What does it mean," I breathe.

"The *S* stands for *Shadwe*, the *P* for *Possesstrix*. Possessed of the Shadow One."

"I—I . . . don't understand."

"You do not wish to understand." The head shifts position, angling down. Then it relevels. "This is the symbol."

A piece of parchment is put to the screen, and through the mesh, the drawing I'm shown is the symbol that I saw. All over my village. At the settlement we spent our first night in. The *S* and *P* together in a swirl.

"That which bears this mark has been claimed by the Dark King."

"No . . ." Except my protest is weak. "How is this possible?"

"Agents of the Dark King went forth to your village and took the souls that resided therein for him. The fire comes when he accepts the victim's essences. After it is finished, the demons mark their new territory with that symbol and move on to the next. They're collecting the souls so that the evil's power may grow and he may emerge from his prison within the Fulcrum. For so long, he has been interred there, but it is in the nature of all things to grow. Plants, animals, humans . . . good and evil as well."

I can't breathe, and put my hand to my throat. "I don't understand . . . why did I not know . . ."

"Your mind would not let you see. It supplied an alternate, logical explanation because you could not live with the truth and also because your time had not come yet."

"The cow bodies." I look to the screen again. "What of them."

"The demons have been watching in these woods for weeks now, counting the take, planning the attack. These sentries of the Dark King may pass through the Fulcrum when he cannot. His force remains trapped, but he has bred these subordinations for the job he needs them to do, which is to harvest souls for his consumption. The black bands are not how the demons get out, but rather evidence of the evil's increasing strength."

I picture the Fulcrum as I last saw it, black from base to top. In a strangled voice, I ask, "If the Sooths knew all this was happening, why did you not say?"

"We did. We warned your mayor repeatedly. He came just days previous with his sons, looking for placations and potions. He did not want the truth. He felt as you do now, facing what he cannot live with and fighting the inevitable."

"What is the inevitable," I breathe.

"The Dark King will triumph if a leader does not rise up, a leader . . . who has courage within them and the power to wield it against that which frightens them most."

"The Queen who sees no one."

"That is correct."

I shake my head. "But she turned me down. I brought her the crown . . . and she refused the calling."

The Sooth's tone softens. "You have traveled farther than you thought you could, gathered skills and allies, and now your fate is culminating. Go into this first skirmish in the War for All Souls and know it is not even a proper battle. It is merely the greeting of the opponent. There is much more ahead for you . . . if you live through this night."

As I exhale, I feel the world spin once again. "I don't know what to do."

"Yes, you do. The point of it all is with you."

"The crown . . ." And then I think of Julion. "All right. If the Queen will not accept it, I have another. There is someone else I can go to. The prince of Prosperitus—"

"Indeed, and I am afraid the one you speak of is already driving his gathered men toward the Fulcrum's altar. He is prepared to fight this very night and will die when he does."

"He's going to die?" I jump back to my feet and the bell rings, sounding like an alarm. Or maybe that's the raucous noise in my head. "I have to do something, then. I have to warn him—"

The Sooth cuts me off. "I have waited generations for you to come unto me, Sorrel, and hear this message. I, and the other Sooths, wish you very well indeed. You will need courage not only to face the enemy, but to confront yourself."

Blindly, I turn to the exit panel. Except then I stop. "Are you safe? Can I help you?"

There is a pause, and then the chuckle that comes back at me is soft. "We are not really here, my dear. That which does not exist on this plane may not be destroyed upon it. But I thank you for your kind consideration."

"I didn't believe in you," I say roughly. "Until now."

"That is all right. Truth does not require acceptance." The sigh that percolates through the screen is as ancient as time. "It was no pleasure to tell you what you came for, I assure you. And given your kindness, let me present you with something in return."

A small door beneath the screen opens and a tiny pouch is passed through. "You will know what it is for and when to use it. Remember, the reason for it all is yours."

The light is extinguished as a plate is slid into place.

After I take what is given to me, I stumble out of the audience box, and the first thing I do is open the neck of the little bag. What rolls out into my hand is a gray pebble, of absolutely no remark whatsoever. I put it back and start walking, my limbs numb and sloppy.

I don't remember anything of my careening path back through the woods. My body knows the way, however, and presently I arrive at the pond, at the beach where Lavante stands in the sunlight, looking over the water as if enjoying the reflection of the puffy clouds. Next to him, Snooze is . . . well, snoozing.

And for an instant, the temporary peace is a temptation to believe in. But I know better.

I stop next to a modest bundle of clothes and a big pile of weapons that sit next to the sapling around which both sets of reins have been wound.

Merc is in the water up to his neck, but not far out from the shore, as if he has taken a seat on the sandy bottom. He's facing away from me, toward the sun, which is even lower now. With idle strokes, he waves his arms back and forth at the surface of the pond, the waves he makes catching the beautiful golden light, creating coins that spill out for lengths in all directions.

When I consider what I was told, I'm loath to ruin his moment.

It may well be the last quiet solitude he has for a very, very long time.

The start of the War of All Souls? The first battle . . . tonight. And we are in the midst of it.

This is what's going through my mind when he dips his head back and then sluices the water out of his hair. After that, he rises up, emerging naked—

Whereupon I see his bare, scarred back for the first time.

At first my eyes reject what I'm looking at. And then the moan that comes out of my mouth emanates from deep, deep inside me.

And even though he turns to me, all my eyes know . . . all that I can see . . .

. . . is the symbol that is etched into his flesh, so deeply the edges are raised like ropes.

The *S* and the *P*, intertwined.

## *Ninety-One*

# My Heart Breaks Further.

As Merc faces me, he does not duck his eyes. He knows exactly what I've seen. Maybe he planned this exhibition of something he's undoubtedly kept hidden in ways that did not get my attention. I wonder if he's aware of what answers I have just received.

I think he is, and it's why he's had to come clean.

When he starts walking forward, his body is revealed in all its power and raw beauty—without any wound at all on his chest. The bandage that was there when we made love last night, the wound that I assumed was beneath it, are gone as if they had never been. My mind instantly fractures at this, splitting into a denial of what I'm seeing and a terror at all that it reveals.

I back away from him—and angle the retreat so that I get to his weapons. I grab the first thing I find that isn't his broadsword because I can't wield it with any reliability—

A dirk. I have his dirk in both my hands and I stick it straight out in front of me.

"Stop," I command. "Or I will—"

"I'm just getting dressed."

His voice is flat, and as I continue to back away, he does indeed merely go over to the pile of clothes. As he pulls on his britches, he's efficient about their fastening, and after that, he's the one retreating from his weapons and our horses: He goes over and stands in the footsteps that he made as he walked into the water.

"What are you," I say in a cracked voice. Even though I know. So I answer myself: "You were sent to kill me. I'm your target."

In devastating succession, I recast everything, all the way back to when this started. "It was you . . . who killed the cows outside our wall. You fed on them as you cased my village, knowing I was there, planning your attack. And that night I sensed something coming after me as I went along the lane . . . it was you."

He doesn't deny any of it. Because he can't.

"When we were at the Outpost." I cover my face with my hands, in an attempt to block the thoughts, the conclusions, that are as inescapable as fate. "What they found the morning after you left . . . the dead sheeplings by the body of the cook? That was you, too, the whole of it. You killed the man and then made it look like it was all done by a demon . . . except that wasn't a staging." My voice catches in horror. "That's what actually happened . . . oh, fates, what are you . . ."

I bend over and retch, my eyes flooding with tears. And then I straighten. "Who sent you." Even though it's obvious, I want to hear him say it. "What sent you!"

There is a long pause. "The Dark King. Your father. And not to kill you, but to bring you home to him."

The ringing in my ears reminds me of when I've ridden Lavante and he's been at a gallop, and I've turned my head to look for Merc, and the wind was so loud.

"You are a demon," I hear myself say.

His voice grows bitter. "Not by choice—"

Abruptly, I remember something else. "Oh, crescent moon, you took my body—"

My stomach revolts again and I jack over to vomit properly. As I haven't eaten all day, I throw up bile and some of the water I drank in a stream, an hour ago. The world spins and jerks and I put out a hand to steady myself. Except there's nothing to grab on to but air, no trunk to catch my balance, no branch . . . no strong arm that will keep me upright.

Merc doesn't come to help me now.

What a wise man—

*Demon*, I mean.

Yet even as my body struggles, my mind remains painfully sharp. "Oh, fates . . . there was no horse. You didn't have a horse to stable when you walked into the Gauntlet because you didn't need one. You came out . . . of the Fulcrum."

I try to stand up fully, but the dry heaving won't relent. My throat is on fire, and I struggle to breathe through the spasms of my entire body.

When there's finally a pause, I look over at him and attempt to focus my straining, watery eyes. "And that's why I can meet your stare. You're already *dead*."

As with the symbols, I had everything all wrong. The blindness to his mortal destiny was not that I was willing to die for him. It's that his death has already occurred . . .

"And all of the things . . . about me." I shook my head. "What I can see about death. The compass. The skills I possessed that I didn't know I had—you were never really surprised, you never asked any questions . . . because you already knew, didn't you. You probably know more than I do about who I am—"

"Listen to me now, Sorrel." He starts to talk quickly, urgently. "However this all started, you need to know that nothing has changed about how I've come to feel for you. I want to protect you, and keep you safe from him—"

"You've lied to me this whole time, about everything! This was all a performance—" I curse and want to slap myself. "You faked crying at that field of dead crops, so I'd be fooled—"

"I did *no* such thing—"

"I can't believe a word you say!"

"I didn't lie about my past!" he yells back. "I was a farmer when my village up north was invaded. I submitted myself to the Dark King because I thought my sacrifice would save my family. It did not. First, he slaughtered the sisters I was supposed to protect, and then he violated my betrothed in front of me and killed her, too!" He clears his throat roughly. "When I stood over those spoiled crops, I was reminded of everything I lost, everything I had willingly given up in the hope that—"

"What did the Dark King promise you." My voice is cold and dead. "What is he going to give you when you present me to him."

As Merc looks away to the fields on the far side of the pond, I'm struck by the suffering on his face. But then I harden myself.

"He said he would give it all back to you, didn't he. The life you had lost."

I think about what Merc himself said, about how the evil gets into people and knows their deepest desires.

"Deliver me, and you get your past." I shake my head. "And now, we're here. Just a couple hundred lengths from the altar of the Fulcrum. You were never going to take me to the north to protect me, you were trying to get me to the altar to be sacrificed—*his* altar."

I think of the stupid arrangement I made with Merc in the beginning, my body in exchange for his help getting to the Outpost. He'd have followed me there anyway—damn him, why did he not just force me?

"How it started . . ." He shakes his head. "Is not how it is now."

"Ended, you mean. We are *over*—"

"Please, Sorrel, I can protect you. I can take you up north where he has not yet come. We can live—"

"Shut. Up."

Merc falls silent, and I try not to notice the way the sunlight clings to his body, creating an aura as if he's not what he is. Then again, he is probably willing the effect, just to seduce me.

Something he has proven to be very good at.

"So we fight now," I hear myself say. "You and me. You're the enemy I'm supposed to meet at the start of the War for All Souls."

And then I answer my own question: "You couldn't force me to do anything because you can't risk me killing myself or getting hurt. That's why you were upset every time I took a risk."

"I'm not lying to you, Sorrel."

"You've always lied to me—"

"If I'm so beholden to the Dark King," he says, "ask yourself why I would take you to the Queen who might be able to defeat him?"

I shake my head again. "Because you always knew she'd say no and I'd fail. You gave me the speech yourself when you were talking about how the King of Prosperitus would only ever take care of his own citizens. You knew eventually we'd come back here to my village, and I'd be determined to go to Prosperitus—and the route we'd have to go on would take us right by the altar at the Fulcrum. This is all perfectly falling into place for you."

"Is that what you think this is? Falling into place?"

"Don't play games with me. We're well past that, you and me."

The two of us stare across the beach at each other, and I find it poetic that it's sand that separates us. Like what I wake up to in my mouth. Like that which makes up the Fulcrum . . . which apparently my mother created to imprison my father.

When Merc moves, I jump back. But he isn't coming for me. He just gives me his back, where that symbol is burned into his skin, the scars running from his shoulders all the way down to his buttocks . . . what I felt when I ran my hands up his spine and was so horrified for him.

He pulls on his shirt and takes his time buttoning up. Then comes the tucking and the holstering, and lastly, the mesh and the leather surcoat. When he picks up his broadsword, I can't hide my flinch.

"I'm not going to fight you." Merc glances to the sun, which is getting lower by the moment. "And I'm surely not going to kill you."

You already have, I think with despair.

He goes over and unwraps his horse's reins from the sapling. As he mounts up, he shifts his eyes back over to me.

"I'll give you as much time as I can, but he's going to call me home. Go and join with Julion. That army is well-weaponized and coordinated. It will be Anathos's best chance. As for you, if you enter the Fulcrum, remember that not all is what it seems."

"Oh, you mean you haven't found things trustworthy inside there? What a crying shame."

He closes his lids briefly, as if I have struck him. "I'm sorry—"

"Spare me the apologies. You are the *cruelest* thing I have ever known—how could you lie to me like that. How could you pretend all this time when you were really just waiting for—"

"Why am I letting you go now?" He cocks a brow. "If I truly am evil, why am I not dragging you to your father this very moment. How about you answer that before you judge me."

For a heartbeat, the logic stuns me into silence. But then I narrow my eyes. "Because Julion is already bringing an army to the altar and that's a wrinkle you didn't anticipate. You have to go warn my father. Without the Dark King, you don't get the bounty you need for the demon defenses to be prepared. It's not about my safety. It's about your security—"

Merc curses at me in a rush of words I don't understand. "I have risked my soul for you!"

"You don't have one anymore!" I yell back. "And you are my *enemy*!"

"I am *not*, and I didn't plan any of this—"

"You engineered all of it! Up until right now, when things are falling apart! You didn't think I'd go to the Sooths, but you couldn't stop me—and then you *had* to come clean."

"It's because I can't live with myself any longer, and I didn't know how to tell you!"

"Lies! You were banking on me being in love with you, and you're manipulating me with some heartbreaking tale that came with an I'll-protect-you-up-north ending. But it didn't work, did it!"

Merc just shakes his head slowly. "You have this all wrong."

"No, I *had* it all wrong. I see the truth now—"

"I didn't think I would fall in love with you!" He wheels his horse around. "And if I'm so evil, why am I leaving you now. Huh? Why am I giving you a chance? I meant what I said. The world is better with you in it and I'll protect you for as long as I'm able—"

"*No*. Your cover is up and you have to run back to your master and tell him that I mean to go to Julion and his army." I jab his dirk at the air, as if I'm stabbing something. "*That's* why you're leaving. Your loyalties are not to me and you will say anything right now because you've been caught!"

Merc stares at me for the longest time, holding the reins to his steed in a brutal grip. Then he says, "I'm not the only one without a soul, Sorrel. You just don't remember when you lost yours yet, but it's coming. Your truth is stalking you and about to jump out of the shadows at you—and hate me all you like, just remember . . . I loved you even though I knew your whole story because who you are is so much more than the curse you carry."

"Curse . . . ?" I breathe.

Merc shakes his head again, and it's as if he's staring at an animal that is so wounded, it has to be put down. "Have you never wondered why you can't see your own death, Sorrel? Before you condemn me, take a good look into your own eyes."

With that he gallops off, disappearing into the tree line, leaving in his wake a kind of destruction that cannot be described, much less borne.

My own eyes?

My own . . . eyes.

On a strangled cry, I stumble over to the shoreline and fall to my knees into the water. Bending over, I stare at my reflection. The disruption in the surface prevents me from seeing anything at first, and surely there's a compassion in that.

Soon enough, though, the pond's surface stills and I stare into my own gaze, seeing only my reflection . . . of a freckled, white-haired young woman whose face is haunted with terror.

Covering my mouth with both hands, I hold in my scream.

So that is why I cannot see my own death.

I am . . . already dead.

## *Ninety-Two*

# The Real Battle Begins.

I stay where I am, in the pond, arms wrapped around myself, my eyes glossing over. I'm dimly aware of the sun sinking down even farther at the horizon, and the darkness prowling around me. I am immobile, numb, and strangely hot. Even with my clothes soaking up the cool water, I feel a burning deep inside me, and images of my village, smoking and ruined, take over my conscious thoughts.

My unconscious ones are too scattered and traumatic to catalogue.

It's as though I'm a house burning to the ground, just like the ones I saw inside the wall, my outer layers eaten away, my interior supports gone, my personal articles obliterated. There are no more chairs or tables for me, no pegs on which to hang my cloak, no bed for me to sleep in or trunks for my storage. Never again will someone make a meal in this destroyed home of mine, and no footsteps will sound out, for I have no floors or stairs.

What I once was, what my purpose had been, what roof I'd had and windows I'd sported, gone, gone, gone.

And in its place . . . something I have been denying for so long . . .

The vengeance, that was always just underneath my consciousness, which I've always seen as this odd, foreign part of me, but which was, in reality, my true nature.

I am my father's daughter.

And in the aftermath of this intractable realization, I discover a weakness within my heart that's of cataclysmic implication if I'm not careful: Of all the brutal truths that have taken me down, it's the one about Merc that I find the hardest to bear.

It should be the revelation of who my father is or the sense that my mother, in hiding me, also took things from me . . . things that I now recognize as skills

I once had, experiences I enjoyed, places I lived. Things I did . . . of which some are intimate—because Merc was right. My first time having sex with him was not that of a virgin, and what does that mean? Did I have a lover, sometime long ago? A man I had deep feelings for . . . a husband? A family? Those headaches I always got if I looked too deeply into a shadowy feeling or passing inclination I now recognize were some kind of mental patch, obscuring whatever is beneath.

My father is evil, but my mother is the thief of me.

Plus I've just learned I am dead, which would explain why I've never had a cycle as women do.

And all of this informs my current destiny: I am going to face the Dark King this very eve. I am going to the altar on my own, before Julion arrives with his men, and I am going there with no weapons, no army, and no defenses, for a greeting which I may very well not survive.

So surely *that*, on top of all of my truths, should count most toward my internal devastation.

But no, none of that is the worst.

Merc's betrayal, and all I did not see when it came to him, is the *most* painful part of this. And as if my mind is determined to punish me for the soppy emotions that helped with the eclipsing, I revisit snippets of him: His first arrival in the pub, the copper he tried to give me downstairs and then in the guest room he was given . . . him yelling at me in the tunnel and then riding the *balas* triumphantly out of the moat . . . I remember his thunderous ride to me when I was down on the bed of the Lake of Lost Souls, having tangled with the skystalker . . . and now he's in that window seat at the Outpost, sketching in his journal, and glaring at Thale when he walked in on that man and me.

I revisit Merc slumped in that cell in the warrior queen's dungeon and him washing my hair and making love to me in that luxurious suite . . .

There's such a temptation to believe what he said just now, about his feelings being true. But what was it that he said about the Dark King?

The evil gets in you and knows your deepest fears and desires.

Merc is, after all, a demon, and I need to believe the reality of what's in front of me, not the persuasive words that were just spoken by him. I must face whatever awaits me with my father on my own, and without the blurring of my feelings.

On that note, I focus once more on my reflection in the water. The gloaming has arrived, and so my eyes are barely visible, yet I see them clearly, the pale outer rim and the dark center hole.

That's as black as my dead soul.

As I rise up from the water, I hear the dripping from my clothing and my body, and feel the cold even more deeply. Staring across the pond, I picture what is not so far away, just a little more north and a little more west than my current position.

The altar. Where the Dark King was supposedly sacrificed.

I thought the compass was sending me to the Sooths. But no, their temple just happens to be between where I am and the ancient seat of the Fulcrum.

That is where I must go.

When I turn to Lavante, his head is up and his alert eyes are on me. I expect him to balk as I walk over. He does not, but perhaps evil is the kind of thing you can become familiar with.

Yes, I know what I must do and where I must go now. And this I must do alone.

No more hiding. Ever.

The stallion's quiet nicker of welcome, so plaintive and lovely, would have brought tears to my eyes earlier. No more. There will be no tears for me now or in the future.

I take off the saddle, take off the bridle, and dump the tack on the shoreline. "You are a beautiful horse."

As I pass my palm down his muscular neck, his golden coat gleams in the last rays of the setting sun. I think of Lalah and Emma, and remember the moment he was given to me, a great asset in return for a bad deed done for all the right reasons. I recall riding him through so many trials, surging over grass, over decayed marble, through mist. He is more than beautiful. He is fierce, courageous, loyal, and smart.

"I will miss you," I say in a low voice.

More than that, I will miss what I knew of the world when he was mine. And I mourn the version of reality I thought I was in.

And then I go still.

Something within me knows what to do, even though I have no idea what is about to happen: I put out both my arms, look down upon the skin revealed as the sleeving rides up, and strip from my eyes all that I was programmed to not see—

There it is.

The shimmer of magic that coats me, hides me, protects me. It's all over my body, a magic shield put in place, long, long ago.

I look to Lavante.

This horse, this beautiful horse, must survive tonight. Not because I'll ever see him again and don't want his death on my conscience, and not because of all that I owe him for his efforts on my behalf. No, it's because the mercy I show in this moment is the last I will give to anyone and anything. His protection will be the gravestone to mark my humanity.

With a flex of my will, I send the shimmer to him, the magic tugging at my corporeal limbs as if it intends to resist the eviction. I prevail, however, the energy leaving me through the tips of my fingers, and traveling through the gathering darkness in heat waves that warp the night air. As the spell reaches the stallion, he jerks and throws his head, then rears up and paws at the distance between us with a whinny of alarm—

There's a clap of thunder, and a flare of prismatic light. Then the shimmers fall all over him and coat his every *nic* and length, as if a rainbow has been broken over his head and back.

The light show fades and he throws his head one last time.

Though I have to deny my emotions, I reach out and stroke his muzzle. "You are the very best horse ever to roam Anathos, and now you must go."

As he nickers softly and nods as if he understands, I'm struck with a fresh loss, and then he's gone, his snow-white tail swishing, his hooves beating the ground while he trots off into the trees, never to be seen by demons or humans alike, free to roam, no master to dictate his future . . .

Or the long life he will lead because I have made it so by giving him what has hidden me for millennia—

A lingering tingle makes me pull up my sleeve and I frown.

My skin is a different color, far darker, and as I pull a lock of hair over my shoulder, the waves are no longer white. They're jet-black, just like Merc's.

I did not have freckles, after all. The masking magic deposited a pale pattern onto my skin and leached the color of my hair out.

Given that I'm someone other than the person I knew, it seems right that I look like somebody altogether different—and that's when I see my own marking. The *SP* on the insides of both my wrists.

Claimed, by the Dark King himself. The whole time.

As this all resonates deep within my soul, I become one with the shadows, just another among the congregation that forms the night and dims the landscape.

Except I am more than shadow. I am demon, the thing all people fear, the soulless undead who roam the forests and mountains under the command of their master—

No, I'm even worse. I am my father's powerful daughter, his next generation, finally vested with the dark magic into which I was born, from which I have been hidden.

And unto my destiny I must go.

As I walk forward and step off the shore, the pond before me does not give way underfoot. Now, the water rejects me, that which welcomed me into its sweet, cleansing cradle only moments before becoming as packed dirt. With the spell released from my skin, my true nature is no longer denied to the elements, and they identify me as unholy and unwanted.

With every stride, I feel myself becoming harder and harder, like molten steel losing its warmth and finding its permanent form. By the time the opposite shore arrives, I have been birthed in a new way, stripped of the lies and deceit that coated me along with my camouflage. And as with my truth, and my intrinsic nature, I am fully revealed as I step onto the ground once more, fully vested in my power.

I cast my hand out and split the forest before me, the trees and undergrowth commanded to bend away.

And that's when I see the demons.

They are threaded throughout the trunks like ticks in a dog's fur, black beasts that have the form of men, the hide of a *balas*, and the oblong eyes of a snake. The abrupt disappearance of their forest cover causes them to wheel about toward me.

They do not attack.

Instead, they fall to one knee and bow.

With my will, I freeze them thus, anchoring them to the ground as if I have staked their dead flesh into bedrock. Keeping them here in this location is not to protect Julion and whatever forces he will be bringing here to fight.

It's to deny my father's aims simply by thwarting the evil.

Two can play at control, can't they.

The path I cut through the vast arboreal thicket stitches itself back up in my wake, further locking my father's forces in, and my anger is such that I laugh at how easy it is to command my environment and subjugate that which I'd regarded with such terror.

It's not the laugh I used to have, shy and timid.

The sound is aggressive and mean.

The roar of the Fulcrum reaches my ears first, and then I am before the great spinning sand, the contamination not just complete now, but being expelled, the black swirling, spitting barrier degrading to the point where it's not even a door to be opened. It's just a curtain to be pushed aside.

The ancient slab altar that marks where my father was supposedly sent into his prison, sits before the twirl like a forgotten relic, its tabletop of granite covered with drifts of sand, its support base all but buried in the detritus from the Fulcrum's demise. I'd heard that for generations sacrifices were made here, animal bribes to the Dark King, small souls offered in hopes the human ones would be left alone. At some point, the practice was discontinued, perhaps because as the weather changed and food became more scarce, there were fewer domesticated meat sources that could be wasted.

The idea the evil would be placated by anything less than the total domination of Anathos is absurd.

Putting out my palm, I stop the swirl, stop it with every remaining sand particle freezing in the air, even the flakes that spin off halting in their descent.

I step through, into a landscape I already know in some deep crevice of my mind—

No, that's not true. I recognize what's before me because I've recently visited a very similar place.

It's the red vista on the far side of that maze of spires after the Crystal Gate, the one with the twisted, tortured trees and the fire holes, only here the flames are black. And here, the bleak panorama goes on for an eternity, the hills rising and falling out to no horizon ever because it does not end.

"Father," I say in a commanding voice. "Come unto me now."

In response, I hear the laughter of a sadist.

And then the voice that I have known in my dreams for as long as I have been hidden among the humans.

*"Sorrel."*

*Ninety-Three*

# The Dark King.

My father comes out of a fissure in the spoiled ground, rising up from the red dirt, surrounded by an aura of the black fire that spits and hisses like vipers in a pit. His evilness is breathtaking, his energy so awful that a wave of sickness goes through me, affecting not just my stomach, but my head. And oh, he is horrific looking. The Dark King is a horned monster who stands upright on two powerful, trunk-like legs, the skin over his musculature red as the landscape, his hideous hands sporting talons sharp as knives, a flowing black mane sweeping out behind him in a wind that seems to blow against only him, for there is not even a breeze around me. There are no weapons upon his body, nothing holstered or tied; then again, he needs nothing of conventional armaments, does he. And he's clothed only by a black cape that billows from his massive shoulders, and a binding to cover his loins.

His eyes are all black, the gaze a void that has a pull to it such that I'm careful not to dwell on his stare, and his smile carries the stinking sweetness of death's decomposition.

"How I have missed you, daughter mine."

The voice is utterly captivating, a seductive purr that weaves into the syllables the promise of riches to the greedy, love to the obsessive needy, sex to the ugly and unwanted, power to the pitiful and petty—if only you are willing to give your soul in return.

"She hid you from me, all these years, hundreds of years. But that makes our reunion all the better, does it not."

Now his smile widens, revealing black fangs like those of the ogres, like what is in the mouths of the black spiders. I see now that those are his creatures, breeding in their prescribed territories, locked into that valley by the dragons that sail high above and keep the populations in check.

As with that contaminated red acreage, those beasts are the remnants of something that once was, just before he was imprisoned.

"Your mother is the evil one, you know. To keep a father from his child. It is unconscionable."

I'm only half listening to him. I can see it now, the statues outside of the ruins of that city, the woman looking away, the man jealously captivated. He built that all for my mother, whoever she was, set those temples and the statues as a lovely trap, the center goddess what he worshipped and sought to keep in place.

A pampered cage, for a twisted love.

"She needed to hurt me." He puts a clawed hand over his broad chest. "And she knew that the two of us together, you and I, are a force unconquerable. But I took care of her. Where she is now is a fitting punishment, worry not. You have been avenged, my daughter, and now we are reunited—and I am free. Thanks to the magic in you."

I snap to attention. "I am not getting you out of here."

"Are you sure about that."

"Very." As a welling enmity boils up within me, I realize for the first time that love is complex. Hatred is not. "And you can't kill me for a second time."

"Oh, I was not the one who did that." That smile lingers like a curse. "And what if I told you that if you give me what is required to release me, I would give you something in return. A familial exchange, the one thing that you want most for the one thing I need most."

"I require nothing—"

"You are lying to yourself. What of that man I sent to you." The words flow through the air toward me like a banner announcing safety, like a heat source in the winter, like a balm for pain. "He was right, you know. Everything he said to you was his truth. He fell in love with you."

"As if I'm going to trust you about anything—"

"But what if you could believe him again. What if you could go back and have what was lost. Do you mean to tell me that isn't of value to you."

For a split second, a yearning claws into my chest. He's right. I only want to return to that place I was in, when the only danger that mattered was the physical kind, when I was united in purpose with a man of strength and protection, the other half of my whole by my side with me none the wiser about what is coming.

What did Merc tell me, though . . . *if you enter the Fulcrum, remember that not all is what it seems.*

"Love cannot exist in a maze of lies." I sharpen my tone. "And truth does not need my acceptance to exist—you can take my memories, but my heart will always know what is right."

"But what if it was all real. What if he loved you, even though he knew what you are."

I try to control my breathing, try to give nothing away. But fates . . . if that were only the truth, and not just words honed to turn my emotions into swords used against me.

Except then I shake my head. "That's why my mother would never have you, isn't it. She knew exactly who you are . . . and you *disgusted* her."

There is an instantaneous change in the Dark King, the seduction gone, a rank rage changing the aura of flames around him from black to red.

"Fine, I will just take what I require."

Without warning, my body is grabbed by a great force, an existential sucking extraction making me feel as though I am coming apart, even as I remain intact: The pain is unfathomable, indescribable, inescapable, tears flooding my eyes as I grit all my teeth and strain against the onslaught. Distantly, I hear the scream that rips from my throat as my arms and legs extend out from my torso and I begin levitating, the center of my chest pulling toward him.

The Dark King's voice weaves in and out of my head, as if he's inside my skin. "Your mother stole a part of me when she conceived you, and if you will not free me yourself, I will require it returned unto me now. The collecting of souls one by one whilst I am trapped in here takes far too long—but the seed of me that's in you will make me instantly whole. Oh, Sorrel, your destiny was always coming back home to me, daughter mine—though having refused my generous offer, I will now take back what is mine on my terms."

I scream again, and then choke as I cough up black grains of sand.

The agony is incandescent, my blood and bones alit with the vicious, drawing pull. I try to fight it, to marshal some magic to send at him, to hold what evil is within me back from him. As he extends a palm to me, however, I feel myself drifting forward—

Not my body, though.

As my physical form falls limp to the ground, my consciousness, my soul, my essential essence, floats toward him.

There's nothing I can do.

He's too powerful.

"We will be one, you and me," he says in his warped, evil voice. "And then I will cast aside this Fulcrum of hers like the sand it is and be free to claim all the souls that are my due—"

*And given your kindness, let me present you with something in return. You will know what it is for and when to use it.*

From out of nowhere, I hear the Sooth's voice.

With the last of my independent will, I order my hand to go into my pocket, and then I refocus on my father.

In a sensory parallel, my awareness registers the feel of the tiny pouch that was given to me, and I surreptitiously draw the thing free of its confinement. My fingers, stiff and clumsy, struggle with the string, but then the pebble, so unremarkable, so unimportant, is in my hand.

"This is as it has always been ordained," my father is continuing with satisfaction as I get ever closer to him. "My missing piece returned—"

Surely this can't work. It's just a little rock.

Yet I'm compelled to toss the—

The moment the irrelevant pebble hits the red dirt, the Dark King hisses and jerks his head in that direction. The drawing suction that connects us is instantly broken as he concentrates on the stone, and I snap back into my floppy body.

Bracing my hands into the red dirt, I push myself up and cough out more black sand. But I haven't been saved from anything. I'm weak, as if I have suffered from a dire illness, and glance up in defenseless fear.

Except . . .

For reasons I cannot understand, my father seems to have trouble looking away from the little rock. He tosses his head and stomps like a stallion, kicking up red dust, digging his hooves in. All around him, black fire explodes out of the nearest ground holes as if in response to his frustration.

With a curse, he bares his fangs and then snaps them at me. "You think that will distract me."

"It's working, isn't it," I wheeze back.

His glower is a promise of eternal torture. "I expected more than parlor tricks from you, *daughter*—"

"Stop calling me that." I wobble to my feet. "I will *never* be a part of you. I came here to destroy you—"

The roar that comes out of him blows me back, but he doesn't pounce. He cannot follow. He's stuck looking at me and then back down at the stone, the latter like a precious gem that he's about to foolishly walk away from.

The idea I've bested him on some level, any level, ushers in a bracing flush of courage and energy.

"Pick that up"—he jabs his finger—"and put it back in the bag."

"No."

*"Pick that infernal rock up and put it—"*

"*No*," I yell back at him.

On a sudden conviction, I thrust my palms forward, and that's when the black fire comes out of me, so forceful that the great Dark King stumbles back. He even puts his bulging, veined arms over his head and seems to beat the air as if he's trying to stop a storm of hornets.

And I know, without consciously knowing, where he must go.

Back into the fissure that was created for him and sealed with the Fulcrum. By my mother. Eons ago. When she collected all of the good, remaining magic from the very soil of Anathos and brought it here to keep us safe by locking him up.

She should have imprisoned me here, too, for I am as dangerous as he. But instead, maybe because she loved me even though I'm a monster, she hid me among the humans, just in case, some time in a future she couldn't imagine, but knew would come to pass, he rose up once again.

And I was the only one who had a chance of defeating him because I am him, and he is me.

As all of this occurs to my mind, I see the fissure he emerged out of reopen in the contaminated red crust. With even greater strength, I scream again, and the dark energy coming out of me redoubles, battering at him like blows, until he is down on his knees and I'm standing over him.

"Sorrel," he says in that seductive voice that promises darkest desires granted. "Do not do this. Together . . . we can have dominion over all of Anathos. Together we can make manifest the destiny I was intended for. Regard now at once my army, ready to do our bidding."

A wave of distortion undulates through the red landscape, the black fires flaring up in a coordinated explosion that brings heat and cold at the same time—and then, as the optical show recedes, I see the horror I suspected, but never wanted to witness.

Legions of demons stand at the ready in formation, thousands of them. *Millions*. They stretch out as the horizon does, into a forever because there is no end. These are all the souls my father has taken, has bartered for with lies, has overpowered with unholy strength.

And Merc is among them.

Then again . . . so am I.

Dearest fate, no human army can defeat this.

The war is lost before it began.

Unless . . .

Unless, I can do more than just survive this greeting, this handshake of which the Sooth warned me so strongly. If I can finish off my father, with a wrath of my own unleashed, I can save all of Anathos.

Surely that triumph will heal me. And if I die in the process? At least I tried.

I think of the Fulcrum, and the black bands, the black flurries, the black flames that surround me.

Gathering all my strength, I pour the very essence of me into my father, not as a gift, or as something he can take, but as a terrible contamination that will corrode him from the inside out, spoil him to his evil core, rot him until he is no more capable of animation and will than the cold dead carcass of a cow taken down by one of his demons—

Against all comprehension, the Dark King begins to move backward toward the fissure. Even as he fights the momentum, he cannot seem to break out of it, his head making rounds of me, the worthless pebble, and the black hole that I am sending him into.

"Wait! Wait—daughter mine!"

I can barely hear him over the grunting that rumbles out of me. I feel as though I'm lifting a house from its very foundation, and the strength required is more than I have—yet I am in the throes of the effort, shaking and sweating, straining and groaning, and it's *working*. The evil is being sucked into the ground now.

"Daughter mine!" The Dark King marshals his voice. "I have something of yours you need to see. Look . . . behind you. Look . . . at what you are doing to him. Look at the one you love—"

"You lie—"

And that is when I hear the one voice I cannot ignore, even though I should.

Merc's:

"Help . . . me . . ."

*Ninety-Four*

# The End.

I close my eyes. And I remember once again what Merc himself told me, even as I never want to think of him again.

*Not all is what it seems.*

"You're a liar," I yell at my father. "He's not here, that is not him, he's not here, that is not—"

The hoarse moan that rises up behind me goes in my ears and through my body. I tell myself this is an illusion created for my benefit only, nothing but a manipulation, a chimera created by dark magic and chosen with deliberation as the only way to get me to stop. And because my father thinks he can dupe me, my vengeance strengthens even more, and for this, I'm glad the Dark King has tried to play to a weakness I no longer have—

The screaming behind me shifts something deep inside my heart—or mind; it cannot be my soul, for I have lost mine, if ever I had one. Though I tell myself not to, though I *order* myself not to turn around, this is my little pebble, my compulsion. The thing I cannot not look at.

My head pivots.

Merc is strung between four black flames, as if he's drawn and quartered. He's naked, twisting against the holds, his wide, pain-crazed eyes focused on the murky gray sky overhead, his muscles in stark clench, his neck veins pumping, his mouth cranked wide so that the insides of his teeth are all showing.

The black flames are tearing him apart while he's alive.

Except he's dead.

So the consumption is perpetual. Even as his flesh is rendered apart, it regenerates on the spot, the stasis of torture unchanging such that he's trapped in the agony. Still, I tell myself this is a lie, an apparition meant to appeal to a side of me I no longer have, if I ever possessed it at all—

The evil laughter that first greeted me as I stepped through the Fulcrum repeats, weaving in and around me like a gust of wind.

I'm reminded of my true purpose.

I turn to resume my assault against the Dark King, but when I put forward my palms, what comes out is nothing like what was before. My father easily casts the energy aside as he straightens from his tuck. Replants his hooved feet. Rises to his full, towering height.

Behind him, the fissure begins to close.

Recalling all the reasons I mustn't be distracted, I redouble my efforts—

Merc's screaming, even if it is an illusion, is not something I can ignore. My focus is no longer complete, and the trap I fall into invisible, but better than iron bars: I don't know whether the torture is real, and if it is, I just cannot bear it.

Even though I hate him, my love is . . . complex.

And that makes the emotion real even though I strive to deny it, the smallest crack in my resolve becoming a fault line that destroys me completely—

"Hear him suffer, and know that it is real, daughter mine. No image thus, but rather a servant who tried to double-cross his master and for what? *Love?*" My father laughs bitterly and starts coming forward. "That castrating force is far, far more destructive than anything I have ever done, a weakening, killing, insidious fissure that sucks us in and holds us captive. I had love—for your mother. And what did she do to me? Stole my child, seduced me into this hell, and imprisoned me here for a millennium!"

Black flames explode into the fetid air at his rage.

And then he puts his own palm out such that it faces me. "You know, Sorrel, I do not think he suffers enough. Let us remedy this, shall we."

Just as a wave of dark energy flows from my father, I do what makes no sense, what I shouldn't, what I can't.

I leap in front of the stream.

The agony is greater than the universe, everything that is cold and hard, that feeds off the suffering and misfortune of others, that sickly rejoices in the deaths of children and animals, in the leveling of houses and families. It is war. It is famine. It is pestilence. It is torture.

It is cruelty.

And now it is me.

The stream lasts forever, and when it relents, I slump down, landing beside

Merc, who has been released from the flames that held him and also crumpled into the red dirt.

As I roll over to retch out a black, viscous stream from my stomach, our eyes meet.

He is real.

I don't know how I know this, but I can sense his essence.

And though he is a demon, the tears that fall from his eyes are also real and they are not for himself. They are for . . . me, and they come from a place of love, even though he is what he is.

Even though I am what I am.

*I loved you even though I knew your whole story because who you are is so much more than the curse you carry.*

I make a decision before I'm aware of coming to any conclusion, and my body moves not from my mind, but from my heart: I reach out my hand weakly toward Merc. And he meets my palm with his own.

As the connection is made, I am reminded of my other truth, the quieter one.

I am half my father . . . but so am I half my mother, too. And whatever she did to me, she was not evil. In fact, she attempted to save all of Anathos.

The Savior. The Dark King.

My history. My origins.

Me.

A tear forms and slips free from my eye. Two sides of the same coin, the good and the evil, and shouldn't it be up to me if I land on heads . . . or tails?

I shift my stare back to the Dark King, who comes over to us with a resonant satisfaction.

The horned monster's smile is one of triumph as he stands over me, his cape waving in the wind. "You came here with such arrogance, my daughter. So sure and certain of your own power, though your mother kept it hidden from you all these centuries, so ready to destroy me. I would be furious at her if I were you, but then perhaps we are not the same, after all. What a pity. And now I'm afraid that *I* will have to destroy *you*."

He brings his palm up. "But first, look around and see your failure. Regard the destruction of your mother's creation, the Fulcrum, no more."

The Dark King is right. The barrier, which I briefly stopped in order to enter, has collapsed, the sands nothing more than a modest circular hill that surrounds us.

"Remember, daughter, we could have ruled together, united within me forever. Instead, you will go where your mother is. For eternity."

Squeezing Merc's hand, I brace for what's going to hit me. I know that the instant the black energy leaves the palm of the Dark King once again, I am over. There's not much left in me now, and no chance of survival with this final onslaught.

The end has arrived, my story culminating here, the fate doled out to me at my creation sealed—

The first of the ghostly forms steps forward from a mystical aperture in the air, as if it is appearing from some other plane of existence altogether. Iridescent and beautiful, the entity is instantly recognizable to me, even before I see the face.

Mare. It is . . . Mare, only she is not old and upon her deathbed. She is young and lovely, elegant and regal of bearing. And she smiles at me before stepping in front of my sprawled, wretched body to face the Dark King—

The aperture in time and space opens again. Ellyne steps out . . . dear Elly, the farrier's second wife, who I attended upon her birthing bed, and in her arms is the infant she lost, his perfect hand pinwheeling in a ghostly arc as she smiles at me.

Before she too turns to my father.

After that it is the baker's wife who appears, along with her daughter, not as the bairn I tried to save twenty years ago, but as the young woman she would have been if she'd survived. Then it's the farmer's daughter who I stepped in to help too late, when she was trampled by the horse. The twins who died in the river, whom I was brought to after they'd gone cold and gray, but tried anyway—ten years ago?

And now there are more of the ones I did save over the hundreds of years I was in my village, those who went on to live good lives and enjoy the time they should have had before finally dying of old age. Men and women they are, all those babies over all the years I didn't know were passing, that I brought back from death. From the illnesses I cheated out of their victims. From the injuries that should have been mortal. I remember each and every one of them, including the babies I lost because I came too late—most especially them I recognize, even if their faces show the maturity they would have enjoyed if I'd just gotten there a little sooner.

Though in life they were all not able to thank me, or even acknowledge me, now they bow their heads to me with gratitude and deference before turning to the Dark King. It doesn't seem to matter whether I was successful in my revival or not; their gratitude to me seems to be tied not at all to the outcome, but more to the suffering I saw . . . and what I tried to do about it.

As I stepped in for them then, so they step in for me now.

There are ten, now twenty. Thirty, then a hundred.

Then a thousand.

My father has been collecting souls . . . but now I see that so have I. And unlike him, I did not want to claim what is not mine to take. I just wanted them to live and be with their families, and love who they chose and have the time upon Anathos that they deserved.

It is the dragon's miracle coming at the right time once again, except this is so much more. This is the culmination of all my efforts, over all the years, everything that I have given to the world without expecting a return, returned back as it was granted.

With love.

And it is delivered by the family I created with what *I* did with the time I had.

The Dark King stands now on the other side of a great wall of light. Through the swirling illumination, he seems confused, but with no surprise, he recovers quickly and he is angered beyond measure.

"You think this show stops me?" he growls, his voice warping.

With an unholy roar, he braces his hooved feet and puts both his palms forth, unleashing his black magic upon the chain of souls.

He's so powerful, it's like the entire ocean comes in on a single wave.

## *Ninety-Five*

# Love.

And yet the shield of souls protects me and Merc.

However much my father projects, however strong his evil is, he is no match for my army of light and the protection they provide. Except it is more than that. As the deluge of evil magic hits the wall of illumination, it is sent back to the Dark King, as a mirror would reflect whatever is before it. He is hit by his own dark energy—

The horned monster is blown apart in a great warping explosion that expands outward above us all in a mushroom cloud big as the whole sky.

I can only stare upward in wonder and disbelief—

As massive as the explosion is, the retraction is just as intense. What extends up and out curdles back on itself, the forceful suction so great that it leaves a fresh fissure in the red earth.

That pulls him down and holds him in.

Before sealing back up.

In the aftermath, the silence is deafening. And then I feel the hand in my own and look at Merc.

I reach for him as he reaches for me. Shaken and weak, we embrace on the ground, holding each other.

As I feel a sprinkling on my cheek, I look up. Black snow is falling, everywhere. On us, on the demon army that remains, on the red ground.

But not on the souls. They are untouched.

My ghostly family turns back around to me, and I see all the calm, glowing faces, of all the people whose lives I changed when I thought I didn't matter. The lesson, I know now, is that kindness is never, ever wasted. It is the sunlight against the darkness of the cold, hard world, and as with how the Sooth defined truth, so it is also the way with mercy:

*Kindness does not need to be acknowledged to exist.*

*And we cannot survive without it.*

All at once, the souls begin to drift off, but not into the split in this plane of existence they came through and certainly not into the fissures in this horrible place.

They go to the Fulcrum.

One by one, the sacred energies take flight and re-form the circumference of the barrier my mother created to keep the people of Anathos safe, and as they begin to circle around, the Fulcrum starts to resume, the bands filling out, the spin starting anew.

Faster. Faster . . . until the sand is recaptured from the ground, and the prison of my father re-surrounds him.

Such that what once was is now again.

I look at Merc and trace his scarred face with a trembling hand. "I love you as you are."

Though he is exhausted and still in pain, he lifts his head with a groan and brings his lips to mine. "And I love you just the same."

His head falls back, for he cannot hold the weight up.

It is as his skull lands back against the red earth that I notice something is happening and have a fresh shot of horror. The black snow that has fallen on the red ground is reconstituting. Flake by flake, it's pulling together, the phenomenon occurring all around us.

My father is not done yet.

He is already attempting to reconstitute himself.

And all the while, along the horizon, his many demons stand at the ready, empty vessels . . . until his will is again strong enough to command them.

"We have to leave," I say urgently. "We've got to get out of here."

If we can.

It takes me two tries to stand on my feet, and I grab Merc by the arm and haul him up.

"Leave me," he croaks. "You must l—"

"Shut up." I heft him a little higher. "Remember how this goes—I'm in charge. And I'm not going forward without you. Back is relative, right?"

We are the halt and the lame as we shuffle toward the Fulcrum's swirling circle of energy. The closer we get, the more I wonder how in the world we'll get through—

An aperture is created, just for us, and it's only as big as what we immediately require.

The moment we're on the other side, the exit reseals.

All I can do is blink. I see trees. I see the last of the light in the sky. I see the stars overhead, especially that one that burns brightest.

"Come on," I say as I set us to walk, though I am about to keel over. "We must get to safety."

Wherever that might be. There are still demons in the forest, and I don't know whether the spell I put on them works as yet, or if my father pulled them back in—

I lose my footing, and though Merc catches me against his chest, he doesn't have the strength to continue. Neither do I.

I tell myself to keep going, but I cannot and we both fall to the sandy ground.

Much as my will wishes otherwise, this is where we are. At least for right now.

In my peripheral vision, I watch the new version of the Fulcrum spin . . . and worry about what's happening inside of it. But then I think of all the souls that lent their energy to its magic.

Anybody can be a hero. And people working together can change the course of an epic war, before it even gets started.

Unfortunately, I fear this was just the greeting, as the Sooth said, and if this was just the handshake? I can't imagine what comes next—

Merc and I stiffen at the same time, and then in spite of our pain and exhaustion, we twist around . . . and watch an army gather up on the rim of the crater we're in.

There must be . . . a thousand soldiers, the armed men all on horseback with their swords drawn.

Before I can think, before I can react, a lone figure starts down the sandy descent. It's a golden knight upon a white stallion. Julion. And as he arrives, he brings his horse to a prancing stop and dismounts. It's as I lift my eyes up to his breastplate and go no further that I realize . . .

The point of this all is mine.

Suddenly, I have the energy to stand, but before I do, I shrug the pack off my shoulders, and take the ancient wooden box out. The top opens all on its own, and the circlet of black crystal seems to float out of its contoured tether and into my hands.

Rising from the sand, planting my feet solidly upon the land of Anathos, I hold the crown of war and shadow up above my own head.

I am the warrior queen who sees no one.

And this is my life.

"I shall unite the Kingdoms of the North, South, East, and West," I proclaim, "and together we will defeat the Dark King."

The moment the weight of the black metal base sits upon my head, a shimmering goes out over the landscape, colors dancing within the darkness of the night, just as I have goodness threading through my black, dead soul.

It's as the mystical illumination fades that Julion removes the plumed golden helmet from his own head. Holding it to his chest, he drops down on one knee and bows to me.

All around the rim, the soldiers who are his take off their helmets and bow over the hearty necks of their warhorses.

Mine to command.

The sacred moment stretches into history, the kind of thing that will be told and retold around hearths and fires, and scribed into books, and taught to younger generations, for the rest of time . . . assuming there is any more of that to come for Anathos.

A legend born, a prophecy fulfilled.

My eyes go to Merc's and I know one last, abiding truth. The love within him is my compass, my direction that will never be lost, my guide that will always return the ghost of my soul to me, if ever I am lost to my dark side.

Always forward, never back we shall go.

Into whatever fate sends our way.

# *Acknowledgments*

There are too many people to thank, but one of the biggest ones is Monique Patterson. I'm so grateful you took on this series and I love working with you! Thank you, too, to Mal Frazier, and everybody at Bramble. I'd also like to thank Meg Ruley, Rebecca Scherer, Casey Conniff, and the wonderful family at JRA (especially Christina Prestia and Sonnie Dean!). Thank you as well to Charlotte Powell, Liz Berry, and Jillian Stein. And this wouldn't be possible without Team Waud, the very best group of absolutely-not-a$$-kissers there are, and my WriterDogs, Naamah, Obie, and Jerjer. I'd also like to express love and gratitude to my family.

Finally, thank you to the readers. Without you, I wouldn't get to do this job that I love.

Always forward, never back.

# *About the Author*

J.R. Ward is the author of more than sixty novels, including those in her #1 *New York Times* and *USA Today* bestselling series, the Black Dagger Brotherhood. There are more than thirty million copies of Ward's novels in print worldwide and they have been published in twenty-five different countries around the world.